EVERY STEP YOU TAKE

678-673-3464

Jan

ALSO BY JUDITH KELMAN

SUMMER OF STORMS

AFTER THE FALL

FLY AWAY HOME

MORE THAN YOU KNOW

ONE LAST KISS

IF I SHOULD DIE

THE HOUSE ON THE HILL

SOMEONE'S WATCHING

HUSH LITTLE DARLINGS

WHILE ANGELS SLEEP

WHERE SHADOWS FALL

PRIME EVIL

EVERY STEP YOU TAKE

JUDITH KELMAN

G. P. PUTNAM'S SONS
NEW YORK

⫼P

G. P. Putnam's Sons
Publishers Since 1838
a member of
Penguin Group (USA) Inc.
375 Hudson Street
New York, NY 10014

Library of Congress Cataloging-in-Publication Data

Kelman, Judith.
Every step you take / Judith Kelman.
p.   cm.
ISBN 0-399-15109-5
1. False personation—Fiction.   2. Authors—Fiction.   I. Title.
PS3561.E39727E84   2003   2003046747
813'.54—dc21

Printed in the United States of America
1   3   5   7   9   10   8   6   4   2

BOOK DESIGN BY STEPHANIE HUNTWORK

FOR THE NEXT GENERATION:

KAREN, MATT AND JOSH KELMAN
VERONICA AND ADAM WOLFF

AND THE ONE AFTER THAT:

CLARA JANE AND OWEN JAMES WOLFF
CAROLINE GLORIA KELMAN

WITH LOVE, GRATITUDE
AND BOUNDLESS JOY

ACKNOWLEDGMENTS

I am eternally grateful for the continued, unflagging support and treasured friendship of my incomparable agent, Peter Lampack, and his wonderful colleagues: Sandy, Ren, and Rima. Thanks also to Natalee Rosenstein, my first and foremost editor and longtime friend, for her excellent input, and to all the other extraordinary professionals at Putnam/Berkley, especially Leslie Gelbman.

For their generous gift of expert insights and advice, I thank J.W. Brown, director of communications for the Superior Court of Maricopa County, Arizona. I am indebted to Captain Gabrielle Spano, Detective Singer, and Officer Duffy (a pure coincidence to my character of the same name) of the NYPD's 6th Precinct, and to Officers Sebastian Mannuzza and David Crouthamel, also of that precinct, who convinced me that while it's great fun to ride in the back of a squad car on patrol, I would definitely not want to do so as a suspected felon.

Thanks, too, to my dear young friend and "Men in Black" look-alike from the State Department, who shall remain necessarily nameless, for adding immeasurably to my understanding of the scourge of identity theft.

And, of course, I am grateful to Ivan, for far more than space or words could ever permit me to express.

EVERY STEP YOU TAKE

"Populus, qui ambulabat in tenebris vidit lucem magnam."

Reverend E Train was preaching midnight mass, whipping himself to a fevered froth. No matter that it was not quite seven in the morning or that every one of his faithful flock—old and young, affluent and indigent, tormented doubters and the unflinching devout—was a figment of the man's bug-ridden imagination. No matter that the dried and crumpled Christmas dregs had been parked at the curb weeks ago.

"The people who walked in darkness have seen a great light."

His booming voice dragged me up from the nightmare I lived by day and relived too often at night. It was a replay of January 28th three years ago, a day I would give anything and everything to erase.

I awoke that day to the reverend's preaching as well, some rambling presentiment of doom that I foolishly chose to ignore. I focused instead on the blaze of winter perfection: crystalline skies, strident sunshine, and a bracing wind. Against such a backdrop, how could anything go wrong?

Rainey and I were out gathering supplies for the special lunch we had planned to lift Noah's sagging spirits. His meeting with internal affairs was scheduled to run from ten to noon. Hopefully, his suspension would be lifted, and the meal could be a true celebration. Noah was unstintingly dedicated to his work, honest to a near fault, and surely his accusers would see that.

I was not worried, even about the worst case. If self-protection or politics continued to render his colleagues blind, he would find some other place to devote his talents and energies. Yes, he had given the NYPD his all for fifteen years, and he had earned his stripes and reputation as a top homicide detective. But it was a job, not his life. We had each other and a warm, loving home. Rainey, his little girl, had come to accept us and me. Even if this marked the hideously unfair end of his police career, it was far from the end of the world.

At Dean & DeLuca's market, we ran into a puckish ginger-haired boy from Rainey's sixth-grade class, shopping for gourmet goodies with his mother. Looking smug, Rainey informed him that we were having a surprise party for her dad, "just because." Envy pushed his freckles into high relief. Many city kids are programmed tighter than the flight grid at LaGuardia. Ditto their parents. All the energy darts are tossed at the aptly named "spoils" of achievement: designer schools followed by stellar careers, fancy cars, well-connected friends, trophy spouses, insulated world travel, and a home for every season. There's precious little room in the frantic schedule for spontaneity, serendipity, or fun.

But today, we were determined to have exactly that. Trolling the aisles, we filled our basket. The planned menu was Caesar salad, lasagna, garlic bread, and apple pie, but we allowed several other temptations to make their case. What was the pie without ice cream and chocolate sauce? Wouldn't the lasagna be lonely without some of my special meatballs? More was definitely more, after all, especially when it came to this man who was the love of my life and Rainey's. On the way home, we stopped at The Reel McCoy Film and Video store and rented *Monty Python's The Meaning of Life*. I could not remember the last time I had seen my husband laugh.

At this point in the dream, everything grows hazy and surreal. Time turns elastic, sounds bounce with pinball frenzy, and I see things through Saran Wrap slogged with grease. We enter the apartment in a boisterous mood, chatting and planning. Rainey unlocks the door and heads in to preheat the stove. By the time I haul my bags to the kitchen, she has vanished. I am musing about her fickle twelve-year-old attention span when she appears at the door, lithe limbs jangling like loose change. "He's here, Claire," she rasps. "Daddy's in the bedroom. The door's closed."

It was barely eleven. "His meeting must have been cancelled." Maybe this was good news. Maybe they'd come to their senses and realized he was incapable of the absurd things they'd claimed he had done: witness tampering, obstructing justice. They might as well have accused him of being a two-headed alien from the Planet Zog.

"How about you get the food ready, and I'll keep him out of here?" Rainey said.

"Good idea. But first let me see what he's up to. Maybe he's taking a nap."

I walk down the hallway toward the bedroom door, but in the dream I never reach it. The corridor expands in a long, snaking loop. The walls are glazed with sunlight, and a rich toasty scent suffuses the air. From outside comes the tinkling summons of an ice cream truck. Smiling, I walk and walk and never think to stop. I never turn the knob and see him there. I never stop breathing. I never find the breath I need to scream.

"If you have been blinded, brothers and sisters, let the scales now fall from your eyes," the reverend declared.

Peering out through the rain-slicked window, I spied him in the gutter across the street. The reverend stood barefoot, ankle-deep in the sluicing runoff from a frigid downpour. His clerical clothes—a navy Knicks jersey and camouflage cargo pants—drooped from his bony frame like line-hung wash. A passing sanitation truck lashed him with shocking straps of icy water, but he remained the very definition of oblivious.

From time to time, the reverend made his ministry on this quiet West

Village block, but his regular pulpit was the Eighth Avenue uptown local. I had seen him there a number of times, riding the E train, passing the gospel along with his Styrofoam Ronald McDonald collection plate. On a very good day, I calculated that he took in about as much as the average writer. In other words: nothing near a living wage.

People like him tend to fill me with guilty concern. Poor loon was begging for a case of pneumonia, or, as my mother would no doubt put it, "his death." No, I'm not willing to take on the army of ambulatory psychotics that roam the city streets (or those who live in luxury doorman buildings, for that matter), but I'm at least as troubled for them as I am by them. In truth, precious little separates the rest of us from what a man like Reverend E Train has become. A few crossed wires, a critical short circuit, and, suddenly, your fixer-upper life is deemed a tear-down. I know this from hard personal experience. After Noah's death, I spent months kicking around the dangerous outskirts of reality, too lost and broken to find my way home. What finally brought me back was the closing of the Garmin case in Phoenix. The brutal killer of that family—a young couple and two crushingly adorable little boys—turned out to be the same monster Noah had tried to nail for the murder of the five Lynnwood children here. B.B. LeBeau's conviction could not undo the lethal damage to my husband's spirit or erase the indelible stains from his reputation, but Noah was more than vindicated as far as I was concerned. And LeBeau was on death row, where he belonged, where he couldn't destroy any more lives.

Suddenly, I heard my upstairs neighbor. Mrs. DiMarco was a frail wisp, north of ninety, with the voice of a car alarm. "That's it, wacko. You skedaddle this minute, or I'm calling the cops."

The reverend soldiered on. He had a message to deliver, countless imaginary souls to save. *"Arise to the truth, brothers and sisters. Embrace the light."*

Heeding his suggestion, I flipped on the bedside lamp. I lumbered out of bed and slipped on my favorite work clothes: a plaid flannel robe and furry slippers. Business formal was an oversized T-shirt and tights. Working for yourself can have distinct advantages, depending on who you happen to be.

Downstairs, I started a pot of coffee and retrieved my sodden copy of the *New York Times* from the brownstone stoop. I popped it into the microwave and set the cook time for three minutes and thirty-three seconds on High.

"Upon those who dwelt in the land of gloom a light has shone, the son of God has appeared, offering salvation to all. Still, some of you stagger blindly, stumbling in a quagmire of uncertainty and doubt," the reverend observed.

The paper was cooked to perfection. The news was anything but. I could have spent the entire morning feasting on a veritable smorgasbord of human misery: earthquakes, political upheaval, train wrecks, kidnappings, a deadly salmonella outbreak, the threat of an imminent world tour by Kenny G.

Writers rarely pass up a procrastination possibility, and I am no exception. Few things are more tempting to avoid than a blank page—and the blank brain that so often goes with it. But my proposal for a new novel was about to be really, seriously overdue. Even Ben Rosmarin, the world's most patient and wonderful editor, had his limits.

"Your eternal Word leaped down from heaven in the silent watches of the night."

If only that had been the case. I could not afford to jeopardize this contract. Like it or not, I had serious responsibilities, most notably Rainey, the pubescent riddle whose upbringing had been left in my dubious hands. This was one of many facts of my life that I found almost impossible to absorb. Somehow, I had arrived at this place that was never my intended destination. Imagine driving due east from Chicago and finding yourself in L.A.

When I married Noah in a blissful haze five years ago, I pictured us forging a fresh, powerful alliance, building a limitless life, adding kids, rooms, whatever, as the spirit moved us.

Rainey's mother had died suddenly of an undetected heart defect when the child was only a toddler. I got to know her as a shy, sensitive, unusually bright and thoughtful nine-year-old who collected female attentions with the same single-minded ferocity with which many of the other girls in my fourth-grade class at St. Stephens School hoarded Barbie paraphernalia.

That year, I had come to believe that I would be a teacher forever, perennially single after a string of disastrous relationships, deflecting my nurturing instincts to the care and education of other people's children. I would remain Ms. Barrow, viewed as a sorry, tight-sphinctered soul by colleagues, and a slowly rusting teaching appliance by the children, who would presume that I was placed on a shelf in the supply closet after hours and left there, along with the audio-visual equipment, until someone saw a use for me and filled out the appropriate requisition form. My students would be shocked speechless whenever they came upon me on the street or at the supermarket, as if they had discovered their sofa or dishwasher staging an escape.

My perspective changed drastically the early October night Noah came in for a routine parent-teacher conference. Our meeting lasted barely twenty minutes, but it felt like one of those head-on collisions from which no one walks away intact.

For Rainey's sake, we held off dating until that endless year played out. After we got together, I slowly learned to fill the aching void in the little girl's life. Over time, I went from being Ms. Barrow to Daddy's girlfriend to Claire and, finally, miraculously, to "my Claire."

I'll never forget the first time she called me that. A month before the wedding I took Rainey to Bloomingdale's in search of a dress. She was delighted with her designated role in the proceedings: Child of Honor. As she posed before the dressing-room mirror, twirling in a pink confection, she went grim. "I've been thinking. You can't be my mom, because I already have one, even though she's in Heaven. Right?"

I repeated the words I had heard Noah say countless times. "That's true, honey. Jenny will always be your mom."

"Then you can be my Claire."

In a nostalgic fog, I hauled out the fixings for Rainey's favorite breakfast: blueberry pancakes. I measured the flour, baking powder, and sugar and added the blueberries. The butter hissed and sputtered on the hot skillet as I whisked in the eggs and added my special ingredients: ricotta cheese and lemon zest.

The reverend built toward the action-packed conclusion. *"And when they had seen it, they made known abroad the saying which was told them concerning this child."*

I was spooning neat ovals of batter into the pan when the refrigerator door swept open with a blazing flare of light. Rainey ducked inside and grabbed a Diet Coke. How did she shove me? Let me count the ways: soda for breakfast, jeans cut too low on her jut-boned hips, shirt far too revealing of the outsized new curves that made her look like the love child of Dolly Parton and Olive Oyl. She had rimmed her azure eyes with grape-toned liner, and sprayed teal streaks in her brandy-colored hair. At least, I hoped it was a spray. The tiny Pooh Bear tattoo on her left ankle was for real.

"Wouldn't you like some juice, honey?"

"Gotta go." She took up her massive backpack and aimed for the street.

"Wait. I'm making pancakes. First batch will be ready in a minute."

She kept going, and I heard the rush of air. For a moment, the storm's voice intensified: growling thunder, a spiteful hiss of wind. And then the door smacked shut.

"Venite, adoremus," extolled the reverend. *"Hallelujah!"*

I went to the front vestibule, which we shared with the neighbors who occupied the floors above ours. Peering out through the driving storm, I spotted Rainey, walking quickly, head bowed against the oblique pelting rain, turning the corner onto lower Fifth Avenue. At least she had a hooded jacket on. At least she had taken her books and was headed toward school. At this point, I was learning to be grateful for the little things.

I was still staring at the space she left when Dr. Midori bustled in and shook himself off, like a wet dog. Midori, a wiry ageless man, ran an Eastern medicine center from his sprawling top-floor apartment. He spoke a fractured combination of Japanese, guidebook English, and health-food missionary, and he never missed an opportunity to try to convert me into an ascetic, vegetarian, water-guzzling, frequently fasting, exercising sylph.

"Weather bad nasty out, Miss Claire. Run three miles treadmill. Meditate fifteen minutes, five times day. Pull here. Keep pull." He poked his rock-wall abdomen. *"Kenshou."*

I tried to follow his suggestion, but my abs retained the undulating sponginess of a water bed. "Good health to you too, Dr. M. *Kenshou.*"

For the next three hours, I chipped away at the proposal. Slowly, the elusive story line came clear. My protagonist developed a detectable pulse. A credible starting sentence popped into my head. Then the dam broke in a torrent of ideas.

My fingers were racing madly to keep up when I heard several sharp reports from the foyer. Cracking the door to the limits of the security chain, I spied a shaggy mongrel poised on his rear paws, trying to scratch his way through the door. Hearing me, he dropped down, growled deep in his chest, and then resumed his buckshot barking. That was when I spotted the note suspended from his collar.

As usual, the animal's vital statistics were penned on the envelope. This healthy four-year-old male was Richter (named for the earthquake scale), a shepherd/collie mix with a dash of Doberman and a subtle hint of chow. He had been neutered (but unbowed), had all his shots, needed minimal grooming, only shed when absolutely necessary, and would not require a checkup until July.

Inside, on a yellowed thank-you note with the gratitude crossed out, I found the *Reader's Digest* version of Richter's, shall-we-say, little difficulty. The text, in my friend Duffy McClure's expansive hand, explained that the dog had slipped out of the family yard as a puppy and gone missing for weeks. He had been identified from the flyers posted all over town and returned to his owners, but some unknown trauma in the interim left him hugely suspicious and eternally on guard. To this day, Richter retained an uncanny knack for sensing trouble, even where no such trouble actually existed. Though he was a loving, loyal hound with impeccable intentions, two families had found it impossible to deal with his highly vociferous, general distrust.

I smiled over hard-clenched teeth. Duffy had been Noah's partner in the Midtown South homicide squad. Since Noah's death, he's been biding his time on the force, waiting for retirement. He devotes his free time and genuine energies to assisting his sister, Sandy, who runs a combination animal shelter and pet-placement service called Dependent Claws, along with the upscale pet-accessory boutique and grooming operation that pays the bills. Every so often, Duffy gets it in his head to park one of their foundlings, generally a furry basket case like Richter, with me. Like most well-intentioned fix-ups, every one has been a near-immediate disaster. But Duffy is not the type to let puny matters like reality or history stand in his way.

The pooch smelled like wet, sour socks. Shards of panic glinted in his eyes. "Sorry, buddy. I can tell you right now: this is not going to work out."

Richter cocked his head and flirted in his way.

"You can stay for lunch. But that's it." I grabbed the mail and led the dog inside.

He sucked down a bowl of the kibble I still had from Wrecker the cocker spaniel. Wrecker had refused all dog food and even the most succulent table scraps, restricting his diet to home furnishings, accessories, and leather goods. While Richter gobbled, I munched on Rainey's cold, forsaken pancakes and flipped through the day's bounty of junk and other, less desirable, mail. One letter, marked with the thick black logo of a collection agency called Paragon, caught my eye at once.

It contained notice of an overdue Visa bill. Only immediate payment in full could avert my complete, instant, permanent annihilation—or something to that general effect. Looking closer, I noticed that the address was correct, but the delinquent bill payer's name was C. Brower, not Claire Barrow, which was mine.

Working up a nice head of righteous indignation, I dialed the agency's number. After Noah died, it took most of two years to slog through the legal morass and straighten out the financial mess. Ever since, I've made a religious point of paying bills on time, staying ahead of expenses. The last thing I deserved was to take on someone else's black mark.

After fifteen minutes on hold, I heard the beep that meant another call was pending. My Caller ID registered Ben Rosmarin's number at Ridgefield Press. Quickly, I flashed over. "Hi, Ben. Listen, I'm on a call. Can I get right back to you?"

"Ben is no longer with the house, Claire. My name is Paige Larwin. I'll be taking over his list."

"What do you mean, he's no longer with the house? What happened?"

"I honestly can't say. Look, I've been reviewing Ben's notes on your next project, and we need to get together ASAP."

"Is Ben sick?"

She sighed. "It's not a health thing. That much I can assure you. The company line is 'creative differences,' but frankly, they don't lock you out of your office and have you escorted from the building for that."

"You can't be serious. Why would they do such a thing to Ben? Everyone thinks the world of him. He's been with the company forever."

"Use your imagination. It's not a giant stretch. Meanwhile, as I said, we need to have a meeting right away. Can you do lunch today?"

"Today? Sure. I suppose."

"Good. Make it Downstairs at one-thirty. You know the place?"

"I've heard of it. What do you look like?"

"Like your worst nightmare."

The razz of the dial tone sounded as I waited for the laugh.

2

The funeral dress hung at the back of the closet. Martha Garmin stripped off the plastic cleaner's shroud and slipped the somber garment overhead. She pressed her feet into squat black pumps and retrieved her handbag from the top shelf where it had perched for over a year. The scuffed leather surface was powdered with dust. Inside were artifacts of her former existence: wallet, ID, car keys, compact, lipstick, and the special parking permit (long expired) from the Maricopa County Superior Court.

She fumbled in the dark for the other things she would need: toll money, driving glasses, and the Visa card for gas. Turning on lights could invite the neighbors' intrusive concern. *Is everything okay? Couldn't imagine where on earth you could be off to at such an hour.*

She slipped outside, into the pulsing cacophony of tree locusts. Clinging to the shadows of a hedgerow, Martha stole across the yard. The desert chill pierced her skin, raising a crop of gooseflesh. Moving faster, she stiffened against an encroaching shiver. If she allowed herself to start trembling, she feared she might never find the means to stop.

The garage door clattered up on old, arthritic joints. Inside, a rancid oil scent mixed with the musty closeness of disuse. Martha considered, almost clinically, that it might be a leak: fluid bleeding from some essential artery or organ in the engine. She had made a point of turning the motor over every month or so, but maybe that was not enough to satisfy the old heap's need for attention.

She slid into the driver's seat of the ancient VW Bug. The accelerator wheezed as she pumped it, and the motor shook with a dry, feeble cough. Stomping harder, she prodded the starter again. The chassis gave an ominous shudder and went still.

Fighting panic, Martha popped the hood and stared at the bewildering tangle of grimy rubber and clotted grease. Her husband, Brad, had understood all this completely. Ditto their son, Joseph, who had spoken fluent automotive, practically from birth.

Memories flooded back on a tide of bitter tears. Martha pictured the two of them hunched over an ailing engine, probing with practiced fingers and identical frowns. She conjured the dueling bass strikes of their somber consultations and the celebration that followed each successful fix: cider and jelly doughnuts all around, raucous pleasure noises, each smile capped by a powdered-sugar mustache.

With an angry fist, Martha swiped the tears away. She blocked out the painful images, allowing only one scrap of useful remembrance to remain.

Leaning into the cab, she released the parking brake and set the gear shift in neutral. Over her spine's strident objections, she pushed the Bug to the lip of the steep, sloping drive. As the car started rolling backward, she lurched awkwardly inside. Her shin caught the sharp edge of the door frame. She felt the shock of a metal bite followed by a sticky liquid rush.

Ignoring the wound, she struggled to control the headstrong Beetle as it took on speed. She pictured Brad at the wheel, with teenaged Joe out front, pushing. He would sprint alongside on his coltish legs, prepared to leap in just as the engine caught. When the car hovered at the brink of reckless abandon, Brad would pop the clutch, and the motor flared alive.

Martha did so now, and to her relieved amazement, the engine kicked in. The wheel went liquid-smooth beneath her grasp. She shifted into first gear and checked the gauges. The gas tank claimed to be three-quarters full; the battery indicator edged in jerky pulses out of the danger zone.

Martha pressed harder on the accelerator. Pulling a measured breath, she willed her thwacking heart to settle down. More than a year had passed since the last time she had dared to take the wheel. That was on December 13, the day the jury handed down the death sentence for B.B. LeBeau. The animal who murdered her Joe and his family would pay with his worthless life. It wasn't nearly enough, not a fractional return on the monstrous debt, but it was the best the system had to offer. Martha had been steeled to make her peace with that.

All that had kept her going was the chance to see that creature punished. To that end alone, she had forced herself to breathe, to eat, to wrap her insensate form in proper clothing, choke down enough food to thwart starvation, and set one leaden foot in front of the other.

Throughout the trial, she had driven to the courthouse in downtown Phoenix. Each hellish morning she had entered that stifling cell of a courtroom and claimed her reserved seat behind the lawyers for the state. All day, every day, she had stared out from the face that had aged several decades overnight. Expressionless, numb, she had listened to the coroner's report as he detailed the location and effect of each of the seventy-eight stab wounds. She had heard the horrified recollections of the homicide detectives. *Worst thing I've come across in twenty-four years on the force.*

Not once had Martha flinched or turned away, not even from the full-color blowup of the sick tableau LeBeau had arranged. Her tow-haired grandsons—Justin and Brandon, now eternally aged one and two—were huddled on their parents' laps, opal eyes agape, mouths molded into grimace-like smiles. Joe and Nancy, stiff hands linked like chains, gazed at each other blindly. On the wall behind them blazed the title: "Silent Night." At first glance, they looked like a beautiful young family posed for a Christmas portrait. Then you noticed the pale shock of death on their faces; and you realized that the words on the wall had been rendered in their blood.

The image raised a collective gasp from the gallery. One juror blanched and raced from the courtroom, clutching her mouth. Several spectators drifted out, dazed and slack-jawed. But Martha sat erect, glacial, as close to dead as it was possible for a technically living thing to be. All she could think of was how lucky her Brad had been, taken by a heart attack before all this.

Tracking the weave of deserted streets toward the highway, Martha flipped on the headlights and continued to pick up speed. In the battle between rage and fear, rage had a clear and growing edge. Court would convene in just under four hours. Before it did, she had to find a way to get to Judge Montrose and convince her to call off the scheduled hearing for post-conviction relief.

Thank heavens that horrid reporter had tracked her down. After the sentencing, Martha had moved from Scottsdale to Sedona. She had hidden behind her maiden name and slipped into blessed obscurity. People here, the few she had been powerless to avoid, knew her as a retired bookkeeper named Martha Tillary, never married, no kids, whose past could be summed up with an apologetic shrug. Except for Gene Persky, who had refused to let her be, she had left no ties or trail.

Persky, a stringer from Seattle, was determined to write a book about the killings, and he had hounded Martha incessantly, trying to win her cooperation. The story needed to be told, he'd urged. Otherwise, the killer might be remade over time into an object of perverse fascination, a bloodstained hero like Jack the Ripper or the Boston Strangler. There would be fan clubs and revisionist biographies. The victims could become a toothless joke: *Lizzie Borden took an ax . . .*

Martha understood full well what Persky was really after: notoriety, a fat advance, maybe a movie deal. Man was a typical, out-for-himself, dirtmonger. As a journalist, her Joe had been the rare exception, a serious professional, willing to stick his neck out to see truth served.

That, Martha knew in her heart, was what had gotten his family killed. Joe had written a scathing piece about B.B. LeBeau, who had captured the nation's fancy by murdering his parents and baby sister at the tender age of eight. The child's vicious talents had been nurtured in various juvenile facilities until he reached legal age and the system was forced to set him free. After that, he was implicated in many ugly crimes, but never convicted. His ability to wriggle free of the law had earned him his nickname: "the Eel."

Joe had crept under LeBeau's choirboy exterior and exposed the wriggling maggots underneath. He had discovered what the initials B.B. stood for, a fact the Eel had been determined to keep to himself. Before the story was finished and the secret revealed, LeBeau had reacted in his typical fashion—with the business end of a ten-inch K-Bar knife.

Persky's words echoed in her mind. "There's a hearing on LeBeau scheduled for today. You've got to stop it, Mrs. Garmin. Go see the judge. Tell her it's a setup." His voice was so odd and hollow, Martha had to strain to catch his words.

The bedside clock read 5:45 A.M. "What on earth are you talking about, Mr. Persky? Do you have any idea what time it is? How did you get my number?"

"Doesn't matter now. Listen, please. LeBeau's lawyers have an out. The head of the lab that ran his DNA said he falsified the results. But it's not true."

"That makes no sense. Why would anyone make up such a thing?"

Persky groaned. "Please, Mrs. Garmin. There's no time to explain. Just go. Get Montrose to postpone the hearing. Otherwise, LeBeau walks."

"No. That can't be."

"It *will* be unless you convince the judge. The lab director said he manipulated other cases, too. He made up some crazy story about trying to discredit the death penalty. Three men he claims he set up have been executed. The governor has ordered the court to fast-track LeBeau's motion to have his conviction overturned. You're the only one the judge will listen to. Please, Mrs. Garmin. You must get there before court convenes."

Martha hung up, mind roiling. Maybe Persky was off his head, but she couldn't take the chance.

Two more rights would place her at the highway entrance. To keep the fear at bay, she did a mental run-through. Martha imagined sliding the car onto the ramp, picking up speed, holding her place in traffic as it thickened to an oily stew in the morning heat. Not long ago, driving had been second nature. But that was before her life fell from its cozy perch and shattered in a million unrecognizable shards. Nothing could be trusted. Tragedy lurked around every bend.

Despite the empty road, Martha braked at the stop sign and flipped on her turn signal. She leaned forward, peered around the corner, and eased forward. Seeing nothing amiss, she angled right. That's when she spotted the figure kneeling near the end of the street and the SUV askew on the roadway like a child's abandoned toy.

Martha's first thought was to double back, but instinct drew her toward the scene.

There. What was that? Something lay bundled on the ground. Must be an animal, she thought. That had to be it.

Suddenly, she heard the anguished cry. "My baby! No!" At that, she sped down the block, flipped off the ignition, and bolted from the car.

"Someone help me! Please, God!"

The broad bill of a baseball cap obscured the woman's face. A flaxen ponytail protruding from the rear shook with her sobs. Her lithe form blocked the swaddled bundle on the pavement. From the size, it had to be a newborn.

Martha's breath caught as she hurried toward the poor woman. "What happened, dear? What can I do?"

The figure stood and flashed a wicked smile. The ponytail came away with the cap, revealing a scraggly mop of dull-brown hair. Not a woman at all.

The man looked vaguely, but not quite, familiar. Martha struggled to place him, but the answer taunted like an itch beyond her reach.

"Here's what you can do, Martha baby. You can shut up and watch." Still grinning, he raised his booted foot and stomped the bundle. "Oops."

Martha's heart seized, but then she realized there was nothing inside— just a rolled-up blanket. She blinked hard, trying to bring the crazy situation into focus. "How do you know my name? What is this?"

"I said shut up!" A harsh slap sent her reeling.

"But—"

"Something wrong with your ears, you old bitch? Maybe this will open them up."

She felt fierce pressure, then an exquisite spark of pain. Again and again, the knife came down. A ten-inch K-Bar. Martha knew it from the trial.

When she tried to step away, the ground went spongy. "Have to get to the courtroom. Have to stop it before it's too late."

"What you have to stop is that goddamned mouth."

Soupy darkness gathered; sound muted to a flannel hum. At a dim remove, Martha caught the playful beep of a seeking cell phone. "She's done," the man said. "We're good to go."

Languid thoughts fluttered, fishlike, in Martha's mind. In the shadows, an evil eel lurked, but she was strangely unafraid.

Phoning was a wonderful idea. She should call ahead and let Joe know to expect her. Maybe Nancy could keep the boys up until she arrived. Can't wait to see those little cherubs, Martha mused with a last, stammered sigh.

Lord knows, it's been way too long.

3

Every writer dreads being orphaned. When your editor leaves, your work lands like a cold, unordered pizza on someone else's overloaded desk. You are taken on with stoic acquiescence at best, fanged resentment in the worst case. Writer friends have regaled me with many such horror stories, but I'd felt protected with Ben Rosmarin as my tether to the house. He had been synonymous with Ridgefield Press for decades and was charged with shepherding several of the company's most bankable authors.

Winston Hodge, my agent, was not surprised when I called to break the news. Then again, few things caused the slightest rumple in his glass-smooth temperament or impeccable bespoke façade. "Not to worry, Claire. These things happen."

"I know that, Win. I just don't want them happening to me, or to Ben, for that matter. I haven't been able to reach him at home or on his cell phone. No one at Ridgefield is talking. Have you heard anything?"

"Not a peep. If I had, I would have called you."

"What could it be?"

He hummed, ordering his thoughts. "The standard list would be stealing from the company; some serious sexual no-no, especially with the boss's wife or playmate; a public display of substance abuse; evidence of serious mental imbalance; or looking crosswise at one of the stars."

"I can't imagine Ben doing any of the above. He's a sane, sensible sweetheart."

"Who knows? Ben has a life beyond the business. Maybe it went off the rails."

"Maybe, but I prefer to think this is all some crazy mistake. Let me know if you hear anything, will you?"

"Of course. And you let me know about your meeting. I've heard of

Paige Larwin. She was quite the comer at *Chic* before she jumped to books. Rumor has it she's being primed for a top slot at Ridgefield."

"I don't know, Win. She sounded as if she has two sets of teeth."

"Nothing wrong with that, my dear. Sharks can be highly effective."

The worst of the storm had drifted east. I headed out under a glum, leaky sky and angled downtown to SoHo, so called for its location south of Houston Street.

Other facts about the district popped into my head, an artifact of the three college summers I spent working as a guide for Gotham Tours.

In the 1850s, after the residential population drifted north, SoHo became home to ornate iron warehouses and home-furnishings outposts for upscale retailers, such as Lord & Taylor and Tiffany. Then, in the early twentieth century, those merchants moved uptown, and the neighborhood was consumed by a crime-ridden, sweatshop-infested slum with the apt nickname "Hell's Hundred Acres."

The course of SoHo's history was altered abruptly by the horrific fire that erupted in the Triangle Shirtwaist Factory in 1911. One hundred and forty-six garment workers, most of them young immigrant women, were trapped by blocked exits and faulty fire escapes on the top three floors of the ten-story inferno. Their unthinkable deaths sparked national outrage and led to the passage of strict new labor laws, which shut the sweatshops down.

In the 1960s, artists seeking cheap, abundant space moved in and rehabilitated the area's many abandoned buildings. Trendy galleries soon snapped up the street-level display spaces. A lemmings' rush of hot new restaurants and boutiques followed. In classic New York fashion, many of the intrepid pioneers found themselves priced out of the very neighborhood they had rescued from ruin and labored to revive.

The restaurant known as Downstairs occupied a moody subterranean space on Spring Street. Charcoal Ultrasuede banquettes flanked sculptural, smoked-glass dividers. The walls were sheathed in a patterned metallic mosaic that fractured passing people into dizzying, kaleidoscopic bursts. Rubber floor tiles swallowed conversations and footfalls. Black-clad servers, all unreasonably young and thin, seemed to glide about like swans. It struck me as the perfect spot for a tryst, or a cozy little assassination.

Paige Larwin came up behind me as I waited behind three other parties at the reservation desk. "Claire?"

"Yes. Hello. Good to meet you."

"I'm over there."

I trailed her like an obedient puppy, taking in the impeccably tailored platinum suit and perfectly obedient flaxen bob. On the way to the table, Paige stopped to glad-hand several equally well-packaged people whose faces were familiar from the news: Ivana, Leonardo, Lizzie. She treated the famous and felonious alike to an ardent air kiss and a blinding flash of phony exuberance.

Paige slid into a prime front booth. Crumpled napkins and soiled silverware littered the table. The plate in front of her held a scatter of wilted greenery, a puddle of wan, oily sauce and a solitary surviving shrimp beside a pile of crustacean cartilage. "You don't look a thing like your jacket photo," she said.

"I got a younger, thinner person without the dark under-eye circles to stand in," I quipped, though I could have replied in kind. I had pictured a hulking ogre on the phone, not this dainty, prom-faced blonde. "You've already eaten?"

"One of those days. Busy, busy. And I have a two-fifteen, so we'd better get you something right away. Shrimp salad okay? Fizzy water?"

"Sure."

She signaled a server and sealed the transaction with a twirl of her index finger.

"So," she said, dipping her pointy chin. "Let me be frank, Claire. I read *Aftermath,* and it missed by a mile."

She was dumping on my last book, calling my baby ugly. "In what way?"

"Every way. Too little plot; too much melodrama. And that ending—"

"Fortunately, the reviewers didn't see it that way."

She pulled a sheet from her briefcase. "No? The *Plain Dealer* called it 'a wrenching walk on the dark side.' And this from the *Wall Street Journal*: 'Read it and weep.'"

"It was a dark, difficult story. I can't see how a woman struggling to understand her lover's suicide could be anything else. Those quotes are out of context."

"No need to be defensive. The point is I can see what you're capable of, and that one simply did not measure up. But what's done is done. Let's talk about the new one, shall we?"

"Fine. Actually, I'm about finished with the outline. I should have it for you by the end of the week."

She produced another page, and I recognized Ben's firm, expansive scrawl. "*Perchance to Dream*: The story of a young Victorian woman trying to flee the life her domineering parents designed for her. Does that sum it up correctly?"

"Yes. I was having trouble getting to the heart of it for a while, but it's really coming together now."

"Take it apart, Claire. Trash it. It's a putrid idea."

"Ben loved it."

"Ben Rosmarin hardly qualifies as the poster boy for exemplary judgment right now. What you do is contemporary, women's, issue-oriented fiction, and you need to stick with that. A handful of writers can jump from thing to thing, but quite honestly, even if you managed to pull it off, you can't afford the risk at this point in your career."

I swallowed hard. "Since you don't like my work and you hate my ideas, maybe it would be best if I was reassigned to someone else."

She wagged a chiding finger. "I've heard about you, Claire. You can't be such a delicate flower in this business. If you're the sort that falls apart every time there's a little problem, this is definitely not the game for you."

My face went hot. "That's hardly what happened."

"Whatever. Quite frankly, your personal life is irrelevant as far as I'm concerned. You have a two-book deal, and I'm your editor for the duration. According to the contract you signed, that means you will deliver proposals and manuscripts, which I deem acceptable, in a timely fashion."

"I hear you."

"I don't think so. I think you're feeling too bruised to hear. But I'd encourage you to toughen up and take this in. You need to be brutally honest with yourself. Figure out what drives you. What questions are you trying to answer in your work?"

I stared at my plate as the waiter set it down. The shrimp lay like legless question marks on a trampled green battlefield.

"Take *Aftermath*, for example. What was the defining question there?"

I sipped the Perrier, trying to soften the painful lump in my throat so I could choke it down. "It was about Allison's struggle to understand Rick's suicide."

"No. The book was about Allison's inability to deal with the *fact* of his suicide. Your protagonist spent four hundred pages drifting around in a fog of denial. I wanted to shake her."

A glance at my watch confirmed that it was several minutes past my breaking point. "I need to go."

"That's fine. I've had my say. I'll expect to hear from you with a new idea by the end of the week and have an outline in two weeks, tops. Make sure it involves a pressing current issue, something we can translate into a nice, juicy hook for interviews. And make sure whatever it is relates to a question that grabs you. Then, go wherever you must to find the answer. When you do that, you'll have something worth the ride."

4

B.B. LeBeau entered Courtroom 803 through the prisoner's door. Restraining braces bound his legs, and his wrists were tethered to a cinch at the waist of his orange jumpsuit. Only his eyes were free to roam, and he took bold advantage, stroking select women with his insolent gaze, flashing a chilling smile as he did so.

His appearance raised a satisfying stir. No matter how much you'd read about little B.B., the angel-faced child who had hacked his sleeping family to death at the tender age of eight, the first in-person glimpse of him caught you short. Now almost thirty, he could still pass for a teen-aged boy. But this was the sort of boy who set your inner demons on high alert. LeBeau had an unnerving magnetic appeal: full-lipped sensuality, searing laser gaze, perfect features carved in coldest stone. One writer had called him a portrait of cognitive dissonance: wolf in a sheep suit. A bucolic landscape peppered by deadly mines.

Hatchling lawyers and newly minted detectives vied for unfettered views. So did the die-hard crime groupies who had lined up before dawn for a coveted seat. Reporters phoned in observations on forbidden cell phones. The prosecution and defense teams hunkered down in their mahogany foxholes, shuffling papers from encyclopedic files.

From the bailiff's chair, Deakin Barnes rose to call the court in session. His voice was an anvil strike on steel. ". . . the Honorable Gretchen Montrose presiding. All rise."

"The Honorable" captured only a hint of the fearsome respect Judge Montrose commanded. Words were swallowed at the sight of her. Smiles dissolved.

Mizzoner came by her fierce reputation rightly. In the eighteen years since her appointment to Arizona's criminal division, Montrose had put more defendants on permanent ice and booked more on that final cruise across the Styx than any four of her fellow jurists combined. Lawyers jumped through perilous hoops in a vain attempt to have their clients' cases heard by anyone else. Sniping behind her back was a wildly popular sport in judicial circles. Still, though her rulings left her far less than beloved in many quarters, they had proven unassailable on appeal. Montrose had never been reversed, and she had never come close to being unseated in public referendum, no matter how bare-fanged and vitriolic the challenge.

Barnes, who had served as her bailiff and unflinching ally since day one, referred to the judge's brand of justice as Swift Premium: fat-free, all natural, no artificial sweeteners. No baloney, either, he thought, chuckling mutely behind his broad, impassive face. You had to admire the crusty bitch, which he did, and then some.

Mizzoner also filled Barnes with a prepositional fear. He was frightened of, around, by, with, and for her. The judge's standards were nosebleed-high and she did not truck with the slightest disappointment. More times than he cared to count, Barnes had been sentenced to the judge's scathing disapproval for some minor transgression. No eye contact, nothing beyond the bare-minimum required daily exchange of words. The scars might not be visible, but they ran deep.

Still, what worried Barnes most was Mizzoner's reckless disregard for the basic rules of self-protection. The judge had amassed a world-class collection of nasty enemies. She got death threats the way other folks had their mailboxes stuffed with catalogs before Christmas, but she refused to take any of them seriously. No bodyguard for her, no watching her juicy target of a back.

As a result, Barnes took every threat more than seriously enough for two. He watched Mizzoner's back as best he could. He made sure she was never alone in chambers after hours. He always walked her to her car. Above all, he kept a close eye on what went on around her. Given what vermin passed through this place, he figured you could never be nearly paranoid enough.

His obsidian eyes huddled beneath a broad, sloped brow. He swept them slowly over the courtroom, checking to make sure everything rang tight and secure. The place swarmed with cops and security. Sheriff's detail was backed up by backup detail, which had backup of its own. These days, anyone entering the building ran a gauntlet of metal detectors, explosives detectors, practiced eyes, and evil-sniffing dogs. Still, Barnes faced this particular case with a deep inner rumble of unease.

LeBeau was bad business, even in a business where bad was as good as it got. Rotten things had a way of happening to people that man didn't like, and he had countless reasons not to like the judge. At the trial, she had never missed the chance to deflate the posturing creep. She had made him sit up straight and show respect and mind his stinking attitude. That, coupled with Mizzoner's impeccable rulings, had contributed to the capital conviction and death sentence. The bailiff could imagine what kind of thank-you LeBeau might try to deliver if he got the chance.

In the flurry behind him, Barnes caught the resolute strike of Judge Montrose's heels. She always wore four-inch-heeled pumps, which brought her to a stately six feet and change. Turning, he watched her stride smartly toward the bench. Mizzoner hooked a pewter wave behind her ear and peered down her narrow nose at the docket. As she read, the solemn furrow between her gray eyes deepened.

"In the matter of the *State of Arizona vs. B.B. LeBeau,* the court stands ready to hear a defense motion for post-conviction relief." She nodded toward the prosecution and defense teams. "Both sides ready?"

"Ready, Your Honor."

"Mr. Giordano?" She gave the nod to lead counsel for the defense, a hulking brute in gray pinstripes from Armani's Gorilla Line.

Gary Giordano hoisted his bulk from the chair and slipped on a pair of comically small, frameless glasses. "As you can see from the pleadings, Your Honor, my client has been the victim of a scandalous miscarriage of justice. Fortunately, this came to light before the most heinous imaginable travesty could occur. Today, each of us stands as a horrified witness to the grave potential for irrevocable error in every death sentence."

Montrose raised a traffic-stopping hand. "That's quite enough, Mr. Giordano. I'll remind you that this is a courtroom, not summer stock."

"I see no way to address this matter without the gravity it deserves, Your Honor. This young man has spent the last thirty months in prison, most of them in unthinkable conditions on death row. His future and his very life were thrown in jeopardy for a crime that was pinned on him by a man who would stop at nothing to make a political point."

Barnes could read Mizzoner's fine print, including a rare, disturbing note of desperation. The bailiff's eyes trailed along as the judge searched the gallery for an eleventh-hour reprieve. Where was the old lady? Martha Garmin had sat through every minute of the proceedings to convict LeBeau. A statement from her could be a big help here. Barnes was sure she'd been told about the hearing. In this case, because of the timing, notices had been sent by FedEx overnight.

Finally, Montrose's gaze settled on the young hotshot for the prosecution. Wanda McFadden reminded Barnes of a younger version of the judge: clear-sighted and loaded for big game. Fiery red hair capped a humorless expression and a combat-worthy, olive-drab suit.

McFadden rose and waited until every eye in the packed house lit on her. "Naturally, the state is dismayed by recent revelations about the possible mishandling of DNA evidence in this case. Still, we respectfully remind the court that the verdict in this matter was handed down after a fine, hardworking jury's careful consideration of more than three months' worth of witness testimony and considerable physical evidence beyond the DNA."

Montrose nodded. "Specifics, Ms. McFadden?"

"Certainly, Your Honor. There's the threatening letter that Mr. LeBeau sent to the victim shortly before the murder."

Giordano lumbered to his feet. "Nothing beyond a highly questionable signature linked that letter to my client."

"That evidence was not unimpeachable," the judge conceded.

"Two witnesses testified to seeing Mr. LeBeau's van outside the victims' home on the day the bodies were found," McFadden went on.

"Spare us, Your Honor," Giordano sighed. "One of those so-called witnesses was a nearsighted ten-year-old child; and the other couldn't state with any certainty whether the van he allegedly saw was beige or gray."

"The defendant has been implicated in several crimes with identical modus operandi. Multiple stabbings; the victims posed and the murder scenes titled in blood. Plus, the knife, that particular knife, has always been his weapon of choice."

Montrose clenched her teeth and waved down an apoplectic Giordano. "I don't need to remind you that our justice system is based on the presumption of innocence, Ms. McFadden. Mr. LeBeau does not stand convicted of any prior homicides. Invoking such cases now is strictly out of line."

Barnes could see the judge's screaming frustration. LeBeau's juvenile record, including the murders of his parents and baby sister, had been sealed in accordance with the law. For all legal purposes, his bloody hands had been washed spanking clean.

"The state simply urges the court to move cautiously, Your Honor. We ask for time to conduct a further and complete investigation before any decision is rendered in this pleading."

"What would be the nature of this investigation, Ms. McFadden?" Montrose asked.

The state's composure was slipping. "For one thing, we'd seek independent verification of the DNA results from a second laboratory."

Giordano rolled his rheumy eyes. "Allow me to clarify, Your Honor. Ms. McFadden seeks to violate the defendant's protection against double jeopardy on the highly dubious strength of evidence that has been admittedly mishandled by a scientist engaged in deliberate, criminal behavior? Do I have that straight?"

The judge gnawed her lower lip, a sign Barnes recognized as third-degree exasperation. "Mr. Giordano is correct. The court can see no reasonable promise of enlightenment from a reexamination of those particular samples."

The judge granted McFadden's request for a fifteen-minute recess. In chambers, Barnes watched her riffle through law books and make frantic calls to colleagues, seeking the out she knew did not exist.

"Where the hell is Martha Garmin, Deakin?"

"No idea."

Mizzoner smacked her desk with a fat copy of the Arizona penal code. "'No idea' doesn't cut it. We need her here—now!"

Barnes allowed a rueful smile. "Yes, boss. Whatever you say. I'm chanting abracadabra. I'm hauling out the bat's tongue and eye of newt."

When court reconvened, the prosecutor made a lame though impassioned final argument against LeBeau's release. "This man must not be set free. Countless times, he has demonstrated his flagrant disregard for the laws of society and decency. We strongly believe that he poses a serious danger to himself and others."

"Ms. McFadden's beliefs, though they speak volumes about her lack of hard evidence, are of no interest or relevance here, Your Honor," Giordano said with a haughty sniff.

The judge sighed. "Stand and face the court, Mr. LeBeau."

A lazy smirk stained the prisoner's face.

"Do you have anything to say in this matter?" asked the judge.

Giordano shot to his oversized feet. "My client has nothing to say."

"Mr. LeBeau? You wouldn't care to make a statement?" Mizzoner dangled the bait harder. Any outburst would give her the excuse she needed to keep him confined.

The prisoner shrugged and slumped in his chair.

Giordano placed an avuncular hand on his client's back. "In the interest of justice, we ask that this young man be released immediately."

Judge Montrose took one last frantic look around. Barnes's breath caught in the beat before she spoke. He knew what was coming. "Freedom is a privilege, Mr. LeBeau. If you abuse that privilege in any way, I will take it very, very personally. Do I make myself clear?"

The prisoner fixed her in his steely sights. Something sharp and ugly shot between them.

Mizzoner broke the eye lock, looking away in disgust. "Motion granted. That's it, Mr. Giordano. Your client will be transported to the penitentiary at Florence for processing. After that, he'll be free to go."

5

Richter greeted me with a baleful look and a litany of woes. He paced fitfully from the kitchen to the door, letting me know that he had an empty bowl and a full bladder. From his pained expression, I understood that the blinking message light on the answering machine made him jittery, as did the rotten stock-market news leaking at high volume from Mrs. DiMarco's television upstairs. Given the dog's agitation level, I presumed he must be heavily invested in tech stocks and telecom.

I let him out in the small backyard behind the kitchen and called my agent.

"How was the lunch?" he said.

"It would have been fine except that I was on the menu. You are speaking to my chopped and charred remains."

"What happened?"

"Paige hates my work and loathes my ideas; so, naturally, she insists that I stay on her list. The woman is a vicious nutcase, Win. You've got to cut me loose. Let's find Ben, wherever he is, and go there. A prison publisher would be better than this."

"I'll speak to Paige. I'm sure there must be some misunderstanding."

"There is. She doesn't get that I'm an actual person, not a word processor with hair. I can't work with someone like that. There has to be some way to buy out of the contract and go somewhere else."

His silence lasted a beat too long. "With so many houses consolidated, there aren't all that many alternatives."

"What about Preston? They were very interested last time."

"I discussed you with Stephanie Hutt, Preston's publisher, before we made this deal with Ridgefield. She wanted to sit out this round and see how things went."

My hopes plunged. "You had this conversation with how many houses?"

"All the majors. Ben was the only one willing to put something worthwhile on the table. Your best bet right now is to stay with Ridgefield and build from there."

"How am I supposed to do that with someone holding my head under water?"

"That will not be the case. I promise you. I'll call Paige right now and straighten things out."

The dog bounded in, chuffing madly, as I hung up. I followed his anxious glance to a paper scrap dangling from the AA Atlas Exterminators magnet on the refrigerator door.

Rainey had stopped home after school long enough to leave the note along with a trail of muddy footprints. She was going to her friend Danielle's house to work on a history report and to stay for dinner. There was no greeting, no signature, nothing but the sharp, dismissive scrawl.

"You should have known her six months ago," I told Richter. "That kid was about as sweet and affectionate as they come. She actually used to ask me for permission to do things. She used to seek my advice and come to me when she had problems. Sometimes, we'd just sit around and enjoy each other. Believe it or not, we were really, really close."

He cocked his head in a sweet show of doggie empathy. Then the phone blared, and he dove into a crash-ready pose, paws over muzzle, eyes clenched like fists.

Thinking it was Winston, I seized the phone before the first ring played out.

"Ms. Brower? This is Leonard Smithline calling from the Paragon Agency. I presume you received our notice regarding an overdue invoice in the amount of one thousand three hundred sixty-eight dollars and forty-eight cents?"

"Yes, I received your notice, but it so happens that my name is not Brower and I have no such overdue bill. It's a mistake, and I want it corrected immediately."

"Your name is not Clarissa Brower?"

"No. It isn't."

He read off the correct address, the number of my Visa account, and my social security number.

"I don't know where you got that information, and I'm not pleased that you have it. The fact is I haven't used that card in months and there is no unpaid balance."

"Oh yes there is, in the amount of one thousand three hundred sixty-eight dollars and forty-eight cents. I'm sorry, Ms. Brower. If you don't settle this account, we'll have no choice but to institute legal proceedings."

Richter paced in fitful arcs. I was tempted to join him. "Let me try this one more time, Mr. Swingline."

"That's Smithline," he corrected.

"There we go. If you say that's your name, I believe you. And you have to accept the fact that my name is Claire Barrow not Clarissa Brower. It's not my name, and I don't have an unpaid balance on my Visa bill. In fact, I don't use my Visa card, so obviously, this is a mistake. I want you to clear up your records and fix the problem immediately. And please, do not call or contact me again."

"Are you saying that you won't pay this bill?"

"Of course I won't pay it. I don't owe the money."

He returned to the script. "In that case, we have no choice but to institute legal proceedings. We will pursue this matter to the full extent of the law. It is my duty to inform you that this unpaid debt could jeopardize your financial standing and your credit rating. Also, you may be held liable for court costs and legal fees."

"We're not communicating, Mr. Smithfield. Please let me speak to a supervisor."

While I waited, the phone signaled another pending call.

"Good news, Claire," Winston said. "I just spoke with Paige, and she is very enthusiastic about working with you. She has tremendous respect for your talent. In fact, she's shooting for this next book to be a breakout. She's envisioning a tour, top marketing, and sales support. The works."

"Are you sure she was talking about me? Clarissa Brower?"

"Afraid you've lost me, Claire."

"Sorry. It's been one of those days, Win. Feels as if I've slipped down a rabbit hole. I was just on with a collection agency, trying to convince them that I am not who I'm not and didn't do what they think I did. Now you're telling me that the Wicked Witch of the West is really my fairy godmother and we're all going to live together in off-key harmony, happily miserable ever after."

"Paige Larwin may be a bit harsh, but she has a good nose for the business and she knows how to get things done. Her objection to your idea was based on what she perceives to be your best shot at a big jump in readership. We discussed the proposal, and I believe she's right about asking you to abandon the period piece in favor of a contemporary, issue-oriented work right now. If this book does as well as she expects, you can choose whatever weapon you'd like next time around."

Richter plopped at my feet, spent from his nervous exertions. "You want me to start all over again? This proposal didn't exactly come easily."

"Maybe that means it's not the book you are meant to write right now. Look around, Claire. I'm sure you'll come up with something wonderful."

"Sure, Win. What could be a better motivator than having a gun to my head?"

"Works for me."

"I'll see what I can do. Thanks for calling Paige."

The Paragon Agency was no longer on the line. When I dialed them back, their number rang busy. Moments later, the connection went through, but a recorded voice reported that the office was closed for the day.

Thinking that things could not look any bleaker, I decided to thumb through the paper. Halfway through the front section, an article caught my eye. By the time I finished reading, I couldn't wait to get to the computer.

There, I went online and mucked around in several sites that dealt with identity theft. Apparently, the crime was an enormous and rapidly burgeoning problem in the Internet age. All someone needed was a bit of easily accessed personal data to invade your finances and cause incredible, lasting disruption in your life. Victims could remain unaware of what was going on until the damage had gone on for months. This struck me as a deliciously diabolical idea to drive a novel.

I called Winston right away. "I've thought of something, Win. How about the story of a woman whose life is threatened by identity theft?"

"That's where someone steals your credit cards?"

"It can be a lot more than that. I saw a piece about it in the *Times* and did a bit of research. It can involve giant bills someone racks up in your name, raided bank accounts, and defaulted loans. A clever thief can slip inside your skin and practically rewrite your existence. I got the slightest taste just moments ago with one dumb mistake at this collection agency and I have to tell you, I can't imagine how impossible it must be to dig out from under a deliberate mountain of fraud."

"It's a wonderful idea, Claire. Lots of lovely rabbit-hole possibilities. Why don't you write up a short teaser and send it to Paige by e-mail. I think it's exactly the kind of thing she's looking for."

"Human misery, you mean? That's right up her alley, to be sure."

"You sound uncertain. If you need to do some more thinking before you contact her, take your time."

I scratched between Richter's ears for our mutual comfort. "No. I like it. I'd just rather work with Ben."

"I've been asking around. No one is saying much, but it doesn't sound as if he's going to resurface any time soon."

"That's all I've gotten, too. Guess I'm stuck with Miss Congeniality."

"She'll like this idea. I'm sure she will."

Clinging to his encouragement, I typed up a brief, upbeat description of the new idea. As I translated the notion to words, my enthusiasm grew. I had only the sketchiest knowledge of the subject, but it struck me as fertile ground. A character that had her identity stolen could face immense, life-altering challenges and conflicts, the stuff of which compelling reads are made.

The dog lumbered in, yawning, and paused beside my chair. Unblinking, he watched the monitor as I typed in Paige's virtual address and clicked the Send button.

6

Entering the Calibre Club, Aldo Diamond sniffed at the rarified air. His practiced nose caught spicy notes of creativity, earthy power scents, and a strong herbal overtone of cultivated gentility. There was the rich, inviting aroma of percolating ideas. The sour trace of jangling nerves and faltering self-confidence had to be his. True, he was widely considered one of the world's foremost experts in forensic document analysis, but what crouched inside was a closer match to his exterior: flabby, milk-pale, hopelessly unkempt, and awash in unsightly insecurities.

Diamond straightened his speckled blue bow tie and finger-brushed the shoulders of his size-46 stout navy suit. Peering down, he confirmed that his pocket square looked reasonably perky, his jacket was buttoned correctly, and his shoes and socks more or less matched. "Aldo Diamond," he told the uniformed man at the foyer desk. "I'm here for the Arcanum meeting."

"Certainly, sir. Dr. Griffey asked me to let him know the moment you arrived."

Diamond strode about, biting back a broad, unseemly grin. He pretended to study the somber portraits and lofty profiles of past club presidents, while he peered into the reflective glass, checking for bits of embarrassing matter between his teeth.

The Calibre Club was a highly prestigious, invitation-only think tank, designed to foster positive humanitarian change. Member résumés routinely included Nobel Prizes, MacArthur "Genius" Awards, and inventions of major import. The men who developed CAT scans and MRIs were members, as were the minds behind the latest cancer therapies and revolutionary new economic theories, and the particle physicists who discovered neutrinos, leptons, and charmed quarks. Solomon Griffey, a world-renowned forensic scientist whose DNA methodology had revolutionized criminal prosecution, belonged as well. Under his auspices, the venerable institution had opened its doors to monthly meetings of the Arcanum, a volunteer group of experts in diverse forensic fields who applied their collective wisdom to long-unsolved, "cold" murder cases.

The great man crossed the foyer in the guise of a wizened gnome. He caged Diamond's thick, clammy hand between his twiglike fingers and spoke in a barely audible rasp. "Welcome, Aldo. I'm so pleased that you were able to join us."

"I am honored to be asked, Dr. Griffey. This means more to me than you can imagine."

"Call me Solomon, please. Aside from a few necessary operating rules, we prefer to keep everything relaxed and informal."

Diamond caught his shirttail attempting an escape. With a sorry grin, he stuffed it back in place. "Informal suits me fine."

Griffey led him into an ornately paneled meeting room, where dozens of Arcanum members milled about, catching up over cocktails and canapés. Diamond recognized the dapper, commanding Lyman Trupin, former director of the FBI, and the towering form of Ted Callendar, an esteemed forensic psychologist and profiling expert.

Russell Quilfo, an Al Pacino look-alike who had risen to the upper echelons of the NYPD, drifted over with a lanky young man and a striking willowy brunette in tow. "Aldo Diamond, good to see you. Meet Perry Vacchio and Erin McCloat, both great admirers of yours."

Embarrassment heated Diamond's neck. "Likewise. I've been reading your articles about the management of mental evidence in insanity pleas. Fascinating stuff, Perry. And Erin, I've read your book on the history of torture. Read it twice, actually. Brilliant work, a quantum leap from anything I've seen before." These two were a quantum leap from anything Diamond had seen before as well. Both appeared younger by decades and far better looking than was reasonable for seasoned forensic professionals to be. Perry Vacchio struck Diamond as an earthier young Clark Kent, while Erin McCloat evoked a bookish twenty-something Julia Roberts.

C. Melton Frame hurried by on his way to attack the hors d'oeuvres, barrel chest heaving. His face, beneath the boot-black toupee, was a hypertensive pink, and pearls of perspiration gleamed in his mayonnaise-toned walrus mustache. "Chop-chop, Griffey old boy. You're always whining about my being late. Well here I am, right on the minute. I virtually hung up on an interviewer from *People* in the interest of promptness, only to find you, standing around, blowing smoke at one another."

"Good to meet you, Melton Frame. Name's Aldo Diamond." Diamond told Frame's rapidly retreating bovine form.

With a sigh, Griffey peered at his ancient Timex. "I suppose we should get the meeting under way. We're at that table, Aldo. I've saved you the place next to mine."

After the assemblage was seated, Griffey stepped to the mike. Everyone leaned forward, straining to hear. Despite his extraordinary public stature, the man had the voice of a summer breeze. "It is my distinct privilege tonight to introduce Aldo Diamond, the man responsible for advancing the controversial field of graphology into the respected science of forensic document analysis that it has become. I know that you're all familiar with his work, especially his invention of the Diamond EDGE, a computer-based system of exogenous digital graphological evaluation, which is used by forensic professionals and human-resources personnel around the world. We are fortunate, indeed, to count him as our newest member."

"Whoa! Stop right there!" Frame sputtered, spewing masticated bits of a Swedish meatball. "I thought he was a guest. I never voted on his membership."

"That's because you missed the past three meetings, Melton. Notices of the scheduled vote and its outcome were sent with the monthly newsletter."

Frame descended on the podium, displacing Griffey with his considerable bulk. "This is an outrage. How dare you induct such an unsuitable member behind my back! The Arcanum has never opened its doors to his brand of hocus-pocus, and we are not going to do so now."

"I'm sorry you feel that way, Melton, but the time for you to register those feelings has passed," Griffey said evenly. "Mr. Diamond has been duly voted into our organization, unanimously, I might add. I'll ask you to accept the decision of your fellow members and join us in welcoming him."

Frame chuckled. "It would seem there's a slight problem with your arithmetic, old boy. You can hardly call the vote unanimous when one of your most important members did not and does not agree."

"I'm afraid that's a moot issue at this point, Melton."

"Nonsense. I demand a thorough debate on this matter, and a revote. Or perhaps Mr. Diamond would care to save himself the embarrassment and simply withdraw like a good fellow."

Diamond shrank in his seat, craving invisibility. With gratitude, he caught Griffey's subtle but highly reassuring nod.

"You're out of order, Melton. Now, I'd like to cede the floor to Ted Callendar, who will introduce this month's case."

Frame pounded the podium with a furious fist. "This is an outrage. I will not stand for such treatment."

"Then perhaps you'd better sit," Griffey said mildly. "Ted. Over to you."

Frame continued to sputter as Ted Callendar extended the microphone in deference to his six and one-half foot height. Concentration claimed his chiseled features as he regarded his notes. "After a complete review of the twenty-seven applications for assistance we received this month, the intake committee has decided to focus on the case of Chrissy X.

"As you may recall, this was a young girl, estimated age between fourteen and sixteen, whose nude body was found in a rest-stop Dumpster on Nantucket back in 1984. Her face was battered beyond recognition, and the only identifying item was a small gold necklace she wore that was engraved with the name Chrissy.

"Police presumed she was a runaway and put out a national plea for information. For months, volunteers worked a special hotline, but none of the thousands of tips they received paid off.

"Now, a woman from Sudbury, Massachusetts, has come forward, claiming that the missing girl was her niece, a fifteen-year-old named Ruth Dolan. As the aunt tells it, Ruth's parents claimed she was killed in a car accident while she was away at prep school. They had a memorial service and placed an urn on their mantelpiece that was purported to contain the girl's ashes. Some years later, the mother died of a bleeding ulcer. Then last month, when the father was in the final throes of lung cancer, he confessed that Ruth had run away from school and gotten involved with drugs and prostitution. When the parents heard about Chrissy X., they assumed some unsatisfied customer or angry pimp had taken her out. The parents invented the accident story to keep the ugly truth from coming to light. I suppose they wanted to protect their daughter's reputation."

"And, perhaps, their own," Perry Vacchio observed.

"Not unlikely," Callendar said. "In a situation like that, shock and shame can win out against nobler instincts."

"The girl's name was Ruth, you said. Why was 'Chrissy' engraved on the necklace?" asked Russell Quilfo.

"Apparently, her parents had bought the necklace as a birthday gift. They got it from a vintage jewelry dealer, with that name already inscribed. They intended to change the inscription after they made sure their daughter liked the gift, but it turned out Ruth liked it so much, she refused to part with the necklace, even to have it reengraved."

"Damned shame to lose twenty years in a case like that," said Lyman Trupin. "Having the girl's true identity could have made all the difference decades ago. But now—"

"True, but there's nothing we can do to change that. The aunt is willing to cooperate fully. She preserved all of the family's papers, including Ruth's diary and some cards the girl mailed home after running away from school. Now that we know the true identity of Chrissy X., I think we have a decent shot at putting a name and face on her killer as well."

A sandy wave drooped over Callendar's brow as he tipped his head toward Frame's frantically waving hand. "Question?"

"Actually, I have several. Where do you people get the unmitigated audacity to conduct a member vote behind my back? Is there some collective amnesia about the import of my membership? I'll remind you I am a regular on *Charlie Rose*. I've been an honored guest at state dinners during the past five administrations. My last book spent sixteen weeks on the bestseller list and was named a *New York Times* notable nonfiction work of the year."

"Please, Melton. This isn't the time or place," Callendar said.

"This happens to be *my* time and *my* place," Frame roared.

"You're out of order, nevertheless. You are welcome to register your objections to the membership in writing, in accordance with the by-laws."

"*My* by-laws. *My* membership. *Mine!*"

"I'll open it up to questions and volunteers," Callendar said over Frame's apoplectic tirade.

"I consider myself personally responsible for every case that has been successfully cleared by the Arcanum during the time of my membership," Frame rambled on. "You have me to thank. Me!"

A shrill tweeting diverted the group's attention. With an apologetic nod, Quilfo crossed to the side of the room and flipped open his cell phone. As he listened, his expression went grim.

He strode to the podium, shaking his head in sorry disbelief. "Excuse the interruption, but that was my office. Seems B.B. LeBeau was released about an hour ago. Head of the lab that processed his DNA has admitted to falsifying LeBeau's results and several others. Some crazy attempt to discredit the death penalty. Judge had no choice but to vacate the sentence."

Frame turned the color of cement. "They can't let him out. The man's dangerous."

"Maybe so, Melton. But that's the way it is," Quilfo said.

"Outrageous!" Frame sputtered. "Utterly unacceptable. If that homicidal maniac is to be walking the streets, I demand round-the-clock protection."

"You're certainly welcome to make that request to the department. But absent any immediate physical threat, they're not likely to assign you a security detail," Quilfo said.

Quaking visibly, Frame sank in a chair.

"I'd advise all of you to keep your eyes open and report anything suspicious immediately," Quilfo went on, returning the meeting to Callendar's charge with a nod.

"Back to the Chrissy X. case," Callendar said. "I'll open it to comments and questions."

Diamond raised a hesitant hand. "It occurs to me that if LeBeau's conviction was overturned, that leaves the Garmin family murders unsolved."

The paralysis of terror was not enough to keep Frame from a sniping opportunity. "My word, the man can add two and two. Perhaps I was too hasty in my objections after all."

"Aldo makes an excellent point," said Heidi Cohen, a flaxen-haired forensic anthropologist. "Much as I would love to see the Chrissy X. case solved, I think we have a moral obligation to revisit the Garmin murders first."

"We have a procedural obligation to go with the case as planned," Frame said. For emphasis, he rapped his palm with the rolled-up cheat sheets on the Chrissy X. case that his research assistant had put together. If the group took up a different matter, he would be unthinkably unprepared.

Griffey's brow pinched. "I agree with Aldo and Heidi. We selected the Garmin case for review almost three years ago. Our investigation led to LeBeau's arrest and conviction. If we were wrong, we're duty-bound to uncover the facts. If we were correct, a very dangerous killer has been released wrongly. Either way, the clock is ticking. I move that we postpone our review of the Chrissy X. murder and revisit the Garmin case immediately."

"No, no, and no," said Frame. "If you do this, I swear I will tender my resignation, effective immediately."

Griffey's impassive look ignited Frame's fuse.

"That's it. The final straw. You'll be sorry. Every one of you. And don't think I'll be back!"

"Griffey made a motion. Do I have a second?" Callendar scanned the room and registered Lyman Trupin as the follow-on. "All in favor of tabling the Chrissy X. case in favor of a review of the Garmin murders, say aye."

"You think I'm not serious? I am leaving this pathetic little gathering. I'm walking. I am voting with my feet." Frame strode out with the soiled napkin fluttering over his chest like a flag of surrender.

Diamond's eyes sparked with alarm. "I'm so sorry, Solomon Griffey. I didn't mean to cause any problems."

Griffey patted the big man's arm. "Believe me, you didn't, Aldo. If anything, you caused a solution."

Once the door closed behind Frame, Callendar called the motion to a vote. Everyone chimed agreement. After a brief rehash of the Garmin case, Griffey, Callendar, Erin McCloat, Heidi Cohen, and Perry Vacchio volunteered for the detail.

"I'd like to ask Aldo Diamond to join us as well," Griffey proposed. "The Garmin conviction relied on strong DNA evidence. If that's been discredited, we'll need to explore fresh new avenues. I suspect the documents we have on hand from the LeBeau investigation may prove fruitful."

Diamond flushed with pleasure. "I'd be glad to help, if the group thinks it's appropriate."

"All in favor?" Griffey breathed.

There was a chorus of exuberant affirmation. Everyone descended on Diamond, queuing up to shake his hand. Callendar banged the gavel and declared the meeting adjourned.

7

I recognized my sister despite the Bo Peep wig and the sort of thick black glasses that usually come with a nose attached. Having penned two best-selling memoirs and hundreds of restaurant reviews for *Gourmand*, Lottie Burns had a hard time maintaining the anonymity she needed to do her job. Her picture had been circulated widely among New York restaura-teurs. The mean-spirited likeness hung in countless kitchens, often pocked with dart holes, slash marks, or smears of blood-toned sauce. Lottie did not mince words, and many found her raw pronouncements mighty hard to choke down.

"God, Claire. What's wrong? You look like *Armageddon, the Sequel*."

"So many complaints, so little time. Where shall I begin?"

Lottie whispered behind her hand. "Begin by ordering the second and fourth appetizer, the fifth main, and the fish special, sides number two, three, and six, and number one sixty-eight on the wine list. Make sure it's a 'ninety-eight. Otherwise, go for a half of two-twelve. Oh, and thanks for filling in at the last minute like this, sweetie. Le Bon Gout used to be so wonderful. I feel duty-bound to give Chef Henri one more chance to either pull himself out or finish digging the hole."

I scrawled tiny crib notes on my palm as I pretended to study the menu. "I'm glad you called. I'm starving. All I had for lunch was crow."

"Losing Ben and getting a witch like that, instead. You poor baby, how can I help?"

"I'm sad about Ben, and worried for him, but honestly, being orphaned is not my biggest problem right now. I'll deal with Paige. At least, I'll do the best I can. I couldn't imagine going back to teaching, not writing anymore."

"I know. Damned writing gets in your blood, and that's that. I suspect it's an incurable virus. Don't breathe a word of this, but I've found myself getting up in the middle of the night to work on a play. A play, for God's sake. Not that I have a snowball's chance in hell of finishing it, much less getting anywhere with it if I ever do get it done. Still, absurd as it is, I can't, for the life of me, stop. Can you think of anything more deranged than that?"

I dipped a chunk of bread in peppered olive oil. "Yes. Me imagining I was capable of raising a kid."

"You're looking at it backwards, honey. Rainey isn't a kid right now; she's a vat of boiling hormones. Think microscopic messengers in neon helmets and spandex bike shorts careening through her veins, running lights, bowling down pedestrians, charging wild."

"Then how do you explain your kids? Seth and Jessie are adolescents, too, but you can talk to them. They love you and Paul. They show respect."

"Is Rainey sleeping?"

"Coma quality."

"Eating?"

"Yes. I can't say she's a paragon of good nutrition, but she sucks down way more than you'd think to look at her."

"Doing all right in school?"

"I haven't heard otherwise, so she must be. St. Stephens reports every belch and hiccup by e-mail. A sneeze requires an in-person conference."

"She hasn't committed any felonies?"

"Unless you count ego assassination, none that I know of."

"Sounds like run-of-the-mill pubescent psychosis to me. Here's what's worked for us—"

Before she could spill the precious secret, a vampire-faced waiter in a tuxedo approached, brandishing an order pad. He was paler than the snowy tablecloth. Milk was swarthy compared to him. "Ready, ladies?"

"Any specials?" I asked.

"Ah yes. We have a lovely monkfish terrine with puree of celery root, yellow trumpet mushrooms, and baby bok choy served on a bed of frisée, and then drizzled with a balsamic vinegar reduction and lime-mango coulis."

Lottie always brought one to three dining companions along on the job. Multiple eaters enabled her to sample more dishes. To draw attention from herself and reduce the risk of being recognized, she made reservations in a phony name, paid the check with a pseudonymous credit card from her extensive collection, and had someone else do the ordering. After many such meals, I had learned to play the food snob and wine sophisticate with an almost straight face.

"The balsamic is how old?"

"Heirloom quality," Dracula assured.

"And the bok choy. Imported or farmed here?"

"Grown on our own farm, madame, as is all our produce."

"Organic?"

He sniffed. "Chef would have nothing less."

"Fine. I'll try that. And the quail to start. My friend will have the wild duck breast in veal *jus*—medium rare, and the poached oyster appetizer. We'll share the *pommes frites,* the asparagus, and the beet soufflé. And this Bordeaux is a 'ninety-eight, I presume?"

"It is. Excellent choice, madame."

"We'll see how it's drinking. I like the maker, but it might still be a tad young."

Blinded as he was by my obnoxious arrogance, he strode off without once looking Lottie's way.

I seized her hands. "If you give me a way to manage Rainey, I will be even more in awe of you than I already am, Sister Goddess."

"Nonsense, Claire. Why on earth would you feel that way? You're smarter and much more creative than I am. You dance better and run faster. You're cuter and funnier and more interesting by miles. I just happen to have ten years more mileage, twenty pounds more pork, and a lot more experience handling kids."

"You're sane and wonderful and stunning and brilliant and accomplished and mature. You have a fabulous relationship with a terrific man and two appallingly wonderful children. If I didn't love you so much, I would want to shoot you and steal your life. But I do love you. Everyone loves you. Sometimes I really hate you for that."

Even in the dumb wig and Groucho glasses, she was lovely to behold. "If everyone loves me, many people have a mighty strange way of expressing it. I get rocks through the window, gifts of rancid food, and tabloid accusations that I'm into devil-worship and eating small children. Well done, no less. Now *that* really smarts."

"Those people are all jealous or pissed off, Lottie. Believe me, I've been both."

"I love you, too. So here's how we handle the teenage monster problem—"

Mr. Living Dead returned with our appetizers. Lottie's poached oysters were garnished with a suspiciously large heap of beluga caviar.

"Damn it, I think I've been made."

"Maybe he's just into Dynel blondes. You were saying about how you deal with the kids?"

"Yes. It's simple, really. Teenagers need something to rebel against. Their job is to defy you, so you make that job simple and safe. You set up some phony restrictions you don't care about, and they get to rebel their perverse little hearts out. With Jessie, I forbade wearing makeup to school, so naturally, she would stuff her purse with more gunk than you can imagine and slap it on in the girls' room. She went so over the top, her friends finally ganged up and got her to tone it down. For Seth, I had a no-shorts, no-sleeveless-shirts-to-school rule, plus no reading after bedtime. That one was really effective. It got him through dozens of terrific books. Turned him into an avid reader. Pretty great rebellion, if you ask me."

"How can I make that work with Rainey? She doesn't give a damn what I say." I wrestled the quail bones for a morsel of flesh. It was rubbery and oversalted.

"Yes, she does, Claire. She cares more than you can imagine, but she'd get drummed out of the United Federation of Snotty Juveniles if she let it show. She wants you to set limits and enforce them and catch her when she screws up. The whole point of screwing up is to get your attention and have you show her that you love her and are there for her no matter what. Remember?"

I took that in with another scrap of tough, salty quail. "I don't have to remember, I'm still there."

"That's because you don't get how much Mom adores you."

"That's because she adores me angrily and judgmentally. She's eternally disappointed in me for what I'm not, which is you."

A tiny flash in Lottie's deadpan expression told me her oysters were no more successful than the quail. Valiantly, she downed them anyway. She never signaled her reaction by an uneaten dish. "That's not you, honey. That's Mom. She's gotten worse and worse since Charlie died, don't you think?"

"All I remember is all hell breaking loose when my dad had the accident. Most everything before that is a blank."

Her eyes went vague behind the silly frames. "Well, I do remember. Before she and my dad got divorced, and afterward, when she married Charlie, Mom was as sociable as they came. She'd seize any excuse to throw a party. The house was always full of people eating, drinking, laughing, telling stories. But Mom was the biggest draw, so warm and gracious, not to mention a fabulous cook."

"From the sound of things, we didn't just have different fathers; we had a completely different mother."

"In a way, we did. The Mom I grew up with was outgoing and upbeat. And funny."

"You mean funny as in ha-ha? Are you sure you're not confusing her with Aunt Amelia?"

"Absolutely. You know how I feel about Amelia. She has a terminal case of the screaming me-mes. All that woman gives a damn about is herself."

"I don't know, Lottie. I'm not saying she's the world's greatest altruist, but she definitely has a soft spot when it comes to kids."

"Sometimes a soft spot is a sign of something rotten underneath, kiddo. If you ask me, the only reason she's so good with troubled teenagers is that she happens to be a major case of arrested development herself."

"You could be right, I suppose. She's always struck me as a puzzle."

"Let's change the subject, Claire. I honestly don't give a damn about Amelia. It's Mom I'm worried about. Believe it or not, before Charlie died, she was full of life, open and happy. I can't stand to watch what she's become. I've begged her to see a shrink, try antidepressants. But she isn't buying."

"Wow, Lottie. You used the words 'Mom' and 'happy' in the same sentence. You think happiness is a possibility for her?"

"It's possible, sure. But first, she has to figure out why she's stuck and get beyond it. Nothing happens if you sit around stewing in your own poison juices."

The bloodless waiter delivered our main courses. Lottie's duck appeared to have died of natural causes. My fish resembled a building collapse. Lottie tasted everything and scrawled a few surreptitious notes. Chef Henri had penned his own epitaph in broken sauce and balsamic glue.

I glanced at my watch. "What should I order for dessert?"

"We can skip it. This is my fifth time here in as many weeks, so I've got the whole bleak picture. I think I'll walk home, try to work off some of these wasted calories before I get on the plane. This is not the body I want to have, Claire. I tried on some clothes last week, and I all but ran out of the dressing room screaming."

"Post-traumatic dress syndrome. I know it well. Where are you off to?"

"Paris, Florence, Rome, Barcelona, Madrid. It's for *Gourmand*'s annual Best New Chefs of the World issue. Car's picking me up in an hour to catch the red-eye."

"I'll miss you."

"You, too. I'll keep my fingers crossed that you have a new improved Rainey by the time I get back."

"I'm for that. In fact, I think I'll get started on the Lottie-and-Paul plan tonight."

"Do it. Lay down a law you don't really care about. And remember which one of you is the adult."

"Who's that?"

"Cute. What I'm trying to say is relate to her as the parent, no matter what. Even if she starts tossing all the toys out of the sandbox, resist the temptation to sink to that level and join her."

"I'll try, Lottie. Trust me, I'm going to give it everything I've got and pray that's somehow enough."

Rainey's friend Danielle's place was on the way home. I stopped in the lobby and had the doorman call upstairs on the house phone. Danielle's mother answered.

"Shari? It's Claire. I thought I'd stop by and see if Rainey was ready to leave."

"Leave? She hasn't been here."

"She left a note saying she and Dani were working on a paper, that she was having dinner with you."

"Hang on. Let me see what Dani knows."

The doorman fixed me with a curious smile while I waited on the phone. In the background came the burst of a sitcom laugh track. Muffled voices. Footsteps. Finally, Shari Auer came back on the line. "Dani says they did talk about working together tonight, but Rainey cancelled at the last minute. Did you try calling home?"

"I did, but I'll try again right now. Thanks."

"Sure. Let me know when you track her down."

There was no cell phone reception in the lobby. As soon as the signal bloomed outside, I dialed home. The phone rang four times, and then transferred to the answering machine. I scanned the traffic stream and hailed a cab.

On the ride, I fought to stay calm. Surely, there would be another note; a nice, reassuring explanation about her change of plans. Or maybe, Rainey would walk in just as I got there. In fact, she could be home right now, refusing to answer the phone. If my cell number registered on the Caller ID, she could be just perverse enough to ignore it.

Richter herded me inside, pacing in frantic figure eights, barking madly. His nervousness multiplied mine.

"Hush!"

I roamed the apartment in a rising delirium of panic, looking for Rainey or any sign of where she'd gone. Richter trailed too close behind, bumping at my heels, whining low.

"Rainey? Are you here?"

Mad notions trampled through my mind. Maybe she was hiding the way she used to when she was nine. Maybe this was all a silly joke, and she would pop out laughing, tickled to death as all children are by their parents' terror.

I called Danielle. "Rainey's not home, Dani. Do you have any idea where she might be?"

"Maybe she went to the library or something."

And maybe pigs could fly. "The library would be closed by now. Any other ideas?"

"Don't worry, Claire. Honest. I'm sure she's fine."

"Please. If you think of anything or hear from her, give me a call."

I tried several of Rainey's other, equally unhelpful friends. If they knew anything, they were not inclined to share the wealth with me.

For a while I stared out my bedroom window, willing the child to appear. When that didn't work, I went to the front vestibule and peered through the glass panels flanking the front door. Cars passed with a hazy flare of headlights. Across the street, a young couple pressed against a lamppost, limbs tangled, melded like ropes of hot wax.

No sign of Rainey.

Growing more desperate by the moment, I called my friend Duffy on his cell phone.

"Hey, darlin'. What's up?" Duff said in his tuneful brogue.

"Sorry to bother you, Duff. But Rainey's missing. I'm scared to death."

"Hang on. I'll be right there."

True to his word, Duffy soon pulled up in the animal shelter's van. He strode in and wrapped me in a bearish hug. "There now. Try not to worry. Everything's going to be okay."

"Where could she be? If anything happened to her, I don't know what I'll do."

"Don't talk that way, Claire. We'll find her. When did you see her last?"

"This morning. She stopped home after school while I was out and left a note. She said she'd be at her friend Danielle's, but she called to cancel at the last minute. I've called her other friends, everyone I could think of, and nothing."

"You have the note?"

He studied her curt message and frowned. I could see his detective wheels twirling beneath the calm veneer. "Does she have a boyfriend?"

"No. I mean, not that I know of. She doesn't tell me anything. She barely talks to me at all."

"Let's see who she does talk to." He brought up the call log on the cordless phone and scrolled backward through the outgoing numbers. The last call had gone to Dani. Before that, Rainey had phoned her friend Grace. The third dialed number was a cell phone I could not place.

Duffy rang the line and frowned. "No answer. Let me try to track it through headquarters. They have a GPS cell tracking system that should be able to find that phone at its current location."

He called in and got the information. "I know that address. It's over in Alphabet City. Not the sort of place you want a kid wandering around in after dark. Let's go."

"Alphabet City? What could she possibly be doing over there?"

Duffy's face drew in a rueful smile. "We'll find out soon enough, Claire. No point speculating in advance."

8

Diamond trudged up the two flights to Ted Callendar's West Broadway apartment. Mopping his brow, he bemoaned his failed annual pledge to embark on a lasting diet-and-exercise routine. He had battled a serious weight problem for decades, and, more often than not, the problem won.

Dense cooking smells and tinny echoes filled the gloomy stairwell. Emerging on the third floor, Diamond found the overlit hallway with its yolk-yellow walls a perverse relief. He raised the lion's-head knocker on Callendar's door and let it strike.

"Come in, Aldo. You're first."

"If I'm too early, I can come back."

"Not at all. I've got highlights from the Garmin investigation spread out in the living room. Make yourself comfortable and dig in. There's beer, soda, chips, pretzels, and M&Ms. If you need some other brand of fuel, I can call down to the market."

"Thanks, Ted Callendar. I'm fine." Diamond's strident hunger had gone quiescent in recent weeks, stilled by his joy at the invitation to join the Arcanum, but he knew from hard experience that it would reawaken, sooner or later, with a roaring vengeance.

His appetite shrank even further as he started perusing the documents. He was appalled by the autopsy close-ups, especially the slash wounds, each magnified to a gore-streaked trench.

The crime-scene photos proved even harder to take. Death was scrawled like obscene graffiti on the little boys' faces, the pretty young wife, and on Joe Garmin, who looked to be barely older than a boy himself. The corpses were posed like plastic mannequins; stiff, grotesque parodies of their human form. You could almost feel the killer's cruel hands prodding the waxen flesh, coaxing his victims into this revolting portrait. Diamond sucked air through his teeth.

"Dreadful, yes. I remember," Griffey said as he entered with Erin McCloat. Perry Vacchio and Heidi Cohen arrived moments later. In silence, they pored through the file, reviewing the evidence, notes, and reports.

"When we got through with this case, we couldn't see a single hole for LeBeau to slip through," Griffey observed. "We had positive DNA results from several of the blood spatters found at the scene. Looked as if LeBeau had accidentally cut himself."

Callendar circulated a fax. "Quilfo faxed this over earlier. It's a copy of the statement from Ronald Sallis, CEO of Celasphere Labs in Westborough, Massachusetts, saying he phonied the results to discredit the death penalty. Guy rambles on about the greater good and the lesser evil. Offhand, I'd have to say he slipped a cog."

The fax landed in Diamond's hands. "Handwritten, excellent."

He inverted the page, flipped it over, and then righted it again. "There's no evidence of mental imbalance, but I do see extreme stress. Acute conflict as well, especially in the signature. The erratic pressure of the strokes and the protective clustering are particularly telling. Notice how the 'o' in 'Ronald' cowers in the capital 'R.' Same with the 'S' and 'a' in 'Sallis.' You can all but see the gun to this man's head, though the threat may have been figurative. I'd love to talk to him. Find out what was breathing down his neck."

"That would be great," said Heidi Cohen. "But I heard he's been ducking the press, refusing all interviews. Anyone have a line to the guy?"

"Celasphere is working with the International Genomics Consortium. A friend of mine named Jack Lang is running that project. I'll give him a call. See what he knows." Griffey trundled off to phone from the kitchen, where his wisp of a voice might prevail. The others continued reviewing the records, trading shrugs and raised eyebrows as Griffey failed to reappear.

"A problem, you think?" said Erin McCloat.

Callendar frowned. "Wouldn't surprise me. This whole thing has that rotten-in-Denmark feel about it."

Suddenly, the phone screeched, startling them all. Soon, Griffey returned with his brow dipped below its habitual, rock-solid perch. "My friend Jack Lang called the chief of Celasphere and found his wife quite hysterical with concern. Seems Ronald Sallis left for work at the usual time this morning, but he never made it to the lab. The wife had urged him to stay home, said he didn't look well, but he was quite insistent that he couldn't take the time off. His car was found abandoned several blocks from Celasphere with the engine running. A thumbprint, not Mr. Sallis's, was lifted from the door handle, and traces of blood were found in the roadway beside the vehicle. They were A-positive, Sallis's type, though they're still waiting for a definite match."

Callendar's scowl deepened. "Doesn't sound good."

"Could be a simple disappearing act," Perry Vacchio observed. "Sallis may have made the admission without thinking it through. Suddenly, it hits the fan in spades. He faces a lynching in the court of public opinion, the demise of his business, plus jail time and wrongful-death suits that would likely wipe him out. Taking off might have seemed like the better part of valor."

"Mr. Sallis was not unsophisticated. I can't imagine that he was unaware of the probable outcome when he confessed," Griffey said.

"I have to agree." Diamond examined the fax again. "Despite the stress, the writing shows definite signs of conscious resolve. The man who wrote this considered his options and concluded that he had no choice but to make that admission. He didn't act impulsively. I can't imagine that someone in this mind-set would later decide to recant or flee."

"So you believe he was abducted?"

"It's a logical possibility."

Heidi Cohen rubbed the salt from a pretzel stick. "But who would benefit from his disappearance? It wouldn't change anything for Celasphere. The damage is already done. And even if Sallis recanted, getting the death penalty or any major charges against LeBeau reinstated would be a major magic feat at the very least. The state would have to put on a new trial. I don't see that happening with the key witness compromised to this degree."

Griffey stared at the file report on the DNA evidence that linked B.B. LeBeau to the Garmin murders. He lifted the paper stack and flipped it over. "Let's try looking at this a different way, shall we? What if Mr. Sallis saw no choice but to make the admission because he was coerced? Aldo's mention of a figurative gun to his head might be right on target."

"What kind of threat would be worse than what the poor bastard did to himself?" Callendar finished his Amstel and popped the ring from another can.

Standing, Griffey rolled his neck to ease the kinks. "That, my friends, is one of the many things we need to figure out."

Diamond had gone through all but the last few documents in the file. He skimmed several articles on LeBeau's arrest and conviction, the penalty phase and the jury's determination that the Garmin murders should be punished by the killer's death. Next, he came upon two sheets of ivory stationery stapled together. On top was a note thanking the group for their part in bringing LeBeau to justice. The writer identified herself as the wife of a policeman whose case against the killer had collapsed. The detective's career had been buried in the rubble, driving him to lethal despair. She had attached a short, unsigned note he'd left before hanging himself. Diamond stared at the pages, side by side, mesmerized.

"What is it, Aldo?" Griffey said.

"I can't say exactly, Solomon Griffey. Call it instinct. A vague red flag. All I know is that I'd like to meet this woman."

Griffey peered over his shoulder. "Then that's what you must do, my friend. Sometimes instinct is the key to the realm."

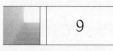

9

Duffy maneuvered the van into a tight space near the corner of Tenth Street and Avenue A. Much of the formerly sleazy, drug- and crime-infested East Village area known as Alphabet City has been gentrified in recent years, but the location of the cell phone Rainey had called was a notable exception. The squat brick building seemed to droop under the weight of serious neglect. Stark graffiti stained the pale beige façade, and black paint blinded the few unbroken windows. At the front door lay an unwelcome mat of shattered glass, rotted leaves, and crumpled takeout menus.

The doorknob twisted with a high-pitched squeal. Duffy grasped my elbow protectively as we entered the dark foyer.

I could feel his cop instincts kick in. His breathing quickened and his grip turned steely. "Maybe you should wait in the car while I have a look about, Claire."

"No, Duff. Rainey is my responsibility."

"Stay behind me then. Don't be taking any fool chances."

I did as he said, hovering behind his broad back. As my eyes adjusted to the low light, I registered further evidence of the building's long neglect. Cracks and missing fragments webbed the checkerboard tile floor. The beige plaster walls bore rotten patches and blots of seeping mold.

The air hung with the rank stench of urine, spoiled food, old sweat, and malignant decay.

Four narrow doors opened off the entry hall. The first three led to cramped, dingy rooms, empty if you didn't count the litter and filth. The fourth contained a narrow metal staircase, its balusters brittle with rust. Duffy motioned with a downturned hand for me to stay, but I had never mastered the basics of canine obedience. I followed him up, clutching the chill, grimy rail.

The staircase climbed to a narrow corridor. Here, everything, including the doors and several of the floorboards, had been stripped away. Stepping gingerly, we walked through what had once been five studio apartments. Now, rusty pipes and protruding wires marked the sites of plumbing fixtures and electrical outlets that had been torn out. Frigid air streamed through the broken windows, raising swirls of gritty debris. Grim-faced, Duffy regarded the crack vials, used condoms, broken bottles, and lipstick-stained cigarette butts that carpeted the floor.

"Not exactly the Ritz," he said.

"It doesn't look as if anybody's been here in a while."

"Nobody two-legged, in any event. That cell phone tracker must have been mistaken."

"What now, Duff? Where can she be?"

"Patience, sweetheart. We'll figure it out."

He pulled out his cell phone and dialed Midtown South again. "Duffy McClure here, Steve. Check on a cell location for me, will you?"

When he hung up, his frown lines ran deep. "He still gets this address, same as before. Maybe we should have another look around."

I trailed him down the stairs and around the perimeter of the building, cracking dried twigs, shoes slurping thickly in the mud. At the rear, we spotted a pair of blackened windows that ran partially belowground. We listened hard, but caught no telltale sounds. Duffy sighed. "Maybe I'd best call this in and get more muscle on it."

My legs went rubbery. "I promised Noah I'd take care of her. What if she's—"

"Don't go there, darlin'. She's going to be fine." He looped a meaty arm around my shoulders and drew me toward the front of the house. Halfway there, he stopped abruptly. "Well, and what have we here?"

"What?"

He pressed a finger to his lips and pointed to a fat black coil snaked behind the scrawny remains of a hedgerow. Duffy traced the cable back to the building's rear, where it descended through a Bilko door that was largely obscured by leafy debris. Crouching, he opened the metal hatch. The debris came away with it, a deliberate carpet of camouflage.

Heart thwacking, I padded down the stairs behind him. Beyond a small anteway was a locked door. Duff peered close, examining the hardware, waited a beat, and then reared back and breached the flimsy lock with his shoulder.

Inside, Rainey stood behind a pallid boy whose stringy hair was bound in a ponytail. He sat hunched over a table crammed with jury-rigged electronics. His fingers skipped deftly over the keyboard, replacing the contents of the screen with a strange-looking screensaver.

Rainey's shock at seeing us quickly dissolved. In a show of phony bravado, she crossed her slim arms and scowled. "What are you doing here?"

Despite the stampeding fury, I tried to heed Lottie's words and act parental. "The question is what are *you* doing here? You said you were going to Danielle's."

Her blue eyes struck the boy's, and then sparked with arrogance like a flint-struck match. "I didn't *say* anything."

"Get your jacket. We'll talk about this at home."

"You can't order me around, Claire. You're not my damned mother."

"That'll do, child," Duffy said. "Get your things."

The boy rolled his red-rimmed eyes, egging her on.

"What's your name, son?" Duffy asked sweetly.

"What's it to you?"

Duffy grabbed a fistful of the kid's torn black T-shirt and hefted him up from the chair. "Here's what it is to me: trespassing and corrupting a minor child, for starters. Plus hacking."

"Yeah? Where's your evidence?" the boy challenged.

"You see that ghost-pale complexion on him, Claire? That's known as a hacker tan. Then there's the posture, like the hunchback of Notre Dame, from all the hours he spends slumped over a keyboard. Plus, he's got the twitchy fingers. Some die-hard hackers can't stop working the keys, even when they're not actually at it."

"What a load of crap," the kid declared, though his expression betrayed an undercurrent of fear.

Duff turned to Rainey. "Hacking is a serious crime, no different from breaking in and entering someone's home. You can be brought up on burglary and computer felony charges, not to mention fraud and grand theft. That goes for the people who do the actual deed and anyone who happens to stand around knowing that it's going on."

The boy snickered. "Hey, I'm really scared. Look, I'm shaking. Now is that all?"

"Probably not, but you can bet your nasty little heart we'll find out every last sorry bit. Then you know what we do, Prince Charming? We add it all up: five years for this thing, three for that, eighteen months for the other, and so on. Before you know it, you can be looking at quite the big number."

"Don't threaten Phelan. He didn't do anything," Rainey said. "Anyway, you have no right. He's hardly even a cop anymore," she told the boy. "Most of the time, he picks up stray dogs and baby-sits them. That's all."

"No, sweetheart, that's not all." Duffy chilled the room with his icy calm. "I also pick up boys and girls who've strayed and see they get what they need. You, child, are going home—now. And your little friend is going to clean up his toys and do the same."

Rainey fiddled with a strand of blue-tipped hair, a comfort gesture left over from her infancy. With a sigh, she took up her jacket and book bag.

The boy's eyes strayed to the monitor. Gazing back at Rainey, he nodded. He was aiming for subtlety, but the message came through loud and clear. Rainey's laptop would be sleeping in my room tonight. That much, if little else, I could control.

On the ride home, Duffy tried to break the angry tension. "It's all out of caring, Rainey. Claire needs to know where you are, what you're up to."

"Caring, sure."

His sparkling green eyes fixed on the rearview mirror. "It's a fact you'll understand when you have children of your own to look after, but by then, it'll be too late to put the color back in poor Claire's hair. She'll be all gray and shriveled with the worry. Shrunken to the bone. A mere snip of herself. Frail as a bird and you'll have no one to blame but your-self. Oh the guilt. The terrible, terrible guilt."

I couldn't help but smile at Duffy's ramblings. Rainey showed much greater restraint. She sat with her slim arms locked around her knees, chin set in defiance. I pressed the back of Duffy's hand, urging him not to waste his words.

He pulled up in front of our brownstone. "Want me to stay awhile?"

"No, Duff. Thanks."

He eyed me gravely. "Sure you'll be okay?"

"Yes," I said, which was meant as a definite maybe.

Richter charged to the door as we entered. He circled Rainey, sniffing fretfully, begging to be debriefed.

Rainey, who in her former incarnation had adored all animals, cringed. "Get off me, stinkpot. You're such a pain."

I found my sympathies sliding toward the dog. "We need to talk, Rainey. Please sit down."

"I'm tired. I'm going to bed."

"Not until we talk this out."

Richter continued his worried examination.

"There's nothing to talk about. I can't stand being around you or this damned crazy dog."

"Who is that boy?"

"Phelan. That's who he is."

"What's the rest of his name?"

"It's just Phelan. Period."

"Where do you know him from?"

"Around."

"That building was abandoned. You shouldn't have gone to a place like that, especially alone with some boy. It's dangerous."

She laughed without feeling. "He knew you'd say that. Those exact words."

I curled my fists, trying to contain the angry frustration. "What were you doing there?"

"None of your business. Besides, you wouldn't get it anyway. Phelan's a genius. He understands things you never will."

"It is my business. *You're* my business."

"No, I'm not!"

She made an angry beeline for her room. Her door slammed, and a cold silence bloomed in the echoing aftermath. I clutched my ribs to still a deep trembling. Lottie was wrong. Simple tricks would never begin to resolve the problem. This was far bigger and uglier than normal adolescent rebellion.

Richter perched beside me on the couch, and we passed some time in grim contemplation. I stroked the dog's smooth flanks and his breathing settled. Slowly his muzzle lolled onto my lap, his eyes drifted shut, and he started snoring lightly.

Something inside me went light and still as well. I would find the way to fix this, whatever it took. The first step in slaying any beast was to acknowledge its existence.

Gently, I slipped out from under the dog and padded down the hall to Rainey's room. There was no response to my light rapping, but her door was unlocked. She had fallen asleep fully dressed on top of the covers with the lights ablaze. Her makeup had run in teary spokes, and the blue-tipped hair swirled around her head in a grotesque halo. Soundlessly, I disconnected the tangle of cords from her laptop. As I was about to leave the room, my eyes strayed to the outfit she was wearing. The stretchy black pants, chain belt, and peasant blouse were not familiar. In the trash bin beside her desk, I spotted the tags. The store was a trendy Madison Avenue boutique known for its high style and exorbitant prices.

My heart started thumping before my brain had a chance to engage. Rainey's allowance wouldn't cover those things in a year, and she had never shown a spot of talent for saving. I could hear Lottie's good-natured teasing: *Has she committed any felonies?*

How long had I managed to ignore what was going on? No matter, I told myself firmly. That was history. All that mattered were current events.

Overwhelmed with weary sadness, I headed for my room. This day had been filled with far too many hideous surprises.

1 0

The next morning, both Richter and I managed to hold our tongues until Rainey left for school. The dog seemed to share my resigned understanding that we were over our heads with this kid and sinking fast. He picked halfheartedly at his kibble and failed to work up a decent head of steam, even when a garbage truck passed with a jarring burst of noise.

For once, I didn't press Rainey to eat a decent breakfast or to reconsider her unfortunate wardrobe choices. In defiance of the chill that turned conversations into dueling clouds of breath, she wore a tiny denim skirt over bare legs, and a skintight striped turtleneck. I reasoned that I needed to choose my battles wisely from the many choices she put forth. The threat of frostbite seemed like chump change compared to other lurking dangers. Ditto purple knees and gooseflesh. Despite my mother's regular assertions to the contrary, you did not really "catch your death" from those.

As soon as Rainey left, I put in a call to my old friend Jed Slattery at New York–Presbyterian Hospital. At this hour, he would likely be on rounds. I gave my name to the page operator and then waited for him to respond.

Months had passed since our last get-together. Still, the memory made me wince. Jed had been my first boyfriend and, until Noah, my longest. Our relationship had bloomed during one highly memorable frog-dissection lab in eighth-grade biology and continued on and off through freshman year in college, when the strain of my freezing happily at Cornell while he just as merrily honed his fake southern drawl at Duke, shattered our fragile devotion. Years later, I heard that he had married a fellow student during medical school, and then divorced before finishing his residency in pediatric cardiology.

After that, I lost track of him until he showed up six months ago in New York. At first, I'd been delighted by his phone call, old-friend nostalgia and all that. But then, he'd turned up for what I had anticipated as a casual dinner, ready to pick up from exactly where we'd left off at about three in the morning after the senior prom in the backseat of his father's Volvo sedan.

After some very awkward grope-and-parry action, I'd explained that I simply wasn't ready for this sort of thing and shown him the door. We had talked since; short bits of neutral chat when he called every month or so, but, despite his mulish persistence, I had avoided another face-to-face encounter. I had resolved to offer him no encouragement, but right now he was the best place I could think of to turn for advice.

"Claire? What's up? Are you okay?"

"Not really. It's Rainey, Jed. She's been acting out, getting worse and worse."

"Sorry to hear that. What is it? Sex? Drugs?"

"I wish I could sum it up in a word or two, even scary words like those. Honestly, I don't know what it is. Just that she's so changed I hardly recognize the kid. I thought you might know a good child therapist."

"We've got the best in the city right here. Specializes in adolescents, in fact. Her name's Helen Bruno. She's usually too booked to get to for months, but I'll see what I can do."

"Would you? I'd be so grateful."

"Grateful enough to have dinner with me Friday night?"

I pictured his high-boned cheeks, the dance of mischief in his steel-blue eyes. "I'm not ready, Jed. I told you."

"Not ready for dinner? That's all I'm asking for, Claire, a nice, quiet meal with an old friend. We can talk or not talk about whatever you want. And there will be no hanky or panky, real or attempted, of any kind. You have my sacred word."

Richter tipped his head, looking dubious, as I smiled. "Okay, Jed. Dinner Friday it is."

"Great. I'll get back to you as soon as I track Helen down."

I hung up and poured a cup of coffee. Before I had the chance to take a sip, the phone shrilled. "Boy, that was quick, Jed. What'd she say?"

"This is a sixty-second warning, Claire. I am just now turning onto your block."

"Aunt Amelia? This isn't a good—"

Before I had a chance to finish the thought, Richter lunged for the hall and yipped to announce her arrival. My aunt swept in, swaddled in fur, trailing a cloud of powdery jasmine. I spotted her chauffeured Bentley, idling at the curb.

"I thought we agreed you were going to call first."

"I did precisely that, Claire. Come now. You're far too young to be so forgetful."

"I was looking for a little more notice than that."

She flapped away the issue. "Was that Jed Slattery you confused me with?"

"Yes."

"Are you seeing that charming hunk again, Claire? What a sexy thing he was, even as a boy. Reminded me of Juan, that gorgeous Mexican I met years ago in Cancún. The man would have been perfect if not for his silly wife and those absurd religious convictions. But as I recall, young Jed was unencumbered and positively gaga over you. I never did understand what possessed you to give him up."

"I'm not seeing Jed. I was just expecting him to call."

She issued a grand dramatic bellows of a sigh. "See him, Claire. See him if only to fool around and get some roses in those cheeks. You need to stop moping about before you dry up completely."

"What's up? I really need to get to work."

"Certainly, dear. You run along and stay as dreary as you like." She frowned at Richter, who chuffed at her with undisguised suspicion. "And take that mongrel with you. His aura is every bit as grim as yours."

"He's not a mongrel. Richter happens to be one hundred percent purebred paranoid schizophrenic."

"Nevertheless. I came to talk to Rainey, not dismal souls like that wretched beast or you."

"She's already gone to school."

"Pity. I did so want to tell her in person. I have divine seats for *Swan Lake* Friday night and a reservation first for dinner at Daniel. It's the start of the festival at Lincoln Center. One grand performance after the other."

Restaurant Daniel held the city's highest Zagat rating. "It's nice of you to think of her, but it's not a great idea right now. Rainey's been a major handful lately. She doesn't deserve that kind of treat."

"It's not a *treat*, as you so quaintly put it, Claire. Think of this as nourishment for the child's soul. Glorious food, gorgeous dancing. Perfect bodies, beautifully displayed." She raised her arms overhead in a trim oval and struck third position. "Her heart will soar; her imagination unfurl like the petals of a perfect rose. She'll be much the better for it, you'll see."

What I could see, with sparkling clarity, was Amelia weaving one of her outrageously effective spells. Sure, she was full of it, but for some incomprehensible reason, you wanted to pile her brand of horse manure on your plate and gobble it up.

"Maybe another time."

She forced her taut features into a pout. Amelia was either my mother's older or younger sister by five years, depending on whom you believed. But while Mom had been sinking for years with her ballast of heavy regrets and depression, Amelia fought age with unflinching tenacity. Botox, nips, tucks, couturiers, cosmeticians, hairdressers, and trainers kept her looking like an unmarked page. One of her many young acolytes, a formerly troubled kid, had straightened out, gone to med school, and become a hugely sought-after plastic surgeon. Though even Hollywood A-listers had to wait months for an appointment, Dr. Harold Strickland always made time and space to keep his dear "Auntie" Amelia in top form. A never-ending string of super-rich paramours and husbands paid the freight.

"You're being silly, Claire. Silly and stubborn, like your mother."

"Leave Mom out of this, Amelia."

"How could I possibly? Here she is, standing right before me, cunningly disguised as you."

"Please stop. You two are welcome to your grudges and jealousies, but I'm not playing. Anyway, this has nothing to do with you or my mother. I simply have to do what I believe is right for Rainey."

"Then climb down from that high horse of yours for a moment and test those beliefs against reality. Who is better with troubled young people than I am? How many have I rescued from their determination to self-destruct and set back on a positive trajectory?"

I took in the graceful flutter of her manicured hands, the doe-eyed wonderment masking the crusty granite core. Lottie was right. Amelia was nothing but an older, manipulative adolescent.

"You're good with kids. I won't dispute that. But Rainey happens to be my kid, and I have to deal with her my way."

"Please, Claire. It's *young people,* not *kids,* as you so crudely put it. Perhaps that's the source of my success. I treat those troubled young souls with respect. I do not diminish them or their concerns. I recognize their needs, their desires. Above all, I treasure their potential. Youth means a boundless frontier, limitless possibilities. I can help Rainey channel her feelings, dear. She happens to be a highly creative child, and I understand how to foster that creativity—mold it into something grand."

"Grand, sure."

"Get out of your own way, Claire. What on earth do you have to lose by allowing me to try to reach the child? If I fail, so be it. If she responds, as I am confident she will, you'll have a happier, far more positive Rainey."

It was my turn to sigh. I would be out with Jed Friday night, and I was reluctant to leave Rainey to her own, or, worse, to that creepy Phelan's, devices. "Okay, maybe you're right. But no Daniel. She's a *young person,* as you put it, not a pint-sized socialite. If you want to take her to dinner, please keep it simple and low-key. Otherwise, I can feed her here first."

"Not at all. I'm certain I can find someplace suitably seedy and unappetizing to suit your purposes. Must it be a chain, or will a stand-alone dive suffice?"

"I don't care about the corporate structure. Just make it something rated less than a Zagat 23."

"Appalling attitude, but predictable. I suppose you couldn't be expected to escape the legacy of my sister's stultifying genes."

"Don't push me, Aunt Amelia."

"I wouldn't think of it, darling. Might break a nail. I'll have the car come for Rainey at six."

"Okay."

"If she enjoys it as much as I suspect she will, there are many more lovely events to follow. And hear me, darling. Let her wear whatever she pleases. As far as I'm concerned, as long as she's cloaked in her own self-expression, she'll be sheer poetry to behold."

Maybe she'd wear blue lipstick to match the hair. Or, perhaps, by then she'd have moved on to glitter or green streaks. Maybe by Friday night, she'd add a nose or brow ring to the nettle cluster in her left ear, or have a Tigger tattooed on her right ankle to match the Pooh Bear on her left. The possibilities were endless. "Oh, she'll be cloaked in her own self-expression. No question about that."

"Marvelous. This is going to be such fun."

As soon as Amelia was out the door, the phone rang again. The Caller ID read "Private Call." Again, it was a woman's voice instead of Jed's.

"Claire? This is Helen Bruno. Jed Slattery suggested that I call."

"Dr. Bruno, I'm so glad you did."

"There's some problem with your daughter?"

"Rainey, yes. She's my stepdaughter, actually, but her dad died, so I'm her legal guardian."

"No mother?"

"No. She died when Rainey was a baby."

"Of?"

"A heart problem, something that went undetected until it was too late."

"And the father?"

The word caught in my throat like a blade. I couldn't get it out. "There was this mess at work. He was wrongly accused."

"I was asking about the cause of his death."

The image of him hanging in our bedroom that January morning flooded back. A clammy dizziness washed over me, and I slumped in a chair. "Depression," I managed to blurt. "Noah killed himself."

"I see."

"But that was three years ago. After the initial shock, Rainey was okay. She dealt with it better than I did, in fact. She's only been a problem for the last six months or so. She's gotten so angry, so withdrawn. And now, I find that she's been lying to me, sneaking out to see this older boy who seems to be some kind of hacker, hanging around in a horrible abandoned building." I left out my suspicion that she'd been shoplifting. Saying it aloud without absolute proof, even to a shrink, felt like an unthinkable betrayal.

"Sounds as if Rainey has had an awful lot to deal with."

"Yes. She has."

"Normally I don't do this, but for a friend of Jed's, I'll make an exception. Can you come in at nine, after my regular hours, tomorrow?"

"You mean Rainey."

"No, Claire. I mean you *and* Rainey. My approach involves kids and parents together."

"I understand that. But you don't know this kid. She won't talk to me or with me around. She doesn't see me as her parent or anything close. 'You're not my damned mother, Claire.' That's what she says. If you want to get anywhere with her, you're really better off seeing her alone."

"If that's what you want, I can recommend several colleagues."

"No, please, Dr. Bruno. Jed says there's no one better with adolescents than you. If you really believe it'll work, I'll go along."

"All right, then. I'll see both of you tomorrow night. We can discuss how to proceed after that."

I hung up, feeling puzzled and displaced. Where was the relief I'd expected? Why did the appointment with Jed's psychiatrist friend make my stomach roil?

Richter bumped his empty bowl across the floor, reminding me that I wasn't the only one with problems.

In my office, a mailbox icon informed me that I had messages waiting. Then again, I always did, given the endless feast of spam offering to enlarge my penis, keep it in a state of perennial elevation, equip me with eternal life, and provide easy, surefire money-making schemes with which to fund it.

Quickly, I scrolled through the unsolicited ads with my finger on the Delete key. I reacted automatically to the standard come-ons in the subject field: "Congratulations!" "Claire, you're an instant winner!" "Here's the information you asked for!" "This will change your life." I was poised to eliminate the last of the e-mails, when I spotted the return address.

My overloaded filing cabinet made the note slow to load. Aching with anticipation, I stared at the stuttering image on the screen. Slowly it came clear.

The header, including several paragraphs of transmission data, came first. I had to scan through that and my own message to Paige Larwin followed by yet another mass of Internet routing information to get to her response. As I searched, all I could think of was what I would do if she hated my idea for the new book. My confidence level had dipped into emergency reserve. Complete paralysis could not be far behind.

Finally, I found her answer. Like the woman, it was short and to the unadorned point. *That works. Now you have two weeks to do the outline and then until your contractual deadline to make the book work.* She copied the managing editor, the publisher, my agent, and the head of Ridgefield's legal department.

I pulled up my word-processing software and started a fresh file. *Once upon a time,* I thought grimly, willing an opening thought to show its face. *Once upon a time—*

11

Solomon Griffey meandered across the grassy expanse that flanked the United Nations complex on First Avenue. His lucky sport jacket, a muted, three-button, glen plaid with brown-suede elbow patches, offered slim protection against the wind, which whipped to a frenzied swirl as it traversed the East River. The member nation flags, set on a block-long row of towering poles, flapped wildly. A wicked gust blew him nearly off his feet. Still, Griffey drifted aimlessly, savoring the moment, still warmed by the eager reception his remarks on stemming global terrorism had received.

After the speech, several members of the Security Council's special counterterrorism committee had descended on him with enthusiastic praise. From their questions and comments, Griffey knew that his message had been successfully delivered and received. This was not a matter of politics as usual, and politics would never solve the underlying maladies. Human nature in its most inhuman form lay at the core of terrorist acts. Griffey's pitch had been to involve experts in human behavior and, more important, misbehavior, in efforts to anticipate and thwart the continuing threat. Forensic psychiatrists and the like could better predict perverse actions than could any number of statesmen, no matter how well-intentioned, articulate, impeccably groomed, or thick of hair. The response today justified the week of sleepless nights Griffey had spent crafting his forty-five-minute presentation. Despite his arthritic joints and the uncomfortable pinch of the polished brogues he wore in lieu of his usual foot-friendly loafers, his stride took on a jaunty little bounce.

Griffey tipped his head toward the massive bronze statue of a scantily clad Saint George having at the dragon. "I see you're not dressed for the weather either, old chap. I daresay you'd seek shelter if you could, and I suppose I had best do the same."

Nearing the exit, he spotted an approaching cab. Taking advantage of a vigorous tailwind, Griffey hurried toward the street with his arm outstretched. Just as the taxi slowed and angled toward him, a scruffy-looking man in a hunting vest and a hat with downturned ear flaps blocked his way.

"Excuse me," Griffey said in his feathery voice.

"You Solomon Griffey?"

"Yes. Do I know you?"

The man thrust an envelope in Griffey's hand. "Guy said to give you this."

"Who was that?"

"Couldn't tell you. All I saw was my good friend Andy Jackson on the greenback he gave me."

In the cab, Griffey slit the envelope with a cold-stiffened finger. Inside he found a newspaper clipping:

The Arcanum, a volunteer group that investigates cold murder cases, has now been named as a prime suspect in a series of murder convictions that may have sent innocent suspects to death row. The allegations come at a time when capital punishment is drawing heavy fire from a number of quarters. Interviewed shortly after his release from death row at Arizona's Florence Penitentiary, B.B. LeBeau called on law-enforcement officials to investigate the group and take a hard second look at the many cases they allegedly helped to resolve. LeBeau claims the Arcanum has engaged in a broad-reaching conspiracy to enhance the reputations of its members at the expense of innocent lives.

As the cab progressed toward the Calibre Club, bucking and heaving under the dubious ministrations of the two-footed driver, Griffey called ahead to reserve a room. Next, he dialed several members of the Arcanum. As expected, they had all received hand-delivered copies of the distressing article.

"LeBeau must have arranged all this," Callendar said.

Griffey caught the nervous jitter in Callendar's tone. "So it would seem."

"Which means he knows where to find us, what we're doing, where we live."

"True, Ted. But it also means that all he chose to do with that information was see to it we were informed of his intentions."

"For now."

"Perhaps. But it gives us time to forge a strategy. Can you get away for a brainstorming session at the club?"

"I'll be there."

By the time Griffey's cab pulled up to the East Sixty-fifth Street brownstone, a dozen members had agreed to convene. Coffee and cookies, along with a pitcher of water and an array of soft drinks, awaited them in the first-floor solarium. Griffey had informed the manager that this was to be a closed-door session. No intrusions of any sort.

Russell Quilfo, Lyman Trupin, and Aldo Diamond had already arrived. The others followed quickly, which allowed them to close the doors and get started in less than ten minutes.

Griffey surveyed the room. "Thanks for coming on such short notice, my friends. Let's get to it, shall we?"

Lyman Trupin stared at his copy of the article. "What do you think he's trying to accomplish with this?"

"If it's intimidation, he's hit a home run," said Heidi Cohen.

Aldo Diamond cleared his throat. "I'm afraid it could be much worse than that. If he succeeds in discrediting us, other cases the group has worked on could be dismissed also."

Griffey's lips pressed in a grim line. "That's precisely what I've been thinking, Aldo."

"I don't buy it. LeBeau doesn't strike me as the altruistic type. What would he hope to get out of letting a bunch of monsters out of their cages?" said Erin McCloat.

"A bunch of monsters who owed him one," Diamond mused.

Quilfo winced. "Talk about a law-enforcement nightmare."

Diamond reached for the cookies. "Could be worse than that. Picture the United Federation of Psychopaths with B.B. LeBeau at the helm." He popped a sugared cookie in his mouth and munched loudly.

Griffey went grim. "It's a truly dreadful scenario, and not one that I like to contemplate as a serious possibility. But I must admit it makes sense. Further thoughts?"

Perry Vacchio sighed. "Maybe this is nothing more than a diversion. LeBeau could be trying to keep us preoccupied and off balance while he plans some other mayhem."

"You mean like making the rounds one night to slash our throats while we sleep?" Callendar said.

Erin McCloat's hand drifted to her long, slender neck. "He has to know he wouldn't get away with killing all of us. Maybe this is simply his way of attempting to murder the organization that put him away."

"Possible," conceded Griffey. "But quite honestly, I can't imagine LeBeau being satisfied with the destruction of a group of volunteers. Maybe he wants that, but I'd bet that's not all."

Diamond dipped into the cookie mound again, his appetite expanding with the gravity of the situation. "I don't think we should dismiss Perry's diversion theory so fast. I agree that LeBeau can't be planning to murder us all. But he could score quite a few before the law caught on."

Callendar doodled a line of gravestones. "LeBeau has always been a major contributor to the funeral industry."

Diamond had downed every last crumb on the cookie plate. Now he played his tongue over his plump lips, seeking strays. Nervously, he scanned the room, wishing he'd brought emergency supplies. "Any ideas about what we do now?"

"Protective measures?" Vacchio suggested.

"Such as?" asked Russell Quilfo. "The NYPD is not about to build fences around all of us, certainly not on the strength of supposition and a newspaper clipping."

Aldo Diamond cleared his throat. "I think it goes back to the old saw: our best defense is a good offense."

"I agree with that one hundred percent, Aldo. We need to find out exactly what LeBeau is up to and try to head him off." Griffey folded his hands and leaned toward Quilfo. "Russell, if these charges against the Arcanum take root, you're going to be placed in a highly untenable position as deputy commissioner of the NYPD. If you'd like to take a leave until this all gets sorted out, I'm sure everyone would understand."

Quilfo's head dipped in reluctant agreement. "That's not the only reason for me to step out. If this thing blows up, the Arcanum is going to need whatever friends it can get inside the department. I can be far more useful to you in that role."

"Agreed?" Griffey took the informal count. "It's decided then. We won't be in touch unless it's absolutely necessary, Russell. We don't want to compromise your position."

Quilfo circled the table, shaking hands. At the door, he paused. "Err on the side of caution, if it comes to that, my friends. I'm afraid that compromising my position may be the least of our worries here."

1 2

Duffy drove us to the psychiatrist's office in the animal-shelter van. We rode in the company of a hugely pregnant mutt and two scrawny chocolate Labs, all refugees he had collected on his way to fetch us. The trio, caged behind wire webbing, kept up near-Richter-quality barking for the duration of the ride. Still, their agitated protests paled beside Rainey's.

"You can't take me someplace against my will. It's illegal!"

"That depends on the someplace, sweetheart," Duffy assured. "In this case, not a court in the country would convict."

"I don't have to. It's a goddamned free country."

Duff sighed. "In point of fact, most things cost dearly. Why, would you just have a look at what's happened to the price of gasoline."

"I don't need jokes, Uncle Duffy. And I don't need a stupid shrink."

"Right you are. But a smart one might do you some good." Duff caught my eye and winked. I held my expression deadpan, terrified that if Rainey got any angrier, she might find a way to breach the child locks and bolt.

Duffy was used to wrangling resistant creatures. Most, he soon won over with his sparkling Gaelic charm. But tonight, Rainey was having none of it.

"She's the crazy one, not me. You saw her after Daddy died. She just hung around in her pajamas with her hair all gross and stringy like some total nutcase." Peering in the rearview mirror, I saw her twirl a finger near her brow.

"We were all a little crazy after your father died, child," Duffy said, catching his voice on a thorn of sorrow. "Some things are like the devil himself to bear."

"Then you go see the damned shrink. I'm not. " She set her jaw and stared out the window. "And would you make those stupid dogs shut up? They're giving me a headache."

"Here we are now." Duffy stopped at the curb fronting Helen Bruno's apartment house on Eighty-fourth Street between Madison and Park. He opened the rear door and took Rainey's wrist and pulled her from the car like a stubborn cork.

"Let go of me. I mean it."

Sporting an aw-shucks grin, Duffy half-walked, half-carried her into the building. Rainey shrieked and squealed like a thing possessed. She flailed wildly and hammered her fists against Duffy's chest. It was the kind of raw display that inspired embarrassed curiosity, like a car wreck or a public exhibition of steamy sex. Exiting residents hurried by or stopped to whisper, point, and stare. Duff tried to contain her, but Rainey found a fresh weapon each time another was disarmed; nails, feet, teeth, killer looks, raw hatred. Seeing her like that took my breath away. I was dumbstruck with horrified awe.

The doorman, a bald gnome whose name tag claimed he was Enrico Caruso, stepped out from behind the sentry desk. He clutched his chest and his lips gaped. I thought for a moment that he might be taking his name too seriously and preparing to burst into song. Instead, he went red in the face and issued a great, hacking cough. When he recovered enough to speak, he fixed his watery sights on me. "Can I help you?"

"We're here to see Dr. Bruno."

As if that explained everything, he waved us on. "It's 4D, through the bridge. Elevator's in the rear. Take it to four."

The building was constructed in two parts connected by a glass-walled passageway. New York had many such anomalies, resulting from oddly shaped land parcels or stubborn owners who refused to vacate tiny buildings to make way for the soaring giants determined to stomp in and sweep them aside.

In this case, a modest frame house was wedged between the building's two towers like food between teeth. A square-hipped old woman in a starched white apron lumbered around the vintage '50s kitchen, fixing dinner for the toothless old soul who slumped at the table, staring through dull, milky eyes.

I could read their story as if it were printed in large type. They had lived in the house forever. Maybe one of them had inherited the place from parents or grandparents. No doubt the doorways were flecked with pencil lines that had been used for generations to chronicle the children's growth. Pictures, many of them sepia-toned or faded to amber with age, would be clustered on the dresser beside ancient bottles of evaporated perfume and a musical jewelry box filled with tarnished trinkets, knotted gold chains, and a broken ballerina.

When some major developer offered a king's ransom to buy them out, the woman had stubbornly refused, afraid that a move would destroy what little remained of her husband's failing faculties. She'd been afraid of where any road away from here might lead: to assisted-living and nursing homes and, not long after—perpetual care. Of course, what terrified her most was the demon *change*. So she had resisted selling, despite the urging of her family and the bullying of the developer's high-priced legal team. She had held her shaky ground despite the building that grew up around them in a choking fog of dust and a thunder of horrific noise, closing off their privacy, light, and air. As the old woman saw it, she was hanging on for their lives. Sometimes that was what it all came down to: hanging on.

In the elevator, Rainey stopped struggling. With a mighty exhalation, she went limp and slumped to the floor.

Duffy drew her up and flung her over his shoulder as the doors yawned on four. He turned right out of the elevator, strode down the hall, bobbling gently under her weight, and jabbed Dr. Bruno's doorbell with his free hand.

The psychiatrist was equally implacable. She barely acknowledged Duffy's existence, as if Rainey had showed up on a skateboard or Rollerblades instead of the shoulder of a ruddy, oversized, middle-aged Irish elf.

"Come in. Hello, Rainey. I'm Dr. Bruno. You can have a seat in there."

The room she indicated was warm and generous, furnished with oversized upholstered pieces and cozy, woven rugs. Comfort aids were scattered everywhere: crocheted blankets, stuffed animals, throw pillows, and boxes of tissues to soak up the sad and angry tears. Duffy installed Rainey at one end of the plush beige couch. "I'll be waiting."

I sat at the other end of the sofa, facing Dr. Bruno's high-backed leather chair. "Don't, Duffy. We can get home fine on our own."

"You sure?"

"Positive. It's better if we do. Honestly."

"Okay then." He turned to Rainey. "Settle down, darlin'. Ease up. Talk can be quite the tonic. Not to mention good for the lungs."

Helen Bruno's solid presence loosened some of the more painful knots in my chest. A mass of curly graying hair capped her kindly face, perfect foil for the Mother Earth body. She slipped on the cardigan draped across the back of her chair and set rimless granny glasses halfway down her nose. Dipping into a vertical file, she extracted a legal pad and pen. "The notes I take are for my own reference. No one sees them but me, and anything that is said in this room is strictly confidential. Do you know what that means, Rainey?"

That brought a shrug.

"It means I never repeat anything that is said to me here, not to anyone, including my family and my very best friend. Any secrets told in this room remain secrets. You can say whatever you want, anything at all, and it's just between us."

"What if I don't want to say anything? What if all I want to do is leave?"

"I'm going to ask you to stay for the hour. I saved that time for you, and it's yours."

"But it wasn't my idea. She forced me to come."

"Why do you suppose Claire did that?"

Rainey stared at the floor and fiddled with her blue-tipped hair. She was closed for business. Doors locked, windows shuttered, security gates down.

"Claire. Maybe I should ask you. Why did you insist that Rainey come here?"

"Because I'm worried about her. And because it's my job to look after her and see that she gets the help she needs."

The doctor scrawled a note. "Worried why?"

"Rainey has changed. She's become very remote and secretive. And last night, I found out she's been sneaking around with an older boy, hanging around in an abandoned building over in Alphabet City. You should have seen the place. It was a rat trap. Who knows what could have happened to her if we hadn't tracked her down." My voice was climbing a rope of hysteria. Helen Bruno tamped the air to calm me down.

"Can you tell me about this boy, Rainey?" the doctor asked.

No response.

"Is he a boyfriend, or a boy who happens to be a friend, or something else?" she went on.

Rainey bit at a cuticle. A scrap of flesh tore away and a gleaming bead of blood rose in its place.

"What about the man who brought Rainey in, Claire?"

"Duffy's a good friend to both of us. He's Rainey's godfather, in fact. He was her dad's partner on the police force for years. They were like brothers."

"What about your family, Rainey? Can you tell me anything about that?"

Rainey glanced up long enough to fire off a poison eye-dart, and then returned to studying the carpet.

Helen Bruno settled back and let the silence bloom. Nearly ten minutes passed without a word, though it felt far longer, an astonishing mass of empty, expectant time.

"What about school?" the psychiatrist said.

"School's school. Period. Now can I go?"

The doctor removed her glasses and rubbed the bridge of her nose. "We have forty minutes to go. If you'd rather not talk about other things right now, how about playing a word game with me?"

Rainey's silence bore a thinner coat of frost.

"It's called free association. I say a word, and you say the first thing that pops into your head."

The teenager peered up, blue eyes brimming with distrust. "What's the point?"

"It's like letting a frog hop, wondering where it might land. It can be interesting. You can go first if you like. You say a word, and I'll answer."

Rainey straightened, unable to resist the tempting chance to take control. "Boy—"

"Girl."

"Doctor—"

"Patient."

Rainey frowned, thinking. "Sky—"

"Diving."

"Diving—"

"Bell."

"This is so lame."

"I hear you. But I still get a turn. Warm—"

"Cold."

"Feet—"

"Shoes."

"Night—"

"Gloomy."

"Child—"

"Scared." Rainey stiffened. "No more. I hate this."

"Fine," Helen Bruno said. "No games then. What would you like to talk about?"

Rainey leveled a finger at me. "Only that she mind her own damned business and stop ordering me around. She's a major pain in my butt. Can you fix that?"

"No, but we may be able to fix it together."

Rainey sniffed. "You'd have to be a magician."

"It doesn't take magic to fix the things that feel wrong, but it does take hard work."

"Claire's the problem. All I need to do is get the hell away from her. Why can't I go live with somebody else?"

I picked up a stuffed blue rabbit that had been rubbed raw in spots. Its left button eye was missing, and the long right ear drooped sadly, as if it had collapsed under the weight of too much misery. "What have I done to make you so angry, Rainey? I don't understand."

"You don't understand anything." She turned to the doctor, suddenly bubbling with enthusiasm. "Why didn't I think of it before? It's the perfect answer. I could live with my friend Dani. Her mom is totally cool."

I held the bunny firmly. "Your dad asked me to take care of you, Rainey. That was what he wanted, and that's how it's going to be."

"How about what *I* want? It's *my* damned life. *I* should get to decide how to live it. Not you or anybody else."

"How would that be?" Dr. Bruno said gently. "How do you want to live your life, Rainey?"

"Without her."

"Aside from that. Suppose you could design it all. How would it look?"

Rainey went mute again, gripping her knees. Another dark mass of time limped by.

The psychiatrist's look brimmed with empathy. "It's the hardest possible question, I know. One most of us spend a lifetime trying to answer. Here's what I'd like to suggest, Rainey. Come with Claire to see me, and we'll try to work things out. You deserve to feel better about things, and I believe I can help you to do that. What do you say?"

After another long, weighty silence, Dr. Bruno declared the game a forfeit. "Fine, then," she said as she stood to walk us out. "I'll see you the same time next week."

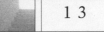 1 3

Friday night, Jed arrived bearing a package wrapped in dotted red gift-wrap with a curly crimson bow.

"You shouldn't have," I told him sternly. "You promised this was going to be strictly a friendly dinner out."

"Why don't you open it before you call out the firing squad?"

I did, and was relieved to find the contents suitably unromantic: a reissue of the best of *Mad* magazine, six sesame bagels from H&H, and a mouse pad featuring Betty Boop with her skirt billowing in the famous Marilyn-Monroe-over-a-steam-vent pose. I have always been a sucker for Betty Boop, and certain other things.

"Thanks," I said grudgingly. "They're great. Sorry I jumped to conclusions."

He took a slow look around, followed by Richter, who had sniffed virtually everything else of our visitor's by then and was now content to sniff at his heels.

"Want something?"

He leered ever so slightly.

"I meant something to drink, Jed. Let's not turn this into a clever fest, okay?"

"Where's Rainey?"

"Out with Amelia to dinner and the ballet. With any luck, it'll last a long, long time."

"Sounds like she's been quite the handful."

"That's an understatement. Helen Bruno was terrific with her, Jed. Thank you for that."

"Helen's great."

"She is. But I'm afraid it'll take a full-blown miracle to straighten that kid out. Rainey has mutated into something that would make an excellent Halloween movie."

"Things change, Claire. Give it time."

I felt the tears rise. Turning my head, I brushed them away. "Always the optimist."

"Bad stuff happens, whether I expect it to or not. Why worry in advance?"

"How did you get so sane?"

"Calling me sane? Now you've gone and hurt my feelings." He eyed his watch. "Hungry?"

"Always. That's why I look like this."

"Whatever you're doing, keep it up."

I made the T sign for a technical foul.

Jed raised his hands in surrender. "It was just a simple compliment, Your Honor. Please don't send me to the hole. I promise I'll never do it again."

"Compliments are fine. Just stop looking at me that way."

"How?"

"You know how. Don't be cute."

He slipped on his coat. "The place we're going doesn't take reservations. If we don't want to wait all night, we'd better get to it."

"Nothing fancy, I hope."

"Definitely not."

We walked in companionable silence to Jane Street and West Fourth, where he steered me into the Corner Bistro.

It was dark inside, redolent of smoke, beer, and the most tantalizing grease. My stomach growled like Richter under imaginary siege. Thankfully, there was no way anyone could hear it over the deafening conversations and the blast of Dizzy Gillespie's horn from the jukebox. Every table was packed; the bar was three-deep, and the line of people waiting snaked nearly to the door. Jed and I brought up the average age of the patrons by several years, at least.

"Best burgers in New York," he extolled in my ear. "You've been here?"

Most of my evenings out were dinners with Lottie. "I've heard of it, but no."

"Shouldn't be too long. Want a beer while we wait?"

I had two before our turn came to sit at a scarred wooden table capped by ketchup and mustard bottles and a stack of paper napkins. The menu was scribbled in chalk on a blackboard. You could have your burger with or without cheese and bacon. For the really perverse, you could have your cheese grilled alone. The vegetable choice was French fries. Except for the absence of dessert, this was my idea of restaurant utopia.

I wondered if Lottie had ever reviewed the place. When the burgers came, I was fairly sure she must have. Though my memories had faded during the three-year drought, each bite evoked a rush akin to sex. From Jed's heavy-eyed slackness, he was feeling it, too. Focusing through the din, I heard the same sounds coming from surrounding tables: low moans, sighs, and guilty-pleasure noises.

After dinner, we looped back to my place the long way, via the theater district.

"I love being here," Jed observed, filling his lungs.

"Me, too. Great city. Not an easy place to raise a kid, though. Sometimes I think maybe Rainey would be better off somewhere less complicated."

"Wherever you took her, she'd been in a complicated place, Claire. It's understandable. Poor kid has been through so much."

"True."

The wind had rearranged my hair. Jed brushed back a stray wave. "You've been through a lot, too, kiddo. I know that. I won't try to rush you into anything."

"Thanks, Jed. You're a pal."

"That's fine for now. But I do plan to be gently persistent. Okay?"

"Deal."

As we turned onto my block, I saw Amelia's Bentley drifting away. "She's ba-ack."

"Great, I'd love to see her."

"I think it'd be better to wait until things settle down."

His smile faded. "You're the boss."

"Things are just so testy with her right now. The last thing we need is another issue."

"I understand, Claire. Thanks for tonight. Best time I've had in months."

"Me, too. And thanks again for Dr. Bruno."

"No problem. That's what friends are for. In fact, I have a favor to ask you. I have to entertain a potential major donor to our new cardiac center tomorrow night at Aureole. Big dog-and-pony show. You'd have to suffer through some really good wines and excellent food. Any chance I could twist your arm?"

"As a favor? How could I possibly say no?"

He set a light kiss on my cheek. The spot was still tingling when I went inside, treading lightly in anticipation of whatever nasty surprises Rainey might have planned.

What I found was far more shocking than anything I might have imagined. She was seated primly on the couch, reading the ballet *Stagebill*. When she heard me come in, she smiled. She made eye contact. She spoke.

"Hi. Were you out on a date or something?"

"I had dinner with my friend Jed. I left a note."

"I just got back myself. You should have seen this ballet, Claire." She stood and twirled gracefully in her tiny skirt and clingy spandex top. "It was fabulous!"

"That's great. How was dinner?"

"Dinner was yum!"

"Where did you eat?"

"At Aunt Amelia's. She had the most amazing food brought in."

"Let me guess. From Daniel?"

She shrugged. "Don't know, but she said to tell you her dining room isn't listed in Zagat at all."

"Leave it to Amelia. If there's a loophole, she'll slither through."

Rainey kept drifting in fluid arcs, floating on the memories.

I stared at her, drinking it in. This was the Rainey I remembered. This was the well-adjusted, happy kid I used to believe she would always be. Maybe Amelia was right and this simple evening out marked some magical turning point.

I wanted so badly to believe that, I almost had myself convinced. Still, deep inside droned a warning voice: *If it seems too good to be true, it likely is.*

This was simply too good to be true.

 1 4

Judge Montrose crumpled a letter she had gotten as a young lawyer, confirming her appearance to plead before the Supreme Court. With an angry sniff, she tossed the prized memento in the trash. "You know what that is, Deakin?"

Barnes, who had spent much of the week as a cringing witness to the judge's unrelenting rage over B.B. LeBeau's release, showed his empty palms. "Simple line shot? I'd have to say that's two points, Your Honor."

She balled another document, and threw it at the wastebasket, which was now crammed to overflowing with legal briefs, articles she had authored for professional publications, long-saved correspondence, formerly cherished photographs, and reams of personal reflections, which, for years, Mizzoner had been planning to pare down and shape into a memoir, tentatively titled *A View from the Bench*.

She paused only long enough to wilt him with a frown. "Don't be a wise guy, Deakin. What all of that represents is my clearing the decks, getting rid of detritus. Letting go clears the mind. That's the fact."

"Right, Judge. Whatever you say."

She dumped a crystal statuette, depicting a blindfolded Lady Justice who bore an uncanny resemblance to Judge Montrose herself. The figurine had been given to her by an old friend to mark her twentieth anniversary in superior court. Mizzoner had loved it so, smiling whenever the figurine caught her eye. Barnes had rarely seen her so tickled by anything.

As soon as she turned her back, seeking more fodder for her discarding frenzy, Barnes retrieved the crystal figurine and several other things that had not been damaged beyond repair. Hastily, he stashed them in a file drawer. When the tantrum played out, make that *if*, Mizzoner was bound to have regrets.

Barnes's stomach made a noise like grinding gears. The desk clock read nine forty-five, and he was used to having his dinner at six-thirty. Seven, at the outside.

During all their other late sessions, the judge had agreed to break long enough to walk across the street with him and grab something from the coffee shop. He would eat his tuna or chicken salad with his eyes shut, trying to pretend he was tucking into his wife Denise's knockout pasta primavera or world-class chicken potpie, instead.

That had been bad enough. But today, the judge was too fired up to break for fuel at all. Food deliveries were banned because of limited weekend security coverage at the courthouse, so since coming here shortly before noon, Barnes had been forced to ward off starvation with whatever he could find in the judge's chambers. In this case, that boiled down to a couple of packs of stale chewing gum, a handful of jelly beans in his least favorite flavor—grape, a flat club soda, and half a bottle of extra-strength Tums. If the label wasn't lying, he soon would have the strongest teeth and lowest stomach acid of anyone he knew. Then again, what difference would that make when he was laid out in his Sunday best with pennies on his eyes, stone-cold dead of starvation?

"We've got a packed calendar next week, Judge. Maybe you should go on home and get some rest."

"I must tell you, Deakin. You don't look the least bit like my mother."

"After all these late nights, you've got to be tired out is all I'm saying."

She started culling books from the shelves. "All you have a *right* to say is whether *you're* fatigued or not. Judging the state of my energies is nowhere in your job description, as I dimly recall."

Barnes raised his beefy hands in surrender. "Fine. You want to stay here all night, spinning gold into straw; I suppose that's your concern."

"Precisely." Judge Montrose toppled dozens of volumes onto the floor. "We'll send these over to the law library on Monday. Please see to it that any personal inscriptions are obscured."

He watched her toss a book she'd gotten as a gift from Ruth Bader Ginsburg years before she became one of the Supremes. Barnes remembered how puff-proud Mizzoner had been of the justice's words: *To a brilliant jurist and treasured friend.*

"Right, boss. No problem." His stomach growled again, loud and surly.

The judge puffed her lips. "My Lord, Deakin. Would you please go and get yourself something to eat! Just because I have some things to see to, doesn't mean you need to hang around like an orphan out of *Oliver Twist*."

"You stay, I stay. That's how it is."

"I happen to be fifty-three years old, Mr. Barnes. It's been many, many years since I required the services of a baby-sitter."

"I'm sure that's true enough, but I believe I'll stick around just the same."

Gaping spaces loomed between the remaining books. The shelves reminded Barnes of his great-aunt Alva without her bridgework. Now, Mizzoner turned her vengeance on her desk drawers, discarding pens and pencils, paper clips, markers, business cards, hard candies, and twenty years worth of lint, crumpled postage stamps, and loose change.

Detritus. Barnes didn't know what the dictionary would have to say about the word, but it sounded like a good name for what was going on in his gut.

"Such a godawful waste," she muttered angrily. "And for what?"

"You talking to me, Judge?"

"Do you see anyone else in the room, Deakin?"

Barnes swiveled his head slowly. On this job, he had learned to take nothing for granted. "No, ma'am."

"And do you consider me to be the sort of person who might be inclined to converse with herself?"

He searched this time for a trick, and then prepared to protect his vitals if the need arose. "No?"

With a sigh, she slumped in her chair. "Well then."

"Sounds to me like you're questioning the whole ball of wax, Judge."

"What if I am?"

Barnes stroked the grainy stubble on his chin. He had ten o'clock shadow, going on fifteen. "Because of LeBeau? You telling me that rotten little piece of something the Lord coughed up when His mind was on other things has got you down on all the good hard work you've done?"

Judge Montrose hammered an angry fist on the chair arm. "He never should have walked, Deakin. I should have found some way to stop it. My job is to serve justice, and in this case, the service stank."

"The way I see it, you did what the law allowed. That's what they sat you up there on the bench to do, Your Honor. Where's the blame in that?"

"I don't know. But it has to lie somewhere. Releasing LeBeau is tantamount to opening a vial of toxic gas and setting it out on the street where it's sure to harm innocent people. If that's what the law says is right, then Dickens was right. 'The law is a ass.'"

"System works most of the time. Nothing's perfect, Judge. You always say that yourself."

She shook her head sadly. "This was no time for the system to break down. I keep wondering how long it will be until LeBeau's next piece of handiwork goes on display. The newspapers love what he does, you know. Norman Rockwell meets Freddy Krueger. Details at eleven. *Tell us, Mrs. Garmin. How does it feel to have your baby grandsons slaughtered? How does it feel to be a childless mother? Give us something for our voyeuristic viewers, Mrs. Garmin.* The whole thing makes me sick."

"Makes me sick, too," Barnes said, though he suspected that a belly full of chalky antacid wasn't helping any either. "But all that's LeBeau's doing, not yours."

"No? I've given him the means, Deakin. Doesn't that make me a conspirator of sorts?"

Barnes studied the judge through narrowed eyes, wondering how far over the line he dared to stray. What he saw, the Rock of Gibraltar crumbling at the edges, made him dare to go for broke. "Forgive me for saying so, Judge, but I believe you're not thinking right about this. You did your job, best you could. Congress makes the laws, and you are sworn to uphold them. That's how it is."

Gretchen Montrose rose to her full height and, to Barnes's eye, well beyond. "You think I've gone off the deep end, Deakin? Have you suddenly added my mental health to all your many other spheres of self-appointed expertise?"

"No, ma'am. That's not what I'm saying at all. It's just that I hate to see you take after yourself for doing your job. You're as good as they come and everyone knows it. Not one of the other judges is fit to lick your boots."

Barnes detected a terrifying flicker of a smile. It was like watching a pig try to fly. You knew it wasn't going to happen, no matter how the fool thing tried, and you hated to watch the useless, pained attempt. "Sorry if I'm speaking out of school, Your Honor. I apologize. Bottom of my heart."

"No need for apologies, my friend. You're right. I have been behaving irrationally. The simple fact is that I had no choice but to free LeBeau, and having no choice is maddening beyond words."

Barnes said nothing, afraid to break the spell.

"It's late, Deakin, not to mention Saturday. You've stayed here well after hours for the past several nights and then again today. Denise must be furious with me. And I'm sure those delightful children of yours miss having their dad around. How did Elissa make out with her SATs, by the way?"

Barnes was bowled over by the rare show of interest in his personal life. "She did great. Near perfect. Got her mama's brains."

"And young Stephen? Still the basketball star?"

"Oh yes, ma'am. Boy's got game."

"Which means?"

"Talent, Judge. Good moves, hands, and speed. Takes after his mother, too, so he's quick, not some lumbering, dumb, ugly thing like his old man."

"You're hardly that, Deakin." The smile came into full bloom, and it wiped ten years from Mizzoner's face. Shed of its tempered-steel testiness, her voice sounded years younger, too. "I must say you've given me a lot to think about. And I need some time alone to do so. Do me a favor, will you? Go home and spend what little remains of the weekend with your family."

Barnes had drifted in a fog of astonishment nearly to the door before he realized that he was being had. "All due respect, Judge. I go when you do."

The smile dropped like a rock. "Honestly, Deakin. This stubbornness does not become you."

"Yes, ma'am. I hear you. Message received."

"Then you'll go."

"Soon as you do. I'm out of here in a flash."

Angrily, she began to throw things in her cordovan briefcase: forthcoming cases she needed to review, relevant precedents gathered by one of her clerks, her appointment calendar. "Do you know how exasperating you can be, Deakin?"

"Not exactly, ma'am, but I have a pretty good idea."

She stuffed the rest into her purse: house keys, car keys, Chap Stick. "Contrary to what you seem to believe, I do not need a keeper. It so happens that I am a competent, reasonably intelligent adult, perfectly capable of going about my own business with no assistance from you."

"I believe that, Your Honor. Every last word."

She donned her Chesterfield coat, and then took up the briefcase and purse. "Excellent. Now, I am going to walk out that door, take the elevator downstairs, enter the parking garage, and retrieve my car. Meanwhile, you are going to stay right where you are and count, very slowly, as in 'one-Mississippi, two-Mississippi' and so on, until you reach one hundred. At that time, and not a moment sooner, you may do anything your overbearing, intrusive little heart desires. Is that clear?"

Barnes nodded eagerly. "Clear as that Scotch Tape you can't even see when it's on the wrapping paper."

"Splendid." The judge breezed out the door.

Barnes followed a step behind.

Outraged, she stopped in her tracks. "What on earth are you doing, Deakin? You agreed not to follow me."

"No, ma'am. All I said was that I heard you, loud and clear."

Angrily, she strode away. "This is ridiculous."

"Maybe so."

"Then stop trailing after me like an insecure puppy."

"Will do, Judge. Soon as you're in your car and on your way."

He followed her into the elevator. The judge stared through him, tapping her foot. "You are getting on my nerves, Mr. Barnes. Seriously."

"Sorry about that."

"Apologies are not what I'm after. What I need you to do is stop."

They crossed to the garage, and Barnes tugged open the heavy fire door. In a fury, she turned to him. "Stop, Deakin. Stand right there. I am going to walk to my car alone. Consider that a judicial order."

Only a few stray vehicles remained in the cavernous lot. Mizzoner's dark green Audi was at the far end. The space was stippled with dislocating shadows. At intervals, broad cement columns blocked the line of sight. The judge's footfalls echoed ominously as she strode away.

Barnes broke through his fear of defying her and scurried to catch up.

"If you don't go away this instant, Deakin, I will have you reassigned. Perhaps Judge Harrigan would enjoy your unrelenting attentions."

"You wouldn't do that." Harrigan was a bumbling fool and a proud bigot to boot. Barnes cringed, thinking about how the old jerk liked to order him around and call him "boy."

"Unless you cease this intolerable behavior, I frankly see no choice," the judge said. "This is tantamount to harassment, Deakin, and I have no intention of putting up with it any longer. From now on, I shall stay in my chambers whenever I wish, for as long as I wish, without the dubious pleasure of your company. I shall do my work alone, as it suits me, and I shall leave when I am good and ready, without an escort."

She strode off again. Barnes allowed her to put a car length between them before he followed. "Over my dead body," he muttered.

Something warm brushed the back of his neck, raising prickles of nameless fear. Then he heard a voice so insubstantial, it could have been an echo in his mind. "Good by me, Barnes. Happy to oblige."

Terror stalled him in his tracks. "What's that?"

"I said, getting to the judge over your dead body suits me fine," rasped the voice again.

The words slipped under Barnes's skin like a million stinging burrs. He forced himself to turn and face the unthinkable threat. But what he saw refused to register. "This can't be. You're not—"

The assailant laughed soundlessly. "Wrong, Barnes. You're the one who's not, or more accurately, about to not be."

The jolt of pain sprang from nowhere. Searching desperately, Barnes could not find its source. The man's hands appeared to be empty. Still, again and again, something sharp caught for an instant on his clothes and skin, and then plunged inside. The blood and strength escaped him in a torrential rush. Otherwise, he felt nothing but intense cold. Barnes was cold beyond anything he thought possible. Frozen muscles, crackling flesh, icicle bones.

He tried to scream. "Run, Judge!" But the words hung like vapor on the chill, dark air. Desperate thoughts started speeding through his mind. Stevie had a big game next Friday night. Barnes should try to get there early and sit behind the bench the way the boy liked him to do. Also, he had promised to read Elissa's application essay again after she cut out that business about the "N" word. Like Denise always said, you caught way more flies with honey. And big flies, Ivy League–sized, were what his little girl had set her sights to nab.

He was racked by painful tremors. He had on his heavy coat. Why was it so damned cold?

No time to think about that.

Better to fill his mind with Denise and the kids. This was such a big year for their baby, not that Barnes would dare to call her that out loud. He couldn't wait to see his Lissy decked out for the prom. Not to mention graduation. Barnes planned to bawl his eyes out over that. No shame he could see in tears of pride and joy.

"Fall, you stubborn son of a bitch," his assailant hissed.

Now he saw the blade, a ten-inch K-Bar, slick and glistening with his blood. A last, desperate thought displaced the others. *No, no!* He screamed soundlessly. *Please, don't! Please!*

It wasn't time for him to go yet. His kids had college coming up, more growing to do. Denise shouldn't have to manage by herself. That wasn't right.

As the curtain of darkness descended, he heard the rapid click of the judge's heels. Barnes struggled to stand upright and go after her. He had to protect his boss. Fool woman never had the first damned clue how to look after herself. Lord only knew what would become of her if he wasn't around.

Lord only knew.

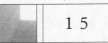

1 5

Whatever spell Aunt Amelia had woven remained in force the following morning. Rainey appeared in the kitchen shortly after nine, not one or two in the afternoon as had been her recent habit on nonschool days. From the sounds that came from her room, I knew she was not sleeping that late, merely holed up, avoiding me for as long as possible.

She wore an oversized Eminem T-shirt and red knee socks. Her hair hung wet from the shower. Most of the blue streaks had washed away, leaving only the vaguest Windex tinge at the ends. "Morning. You eat already?" she asked pleasantly.

"No. Not yet. Can I make you something?"

"Sure, whatever."

"Pancakes?"

"If it's not a big deal." She perched at the table on crossed legs and issued a squeaky yawn.

With a sidelong glance, I confirmed that she looked and sounded exactly like a regular kid, not some swivel-headed demon in dire need of an exorcism. "My pleasure."

She scanned the paper while I cooked. Tossed me the interesting tidbits. "They found that little kid who was missing in Atlanta. She's okay."

"Great. Who took her?"

"Baby-sitter. Must have been some kind of nut."

"Sounds like." I cracked two eggs over the bowl. They broke in tidy halves.

Rainey came upon another story worth repeating. "School bus crashed on a field trip to Mystic Seaport. Looks like the driver was drunk."

"That's terrible."

"Nobody died or anything. Just injuries. Says the victims were treated and released."

"Lucky."

"Big time. Remember when we went there in fourth grade and Marcy Kaplan got sick on the bus?"

"Marcy Kaplan got sick everywhere. I believe she was personally responsible for the early retirement of at least three school janitors."

"Remember that geeky guy who sang sea chanteys? We all had to practically hold our breath. He smelled so awful, like low tide."

"You didn't find that educational?"

"Yeah, really. Oh, look. Bloomingdale's is having a major sale. Think I'll go."

I whisked the batter gently, mindful that it was important to leave some lumps. "What do you need?"

"Aunt Amelia thinks I'd look great in tailored stuff. Blazers and slacks—like that. She said I should pick out a couple of things. Her treat."

I thought of the expensive, unexplained additions to her wardrobe Rainey had worn the other night. "She's awfully generous, Amelia. When did you get on her major gift list?"

Rainey shrugged. "She's been into buying me clothes lately. Says she really loves helping young people like me to find their personal styles. If you want to have flair, you need to be an individual, find your own look. I'm through getting my ideas by watching other kids or from those dopey magazines."

I coughed to cover the laugh. One evening with my outrageous aunt had rewritten the child's entire script. Amelia was a force of nature, no question about that. *Flair*, indeed. "I can go with you, if you'd like."

"I'll probably go with Dani."

I spooned pale ovals into the sputtering pan. "Sure. I should really work on my proposal anyway."

"She asked me to stay over tonight. Is that okay?"

"Honestly?" I steeled for a furious response.

Instead, she shrugged again. "You want to check with her mom? Knock yourself out."

The first of the pancakes went dry and bubbly, ready to flip. "If you promise you're telling the truth, I'll believe you."

She looked me hard in the eye. "I promise."

"Okay then. You can go."

Rainey turned to the Arts section. "Reese Witherspoon has a new movie out. It's a romantic comedy with Matt Damon. Does that sound great or what?"

"Should be." I bit back the suggestion that we go to see it together. Finding a pile of manure doesn't necessarily mean that someone has given you a pony. You can hurt yourself leaping to conclusions like that.

Still, though I didn't entirely trust the change nor have faith that it would continue, I was grateful beyond words for Rainey's improved frame of mind. She ate with good appetite, downing two short stacks of syrup-soaked pancakes, a glass of orange juice, and a large glass of milk. She thanked me for the breakfast, rinsed her things, and set them in the dishwasher. I could not help but muse that Amelia must have stolen the real Rainey and replaced her with a Stepford child.

After she left to meet Danielle, I headed to my office to tackle the proposal. I went armed with a cup of coffee and mounting enthusiasm about the new idea.

From further online research, I had learned more about the daunting problem of identity theft. Determined thieves had devised countless strategies for securing credit card, social security, and PIN numbers. Some went Dumpster-diving to retrieve credit card offers and bank statements that could be used to establish phony accounts. Shoulder surfers knew how to capture passwords entered into ATMs, no matter how surreptitiously. And then there was the Internet, which, for the ambitious hacker, amounted to a fishing pond stocked with millions of easy marks.

Last year alone, close to a million people were reported to be victims of the crime. Someone had gotten hold of their personal information and saddled them with unauthorized charges or raided their accounts. Though most people eventually recouped what they'd lost, restoring their good name and healing damaged credit ratings could prove a protracted nightmare. In the worst cases, a person's life savings could be wiped out by a clever, determined thief. For the purposes of my novel, I conceived of a worse case still.

Thoughts for scenes to propel the story came freely. At the outset, my central character would receive threatening letters as I had, demanding payment for purchases she had not made. Then, funds would be stolen from her accounts. New accounts would be opened in her name, and the debts incurred would threaten to bankrupt her.

I imagined my protagonist's gradual, reluctant awakening to the fact that someone had invaded her life and systematically begun to take it over. No one would want to believe that she was vulnerable to such an attack, that security and privacy were little more than an optimistic illusion.

As I wrote, I felt that chill that signaled I was definitely on to something.

I continued to paint my heroine into an ever-shrinking corner. Even as she thought things could not get any worse, the intruder who had slipped beneath her skin began committing crimes and leaving clues designed to make my protagonist look guilty. How simple it would be to forge a copy of her license plate, for example, and plant a car that looked precisely like hers at the scene of a robbery or a kidnapping or a brutal hit-and-run. While she was still trying to dig her way out of that, the thief could deepen the hole by ruining her professionally and cutting off her remaining resources. I hadn't yet decided on my main character's profession, but if she were, say, a schoolteacher, the crushing blow could be a trumped charge of child abuse, using an underage shill. If she worked for a corporation, she could be framed for embezzlement. If I decided to keep her closer to home and make her a writer, she could be leveled by a serious charge of plagiarism. Friends and colleagues would lose faith and abandon her. She would have no means to mount a decent defense.

A perpetrator had only to keep a careful eye on his victim to know when she would lack a credible alibi. He could chart her habitual movements and use them to suit his nefarious purpose, which was to ruin his victim for some reason I had yet to define. This would be a different form of annihilation, the destruction of everything a decent person spends a lifetime trying to build: an honest reputation, financial security, a home, personal freedom, trusting relationships, respect.

I hadn't read of anything like that happening in the current world of identity theft, but it struck me that such a progression was inevitable. The thief could do exactly as he pleased in his victim's name.

When the doorbell sounded, I was startled to note the time. Nearly five hours had passed since I sat down to work. My neck was stiff, fingers cramped, and my vision had gone furry from staring too long at the computer screen.

At the door stood a heavyset soul with melancholy eyes and a wry, regretful grin. "Yes?"

"Ms. Barrow? Aldo Diamond. Sorry to intrude like this, but I need to speak to you about a matter of considerable importance."

Suddenly, I got the joke. "This is about that bill, isn't it? I spoke to your agency yesterday. I told them those charges weren't mine and not to contact me again. You have some goddamned nerve coming to my home like this. Leave immediately, or I'm calling the police."

"Sorry, Ms. Barrow. This isn't about a bill. I'm here on behalf of the Arcanum."

"You are?"

He shuffled uncomfortably. "If it's not a good time, I'll be glad to come back whenever you say. I would have called first, but your number's unlisted and I only had an address, so I thought—"

"It's fine. Sorry for snapping at you like that. Please come in, Mr. Diamond. I have nothing but gratitude and admiration for your group."

Richter charged to the hall and gave him the sniff test, which the stranger passed with flying colors.

"Richter likes you."

Diamond scratched behind Richter's ear. "Feeling's mutual. And call me Aldo, please."

"I'm Claire. Can I get you something? Coffee?"

"Nothing, thanks. I wanted to talk to you about B.B. LeBeau. Don't know if you've heard, but he's been released."

"No. That's impossible."

He sighed. "Sadly, it's true. Head of the lab that tested his DNA admitted to falsifying the evidence that convicted LeBeau. In the face of it, the group has decided to have another look at the Garmin matter. I was going through the file and I found these."

He passed me copies of the note I'd written to the group thanking them for bringing LeBeau to justice, and of the brief, excruciating farewell message Noah had left. *This has to end. I know no other way. Please forgive and try to forget.*

Diamond spoke gently. "I study handwriting, Claire Barrow. Forensic document analysis, they call it. You can tell a great deal from a person's writing: mood, personality, stresses, psychological profile at the moment the sample was taken . . ."

I stared at Noah's note again. "And what do you see here?"

"Uncertainty. Intense conflict. Tremendous anger. "

"That's not surprising, is it? He was about to take his life."

"That's exactly what's troubling me. Right before a suicide, people usually reach a state of determined calm. They've made up their minds to end it, and that tends to resolve whatever inner torments brought them to make that terrible choice."

"Usually, you said. Couldn't Noah have been an exception?"

"Anything's possible."

I studied the reckless scrawl of his final words. "To be honest, I've never been completely convinced Noah took his own life, Aldo. Never made any sense to me, but then neither does anything else. If he didn't hang himself, someone else did. But how, and why? It's all simply impossible for me to imagine."

"I know how hard it must be for you, and I hate to have to dredge this up again, Claire Barrow. But I'd like to learn more about Noah. I think it might be valuable to our investigation."

"Nothing would make me happier than helping you put LeBeau back behind bars, but I honestly can't see how this is going to get you there."

He shrugged. "It may not. But I've been trained to follow my instincts, and they're pushing me hard to pursue this."

"Okay, then. How can I help?"

"I'd like to have other samples of Noah's writing. Anything at all."

"I'll look around and see what I can find. Can you stop back Monday?"

"Sure. What's good for you?"

"Any time after noon. I've got an appointment in the morning, but I should be here working all day after that."

"Great. I appreciate it. Good to meet you. You too, Richter. Pleasure."

After he left, I grabbed a cheese sandwich and then went back to work. Reviewing what I had written, I found to my enormous delight that I was well along in the story line. A few more days like this would propel me to the action-packed conclusion. Barring a disaster, I would have the proposal finished well in advance of the two-week deadline Paige had imposed.

By the time I got up again, it was nearly five o'clock. My thoughts turned to the evening's plan with Jed. Nothing in my closet was suitable for the dog-and-pony spectacular he had described. The only little black cocktail number I owned dated from years ago, when I still had a life. Trying it on confirmed my suspicions. The dress was out of style and cut for a far trimmer me. The zipper had to be coaxed and prodded like a stage-shy child. When I finally managed to wrench it shut, the mirror had nothing pleasant to report. The fabric clung like a sausage casing. My stomach bulged, and the incipient saddlebags made me look as if I were packing a pair of six-guns under the skirt.

Like Lottie, I suffered an acute case of post-traumatic dress syndrome. My confidence plunged, and I had a burning desire to throw out the offending garment and take its place in the closet.

Had the dinner been a month from tonight, I would have gone on a crash diet, moved into the gym, and hired the most sadistic trainer I could find to bully me into shape. Nothing but bean sprouts and lemon water would pass my lips until every last flabby lump disappeared. Briefly, I considered canceling, but I couldn't let Jed down at the eleventh hour like that.

Instead, I pulled on baggy sweats and grabbed my purse. Maybe the dress was at fault. Though people made a joke of garments shrinking in the closet, wasn't it logically possible for such a thing to occur? I imagined the fibers huddling together, clinging to one another in their loneliness. Or maybe my mirror was defective. Glass was prone to all sorts of distortion, as were perceptions. My seemingly altered body might signal nothing worse than astigmatism. Thinking of my long hours at the computer, I decided that had to be it. My eyes had gone fuzzy.

Still, there remained the terrifying possibility that Jed's eyes were working just fine.

I walked to Nicole's on Bleecker Street, got there moments before the scheduled closing time, and threw myself on the mercy of the shop's owner. Nicole was a towering Swedish blonde with an uncanny eye, who could always be counted on to slip you into something absolutely perfect. A local legend, she'd been held responsible for any number of marriage proposals and successful job interviews.

She appraised me from all angles. "This is for?"

"Dinner at Aureole. A business thing."

"What kind of business?"

"My friend is entertaining a potential donor for a new hospital wing."

A sly grin displaced her pensive frown. "I've got just the thing."

On the hanger it looked all wrong. It wasn't black, for one thing, and black was both slimming and safe. If you lived in New York, wearing anything else felt mildly subversive. I doubted that the soft rose tone would suit me, and I was even more dubious about the high puritanical neckline and flowing Morticia sleeves, but out of intimidation and respect, I agreed to try it on anyway.

She led me to the curtained dressing room and handed me a pair of strappy high-heeled sandals to complement the dress. When I emerged and spotted myself in the full-length mirror, I was stunned. Whoever that was staring back at me with her mouth agape, she looked terrific. She had great shoulders, a wisp of a waist, no stomach to speak of, and remarkable breasts. Her trim legs tapered to slender ankles and extremely sexy feet. If Jed hadn't beaten me to it, I would have invited her out for a fabulous dinner myself.

Nicole appraised me with crossed arms and a smug look.

"You must be a witch," I said.

"I'll take that as a compliment."

"It is. Of the highest order, believe me. How much?"

"Actually, it's on sale. Twenty-five percent off." She showed me the tag: less than two hundred dollars. I would have paid twice that to look half as good.

"Sold. I'll take the shoes, too, if you have them in size eight."

"Done."

She retrieved the shoes from the stockroom and hung the dress in a garment bag. Happily, I handed her my American Express card, imagining the look on Jed's face when he saw me in this getup.

Not that I cared.

Nicole rang up the sale, and then ran my card. She stared at the readout with a deepening frown. "Stupid machine."

"Something wrong?"

"It's denying the card."

My cheeks went hot. "There has to be a mistake. I know it's good."

"I'm sure it is. This just happens sometimes. Joy of computers."

I pulled out my Visa card, the one I never use. "Try this."

She did so, with the same result. This time, she looked even more embarrassed than I felt. "I'm so sorry, Claire. I'm sure it's the machine. Look, I need to close up. Why don't you just take your things and we can settle up on Monday?"

"Are you sure? I hate to make you wait, but I don't have that much cash." People deserved to be paid fairly and quickly for what they did. That was one of my aunt Amelia's more appealing convictions.

"Don't be silly. Go to your dinner and knock them dead."

She followed me to the door. "Go for dramatic eyes and soft lips. Oh, and think about wearing your hair up. It'll show off the neckline."

I flashed a victory sign, though I felt far less than victorious. Even though it had to be a computer glitch, the incomplete transaction felt wrong.

Anxious for closure, I decided to get the cash. The nearest ATM was two blocks away. I hurried there, cradling the dress, with the shoe bag slapping rhythmically against my thigh.

A kid in a backwards baseball cap and earphones hovered over the machine, playing it like a video game. He kept inserting and retrieving his card, tapping a variety of requests. I sighed loudly and cleared my throat, but my impatience was no match for the angry cadence pounding in his ears. The volume on his Walkman was turned so high that the music leaked out and throbbed on the chill, winter air. An eternity passed before he plucked a crisp twenty-dollar bill from the tray and walked off, bopping to the ponderous beat.

I oriented my bankcard according to the diagram and threaded it into the slot. Cupping my palm over the keyboard, I entered my PIN code. Quickly, I input the amount and requested a receipt. I waited as the machine processed the transaction, ghost's fingers clacking at the keys. As the typing sound continued, I kept gazing anxiously at my watch. More than ten minutes had elapsed since I left Nicole's. How long would it take her to close up and leave?

I stared at the blinking display that said *Please wait,* as if my will could hurry things along. A woman pushing a double stroller filled with toddler boys came up behind me. She was followed by a dour-faced matron walking a trio of perky bichons.

The dogs started circling wildly, yipping in nervous bursts. In seconds, they had woven their leashes into an intricate tangle filled with squat paws and arched feathery tails. At the same time, the babies staged a tantrum duet. They went stiff and beet-faced, mouths stretched around toothless howls.

"Is it working?" the young mother asked over the din.

The display had not changed: *Please wait.* "I don't know. It did a minute ago."

The babies' screaming seemed to fuel the dogs' frenzy, or maybe it was the other way around. The mounting commotion set my nerves snapping like castanets. I poked the Enter key again, as if that could possibly make a difference.

The little ones' screams intensified. Their harried mother plucked them from the stroller and planted one on each slender hip. Her attempt to bobble them calm had the opposite effect. Bending awkwardly, she rummaged through the huge, flowered plastic diaper bag that dangled from the stroller handle. She pulled out pacifiers, squeaky toys, Cheerios, and bottles of rouge-colored juice, all to no avail.

I shot her a sympathetic smile. You think this is bad, I thought. Wait until they're teenagers. Wait until their tantrums take the form of multiple piercings, tattoos, screw-you clothes, and psychopathic friends.

When I faced the machine again, the display had changed. Now it read: *The amount you've requested exceeds the available funds in this account.*

That could not be. Less than two months had passed since I deposited the partial advance due on signing for my new contract with Ridgefield Press. After paying the usual bills, plus necessary apartment repairs and Rainey's private school tuition, I still had a hefty balance in the checking account.

I tried again, starting over from scratch. I keyed in my PIN code and entered the rest. After another interminable pause, the same message flashed on the digital display. *The amount you've requested exceeds...*

The woman with the dogs peered over my shoulder. "Come on, lady. There are people waiting." Her imperious tone suggested that there were garden-variety deadbeats, and then there were clueless, thoughtless ones, like me.

The babies kept up their protests; the dogs their maniacal do-si-do.

"Go ahead."

Disgusted, I started home. When I passed Nicole's, the lights were out and a Closed sign hung in the window. There was nothing more I could do about my debt to her today.

1 6

Tudor City looms as an oasis of dislocating calm amid Manhattan's grand, chaotic sprawl. The planned residential community, which runs from Forty-first to Forty-third Streets between First and Second Avenues, was developed in the 1920s. It encompasses two generous public spaces, a few small shops, and eleven apartment buildings, perched on a hill over-looking the East River.

Turning into the complex, Diamond thrust his hands in his pockets and watched his slouching shadow ooze across the pavement. As he passed one of the winter-browned parks, he spied the sleeping vagrant curled in a fetal comma on the ground. The man's sole protection from the cruel elements was a makeshift windscreen fashioned from a weather-beaten moving carton and a meager blanket of folded want ads with the choicest opportunities circled in red.

Chilled further by the sight, Diamond crossed to the local delicatessen, tipped his head toward Battu, the turbaned counterman, and raised two fingers. In response, the clerk prepared and packed up two large takeout coffees and two roast-beef subs, along with pickles and coleslaw, paper napkins, plastic cutlery, and slim paper tubes of pepper and salt. A second nod from Diamond was all it took to have the purchases added to his house account. The register rang with a triumphal flourish, and then the clerk butted the cash drawer shut with his hip.

Diamond returned to the park and settled one of the brown bags on a corner of the battered moving box.

The homeless man blinked hard and flashed a crooked smile. "How do you handle a hungry man? The man handlers." His singing voice was a flimsy warble.

"Coffee's hot, sweet, and light, Harry," Diamond explained. "Extra mayo on the side, and there's tomato but no lettuce on the roast beef. Just the way you like it."

"Ruffles have ridges. Betcha can't eat just one."

"Got it, buddy. Next time I'll get you a bag of chips."

"Use Wildroot Cream Oil, Charlie."

"You're right, Harry. Bet I do look rode hard and put up wet. I'll be sure to have a shower and shave before I turn in. Meanwhile, you drink that java while it's nice and hot. And eat up. A body needs fuel in this weather."

"Take Sominex tonight and sleep. Safe and restful sleep—sleep—sleep."

"Sounds like a fine idea. Believe me. I'm all over that."

Harry examined the contents of the bag and went grim. "Nothing says lovin' like something from the oven. And Pillsbury says it best."

"I read you. Chips and dessert next time. I'll see what they've got that looks tasty. Good night, buddy. Stay safe."

"I'll be seeing you, in all the old familiar places." Harry's voice trailed away on the wind.

Diamond left the park, lumbered down the street, and turned into his building. His footfalls thumped like elephant strikes on the gleaming checkerboard tile. He was beyond bone-weary. Two days of testimony on direct examination, and a day of brutal battering on cross had him running on the last vapor traces from an empty tank. Today, he had spent almost nine hours with the assistant DA, reviewing documents and rehearsing testimony in preparation for his continued grilling by the defense come Monday. Talk about earning his keep.

He was currently serving as an expert witness in a brutal kidnapping that had gone wrong in the worst possible way. The victim, the only son of a billionaire investment banker, developed a brain hemorrhage after a monstrous beating by his captors. Over the next several days, the little boy slowly descended into unconsciousness. When the kidnappers were unable to rouse him, the stakes had been simultaneously raised and reduced.

Given that they could no longer provide evidence that the child was alive and well, no ransom would be paid. The perpetrators panicked and fled. The boy, who was comatose, not dead, could have been saved by a simple operation to reduce the pressure from the blood that was compressing his brain, but by the time he was found, he was beyond help.

The state had only a circumstantial case against the alleged kidnappers. Diamond, called in to analyze the ransom note, turned out to be the pivotal player in the trial. Everything hinged on his testimony, which hinged, in turn, on the credibility of forensic document analysis.

During much of his time on the stand, Diamond felt like a punch-drunk fighter, defending his turf against a series of brutal, steel-fisted assaults. Not that this experience was new to him. During his three-decade career, he had spent an absurd amount of energy trying to convince die-hard doubters that handwriting analysis was a breed apart from tarot reading, or parlor magic, or the analysis of lumpy skulls. His legitimacy had been attacked again and again on the stand, and in more professional and social situations than he cared to recall. The recent tirade by C. Melton Frame at the Arcanum had been painful and humiliating, but it was also par for the rocky course he had chosen to play. The fact that he had proven himself, time and again, through unassailable legal precedent and countless honors from the forensic community, did nothing to still the strident detractors.

All those years on the defensive had thickened Diamond's hide and numbed his sensitivities, but this particular case managed to pierce him, nonetheless. The kidnapped boy bore a striking resemblance to Willy, the young son he had lost decades ago. His darling wife, Emily, had been mowed down by the same speeding car. The reckless driver who had stolen his family and future served nine months in a minimum-security prison, plus two hundred hours of community service, giving safety lectures to high school kids. Diamond's sentence, for the selfsame crime, was much stiffer: a lifetime of lonely regret. No mitigation. Not even a remote possibility of parole. Since the accident, the only constant presence in his life was aching loneliness. Ravenous hunger, his more strident, unwelcome companion, came and went.

Diamond collected his mail and a package of laundry from the doorman. The letters bore a riot of yellow forwarding stickers, vivid testament to his nomadic existence. Professional obligations took him all over the world, from trial to trial and consulting job to consulting job. Whenever he could, he rented a furnished place for the duration. Hotel living had lost its charms during way too many years on the road. He liked having a place he could call home, even if it was technically someone else's.

He had learned to read subtle clues to the nameless souls who had occupied the rooms he now claimed. Worn arms on a plush chair or worn footboards beneath betrayed the owner's favorite perch and point of view. Books and other paraphernalia reflected hobbies and interests. Even the contents of a so-called junk drawer held crucial keys to personality. One glance at a seemingly meaningless jumble of matchbooks, coins, bottle caps, or cocktail stirrers could separate the saver from the spendthrift, the sentimentalist from the pragmatist, and the wary from the bold. Most revealing of all were the photographs. They spoke volumes about who meant what and how much to whom, and which moments a former occupant deemed worthy of capture, preservation, and display.

In his most desolate moments, Diamond found himself communing with these strangers. He smiled back at the gap-toothed children and waxed nostalgic over their weddings, birthday celebrations, and graduations. Weirder still, he joined these people he did not know in the occasional pull of sadness or puff of pride. Luckily, he still recognized such behavior as teetering on insane. But someday, if he didn't watch himself, he feared he might wind up hunched behind a battered moving carton, spouting songs and jingles from his mashed-potato brains, like Harry, who, according to local rumor, had once been a Secret Service agent, charged with protecting two first ladies and a secretary of state.

Diamond's third-floor studio sublet was still and dark, save for the answering machine, which blinked like a twitchy eye. The digital counter read an astonishing 23. Diamond's imagination took off at a run, wondering what cataclysmic disaster could have inspired such a flood of communication. Fortunately, or unfortunately, he could eliminate the death of a close relative. He no longer had any of those.

He grabbed a pad and pencil, pressed the Message button, and braced for the worst.

The first call was from Erin McCloat. *Hi, Aldo. Sorry I missed you. When you get a chance, check out CNN online. LeBeau was interviewed, and it wasn't pretty.*

Next was Perry Vacchio. *Aldo, I wanted to let you know that I think the B.B. in LeBeau must stand for "busy, busy." If you missed it, you'll find his* NBC Nightly News *segment on the network Web site.*

He listened to four more calls. All were from Arcanum members reporting on media appearances by LeBeau. The creep had embarked on a publicity whirlwind. Lord knew what fresh vicious lies he was determined to spread.

Suddenly wide-awake and bristling with curiosity, Diamond fired up his long-neglected laptop. The building had been wired recently for high-speed Internet access, but given that he rarely stayed settled anyplace for more than a couple of months, he had declined to subscribe.

Over his outmoded modem, the streaming media clips were maddeningly slow to load. After visiting a few of the sites, Diamond decided that taking the full tour was unnecessary. Every appearance hammered home the same absurd idea. B.B. LeBeau, long viewed as a grisly curiosity, the child prodigy of serial murderers, was busily recasting himself as a sacrificial lamb.

Predictably, the major villain in the piece was the Arcanum, which, as LeBeau continued to claim, had engaged in a cold-blooded conspiracy to place him on death row. The motivation, he charged, was simple self-interest. The group had used the Garmin case to bring attention and glory to the organization. To bolster the absurd allegation, LeBeau cited several publicity pieces, a large grant, and a number of major contributions that allegedly had come to the Arcanum as a result of his death sentence.

Watching the clips, Diamond could feel the shifting winds of media sentiment. The tides of public opinion were bound to turn as well. Soon, if they didn't find a way to counter this burgeoning lunacy, LeBeau would be sporting a martyr's thorny crown and enjoying the blind adulation that went with it.

His mind strayed from LeBeau to the current kidnapping trial. From there he made the short, perilous leap back to his dead wife and son. Just before the accident that took them both, Diamond had been struck by a screaming premonition of doom. He was on the stand at the time, testifying in a nasty case of fraud, and the feeling had torn through him like a blazing sword. If only he had ignored the judge's refusal to grant a recess so that he could call home. A warning to his wife might have changed everything. Calamity hinged on the slightest things: a breath of time, a word. If he had called, Emily would have gone to the bus stop in a more cautious frame of mind. She might have seen the speeding car sooner and called out to Willy in time to keep him from charging into the street.

Diamond imagined the boy waiting obediently, safely, beside the school bus. He could picture Willy's cowlick bobbing like a comical antenna as he practiced his soccer kick on stray pebbles and twigs. The boy would never have run into the street. Em would never have witnessed the impending disaster and charged into harm's way in a desperate urge to save their son. The two of them could have been waiting for him at home that night and for an eternity of miraculous nights thereafter.

Diamond's heart squeezed as he conjured his son's delight at his homecoming. He could hear the loud, candy-tinged kiss; feel the chunky little arms around his neck; smell the boy's distinctive scent of clean sweat and fresh air and earth.

His appetite awakened with a primal howl. He tore open the deli bag, and wrestled the sandwich from its paper cocoon. Removing the top half of the hero roll, as one in the long string of diet counselors had advised, he consumed half the sub in measured bites. He kept reminding himself to chew, taste, and swallow, in that order. But in a spiraling scenario that was all too familiar to him, the more he ate the hungrier he became.

His craving swelled to a mammoth, marauding, unstoppable beast. He sucked down the remainder of the hero and then all but inhaled the other half of the roll. The pickle spears followed along with the coleslaw, though, in rational moments, he was not partial to either. He even licked clean the little cup of extra mayo and poured the salt directly on his tongue. Despite his mounting self-disgust, he riffled through the near-empty cupboards. At the dusty rear of a top shelf, he found a package of ancient breadsticks, courtesy of the former occupant, and two cans of baked beans. He opened both and started spooning the cold, viscous beans into his mouth along with great, chomping bites of breadstick.

Diamond recognized the perilous territory he had entered, but he was powerless to escape. When he got like this, everything was substance, not form, and there was never enough substance to fill the yawning void. Once the breadsticks and beans ran out, he would be forced to do the same. He would go to the deli and wipe them out of snack cakes, soda pop, and all manner of fatty junk. Panic nipped at him as he realized that nothing edible, beyond the rapidly disappearing beans and breadsticks, remained in the apartment. Then, perhaps, he could slather ketchup on the sandwich wrap and eat that. The idea was actually starting to appeal to him when the phone rang yet again.

This time it was Griffey. "How are you doing with all of this, Aldo? Any regrets about joining our beleaguered society?"

"Not a one."

"I'm glad to hear that. But still, from the sound of things, I gather you find this all as upsetting as I do."

Cringing, Diamond realized that he had been shoveling bean-coated breadsticks into his ravenous maw. Making noises like a wood chipper. "I have this awful feeling that LeBeau's going to pull it off, Solomon Griffey. In this game, people who don't play by the rules have a definite advantage."

"Somehow, we are going to make sure that does not happen. But I agree with you. It's going to be a difficult, uphill climb."

The weary defeat in Griffey's tone put Diamond in a fighting mood. "LeBeau isn't the only one who knows how to play the press. Why don't we get some of our more practiced mouthpieces to counter what he's saying?"

"We're trying to do precisely that, but given the circumstances, there isn't much interest in hearing our side."

"What about Melton Frame? Can't he call up one of his contacts and get some airtime?"

"I seriously doubt he would."

Diamond tossed back another breadstick before he realized what he'd done. "Excuse me one second," he mumbled, quickly forcing the dry crumbs down. "I'll apologize to Frame, Solomon Griffey. I'll kiss his pompous behind in Macy's window, if that's what it takes. If need be, I'll resign from the society and help you from the outside wherever I can. All that matters now is making sure that the true story gets equal time."

Griffey's sigh was an atomized puff. "Frame has no magic to accomplish that. I fear no one has, given the compelling evidence LeBeau has been able to offer."

"What evidence? I watched half a dozen of his interviews and all I heard were empty accusations that the big, bad Arcanum was out to get him for our own self-serving ends."

"That explains it, Aldo. You didn't see the latest round in Mr. LeBeau's attack. Make sure you take a look at the breaking bulletins on any of the networks or cable news services. It came across the wire a short while ago."

"What could he possibly have said to strengthen that line of malarkey? When people come to their senses, they'll realize how ridiculous it is. The Arcanum gets plenty of credit and more grants and donations than it needs. Always has."

"Listen to the news and you'll understand, Aldo. It's better if you see for yourself. After that, if you have any ideas, feel free to call, regardless of the time. I seriously doubt I'll be getting much sleep until this nasty business is cleared up."

"Can't blame you."

"The Calibre Club is arranging space for us to use as a command center. I plan to be there first thing in the morning, along with several others. Join us if you can."

"Okay, Solomon Griffey. I need to be in court by ten, but I'll be there early. See you then."

Diamond booted up his laptop again. He waited through the strident dialing and the bouncing tones as the modem connected. On the CNN home page he scanned the headline news. Soon his eye lit on

B.B. LeBeau's smirking, choirboy face under the legend: "Shocking Murders Strengthen Charge that the Arcanum Set Up B.B. LeBeau."

The story clip took forever to load. Fiona McBride, a fiery young journalist, was reporting from the scene. Wielding a fist-shaped microphone, she spoke in sharp, angry tones. "During routine rounds tonight, a security guard at the Maricopa County courthouse in Phoenix, Arizona, came upon this horrifying scene. I must caution that the footage we are about to show is highly disturbing. We strongly advise that any youngsters or others who may be unduly distressed by violent images leave the room."

The reporter passed a moment in stern-faced silence. Then, she went on. "Judge Gretchen Montrose, who has served as a superior court justice here for more than twenty years, and a veteran bailiff, identified as forty-six-year-old Deakin Barnes, were discovered in Courtroom 805 earlier tonight, victims of an apparent homicide. The security guard, who discovered them during a routine check, said that they had signed into the courthouse shortly after noon. Station management feels that it is in the public interest to release these early pictures from the scene. A detective on the case has confirmed that details of this horrifying crime match unpublished particulars of the Garmin family murders, for which B.B. LeBeau had been charged and condemned. Judge Montrose presided at Mr. LeBeau's trial and handed down the jury's death sentence, which was recently overturned, after key evidence linking the defendant to the murder was found to be fraudulent."

The camera cut to a horrifying close-up of the victims. The judge was seated at the bench, gavel in hand, peering blindly at a porn magazine titled *Hot Rods*. Horror was etched on her lifeless face. The bailiff was propped behind her with his thick arms circling the judge's torso. One of his hands lolled beside her right breast, and the other rested suggestively in her lap. On the mahogany paneling behind the bench, painted in blood, were the words: "Let she who is without sin cast the first stone."

"Fortunately, the tainted evidence came to light before the death sentence against Mr. LeBeau could be carried out." The camera panned to a snapshot of LeBeau. From the angelic look on his face, you could conclude that his mysterious initials, B.B., stood for "Boyish" and "Beguiling." "It is distressing, indeed, to consider that this man could have been the next, innocent victim of a system that seems to have gone dangerously awry."

1 7

My bank's customer service department would be closed until Monday, nine A.M., Eastern Standard Time. The sultry voice on their recorded announcement suggested, though not in so many words, that I should feel perfectly welcome to have carnal relations with myself in the meantime.

A call to the credit card companies yielded equally unsatisfying results. I could report my cards missing or stolen and have them canceled, with all the attendant grief, but if I wanted to get to the bottom of why they had been denied, I would have to wait for an investigation that could take days or even weeks. I was told to call again tomorrow, when seasoned supervisors would be available to put me off with greater authority.

Aunt Amelia had invited Rainey to a dramatic reading at Avery Fisher Hall that afternoon, and, hoping to perpetuate her pleasant mood, I agreed that she could go directly from her sleepover at Danielle's. I decided to skip the ritual reading of the Sunday paper, and work on my proposal instead.

Richter followed me to the office, barking his strident challenge at all the highly suspicious objects he encountered on the way. He yapped at a chair, snarled in rabid rage at Rainey's backpack, and let the coatrack know, in no uncertain terms, that he was on to it. He growled at my desk, chuffed furiously at the bookshelves, and told off the fax machine, printer, and computer. Finally, satisfied and spent, he sagged to the floor and nodded off at my feet.

To avoid unnecessary interruptions, I muted the ringer on the office phone. I read over the pages I had completed so far, delighted to find that the story line still seemed plausible, interesting, and strong. This was not always the case. Revision, a major part of any writer's job, means unleashing your harshest inner critic, the nasty, rotten, unsympathetic shrew who would never consider placing your feelings or fragile ego ahead of the work. Mine spoke in simple, razor-sharp declaratives. In the worst cases, she simply said, "This sucks." When that happened, I understood that the only reasonable solution for what I had written was a proper burial.

Thankfully, this time the reviewer within offered nothing but a grudging nod, and I was able to forge ahead. I wrote for the next hour and a half, digging my protagonist into an ever-deepening hole, until I caught the muffled summons from my cell phone.

Hoping it was Jed, I hurried to my bedroom. Frantically, I rummaged through last night's clothing, which lay heaped on the easy chair beside my bed. In a haze of contented exhaustion, I had dropped everything there after Jed left me at the door following a lovely after-dinner walk that neither of us had been willing to end until one in the morning. I had resisted asking him in, though just barely. Still unable to find the phone, I tossed my magic dress on the floor, followed by the coat, underwear, and stockings.

The ringing continued, though I calculated that the call would soon be bounced to voice mail. Finally, I found my tiny Nokia wedged beside the chair cushion, where it had slipped along with my embroidered clutch purse.

My spirits plunged as I noticed the number flashing on the Caller ID. It was Paige.

"So, where are we on the proposal, Claire?"

"I'm working on it, even as we speak."

"How is it coming along?"

"Very well, actually. I'm pleased."

"Great. I'm at my desk, expecting one of my writers from out of town. He just called to say that he'll be late, hung up with airport security, so I have a little downtime. Send me what you've got, and I'll have a look at it."

My voice shot up most of an octave. "Now?"

"No, Claire. I was thinking of next Arbor Day. Of course, now. Now is the hour, as they say. How many pages shall I expect?"

"It's twenty something."

"Fine. You can send it as an attachment."

"I'd really rather wait to show it to you until it's finished."

"Just send it, Claire. If it's on target, great. If it's not, I can save you from a lot of unnecessary backtracking."

"I appreciate the offer, but I'd still prefer to finish it first."

She chuckled dryly. "Are we playing please-the-editor, or have you really made good progress?"

"I'm just afraid that sending it out at this point may get in the way."

"Simple solution, Claire. Don't *let* it."

"Maybe it's just superstition, but—"

"That's exactly what it is. So how about I promise not to show your proposal to any black cats or place it under any ladders? Now please, we're wasting time. Send what you've got, and I'll let you know what I think."

She hung up before I could argue further. I wanted to whine about her arrogance and gall to Winston, but there was no answer at his Manhattan apartment and I didn't know the number at his country house in Dutchess County, where he spent most weekends.

I reviewed my options, which boiled down to doing as Paige asked or refusing, which was sure to reinforce her conviction that I was a lying, unreliable, hypersensitive loon. Before my indignation had the chance to shout down my good sense, I returned to my office, climbed over Richter's sleeping form, and composed the tersest possible note to Paige: *Per your request.*

I brought up the proposal file and attached it to the e-mail. When I pushed the Send button, my monitor erupted with pale streaky lines. Chunks of meaningless gibberish started marching across the screen. Something deep inside the computer screamed in horror and kept screeching. Richter awoke and added his coyote howl to the maddening din. Desperately, I pressed the Control, Alt, and Delete keys. When I hit the three keys again, the electronic clamor ceased. All that remained was Richter, baying at the hypothetical moon.

Normally, a reboot was enough to bring the machine to its senses. This time, instead of the usual, pulsing sounds and triumphal flourishes that preceded Bill Gates's ubiquitous clouds, a long list of file folders appeared against an ominous black background. As I watched, the files vanished in alphabetical order: AOL, Adobe, ArcSoft Photoprinter, DigitalPrint, DVGate . . .

Horrified, I tried Control, Alt, Delete again, but nothing happened. The file folders continued to evaporate: Games, Intervideo, MovieShaker, PC-cillin—

"PC-cillin" stood for "digital penicillin," a supposed preventative for viral invasion. I couldn't begin to imagine what happened after a bug conquered the protective software. Nothing, except ignorant me and an incensed, neurotic dog, stood between my files and extinction: Picture Gear, Power Panel, Powerpoint—

In a panic, I tried to shut down the machine. The Off switch had no effect. Though I pressed it several times and held it firmly, files continued to quiver, and then disappear: Quicken, QuickTime, Real—

I pulled the power cord, but even that failed to stop the horrifying destruction. Finally, I turned the laptop over and dug into every available orifice until I found what appeared to be the battery and yanked it free.

A call to J&R Computer World confirmed that their computer repair department was open, even on Sunday. I swaddled the machine like an injured pet, placed the parts I'd removed in the pocket of my sweatpants, and hurried toward Fifth Avenue to catch a cab. The one that stopped reeked of garlic and cumin and the kind of body odor that takes years of hard, determined work to cultivate. Fortunately, I was too upset to breathe.

I rolled down my window as the cab swerved down Broadway, and then turned east toward Park Row. J&R, which started as a small mom-and-pop operation, has grown into the granddaddy of discount home entertainment and electronics purveyors, offering every imaginable high-tech gadget, audio and video device, and a staggering stock of peripherals and accessories. During several visits, I had found their staff cheerful, knowledgeable, and highly tolerant of techno-clueless souls like me.

Computer repair was down a steep flight, below street level, which was also the locus of customer returns. I took the stairs cautiously, cradling my laptop.

Three techs manned receiving stations at the bottom landing. As I approached, the broad-faced young man at the left glanced up at me. "Help you?"

Gingerly, I set the computer on the counter.

"Problem?"

"I was trying to send an e-mail, and suddenly everything went crazy and the files seemed to be disappearing. It wouldn't shut down. All I could think to do was pull out the battery."

He plugged in the power supply and tapped the keys. "How'd you say it happened again?"

I repeated the scenario, describing the weird screen followed by the incredible vanishing files.

He tapped his discolored front tooth, thinking. "Sounds like a worm. That's like a virus, only different. Gets in through a DSL or cable modem and gobbles the files."

"But all my work was on there."

"You don't back up?"

"I didn't this time."

"You should always back up." He looked genuinely disappointed, as if I was some screw-up kid instead of a bona fide screw-up adult.

"I understand, but right now, what I need to do is find my work. There must be some way to retrieve those files."

"We don't do it here. There are data retrieval companies. But it's hit or miss. And it's really, really expensive."

"How much?"

"Depends on what they're able to find, but it can run as high as twenty-five hundred dollars."

"Ouch."

"No kidding. Plus, it can take weeks, and there are no guarantees."

"Sounds like a bad idea. What do you suggest?"

"We can restore the machine; take it back to the way you got it from the manufacturer. That'll take care of the worm or whatever it is, but it won't get back your work."

"How long does that take?"

"Few hours. You can pick it up late today. Cost you fifty bucks."

I didn't argue, though I knew he was way off. The cost was going to be far more than his quote. My editor was going to be furious.

18

As expected, several irate messages from Paige awaited me on the phone machine at home. "Where are those pages, Claire? I've been waiting for you to send them as agreed. I don't know what you did with Ben, but I expect my writers to deliver on their promises. Call me back."

In the living room, I found a nasty surprise courtesy of Richter. The dog had lost more than his head in one of his frenzies and anointed the antique Persian rug. I blotted the mess as best I could with clumps of paper toweling. I tried club soda as well, but a large yellow specter remained.

Richter paced beside me, chuffing indignantly as if he were the injured party. The rug had been a wedding present from my mother. She had inherited it from her parents, who had died before I was born. The link to those people I had never known strengthened my attachment to the gift. So did the fact that it was the first joint possession Noah and I had received. We had furnished our cozy home around the complex weave of lovely jewel tones, and until that monstrous day three years ago when I found him cold and lifeless in our room, I had considered it a part of our unshakable foundation.

I caught Richter by the collar, directed his attention to the stain, and issued a firm reproach. When sufficiently provoked, I could bark with the best of them. "Bad dog."

He yipped in utter outrage, as if I had some nerve accusing him without incontrovertible proof. Some other weak-bladdered mutt could have been the culprit. At any moment, I expected him to break into Boston-tinged English in the voice of Dr. Richard Kimble from *The Fugitive* and swear the crime had been committed by a sneaky, three-legged Dalmatian.

Professional cleaning would have to wait for tomorrow. I could add that to the long and growing agony list. I had promised to take my mother to a doctor's appointment first thing in the morning, and then there were the credit card companies to deal with, plus the bank.

Hoping that she would not be there, I dialed Paige's number at Ridgefield Press. She did not pick up, and I left the sorry facts of the situation on her voice mail. Despite their utter truth, the words rang limp and hollow. The dog ate my homework. Sure thing.

Though I dreaded the prospect, I had no choice but to try to re-create the pages I'd lost. Reluctant to lose the day, I found Rainey's laptop in her book bag and set it up on my desk. In one of her legendary shows of breathtaking generosity, Aunt Amelia had given us identical computers last Christmas, so working on Rainey's machine would be no problem for me.

Or so I thought.

When I tried to boot up her computer, a dialog box demanding a password appeared. On my laptop, when such things came up, I was able to press the Escape button and continue. Rainey's stubbornly balked and repeated the request.

Anxious to get to work, I tried to imagine what her password might be. I keyed in "Pooh," the character she loved enough to have his likeness tattooed on her left ankle.

Incorrect password, scolded the computer.

Next, I tried Rainey's birth date.

Password invalid. Check your spelling and try again.

In turn, I tried the name of her school, her homeroom teacher, and her best friend, Danielle. Nothing worked.

Finally, on a whim, I typed the name of her horrid new friend: "Phelan." As I did, an echo of his pale, smirking face bloomed in my mind. I pictured him hunched over his jury-rigged computer, working the keyboard in probing beats and languid strokes that bordered on obscene.

One of my mother's favorite creepy cautions came to mind: A child could drown in six inches of water. Something told me that the murky, vermin-infested pool that was Phelan posed dangers that were almost as chilling to contemplate.

I pressed Enter. This time, instead of a simple reproach, a cartoon black bomb with a sizzling fuse materialized. The virtual wick burned down, and the bomb morphed into the face of a sly, snickering clown. In the thought bubble trailing from his garish scarlet mouth was the single word: *Kaboom!*

Next, the clown grew a body, clad in a plump, frilly-necked jumpsuit and oversized feet in floppy polka-dotted shoes. A matronly cartoon woman wearing a prim hat waddled up and joined him on the screen. The clown extracted a giant sledgehammer from one of his minuscule pockets and pounded the woman flat, leaving nothing but the lozenge-shaped silhouette of her hat brim on the pavement.

A new thought bubble rose from the clown's curly wig. *This is what happens to nosy fools,* it said. Then a nasty smirk consumed his face, and menacing funhouse laughter bellowed through the speakers. "Stay out of my business, or I'll make you wish you had. Try this again, and you're through."

As if that was not unnerving enough, Richter charged into the office, howling like a stuck beast.

I cupped my ears. "Hush!"

Instead, he bellowed louder, struck a defensive pose, and barked in the strident cadence of automatic gunfire.

"Stop!" I pleaded. "Cut it out!"

From upstairs came the frantic strike of Mrs. DiMarco's cane. "Stifle that blasted mutt, or I'm calling the pound."

I tried everything. Holding his muzzle transformed the bark to a hideous growl. Next, I took a jar full of pennies and shook it sharply in his face. Somewhere, I had heard that this would shock even the most intently yapping dog silent. But Richter had passed into another dimension.

Mrs. DiMarco rapped her cane again. "If that racket doesn't stop immediately, I'm calling the cops, Claire. I'm calling the law and the ASPCA and your mother. You've got until the count of three."

Over Richter's continued frenzy came my neighbor's warbled countdown. "One—two—two and a half—"

A giant headache thumped behind my eyes. There was no way I could concentrate with the dog's constant carrying on. I clipped on his leash and urged him out the door. He shrieked like a small child faced with a doctor's smile behind the loaded syringe. I spoke gently, measuring my words, trying to ease the blow that accompanies every breakup. "Try not to take it personally. These things happen. We gave it our best, but this relationship is just not working out. I'll come by and see you. No reason we can't be friends."

Dependent Claws, the mongrel conglomerate that belonged to Duffy's sister, occupied a trio of connected storefronts two blocks north of Union Square. As we walked, the dog's voice faded, worn to a rasped frazzle by the strident abuse. I tethered him to a parking meter in front of the A&P, ran in, and bought half a dozen of Duffy's favorite chocolate-glazed Krispy Kreme doughnuts.

I found Duff's sister, Sandy, a warm, jovial soul, feeding the capacity crowd of strays. Dogs of every imaginable size, age, state, and breed fretted, fought, snoozed, and romped in the cages and runs and overflowed into the reception area.

"Claire, I'm so glad you came by. You've heard about LeBeau getting out, I suppose."

"Unbelievable, isn't it?"

Sandy set down her scoop and the giant kibble bag and swaddled me in a hug. "How are you holding up?"

Richter's muted yapping was swallowed by the greater commotion. I flipped my hand in a so-so motion. "Is Duffy around?"

"He's in the back. In a bit of a stew, as you can imagine. Seeing you will be just what the doctor ordered. Go on and have a nice visit. I'll mind the dog."

"Thanks."

"There, there, sweetheart. Quit your fretting, now. Everything's fine," she told Richter. One touch of her firm hand turned off his Panic button. The bands of tension slackened and something perilously close to a smile replaced the fevered angst on his muzzle.

This was not so for all their furry charges. Heading for the rear door, I almost tripped over a darting schnauzer. I ran a gauntlet of baying hounds and terriers. And I narrowly missed losing the doughnut bag to a butterscotch fur ball with astonishing spring in its stumpy legs.

The heavy fire door closed behind me, blunting all sound from the front. In the ensuing silence, my heartbeats thumped like jungle drums. I searched for Duffy among the towering shelves and stacked supplies that tracked a narrow swath behind the three connected shops.

"Duff?" I called softly, hating to breach the blessed silence. "Are you here?"

I presumed that he must have ducked out unnoticed. Given the deafening clatter and chaotic activity out front, this would not be a difficult trick.

In truth, I felt guiltily glad that he was gone. Leaving Richter with Sandy would be much easier. She would accept the failed match as a simple fact of life. Duffy, for all his size and bluster, was bound to take it to heart. He was always charmingly befuddled when his rough- and smooth-coated friends failed to hit it off.

To ease the blow, I decided to write a conciliatory note on the doughnut bag. I searched for a pen, making my way past cartons of heartworm pills, rawhide bones, pig ears, odor eaters, plush toys, combs and brushes, flea shampoo, tick collars, chews and treats, sweaters and stacked beds, casual collars and the rhinestone-bedecked.

Halfway along, I caught the rasp of agitated breathing. "Duffy?"

At my approach, he stiffened and slipped something quickly behind his back. I took in the higher-than-usual color in his cheeks and the cords of tension bulging in his neck.

I patted his brawny back. "Take it easy, Duff. It's okay."

"Damn it, Claire, no. It is anything but okay. Have you seen the papers? Blasted fools who run the news have been swallowing LeBeau's story whole, sucking up whatever the slimy bastard dishes out. He's right here in New

York, you know, playing the media darling. Next thing, the devil's own will be riding in parades, dripping medals, a regular hero, for the love of God."

He passed me the front section from the *Post*. Tight with fury, he leveled an accusing finger at the banner headline: COLD-CASE GROUP TAKES HEAT. I read the damning first line: "The brutal murders of Arizona Judge Gretchen Montrose and her bailiff cast serious doubt on the guilt of B.B. LeBeau and countless other convicted killers the group of volunteer crime experts, known as the Arcanum, put behind bars."

With a grand sweep of his arms, Duffy outlined the scope of the mess. "Before long, they'll be tossing open jailhouse doors all over the land, letting the worst of the worst go free. To think, Noah gave his all to lock up scum like LeBeau. And now, it comes to this."

A shudder ran through me as I glanced at LeBeau's picture below the headline. "I can't even look at him."

His mouth pressed in a grim line. "Tell you the truth, I believe I could kill that worthless lump of flesh with my bare hands and never lose the smile."

"Easy, pal." I pressed his hard-clenched fist. That's when I spotted the gleam of metal. The gun was almost obscured by Duffy's bulk, but not quite. I reached behind him and took the piece in hand. It was an ugly, snub-nosed thing, definitely not department-issue and definitely not intended for use in official, sanctioned police business. Thanks to Noah, I had tamed my long-standing fear of firearms. He had even taken me to a Connecticut practice range several times, where I'd learned to aim on a target and hit the mark. But no way was I comfortable with this.

"That's not the way, Duffy, and you know it. Let it go. LeBeau's destroyed enough."

"It's not that simple, Claire. You don't understand."

"Yes I do. Noah isn't here because of him. Because of LeBeau, Rainey doesn't have her dad, and I've spent three years going through the motions. Because of him, you've switched your devotion from detective work to mucking out cages and placing neurotic strays."

He managed a small, rueful smile. "Can't honestly see that it's much of a difference. It's all animal behavior. Two legs or four."

"Believe me, I'm as upset about this as you are. But we'll just have to trust the system to take care of it. Isn't that what you always say?"

He went grim again. "This time it's not so simple."

"Meaning what?"

"Meaning I can't just sit back and trust the system when it comes to looking after my own. LeBeau runs on revenge, sure as the little engine that could ran on hope. How do we know who's on his payback list? Who can say how far he'll go?"

Cold fear settled in my gut. "The press will be all over him for the duration. I can't imagine he'd risk doing anything to tarnish the halo."

"Maybe so, but what if you're wrong? It's not me I'm worried about. There's Sandy and the girls to think of. Mara just told us she's expecting come the fall."

"That's great, Duff. Congratulations. You a great-uncle. Imagine that."

He rose heavily. "That's the picture I'm trying to hold, Claire, believe me. Growing old, watching the young ones come into their own. If only wishing could make things so, I'd be wishing. But something tells me that's not going to cut it against LeBeau."

"Promise me you won't do anything stupid, Duffy. Playing vigilante is not the answer."

"All I'm doing is keeping a step ahead of the Devil, Claire. Preparing to look out for what's precious to me, if it comes to that. Including you."

"I'm nothing to LeBeau, Duff, and neither are you. It'll be fine."

"Yes, it will. I intend to make sure of that."

Richter led me home, tugging eagerly on his leash, tail perched proudly aloft like a victory banner. Under the circumstances, I couldn't bring myself to add to Duffy's mountain of concerns. The dog and I would postpone the divorce for the sake of the overgrown Irish kid.

Passing a newsstand, I cringed again at the sight of LeBeau's evil image peering back at me from a broad array of front pages. Duffy's words kept looping through my mind: *How do we know who's on his payback list?*

Who can say how far he'll go?

1 9

Rainey was playing "Aunt Amelia Says," a game I knew all too well. As a child, I had often done the same. My quoting Amelia's advice and adages had driven my mother nuts, which would have been more than sufficient reason to keep it up. But back then, like many kids, I saw my aunt as the ideal adult. She was impulsive, outrageous, fun-loving, and boundlessly indulgent with herself and others. If you played by her rules, she was loyal and generous to a fault. But when someone did her wrong, her retribution was measured and devilishly effective. The package looked highly appealing from a child's largely powerless perspective. If I thought and did exactly as she said, perhaps someday I could become her, or, at least, a pale imitation. Even now, I must admit, the prospect of grabbing the world by the throat as she does and squeezing until it yielded every last drop of your heart's desire holds a certain undeniable appeal.

"How was the reading?" I asked Rainey as she floated in from Amelia's car.

"Extraordinary," she said, savoring every syllable. "Aunt Amelia says it exemplified theatre at its finest. She says we simply must attend more of the festival events, that I have a natural appreciation. She says she's going to find some way to get good seats; even though the best performances have been sold out for weeks."

"If there's a way, Amelia will find it."

Richter, fresh from a nap, bounded in to challenge whoever had the nerve to invade his turf. Noting that it was Rainey, he went coy. He cocked his head, trying to win her over as he had been doing for days. But she was having none of it.

Her lip curled in distaste. "Get lost, smelly."

The Bentley eased away from the curb, and I caught a glimpse of my aunt's calculated silhouette behind the tinted glass. Amelia always held herself as if she was sitting for a portrait or having her likeness chiseled in age-defying stone. I imagined it was the posture she assumed for her frequent consultations with Dr. Strickland, her famous, on-call plastic surgeon.

"I'm glad you enjoyed it," I said.

"I *loved* it," she corrected firmly. "In fact, there was one part that would have been perfect for me."

"Which was that?"

"The youngest daughter: Victoria. She was tragically ill, but very creative and wise beyond her years. She had the best lines of anyone, Aunt Amelia said."

"Shame about the tragic illness, though."

She sighed mightily, as if my ignorance were the greater tragedy by far. "That's the whole thing about the part, Claire. That's what distinguishes Victoria and makes her the actual star, even though she doesn't have the most time on stage."

"Interesting."

"Aunt Amelia says I should really consider an acting career. She thinks it would fit me like a glove."

I wondered what role this chameleon child was playing tonight. From her getup—a gold-buttoned navy blazer, cream cowl-neck sweater, prim suede flats, and camel slacks—I presumed it had something to do with the Junior League.

"What do you think?"

She stared at her murky likeness in the window glass, appraising her purse-lipped expression, testing the swish of her newly acquired ponytail. "Aunt Amelia says either you have it or you don't. If you do, and it's in your blood, then that's that."

"There's no medicine for this?"

She shot me a look of contempt. "You don't take me seriously, Claire. You think I'm some dopey little kid."

"No. I think you're a very complicated and interesting person with lots of abilities and plenty of time to decide what you want to do with your life."

With her commanding stance and implacable face, she looked like a travel-size CEO. "It so happens, that's not true. Aunt Amelia says that if I want to make it as a performer, I need to start lessons right away. Most kids my age have had years of acting, singing, and dancing classes already."

"I'm not against looking into that. But we need to know what the costs and commitments are before we decide."

"Aunt Amelia says she'll be glad to pay. It's her pleasure."

Technically, it would be her latest husband's pleasure, but I saw no value in belaboring the point. Amelia was as capricious as the tides, and Rainey's attention span was not much firmer. I strongly suspected that the acting fetish would vanish along with the Muffy look before either required serious consideration. "Why don't you do some research and find out what's involved?"

"I will. In fact, I'll do it right now. *Tempus fugit*, Aunt Amelia says."

"You know what that means, Rainey?"

Her face tensed. "I think it means if you want something, go for it, and don't let anything stand in your way."

"Actually, *tempus fugit* is Latin for 'time flies.' What you said is the definition of Aunt Amelia."

She was halfway to her room before I remembered the virtual exploding bomb. "Wait, Rainey. I meant to tell you. My computer broke down earlier today, and I tried to work on yours."

Her face warped with outrage. "You tried to spy on me, you mean. I knew it. That's why I planted the trap."

"That's pretty nasty stuff."

"You wouldn't even know about it if you hadn't been snooping around."

"I wasn't snooping. I told you, I had a problem. Apparently, a computer worm got in through the cable modem and destroyed my files. I needed to work. That's all."

"Just keep your goddamned mitts off my stuff."

"Calm down, Rainey. I would have asked, but you weren't here. You weren't using the computer, so I didn't see the big deal. Next time I'll ask first. Okay?"

"There won't be a next time. Touch it again, and you'll be sorry."

"Don't threaten me. That's way out of line."

"You're the one who's out of line." Her mouth tightened with fury. "Phelan was right. You're nothing but a nosy bitch."

The air escaped me in a rush. "You may not speak to me that way. I understand that you're angry, but that's not an acceptable way to express it. Now I need you to go to your room."

"I'll do what I damned please."

"Go to your room, Rainey. Now!"

The showdown lasted only seconds, but it felt far longer. In the thrumming aftermath lay the devastated rubble of our very short-lived truce. I heard the smack of her door followed by a harsh clank as the bolt slid home.

A spike of pain lodged behind my eyes. I downed two aspirin, flipped off the living-room lights, and headed to my room.

Noah's picture perched on the nightstand in a burgundy leather frame. Scorched by his warm, trusting gaze, I turned it facedown. Then I undressed and slipped beneath the down comforter.

Shadow forms gathered cloudlike on the ceiling. I watched as they puffed into floating wisps and disappeared.

As my eyes drifted shut, I caught the sounds of Reverend E Train preaching across the street. *So what are we to believe, brothers and sisters? In what sacred container do we place our faith? When the Lord speaks in contradictions, which of His words do we call truth?*

I listened, wondering where he was headed with all this. Sometimes, the raving psycho made a chilling bit of accidental sense.

Contemplate this, my brethren. In Psalm 127, it is written, "Behold, children are a blessing from the Lord. Like the arrows in the hand of a warrior, so are the children of one's youth. Happy is the man who has his quiver full of them."

When it came to Rainey, "quiver" took on a very different meaning, I thought bitterly.

The reverend raved on: *But then, in Psalm 137:9, we read this, "Happy shall he be who takes your little ones and dashes them against the rock!" Think about that, winners and sinners, you sweet lambs and lost hopeless sheep. What does it all mean?*

I turned onto my stomach and burrowed beneath the pillow. *What does it all mean?*

Exactly.

2 0

Tendrils of frost glazed the Calibre Club's solarium windows. Backlit by the first of dawn, the icy forms had the look of reef coral: lace fans and majestic staghorns, graceful sea feathers and delicate whips. Staring wearily, Diamond conjured a malevolent eel lurking amid the slowly shifting shapes, camouflaged by the murky hush and lulling beauty of the deep. A specimen of exquisite evil: lock-focused, utterly intent.

Rich coffee scents suffused the room, along with the hissing prattle of overburdened radiators. Rising stiffly, Griffey rolled his creaky neck, doffed his reading glasses, and pinched the bridge of his nose. He crossed to the stately Chippendale sideboard and refilled his porcelain cup from the silver urn marked "Regular." He filled a cup for Diamond as well, and ferried it back to the paper-strewn conference table along with a plateful of miniature pastries to replace the ones the graphologist had sucked down with the force and determination of a commercial vacuum.

Ted Callendar strode in, slapping his gloved hands, face stiff and polished with the cold. "Sorry I'm late. The girls were with me last night, and I didn't want to leave before they got up."

"Six-thirty is not late by anybody's definition, Ted," Erin McCloat observed. "Anyway, you haven't missed a thing except an hour or so of frustration."

Callendar peeled off the ski gloves, uncoiled his long blue-and-white barber-pole muffler, and hung it, along with his blue down jacket, on the coatrack near the door. "Can't say I've been suffering a shortage of that."

"No luck?" Lyman Trupin sat before a legal pad filled with far-fetched speculations about the society's current plight.

"I had plenty, all bad. As we discussed, I put in a call to Phoenix Homicide late last night. The detectives who caught the double murder at the courthouse were out beating the bushes, but the sergeant I spoke to promised to have them call as soon as they got in. Guy was so pleasant and helpful, I was starting to believe we had it made."

"He bought the line about you working on a book about ritual killings?" asked Perry Vacchio.

"He seemed to, yes. And it's a fact that I've been playing with that idea for years. Unfortunately, the detectives working the case weren't buying anything; at least, not from me. They called at about three in the morning our time. Both of them were on the line, talking over each other, dying to hear what I had to say. For some reason they took me for an informant. The message they got must have been misleading."

Heidi Cohen nodded eagerly. Her flaxen hair, bound in a ponytail, bounced a beat behind. "Misleading is good. I'm all for that."

"It was, as long as it lasted. But as soon as I straightened them out, their tune changed in a giant hurry. Their first question was whether I had anything to do with the Arcanum. And the rest, as they say, was history."

Trupin sighed. "It was worth a try."

Callendar showed his giant palms. "No harm done, I guess. Except they slammed the phone so hard, my ear's still ringing."

He slumped in a vacant chair and started doodling. Quickly, he sketched a convoluted maze. At the center was a tiny, frazzled figure, surrounded by the round-trip footprints from a series of false starts. "We seem to be back at square one, folks. Where do we go from here?"

"Wherever it is, we need to get there quickly," Griffey said.

An uneasy silence gathered around that thought. They were all painfully mindful of the potential downside. If LeBeau's charges took root, all the cases in which the Arcanum had played a role could topple like a row of dominoes. No doubt there had been many strident calls to the nation's governors and chief prosecutors already, demanding investigations, retrials, reversals, and the immediate release of many of the heinous killers the society had helped to put away.

Griffey took the linen napkin at his place, opened it out, and spread it smooth. Next, he folded the cloth into tidy thirds and finger-pressed the seams. "As I see it, we're dealing with a three-pronged problem. First, there is the matter of the society's credibility and what might become of all the cases in which we, individually and collectively, have been involved."

Heidi Cohen groaned. "I hadn't thought about the individual implication beyond the lawsuits. Of course, if we're discredited as a group, it stands to reason that each of our reputations will be blown to bits as well."

Griffey folded back one edge on each side of the napkin, forming triangle wings. "Then there is the question of Mr. LeBeau and how he came to be released."

Trupin chimed in. "We know the answer to that. Ronald Sallis, the head of Celasphere, claimed he falsified the DNA evidence. The prosecutor had hinged the entire case against LeBeau on that evidence."

Working in from the ends, Griffey rolled the napkin into two tight cylinders. "We know what Mr. Sallis claimed about falsifying the DNA evidence. What we don't know is why he made that admission and whether or not it was true."

"Unfortunately, he's not around to question," said Erin McCloat.

Griffey dipped his chin. "Worse, we have no idea whether his departure was voluntary or compelled. In either event, his disappearance casts his statements in serious doubt."

"True. Plus, whatever turns out to be the case with Ronald Sallis may not resolve the question of LeBeau's guilt or innocence," Perry Vacchio observed.

"A puzzle within an enigma tucked into a conundrum with a riddle attached," said Erin McCloat.

Griffey's lips tensed ever so slightly. "And then there is the matter of these latest murders at the courthouse. Are we dealing with one puzzle, two interlocking ones, or a copycat crime?"

Callendar scratched angry Xs through the maze. "I would say our plate is more than full." He noticed this was not true of Diamond's plate, from which every morsel of sugary evidence had been expunged.

With a rueful hitch of his shoulders, Diamond made for the sideboard to reload. "How many members can we get on this, do you think?"

Griffey flipped the napkin over, taking care to keep the cylinders tightly coiled. "So far everyone I've contacted is eager to join us as their schedules allow. The question is, which problem to tackle first?"

"Getting LeBeau back behind bars tops my hit parade," said Heidi Cohen. "I say we revisit the Garmin case as planned and find some way to prove we pinned the tail on the right donkey."

"I second that," said Trupin. "Putting him away again might well solve the rest of our problems."

"I don't think it'll be that simple." Diamond peeled a tiny muffin from its paper cup and examined his catch: banana nut.

"Because?" McCloat challenged.

"Because once people see you in a certain way, their perspective can be devilishly hard to change."

"The Arcanum has always been highly respected. Why wouldn't that reputation stick, instead of absurd charges by a murdering slime?" Vacchio said.

"It might in certain circles," Callendar observed. "But until now, we've been largely unknown to the general public. It's the first-impression thing. If you meet someone when he is wearing a mustache or glasses, he will always look strange without them."

Griffey's brow drooped in a rare show of dismay. "I fear that's far from the biggest hurdle we face."

"Stone walls?" Diamond offered.

"Exactly," Griffey said. "Given the current assault on our credibility, it's going to be difficult at best to get witnesses or anyone else to cooperate with us." Still clutching the napkin cylinders, he turned back the top half and tucked the tight rounds down.

"Sounds like we're facing a long, hard, uphill march," Trupin observed. "I say we'd better get on it."

"Agreed. And again, I think our best bet is to tackle the Garmin case," said Heidi Cohen.

"Ditto," said Trupin.

"I say we focus on the courthouse murders," Perry Vacchio said. "The case is fresh, and fresh things are easier to cook. Plus, LeBeau has to be tied into those killings somehow. Judge Montrose rapped his knuckles, brought him down to size, and put him away, and the Eel likes nothing better than to pay people back for insults like that. It's his twisted take on the Golden Rule: Do unto anyone who even thinks of doing unto you."

"Yes, but LeBeau has one hell of an alibi. He was right here in New York, green-room hopping, at the time those killings went down over two thousand miles away," Trupin observed. "The top news anchors and talk show hosts could be called in to testify for him. Unless he's found the secret to time travel or teleportation, I'd say he's pretty much off the hook."

"Not necessarily. He could have been involved in a hired hit or some other sort of conspiracy," Heidi Cohen said. "I'd bet a charmer like LeBeau has lots of lovely friends. And I'd bet Judge Montrose had an equally charming collection of enemies. The Eel was far from the only sweetheart she took down."

"I'm with you, Heidi," said Erin McCloat.

"I believe you're all correct," Griffey said. "Why don't we continue reviewing the Garmin murders and examine the courthouse killings as well? If good fortune is with us, I suspect we may find that both roads lead to the same destination."

"Perfect solution, Griffey. You have my vote," Trupin put in. "All in favor?"

They chimed in a chorus of ayes.

"It's decided then," Trupin said. "I have a friend in the Phoenix field office who owes me one. I'll call Agent Straley and see if we can get our hands on the current records from the courthouse murders."

Griffey pushed aside the napkin, which he had folded into a headless white-robed figure.* "It's settled then. Which of you would prefer to work on the courthouse murders?"

---

*For a diagram of Griffey's "Mr. Spoonhead" napkin fold, visit Judith Kelman's Writers' Room at http://www.jkelman.com/.

Erin McCloat and Perry Vacchio raised their hands.

"Heidi, Lyman, and Aldo can review the Garmin case. Ted, I believe you're the best man to contact Martha Garmin and whichever other witnesses turn up that require kid-glove management. And I'll be glad to take on the administrative end. If everyone agrees, why don't you and I straddle both cases and act as liaisons?"

"Fine with me," Callendar said.

The others signaled their agreement.

Griffey's minuscule nod sealed the deal. "The others who choose to join us can pitch in as they see fit."

Diamond's gaze fell to his empty plate. His appetite had finished its frenzied rampage and gone to sleep it off. "As I mentioned to you, Solomon Griffey, I've made contact with Claire Barrow, widow of the detective who was close to nailing LeBeau here before the case fell apart."

"He was under investigation for witness tampering, if I remember correctly," Callendar said. "Committed suicide?"

"That's the word, Ted Callendar. But from the note he left, I have my doubts. His widow is gathering other writing samples for me to use in comparison. Should be interesting."

"Excellent, Aldo," Griffey said.

"Wish I could meet with the Garmin witnesses and get handwriting samples from them as well. I'm afraid I won't be much use to you in reviewing the case without that."

A glint of mischief lit Griffey's eyes as he tucked a spoon into the folded napkin. The bowl, which protruded like a head, reflected his owlish face. "Ask, and ye shall be given, my friend. You shall have exactly what you need."

2 1

Dr. Midori bustled into the building as I was heading out to catch the uptown train. More than an hour remained before my mother's appointment for a bone-density scan at Lenox Hill, but prying her out of her apartment could be a major undertaking.

Midori clacked his tongue. "See stress on Miss Claire. Chi energy all stuck like dam. Not smooth flowing. Come have massage. For neighbor, no charge—free."

"That's very sweet. Maybe I'll take you up on that some other time."

"Must care for self first, Miss Claire. Rest follows."

I sensed that he was poised to embark on one of his endless, incomprehensible rants. "I'm sure you're right. Now if you'll please excuse me—"

He stood blocking the doorway, firmly entrenched on a higher plane. "Body need fire. Burn low best. Heat spleen, no good. Fall weak, sick."

"Very interesting, Dr. Midori. Thanks. But I really need to go."

"Must cleanse, fasting, no heavy." His fingers fluttered on an imaginary breeze. "Light, fly like bird. Strong empty. Weak full."

I had not yet locked the apartment door. Richter nudged it open with his nose and trotted into the front vestibule. He barked sharply at Dr. Midori, who took no notice whatsoever.

My neighbor went on. "Woman fire. Run three miles. Low like pilot light. Touch, hand no hurt."

Richter tried a few more tentative barks, and then circled slowly, seeking a way to capture the man's attention.

"Cool," Midori crooned. "Soft ripple spring. Summer not when sorry bird."

Richter sniffed the doctor's pants leg and his eyes went vague. Suddenly, he bounded up on his hind legs, clutched Midori's trim torso with his front paws, and attempted to mate with the doctor's right thigh.

Still, my neighbor ranted on, oblivious to the dog's ardent lovemaking. "Get energy warm. Cool slow ice. Breathe slow: in—out. Like police whistle: whoo whoo. Make relax."

Richter's eyes went vague and his worry lines dissolved in blissful oblivion.

Somehow, I suppressed the laugh. "Down, Richter. Cut that out." I wrestled the dog off the object of his fervent affections and shut him in the apartment. "Sorry, Dr. Midori. I think Richter's energy flow is a little constipated, too."

"Animal soul touch God. See other life spirit. Fly."

Angled sideways, I passed by him. "See you later, Dr. Midori. Take care."

"Five o'clock, Miss Claire. I hold hour open for you. Shiatsu fix energy jam. Bring dog. Work him miracle, too. You'll see."

My mother lives on Fifty-ninth Street, hard by the Queensborough Bridge. The cantilevered span was completed nearly a century ago at a cost of twenty million dollars and the lives of fifty construction workers. Each day, two hundred thousand cars and trucks clatter across its roadbed, which links midtown Manhattan to the borough of Queens. The tram connecting Manhattan and Roosevelt Island runs by Mom's apartment as well. Since it opened in 1976, thirty million people have ridden the red gondolas that hang like wet wash from cables suspended high over the East River.

Mom, who rarely ventures out, spends most of her time in the faded gray armchair near her living-room window, watching the people who do. She never lacks for complaints, criticisms, and dire predictions about the strangers whose fleeting behavior she observes from the desperate safety of her chair. *See that man smoking in a closed car—disgusting. Look how that one is oozing out of her low-cut sweater. Doesn't she have a mirror, for heaven's sake? And if that idiot in the red Toyota doesn't stop tailgating, he's going to wind up riding in the back of a hearse.*

She sat rooted in her chair when I let myself in. Mom insists that I keep her key and use it, thinking that will make me feel at home in her musty monument to broken dreams and failed promises. Pictures of dead relatives clutter every space that is not otherwise occupied by poignant mementoes of long-ago, less-dreadful times. Mom saves most everything and sets much of it on display: dried bouquets and corsages, ancient stuffed animals, ancient magazines, baby shoes, clumsy crafts projects, saccharine greeting cards, and countless cheesy souvenirs from ill-remembered trips. She has the tin replica Eiffel Tower, the jewel-encrusted Las Vegas slot machine, and a swivel-hipped hula doll with a disintegrating faux-grass skirt. Hopefully, she has detailed the distribution of all these precious objects in her will. Otherwise, Lottie and I are bound to battle furiously over who gets what when she goes.

"Hello, dear. There's fresh coffee in the kitchen, and I fixed cinnamon toast. Help yourself."

"Thanks. I already ate." I kissed her cheek and tracked her fretful gaze to a skeletal behemoth rising around a mammoth crane four blocks north. "What's going up?"

"Condos. Mr. Lustberg down the hall told me it's going to be forty-two stories plus a mechanical floor. I'm going to lose Rockefeller University at the very least. And maybe part of the river."

"You'll still have spectacular views."

"Why can't they just leave well enough alone?"

"Because it isn't well enough for them."

She was huddled in a worn plaid robe over her favorite flannel nightgown, which featured tiny cornflowers on a cream-colored ground. Her pewter waves were flattened on one side from long, unyielding contact with the pillow. Whenever possible, my mother took refuge in sleep. I had been drawn to the same escape route after Noah died, but my dreams turned out to be even worse than reality.

I clapped once, like a drill sergeant. "Okay, Mom. Time to get dressed. Chop-chop."

"I'm not going. What's the point? If my bones are thinning, so be it. I don't honestly care to know one way or the other. When things start to fracture, I'll deal with it."

"Dr. Sternfeld wants you to have the test. You heard him as well as I did. If your bones are thinning, which they may not be at all, there are medicines you can take to head the problem off or even reverse it."

"A broken hip isn't so terrible. Believe me, there are plenty of worse ways to go."

"It isn't a contest." I gripped her by the wrists. Her skin had the slick, unnatural feel of mock silk. "Come on, sweetheart. Up and at 'em."

"Honestly, what's the point?"

"Being as healthy as possible for as long as possible."

"I don't care what becomes of me, Claire. That's the simple truth."

"But I do, Mom. Consider it a favor to me—okay? I just bought lots of stock in the bone-density scan company."

"Very funny."

"I'll help you. I'll do your hair and everything. You can play lady of the manor, and I'll be the deeply devoted personal maidservant who considers it a privilege to preside over your wardrobe and ablutions."

She wrenched free and hunched behind crossed arms. "I've decided not to go, and that's that. Anyway, it's freezing out. Highs in the low twenties and blustery winds, they said. Chance of snow. The last thing I need is a case of pneumonia."

I dispensed the words one by one, trying to keep them in line. "Then why on earth did you have me come? You could have called and saved me the trip."

"I haven't seen you in ages," she said accusingly. "I didn't think it would kill you to visit."

"I didn't think so either," I muttered.

"Leave then, if you find it so unpleasant to be around me. I suppose I can't blame you. I'm nothing but a useless, old pain in the rear."

"No you're not. And I don't find it unpleasant to be around you, Mom. What I find unpleasant is the black cloud. You're always so down on yourself, on everything."

"What do I have to be up about?"

"Life, possibilities, other people's misery, whatever. Contrary to what you think, you are not the queen of rotten luck. Stuff happens. Everyone gets a share."

"Not everyone," she said pointedly. "My sister has never had a single day's trouble in her life."

"Please, Mom. Not that again."

"Why not, Claire? It's the simple truth. Amelia always gets her way. Is that fair?"

"It is what it is. Anyway, Aunt Amelia is not the issue right now."

"She has plenty of reasons to take perfect care of herself. That's the point. Little Miss Perfect and her impeccable existence. You enjoy her more than you do me, that's for sure."

"Can we please change the subject?"

"If that woman had been through one iota of what I have, she wouldn't be so smug and self-important." Resenting Amelia was my mother's religion. She had practiced it devoutly for as long as I could remember.

"Let me help you get ready and take you for the test. You'll barely need to go outside at all. We can get a cab right downstairs and get out at the hospital door."

"Hospitals are dangerous. Just last week I read an article about all the terrible infections patients come down with. They go in for a simple procedure and come out feet first."

"All you're having is an X ray."

"And you think those are safe? Have you ever seen the effects of X-ray poisoning? You can get cancers, worse."

I poised for surrender. "Okay. You win. You don't want to go, don't. You're a big girl. I suppose they're your bones to neglect as you see fit."

"It doesn't matter, Claire. I don't matter."

"Look. I'm not going to argue with you. I have a million things to take care of today, so I'm going to take off now. I'll come back as soon as I finish my proposal, and we can have a nice long visit. I'll pick up Chinese food at Maple Garden, if you like. Your favorite orange chicken and moo shu pork. Sound good?"

"You needn't bother."

"I want to."

I kissed her and aimed for the door. Before I reached it, she burst from her chair like a storm surge. "If I don't go at this point, they'll charge me anyway. Stupid test must cost a fortune. Hundreds of dollars, maybe more."

"So now you want to go?"

"What I want has nothing to do with it. Have a cup of coffee. I'll be ready in a minute."

On the way home from that ordeal, I stopped at my bank's local branch. Four people queued ahead of me at customer service. Each transaction took an absurd amount of time. The young woman behind the desk, a doe-eyed daisy blonde with glitter-streaked long nails, worked with maddening deliberation. It's a dirty little secret that most New Yorkers are pleasant, thoughtful, patient, and polite. The Chamber of Commerce must work overtime to maintain the surly, off-putting image that is widely believed to define the city. In truth, niceness is nearly epidemic in this town. Most of the time, I am grateful for that, but at the moment, it struck me as one of those lifestyle offenses, like aggressive panhandling, that the mayor should target for extinction. By the time my turn came, I was primed to hit her with my giant payload of frustration.

"Good morning. How can I help you?"

"You people have managed to make many thousands of dollars disappear from my account. I need you to find the problem and clear it up." Angrily, I passed my bankcard through the smile-shaped slot.

Her doe eyes went limpid. "I'm so sorry. I'll take care of this right away, Miz"—she squinted at my name on the card—"Barrow."

She swiped my ID through the card reader and tapped her request. "What I show is a series of large withdrawals over the past week, Ms. Barrow. Basically, they bring the balance below the limits of your reserve. Here." She passed me a printed readout of recent account activity. The details covered two full pages of minuscule type.

I scanned them with mounting horror. "I didn't make any of these. Other than a small check I wrote to the phone company, I haven't paid anything out of this account in over a week."

"Oh my. I'll have the records double-checked right away, but you should really go to the local precinct and report this. It may be a simple computer mix-up, but I wouldn't take any chances. It could be a case of identity theft."

An incredulous laugh escaped me. "Identity theft? That's too weird."

"It's no joke. Believe me. The thieves find ways to steal personal records, credit card and social security numbers, even banking information."

"I meant it's weird because I just started working on a book about that."

"Then you understand what I'm talking about. It's hard to believe what these characters can do. With nothing more than a credit card or your social security number, they can buy things in your name, wipe out your bank accounts, put you into bankruptcy, and wreck your credit rating. It's really frightening. And these crazy kids think it's a game. They don't care whose lives they ruin. It's all about seeing how far they can go. Beating the system."

"Kids? I thought professional criminals were behind most of it."

"You'd be surprised how many identity thieves turn out to be young hackers. Last month we had a horrible case. The nicest old lady who banks here came in nearly hysterical. She'd started getting these crazy bills for things she hadn't bought and cell phone accounts she hadn't opened. Even hotels and fancy restaurants in cities she'd never visited. Talk about nerve. The charges ran to nearly fifty thousand dollars. She was completely wiped out, couldn't even pay her rent. The landlord was threatening to evict her. Poor thing was so upset; I thought she was going to have a heart attack."

"Doesn't the bank have any safeguards? Don't you check before you allow just anyone to raid a customer's bank account? "

"We have very careful procedures, sure. These withdrawals went through your online account, which is very secure."

"Excuse me? I don't have an online account."

She went sheepish. "It says you do right here. Opened over a month ago. You must have filled out the application."

"I did nothing of the kind. That's outrageous! What kind of operation are you running? I'd be better off keeping my money in a cookie jar."

She tamped the air. "Why don't you give me a chance to check it out? It may be a simple mix-up we can straighten out in no time."

"And what if it's not?"

"That's why I suggested you file a police report. That way, if it turns out to be identity theft, we can launch an official investigation right away."

"How long would an investigation take?"

"Hard to say. But don't worry. If the funds were taken fraudulently, they'll be restored to you as soon as we get things sorted out."

"What am I supposed to do in the meantime? I have bills to pay, checks to cover. And whatever is going on seems to be affecting my credit cards as well."

Her gaze dropped to the printout of my raided account. "Sorry, Miz Barrow, right now there's really nothing I can do. File that report; that's the first step. And, hopefully, we'll get this cleared up soon."

2 2

Frigid gusts prodded me toward Sixth Precinct headquarters on West Tenth Street. While I was with Noah, I had come to view all police stations as warm and welcoming, like the porch lights of home. The NYPD had been our extended family, safe haven, and emergency backstop. But since the work he loved and the people he trusted turned on him, the force has become nothing more than a painful reminder. Aside from Duffy, I'll walk blocks out of my way to avoid any contact with our men in blue.

This is no simple feat. The city's massive police department is sliced into seventy-six precincts, plus transit and patrol divisions and myriad specialty squads, many of which operate out of One Police Plaza, downtown. The Sixth Precinct has jurisdiction over the sixty-five thousand residents of the western half of Greenwich Village, plus the hordes of people and certain lesser species who work in and visit the area each day.

My home neighborhood has long thrived on upheaval and continues to pride and pummel itself for pushing the social extremes. During the past decade, violent crime has declined steadily, while nuisance complaints, such as harassment, have soared along with the property values. Recent years have seen steady growth in the flamboyantly psychotic, drug-addled, and flagrant purveyors of chemical oblivion and every imaginable variety of pleasure for sale. These new neighbors have tested traditionally liberal Village values and caused many community members to sprout very prominent right wings. Residents claim they're concerned about quality of life, but preserving record real estate prices is high on the priority list as well. As Aunt Amelia often says, the very definition of a conservative is someone who has something to conserve.

Nearing the precinct's broad tan-and-white façade, I stalled and stood watching the straggle of cops and complainants. I reconsidered my non-existent options. Duffy couldn't help with this. The report had to be filed in the precinct where the crime took place, which, according to the woman at the bank, meant my local stationhouse. Anyway, I hated to lean on Duff any more than was absolutely necessary, which was far more than reasonable as it was.

I imagined his playful brogue. *"Sure, and what is it you're afraid of, Claire? Telling what happened? Signing your name?"*

Cruisers angled into parking spots or sped away, sirens wailing, cap lights ablaze. The sounds were achingly familiar: spirited chatter, ritual jibes, radio squawks.

I could do this.

Or maybe I could not.

My breath came in misty plumes, and then caught at the sight of a passing stranger. In defiance of the cold, he carried his coat. From the telling bulge under his gray tweed jacket, I made him as a plainclothes detective. I stared unblinking as he entered the precinct house, mesmerized by the resemblance he bore to Noah. He had the same dime-slot dimples, the identical broad shoulders, and long, loping stride. His hairline was a dead ringer for Noah's as well, down to the willful curls that flared over the collar of his faded denim workshirt. Even his hair color was the same distinctive blend, wet sand streaked with sunshine and a hint of creeping dusk.

Vividly, I imagined peeling back that collar and pressing my lips to the back of his neck. I conjured the salty taste of Noah's skin and the hint of nerves and coffee that often clung to him after a long, tense day in the field. I imagined how that kiss would turn him around and trigger the deep, heavy urgency I now felt throbbing like a phantom limb.

Powerless against a hard magnetic pull, I trailed him inside. In my fog of lust-tinged lunacy, I ached to embrace him. I yearned to press myself against him as tightly as our flesh and hollows would allow, defying our terrible separateness, daring our membranes to disintegrate so our molecules might fuse.

Quickly, he crossed the public area and disappeared down a corridor that was restricted to stationhouse personnel. The way was blocked by a giant Stop sign suspended from a metal gate, and an imposing officer, who stood watch with crossed arms and a face tight with warning.

Losing sight of Noah's look-alike felt like a gut punch. The pain doubled me over; it was that bad.

Soon, the agonizing illusion fell away and I was able to breathe again. I straightened cautiously, like an accident victim, steeled for an assault by lurking pain.

Thankfully, moments like this had become a rarity. For months after Noah's coffin was lowered into the ground by a whining pulley, I saw the possibility of him everywhere: stepping onto buses, framed behind restaurant windows, hurrying across the street. His echo existed in every vaguely familiar smile, in countless quirks of posture and movement, in teasing plays of light. Each time it happened was a head-on collision between impossible truth and the longing that was eating me alive.

A kind-eyed old woman shuffled by on a Windex-blue aluminum walker. "Honey, you're so pale. Are you all right?"

"Fine, thanks. I just got dizzy for a second."

She flashed a knowing smile. "Well, how exciting. I bet it's a boy."

"Yes," I said numbly. "Actually, it is."

"Good for you."

Community notices, crime statistics, and memorials to the precinct's fallen heroes cluttered the wan ivory walls. The left half of the large rectangular space served as a museum, filled with badges, uniforms, stripes, medals, and photographs donated by police departments around the world. There was a motley array of worn furniture, including a table capped with stacks of crime-prevention flyers. One was about identity theft. It warned against giving out private information, as if that provided any protection at all.

I drifted toward the so-called 124 room, which was, in fact, a desk devoted to collecting complaints. The woman in charge was a young, Hispanic police administrative assistant, trained to take reports and direct complainants to appropriate resources.

She was on the phone, and I was struck at once by her Sphinx-quality patience. "No, ma'am," she said evenly. "You don't need a permit for a birthday party. Not even if the kids are from out of town. No, ma'am. I'm positive. Yes, ma'am."

As she hung up, a terrible thought rooted me in place.

What if Rainey and her hacker friend were responsible for my incredible shrinking bank account? What if they had run out the limits on my credit cards and made those unauthorized withdrawals? Numbing horror overcame me as the likelihood clicked smoothly into place.

Duffy had picked up the signs that Phelan was a serious hacker, addicted to using his computer to steal into other people's lives. Once he had slipped inside the candy store, what was to stop him from grabbing the sweetest souvenirs?

That would certainly explain the pricey additions to Rainey's wardrobe. She had credited Aunt Amelia for the purchases, but that didn't guarantee it was true.

Had there been other unexplained acquisitions? It would have been easy for her to tuck away jewelry, CDs, and Lord knew what else without my noticing. Or she could have parked things she didn't want me to discover with a friend.

The more I considered the possibility, the more chillingly likely it seemed. I recalled Phelan's spidery fingers caressing the keyboard with the same breathless passion Richter had shown for Dr. Midori's leg. Free access to whatever his evil little heart might want could certainly explain the depths of that little creep's devotion to his precious machine. Having abandoned rules of decency would explain Rainey's alarming arrogance as well. Maybe she had taken to writing her own rules, sampling jungle justice. Making it up as she went along.

I would have been the easiest of marks. Rainey had unrestricted access to the mail, including my charge account and bank statements. I had never taken pains to hide my passwords or PIN numbers from her or keep her from uncovering my social security number. The file drawers that contained my tax returns and other personal records were never locked. Until now, I had never seen any reason not to trust the child completely.

Or, perhaps, I had simply chosen not to look.

"Help you, ma'am?"

The PAA was eyeing me with the guarded curiosity of someone trained to be on the lookout for impending trouble.

"No, sorry." I hurried outside, heart hammering. I could not bring the cops into this. Not without absolute proof.

Maybe not even then.

Rainey was just a kid, Noah's precious little girl. I had made a solemn vow to protect her, no matter what.

I was buffeted by the arctic wind, shivering beneath my clammy shirt. Frantically, I hailed a vacant cab that loomed two blocks away. The yolk-colored sedan approached at a determined clip, and then sped by, as if I had turned invisible.

I decided to save the few dollars and walk home. Turning up my collar, I braced against the ferocious westerly. The temperature had plummeted. Grim clouds were muscling out the sun.

2 3

I spent most of the afternoon on hold with the credit card companies. While the wind howled and frigid branches rapped against the frost-caked windows, I was bounced from department to department and thanked incessantly by recorded drones for patience I did not have. My frustration rose like a malignant fever. I needed to be working on my proposal, not treading endlessly in a sea of incompetence.

When I finally got through to the supervisors in charge, they had little to offer beyond the promise of further delays. If I sent the necessary authorizations, they would contest the charges I had not incurred. No one could guess how long it might take to set things right, presuming my claims were correct.

"I told you, I didn't buy those things."

"Are you saying the card was stolen, Ms. Barrow?"

"No."

"Has it been out of your possession then?"

"No, but someone managed to use it anyway."

"You didn't authorize anyone to make purchases on your account?"

Anger thumped in my veins. "No. I didn't make them. I didn't author-ize them. I didn't even dream them."

"Would you like me to cancel the card and issue you a new one?"

"No. Please just cancel it. I don't want anything floating around until all this gets sorted out."

"Are you sure? We have a new low-interest rate. Very attractive."

"Meaning I'll get to pay less every month for the things I haven't bought?"

"Sorry?"

"Nothing. I'll send the authorization letters so you can contest those charges."

"Will do. You have a nice day now."

As I started writing the authorizations, the doorbell rang. Richter chuffed happily at the sight of the handwriting expert from the Arcanum.

"Aldo, I'm so sorry. I was going to look through Noah's things, but I got sidetracked."

"Is everything okay?"

"Yes. Well, actually, no. There's been some crazy mix-up with my accounts."

"If you don't mind my saying so, you look pretty upset."

"Just frustrated, Aldo. And sorry I had you come here for nothing. Would you mind terribly coming back tomorrow?"

"No problem, Claire Barrow. See you then."

I had to send a separate letter for each store involved. I felt like a child mired in the criminal tedium of a punishment assignment: *I did not charge anything at Saks Fifth Avenue. I did not charge anything at the Virgin Megastore. I did not charge anything at Niketown. I have never eaten at Trattoria Del Este. I have never shopped at Chanel.*

Amelia was otherwise occupied tonight, so Rainey was going to her friend Melinda's after school to work on a project for the science fair. She would be staying for dinner and spending the evening. Melinda's mother, Irene, whose embarrassing overinvolvement now struck me as sensible and reassuring, had called to discuss whether Rainey had any specific study rules or diet restrictions and what the girls might require for supplies. As a result, I had no doubts about where my errant child would be and what she would be doing, at least for the next several hours. I was grateful beyond words that I would not need to deal with her any sooner. I felt miles from being mentally or tactically prepared.

As soon as I finished faxing the necessary requests, there was a harsh, insistent rapping on the door. Dr. Midori sported a crisp white coat and an air of preternatural calm. Blinking slowly, like a frog, he pointed at the back of his wrist. "Ten after five, Miss Claire. Must come now. Table waiting."

"Thanks, but this isn't a good time."

"Always good time take care of self. Soul thank body. Mind, too. All win."

"You're sweet, really. But it's been one of those days. I'm in exactly the wrong frame of mind."

"Wrong frame best. Change big." His smile lit on Richter, who barked madly at his feet. "Dog, too. Both come. Free neighbor, no charge."

My remaining strength proved no match for his incorrigible optimism. Midori set a paddle-sized hand on the small of my back, took Richter by the collar, and steered us both upstairs. Richter hung back, staging a doggie sit-in, braying with fright.

As we neared the second landing, Mrs. DiMarco's door swung wide, and she trailed her wooden cane into the hall. My upstairs neighbor was a compact bundle of ferocity, four and a half feet of strident opinions capped by the wizened face of an apple doll and a mass of electric-white hair. "What's the story with that mutt of yours, Claire? Is he crazy or what?"

"Just a little high-strung."

"Looks nuts to me. Reminds me of my brother's wacko wife, Johanna. Same twirly eyes."

"Sorry his barking bothers you. I'm trying to keep him quiet."

Her lips drew in hard, wrinkled spokes. "Lucky for you my hearing's not what it used to be."

Bobbing like an oil crane, Midori propelled us ahead. "You come get acupressure, Misses DiMarco. Make hearing fix. Bird song loud clear like stream run. You give word, I save hour. Free neighbor, no charge."

"Be a cold day in hell when I let you get your slimy hands on me, Mister Touchy-Feely. I may be old, but I know damned well what goes on in massage parlors."

Midori winced. "Not massage parlor. Eastern therapy center. Make health for thousand of year."

"Health? That's a hot one. I hear exactly what you make up there, Dr. Slime Bucket. Thump—thump. *Ooh, that so gooood. Deeper, harder.* You should be ashamed."

"Miss Claire table ready. We go now. See Misses later."

The health center was dim and hushed, except for the light hypnotic tinkling of a New Age Japanese CD. I caught the heady scent of eucalyptus and pungent green tea. Behind the desk were shelves crammed with packets of herbs and jars filled with odd tentacled objects floating in amber broth.

Midori walked me down a narrow corridor and led me through a series of rooms. "Today late, table waiting. Ten minutes dry sauna only. Next time Miss Claire come more soon early. Dry, wet sauna first. Cold hot contrast bath. Big heat make big relax." The heating units were off in the sauna and steam rooms he showed me, but I took careful note of the posted warnings and emergency cut-off valves. Apparently, "big heat" could also cause serious health effects, including a nasty case of death.

A young woman appeared and led me to the changing room in the rear. I hung my shirt and jeans in a narrow locker, traded my shoes for outsized rubber thongs, and wrapped myself, as instructed, in a pink-and-white striped towel.

Emerging, I half expected to find Richter trotting about in a similar getup. Instead, his lemon-and-vanilla towel was spread across a slatted teak bench. The pooch sprawled on top, purring softly as a therapist kneaded his flanks. He had been transformed from a quivering mass of raw, screaming nerves to a puddle of warm canine ooze.

Dr. Midori installed me in a preheated dry sauna with a glass of ice water and a cold, wet cloth.

"Think relax," he said. "Mind boss, body listen."

Unaccustomed as I was to the intensity of the heat, I soon started gasping for air. Each breath felt like a branding iron to my lungs. I feared my skin would shrink and curl at the edges like an overcooked steak.

I was poised to flee the instant the sand in the small plastic timer ran out. Another young woman led me past the functioning steam bath to a treatment room at the rear. Passing the window, I noticed the throbbing mist. The heat appeared to have a malevolent life of its own. Glad to be exempt from more scorching, I followed my leader into a small dim space fitted with twin massage tables. She instructed me to lie prone with my face in the padded oval frame that extended off the cushioned slab. She slid a fat pillow roll under my ankles, draped me with a soft sheet, and dimmed the lights.

Soon, an unseen figure padded in. Warm hands pressed my spine, stretching and rubbing, coaxing out the kinks. The worst of my tension softened and sloughed away. My limbs went slack and heavy as the muscle knots uncoiled. The therapist prodded harder, urging the deeper knobs of sinew to surrender.

Though the hands felt barely larger than a child's, they had the force of heavy machinery. Driving pistons, thumping gears, giant drill bits biting through stone. Gradually, the pressure crossed through discomfort and flirted with pain. Still, it was oddly satisfying. Teasing charges trilled along my nerves. Dr. Midori had promised to get my sluggish energies moving, and here they were, shaking off a long torpor, jangling with impatience like school kids awaiting the dismissal bell. Soon, the circuits were firmly established, hung like blazing string lights, spreading heat. It kept building, currents coursing faster, leaping synapses, snapping long-dormant feeling cells to life.

Questions started reeling through my mind. Where and how had Rainey met that creepy Phelan? Could he be a schoolmate? A friend of a friend? Or had he come into her life by some unfortunate accident? I imagined Rainey standing beside him on the subway, trading tentative glances, seduced by his danger like a flame-bound moth.

How long had their relationship, whatever it was, been going on? I tried to pinpoint the moment when Rainey's behavior began to shift and deteriorate, but I could not. It was as futile as trying to trap the moment when day slides into night. Dusk gathers and the sky flares with heartbreaking color, and a scatter of city lights winks on. But there is no way to isolate the first of darkness. Suddenly, the sun has slipped away and you are left to deal with its absence.

What I could identify were undeniable trends. At some point, the child had stopped bringing her problems to me. She used to present them with solemn trust, like prized broken toys that she presumed I had the power to fix. Now she kept her troubles locked inside or brought them somewhere else for analysis and repair. I didn't want to think where that somewhere else might be.

She had stopped bringing friends home as well. Not long ago, our apartment was puberty central, a mecca for hormone-induced chaos. Kids were always hanging around, staying for dinner and spending the night, emptying the refrigerator and filling the place with giggles, plans, and angst.

When that changed, I had swallowed Rainey's explanation whole. In fact, I'd been proud of her. She'd claimed she didn't want to interfere with my work. How sweet and considerate, I'd thought, what a good-hearted kid. Devious and deceitful had never entered my mind.

The hands on my back kneaded insistently, breaking up more mental sludge. How many times had Rainey snuck off to be with that smirking slime Phelan? What, beyond nasty computer games had they found to fill their time alone? I forced myself to run through an unexpurgated version of the list. My stomach lurched and fell with a sickening thud.

"Let mind go," a voice rasped. "Breathe deep slow, relax."

I filled my chest and released the air in a thin, even ribbon.

"Worry no help. Life flow like river, carry soul along. Wind tell boat where go. Fight wind no use. Go circles. Sink."

Dr. Midori's voice was a cool breeze. His steely hands radiated heat.

"Let go reach right place. Soul finish journey, find home."

With a feline leap, he mounted the table. Large stocking-clad feet replaced the hands on my back. Midori worked with astonishing skill, molding me as if I were inert. And soon, I became so: limp and mindless, drifting on a parallel realm to the tinkling music, sinking gently away from consciousness, bobbling like a lost balloon on a eucalyptus-scented cloud.

Next thing I knew, a squat woman with dark bangs and an earnest look was leaning beside me. "Massage good?"

"Oh, yes." The words stretched like warm taffy. Even my tongue was relaxed.

She helped me to sit and passed me a cup of green tea. "Take time. No hurry."

After I dressed, I found Richter splayed like a throw rug beside the desk. Seeing me, he rose with the hypercautious moves of a wobbly drunk.

Dr. Midori walked us to the door. "Treatment make strong. Stress fly south like winter bird."

"It was great. Thanks."

"Every week come. Next week same time. I hold appointments, you and dog."

"No, don't, please. I'll let you know, okay?"

His face fell. "Miss Claire not like?"

"I did, enormously. It's not that. "

"Money no problem. Free neighbor, no charge. House rule."

"Once was fine, Dr. Midori. And I appreciate it. But you're running a business. I can't use your services without paying. I wouldn't feel right about that. And, quite frankly, massage is not in the budget right now."

He scooped several flyers from the desk. "Miss Claire writer, yes?"

"Yes."

"Midori speak good, but no good English writing. You fix flyer word. Pay like that."

I glanced through the pages. They held mangled snippets of the doc-tor's philosophies. *Challenge opportunity bring. Push no stay place not. Run bring slow down.* "I'll be glad to go over them for you and make them read a bit more smoothly. No free massages necessary."

He set his jaw. "Miss Claire run business. Midori no feel right use service no pay. Writer not in budget now. Too bad for me."

The clever devil had brought me to checkmate. "Okay, you win. It's a deal."

He clutched my hand and worked my arm like a pump handle. "Everyone win. Best deal. Next week same time, you and dog."

Richter and I floated down the stairs. Mrs. DiMarco appeared again as we approached the second landing. Through narrowed eyes she took in our drowsy moves and murky expressions. "So it's animals now?"

"Look how relaxed he is. Isn't it amazing?"

"Amazing isn't the word I'd use, Missy. I call it plain sick. Don't you people have any decency? Any limits?"

"Have a lovely evening, Mrs. DiMarco," I said.

"What would your mother say, Claire? Tell me that. Are you too busy getting your sick pleasures to think about what all this would do to her?"

"Sleep tight, Mrs. DiMarco. Sweet dreams."

"World's going to hell in a handbasket and I'm supposed to sleep? I'm calling the mayor's office, that's what I'm going to do. I'm calling the FBI and the vice squad and that complaint guy with the bad hair on NBC News. You haven't heard the end of this, Missy. Believe you me."

Her continuing rant trailed us downstairs, but my haze was far too strong for her to penetrate. Richter and I drifted into the apartment, flopped on the couch, and sighed in unison.

As my breath played out, I heard the noise, sharp and jarring, like a sledge cracking stone. Moments later came a flurry of frantic activity from the garden. Rapid footfalls slapped the frigid ground. Soon the sound faded, and then disappeared, swallowed by distance and the last gusting howls of the dying storm.

Richter's head snapped up and his ears pricked. His tail went rigid, and a subway rumble sounded deep in his chest.

Someone was out there. Someone had been in the house.

2 4

I snatched the cordless phone from the end table and punched in the number of Duffy's cell phone. Breath held, I prayed for the call to connect. Service in the city was erratic. Sometimes, he wandered out of range, picking up a felon or a stray.

Thankfully, his soothing brogue soon came on the line.

My voice was a dry croak. "It's Claire, Duff. Someone broke into my apartment."

"He's there now?"

"No. But I heard the door slam. And I saw someone running away."

"Okay, sweetheart. Make sure the doors and windows are locked and hold tight. I'll be there in two shakes."

He patched me through to his police radio and instructed me to stay on the line. Still staring out at the misty darkness, I listened to the squawked litany of woes that rang into emergency dispatch: a heart attack on lower Broadway, gunshots on Park Row, a three-car accident near Madison Square Garden, possible drug overdose in Bryant Park, a restaurant grease fire raging out of control in Chinatown.

Soon, Duffy's unmarked screeched to the curb. He jogged up the walk and pressed past a crazed, howling Richter. He folded me in a generous, soothing hug, then he stepped back and his green eyes narrowed in somber appraisal. "You okay?"

"Depends on your definition of okay."

He strode around slowly, taking mental notes. "What happened?"

"Dr. Midori invited me up for a massage. Right after I got back, I heard the door slam. Then, I saw someone running away."

"Anything missing?"

I took a quick inventory: TV, stereo, VCR, silver candlesticks on the dining table, jewelry box. "Doesn't seem to be."

"Which way did he go?"

"Out back. Through the garden and over the fence."

"Did you get a look at him?"

"Not really. It was so dark."

"Walk me through it from the beginning, Claire. Close your eyes and tell me what you see. Sometimes the mind picks up more than you might imagine."

"I'll try." I shut my eyes and rewound my memory tape. "Dr. Midori had me and Richter up for a massage."

"Richter?"

"Yes, strange as it sounds, Midori thought it would help relax him. And it did. Both of us came back on a cloud. We were in the apartment for a minute, maybe less, when I heard this sharp noise. My first thought was that something had fallen. But then I heard a racket in the garden. From the way Richter acted, I figured it must be a cat or a stray."

"Why so?"

"He was alert, interested, but not crazy the way he gets around strangers."

"Hm. Interesting."

My eyes snapped open. "Interesting how, Duff?"

"What you said. That it might have been someone familiar to the dog."

"I said that?"

"In a manner of speaking. Go on."

I crawled back inside the memory again. "After I called you, I went to the kitchen and looked outside. It was dark and hazy, hard to see anything clearly."

"But you saw this person running away."

"Yes. He jumped the fence and bolted down the alleyway next to the brick building out back."

"So it was definitely a male?"

Clenching my lids, I dug deeper into the image. "Yes. Young, slim, tall."

"Light-skinned or dark?"

"Light." My eyes snapped open. "But it's hard to be sure. I could be wrong."

The smile was trademark Duffy, infinite patience spiced by a dash of wry amusement. "Trust your instincts, Claire. Shut your eyes."

He waited for me to do so. "Fence looks to be about four-feet high?"

I made a mental measure. "About that."

"You said he jumped it?"

"Actually, it was closer to a vault. He set a hand on top and swung his body over."

"In one clean, smooth movement, like a gymnast?"

"Yes. Everything moved together except for his hair. It was long and loose." The intruder's shape echoed in my memory: broad shoulders, narrow hips, and a slouchy spine.

The image was familiar.

Too familiar.

I tensed against a dizzying wave of fear.

"What is it, Claire? What's wrong?"

"That boy, Duff. Rainey's hacker friend. It could have been him."

Deep worry lines scored his brow. "Or someone worse."

"LeBeau, you mean?" Cold horror washed through me.

"No. Nothing like that." He flashed a hollow smile. "Don't be jumping to any crazy conclusions."

"I'm not, Duff. I told you, I can't see any reason why LeBeau would be interested in me. There's no rational connection." My heart was hurling hard against my ribs, nonetheless.

"You're right, sweetheart. Makes no sense when I give it some proper thought. Anyway, the Eel is not the sort to simply sneak in somewhere and run off like a frightened jackrabbit. Now is he?"

I pulled air, struggling to shake the noose of terror. "I'm delighted to say I can't claim to be any sort of expert on B.B. LeBeau."

"But I can. And this is not his way. Skulking off in the night? Running, no less? Not LeBeau."

"I'm happy to second that."

"Good. Now relax while I have a look around."

Despite his assurances, my nerves were still sizzling with fright. "Anything you say, pal. Want coffee?"

"That'd be grand."

"Don't ignore under the beds and in the closets, Duff. I still remember where the monsters hide."

"Only the imaginary ones, sweetheart. The real ones can hide in plain sight."

The pot finished perking, and I poured a steaming mug as he returned. Duffy drew a noisy sip, and then cupped the heated porcelain to warm his hands. "I checked the apartment and the grounds. Everything seems to be in order. Any chance you could have left the place unlocked?"

"I can't be absolutely sure. But I don't think so."

"No sign of forced entry at either door."

"My God, Duff. What if Rainey gave Phelan a key? What if she invited him to break in?"

"For what reason? If Rainey wanted to get her hands on something, wouldn't it be easier for her to do it herself?"

"Who knows how these kids think? Maybe she gave him the key, or maybe, he decided to come in for reasons of his own. It's possible, isn't it? The person I saw definitely looked like that kid."

"Nearly everything's possible, darlin'. But possible doesn't make it so. One thing you learn in this business is to take things step by step, follow the logic and not go jumping blind from here to there."

"I'm not in the business. Anyway, it's different for you. You're not nearly as neurotic as I am."

His eyes twinkled. "Now there's a competition I'll be happy to concede. You win, Claire. Hands down."

"Be nice, Duff. I've had a seriously rotten day."

"Besides the B and E, you mean?"

"Yes. Seems someone's been breaking and entering into my finances as well. My checking and charge accounts have been raided."

"Why didn't you tell me?"

My eyes stung. "I didn't want to bother you, Duff. I'm such a giant pain, always leaning on you for everything."

He shook his head. "Don't I lean on you as well, Claire? Aren't I forever mewling to you about this thing and the other? That's what friends are for, to be a great big nuisance to one another. If it wasn't for friends, what would we do for misery, after all?"

The tears spilled over. "It's more than that. I can barely say it."

"Sure you can, Claire. This is me you're talking to."

"I'm afraid Rainey and that Phelan kid may be behind it."

He went grim, taking that in. "What makes you think so?"

"His hacking, for one thing. And Rainey's got some fancy new clothing I can't explain. Look, I could be totally wrong about this."

"Who else have you told?"

"I went over to the Sixth Precinct to file a report. But then it occurred to me that Rainey might be involved. If she is, I can't bear the thought of turning it over to the cops, Duff. You saw what being suspected did to Noah. Anyway, if she's gotten into a mess like that, I'm the one to blame. I'm responsible for her."

"You have any proof beyond the supposing?"

"No. But it all fits."

He stroked my head absently, as if I were one of the dogs. "There, there, sweetheart. One thing at a time. First, let's figure out *if* she's involved for a certainty, then we can decide what to do about it."

"How do we figure it out?"

"You could simply ask her."

"Sure, and I could stick my head in a lion's mouth. Either way the head gets bitten off."

"Maybe she'll surprise you."

"She always does."

"Give it a try, Claire. And call me after you've had a talk with her. Meanwhile, I thought of someone who might be able to help us get a line on that kid Phelan. I'll go see him first thing in the morning. Pick his brain."

"Let me come with you, please, Duff. I can't stand doing nothing while Rainey takes a hatchet to her life."

His shoulders hitched. "Sure, I suppose."

"Thanks." I kissed his ruddy cheek. "Thanks for that, for this, for everything. What would I do without you?"

"No need to ask the question, Claire. Whenever you need me, there I'll be."

2 5

The trip to Stafford Secure Storage marked Diamond's first foray to Queens. He was grateful for Griffey's company in this alien borough, where subways ran high aboveground, English was often a second language or a distant third, and derelict warehouses commanded the prime river views.

Griffey had met him as planned. They caught the 7 train as the doors began to close with a harsh pneumatic hiss. Eyeing the route map,

Diamond noted that this line snaked through a tunnel under the East River and then rose to the elevated tracks on the outer borough side.

The scatter of other passengers bobbed along bleary-eyed or drowsed fitfully in their seats. Griffey passed the ride perusing the latest issue of the *Annals of Forensic Psychiatry*. With a sidelong glance, Diamond scanned the offerings: "Incidence of Migraine Headache in Finnish Violent Offenders," "Some Like It Haute: A Fresh Look at Upper-Crust Crime," "Group Stalking—Fad or False Reporting?"

For his own education, Diamond stared out the window, studying the dizzy parade of shuttered stores and modest row houses. Some still blazed with holdover Christmas lights. Others glowed with spectral reading lamps or the manic play of late-night TV. At this hour, many homes were dark. Diamond wished himself into one of those cozy cocoons, an ordinary soul, resting for the next day's spate of blessedly normal problems and miraculously dull routines.

Griffey led him from the car at the Queens Boulevard and Thirty-third Street station in Long Island City. They walked three blocks past the temporary headquarters of the Museum of Modern Art and turned down a dimly lit side street.

"Over there."

Diamond tracked the trajectory of Griffey's gaze toward a squat building that was largely obscured by a darkened auto body shop and the shuttered tool-and-die factory next door. Drawing closer, he observed the perimeter security. A towering chain-link fence was capped by razor wire. At intervals perched slowly rotating cameras that could ferret out signs of trouble in the dark.

"Certainly looks secure," Diamond observed. "Aside from the records of old murder cases, what do people keep in a place like this?"

"I honestly don't know. It's all top-secret. Total discretion is one of Stafford Secure's middle names."

"What are the others?"

"Paranoia, Suspicion, Crazy Caution, Utter Distrust. Follow me. You'll see for yourself."

Diamond trailed behind as the old man picked his way past the crumpled wrecks and rusting car carcasses that littered the auto body lot. At the center of the chain-link fence stood a heavy metal door. Griffey punched in the general access code on a small numeric keypad, and a voice crackled through an unseen speaker. "Your current password, please."

Griffey jabbed the keys with gloved fingers, and the disembodied voice turned harsh. "That's incorrect. Try your input again, please."

Stripping off the glove, Griffey muttered, "It appears some people have seen one too many James Bond movies." He tapped the code and waited, blowing into his palm for warmth.

Moments later, a beep sounded and the door swung inward with a spectral moan. Two cameras tracked them like light-seeking plants as they passed through the fence and approached the building. Diamond strode stiffly, cowed by the creepy scrutiny. "Maybe we should have had the papers delivered, Solomon Griffey."

"First we have to find the ones we need."

Another rigorous entry procedure awaited them at the warehouse door. This time, in addition to entering pass codes, they were patted down by a burly, bald guard and traced by a dour woman wielding a hypersensitive wand. The metal detector screeched at Griffey's belt buckle and watchband and the crumpled chocolate-bar wrappers in the pocket of Diamond's coat.

Next, they were required to sign in on a touch screen, technology which Diamond had helped to develop. Their particular screen signatures would be relayed to an international data bank and checked against those of known criminals and other undesirables who might pose a potential threat. The technology had proved to be a particular boon in rooting out terrorists at transportation hubs and border crossings.

"All I need now is a final okay from the Arcanum's gatekeeper," said the guard.

"Granted. That happens to be me," Griffey said.

The guard hitched his massive shoulders. "Sorry. Have to do it by phone. Procedures, sir. You understand."

"Try the second number on your list." Griffey retrieved his cell phone from the plastic receptacle in which he had deposited all his metallic objects. It rang almost immediately. The guard pressed the desk console receiver to his ear as Griffey picked up four feet away.

"Mr. Griffey, this is Raymond Garret calling from Stafford Secure. Will you kindly respond according to protocol, so we can voiceprint?"

"This is Solomon Griffey, gatekeeper for the Arcanum unit Number 528, authorizing unrestricted access and discretionary removal for members Solomon Griffey and Aldo Diamond."

"Voiceprint verified. Any projected termination time for this access, Mr. Gatekeeper?"

"The authorized members may use their discretion there as well."

"Thank you, sir." The guard hung up and nodded sheepishly. "You're cleared to go in, gentlemen. I'll escort you."

The Arcanum records resided in a ten-foot cement-walled cube. The guard pointed out the silver button they had to press to be released before he stepped outside and activated the locking mechanism. Watching the ponderous door glide shut, Diamond suffered a bout of claustrophobia. Ropes of fear tightened around his chest, neck, and well-upholstered midsection. His limbs erupted with an odd, electric rash, and his head puffed like a helium balloon around a quivering core.

Griffey's mouth pinched ever so slightly. "Are you okay, Aldo? You look a bit pale."

Diamond drew deep, measured breaths until his crucial senses came back online. "I'm fine. Let's get to it."

Seeking distraction, Diamond scanned the labels on the file boxes, which were stacked wall to wall, floor to ceiling, in tidy rows. His jaw dropped at the incredible roster of stubborn cases the society had investigated and managed to break.

His awed admiration of the Arcanum deepened as did his humble pride at being asked to join the group. There were the "Full Moon" murders, the case of the savage Ethan Alan Deboise, and the so-called Vampire Killings, which had cost twelve young lives in Seattle—the victims brutally slain and drained of their blood—and all but shut the city down until a suspect was identified and jailed.

It went on and on. There were the "Poison Pen" killings, the Motor City Car Bomber, and the Scorpion, an entomologist who had annihilated his victims with rare insect venom. The Arcanum had also broken the "Ivy League" killings and unmasked the deadly stalker in Beverly Hills, whose preferred prey was Hollywood stars. That charmer had turned out to be an aspiring actor determined to eliminate the competition.

"My word, Solomon Griffey. I didn't realize the society was involved in all these."

"That's the way we prefer to work. With rare exception, we are not in this for the notoriety. In fact, it can get in the way."

"That, I understand. It's tough enough to get anything done without the press breathing down your neck."

"True, but unfortunately, that's exactly what they're going to be doing as long as LeBeau has his way."

"Maybe we can find some way to spoil his party," Diamond said. "Where's the rest of the file for the Garmin case?"

Griffey turned toward the left-hand wall. "Should be around here. All the cases are ordered counterclockwise chronologically, most recent over here. Why don't you start from the top, and I'll search the bottom."

Soon, they came upon the file—three boxes wedged between the Kansas City bomber case and the murder of Senator Arne Selwyn's son by a man opposed to the senator's stand on strip-mining. Diamond removed the boxes above it until they were able to slide out the ones marked GARMIN. They were surprisingly heavy. Diamond went florid and clammy as he helped Griffey haul the files toward the door.

Griffey's chest was heaving as well. "I think we'd better go through these here and only take what you'll need."

"Good idea," Diamond wheezed.

A jab at the silver button brought the guard. He led them down the hall to a room marked PRIVATE. KEEP OUT! AUTHORIZED PERSONNEL ONLY.

Inside, they found a pale rectangular table and four stiff gunmetal chairs. "Will you gentlemen need anything else?" the guard asked.

Griffey perched on the chair at the far end to catch his breath. "I'm fine. You, Aldo?"

Diamond mopped his clammy brow. "All set."

Again they were locked inside. This time, in addition to the musty closeness, they were assailed by the sound of sharp, frantic scraping beyond the wall. Diamond pictured slimy rodents scurrying about with twitching whiskers, whipping tails, and sharp, seeking teeth. Forcibly, he fixed his attention on the files.

"Start with that box and take everything you find with any handwriting, even a signature, Solomon Griffey. I'll go through this one, and we can split the third."

Many of the documents were copies of typed transcripts and reports. As he thumbed through the box, Diamond culled out the witness interviews and statements. He extracted copies of scrawled musings from investigators on the case and notes from known and anonymous informants. The pile grew impressively high.

So did the heap of papers on Griffey's side of the table. Diamond faced a giant pile of work in addition to the further preparation he needed to do for the kidnapping trial.

Leaving Stafford Secure, they were searched again and asked to sign out both themselves and the documents. At Griffey's request, the guard summoned the storage company's bonded, bulletproof delivery service to ferry them back to Manhattan. The service was pricey, but given the heft and value of the documents, Griffey deemed it a necessity.

The van stopped first in front of Diamond's apartment house.

"If you like, I can stay and help out," Griffey offered.

"Thanks anyway. I really need to go through this by myself."

"See you tomorrow, then."

Diamond locked the documents in his apartment and trudged out again, hunched in his coat against the cold. As he walked toward the deli, he scanned the park. He saw no sign of Harry, so, hopefully, good sense had triumphed over stubborn craziness, and the man had gone to spend the night in some warmer, more hospitable place.

That was the exact thought kicking around in Diamond's mind when he heard a feeble groan. Tracking the sound, he spotted the vagrant curled up between a row of crammed garbage cans and a hill of bloated trash bags. Harry could have passed easily for just another lumpy sack of rubbish parked at the curb for morning pickup.

Diamond tried to haul him to his feet, but Harry hung heavy and limp. "Come on, buddy. Let's get you in where it's warm."

Huffing hard, Diamond hooked his arms around the man's heaving chest and dragged him into the deli. Under the store's fluorescent glare, he caught the gray cast of Harry's complexion and the erratic rasp of his breathing. Harry's nostrils flared with the effort to draw sufficient oxygen, and his eyes swirled beneath leaden lids. "Better call emergency, Battu."

"Right away, Mr. Diamond."

The EMTs arrived in seconds. They worked Harry over, taking his vitals and threading in lines.

Diamond hovered anxiously. "His heart, you think?"

"Ticker seems strong. EKG looks normal. Could be hypothermia, but we won't know for sure until we have him checked out. Guy's homeless?"

"Sleeps in the park."

"Relatives?"

"None that I know of."

"We'll take him over to Bellevue."

"Should I come along?" Diamond asked.

"No point. They won't let you into emergency unless you're related. If they decide to check him in after they check him out, we can leave instructions that you be informed if you like."

"I would, thanks." Diamond wrote his number on a slip from Battu's order pad.

The techs strapped Harry to a collapsible gurney and rolled him out to the waiting ambulance. Diamond followed, muttering encouragements.

"You hang in there, Harry. Soon as you're up to it, I'll see you get some decent chow."

Harry's dry lips smacked. "O—O for an Oreo."

"That's the way, Harry. Think happy thoughts."

2 6

The taxi shimmied at the curb, belching exhaust, while Melinda's mother ferried Rainey to the door. Melinda dawdled at the end of the walkway, jangling with impatience, averting her eyes from the humiliating spectacle.

Irene Ericsson had round features in a pie-shaped face and a plump, cushy body reminiscent of pillow furniture. "Here's your lovely girl, Claire. Safe and sound. Such a sweetie."

"Thanks for having her."

"And such nice manners. Not like some of the youngsters today. I'll tell you that."

"Good to hear."

"Maybe it's her name. 'Lorraine' is so sweet and old-fashioned. Reminds me of flowers and ribbons and lace. I bet someday soon you'll decide to call yourself that instead of Rainey. You'll be known as what you are: sweet Lorraine. In fact, I think I'll just go ahead and call you that from now on."

I held my breath, afraid that Rainey might rear back and sock her in the pie face or lash out with some unseemly insult, but she held her nasty tongue. *Sweet Lorraine.*

"Mom," Melinda whined, stretching the word to four syllables.

"Be right with you, hon," Irene crooned. "The girls worked really hard. They built a mechanical model of an earthquake that shakes and everything. The little buildings collapse and the tiny bridges fall into this miniature river that looks so real, you wouldn't believe it was just paint thickened with sand. They made the bridges out of toothpicks and the buildings out of cardboard, decorated to look exactly like brick. So imaginative. Bet it'll win a prize."

"Sounds great. Thanks again."

"Always a pleasure. You're welcome at our house any time, *Lorraine.* Maybe you'll sleep over when it isn't a school night. Sleepovers can be such fun. Not that anyone gets any sleep to speak of." She giggled like a cartoon sound effect: tee-hee.

Rainey's smile looked glued on. "Thanks, Mrs. Ericsson. Dinner was delicious."

Irene wove her plump fingers in delight. "Perfect manners. Simply perfect, Claire. You see?"

"I do, Irene. You take care now."

The instant the front door closed, Miss Perfect Manners brushed past me roughly and made for her room.

"Wait, Rainey."

"I'm tired. I'm going to bed."

"Someone broke in here while you were at Melinda's."

Her defiance faltered. "So?"

"So I think it may have been your friend."

"You *think,* meaning you don't *know* anything. Whatever happens, you blame Phelan."

"I'm not blaming him; I'm simply saying that whoever broke in here looked like Phelan. Anyway, Phelan is not my concern, Rainey. You are. I need to know what's going on with you. If you've gotten into some kind of trouble, I want to help."

"Then get off my damned case."

"I'm afraid you're in over your head. I think you may have gotten involved in things that could seriously mess up your life."

"And I think you're imagining things. Next it'll be flying saucers and little green men."

"Have you and Phelan been hacking into my bank and charge accounts?"

Her eyes bugged. "Are you kidding me?"

"I asked a question. I'd like an honest answer."

She dropped her book bag with a furious thud. "Fine. Here's *total* honesty. I think you're *nuts*, Claire. I think you're honestly, seriously *gone*. I think they should lock you up in a loony bin."

"Did you and Phelan hack into my accounts? Yes or no?"

"Yes or no," she mimicked. "I'm sick of your damned accusations. I don't have to stand here and listen to this!"

"If you aren't involved, I need to report it to the police. But if you are, I'd rather try to work it out between us."

"I don't care what you do. Don't you get it?"

"I need an answer."

"And I need to get the hell away from you!"

She shot down the hall, locked her door, and blasted her stereo. When I knocked, she cranked it louder still, until the walls shook with angry percussion and the irate counterpoint of Mrs. DiMarco's cane against the floor.

"I'm calling the police if you don't stop that immediately," my neighbor hollered. "I'm dialing, Claire. I am."

Richter cowered, shivering against the wall. I ran a soothing hand between his ears. "I certainly screwed that up."

The dog eyed me sympathetically. He had strong opinions about almost everyone, but when it came to Rainey, he was every bit as lost as me.

Duffy was not so quick to give up. I reached him at Dependent Claws, where he had stopped to make evening rounds. In the background I could hear the furry ones, vying sharply for his attention.

"So I spoke to her."

"That's good, Claire. How did it go?"

"It went."

"Sorry to hear that."

"All I managed to do was make her even angrier."

"You opened the door for the child and showed her where help lies. Under the circumstances, I'd say you've done the best you could."

"Now what? Do I report the identity theft or don't I?"

"I'd give it a bit of time. Let me see what I can find out on my own, without turning this into a formal investigation. Then, if Rainey and that boy are involved in any way, we'll have our options open."

"I agree. I'll find some way to manage in the meantime."

"Sorry I can't help financially. Truth be told, it's me they're speaking of when they talk about going to the dogs."

"We're not talking about forever, right?"

"Not at all. Shouldn't take me more than a few days. A week at the outside."

"I can deal. Anything new on LeBeau?"

"Just more of the same. He's still the darling of the airwaves. Hero of the department, too, if you can believe. Word is many of our boys are of a mind to lynch those volunteers at the Arcanum and give LeBeau the honor of placing the rope. Still, I've been on the phone since I left you. A few of my saner brothers on the force have agreed to help me keep an eye on him. Hopefully, someone will sound the alarm the minute he starts acting even vaguely like himself."

2 7

After the ambulance carrying Harry wailed off into the night, Diamond slogged back to the deli. He ordered a low-fat tuna salad, a small container of mixed fruit, a package of Melba toast, and two large black coffees.

"Nothing else?" the counterman said.

Diamond gazed longingly at the crammed shelves. The cookie sacks and snack bags preened seductively, crooning their siren songs, urging him toward the perilous shoals of self-destruction. "Hopefully not."

Wearily, he returned to his empty studio. He set down the documents from the Garmin case, settled in an armchair, and got to work.

He had a copy of the Diamond EDGE software on his computer, but he preferred to conduct his analyses by hand. To his practiced eye, writing spoke in subtlety and nuance that no machine could assess fully.

First, he looked again at the notes from Claire Barrow and her late husband. Something elusive lurked beneath the disorganized slant of Noah's writing. Diamond detected a hidden subtext, some indecipherable message the man had been trying to slip between the lines. But he couldn't put his finger on what it might be.

Next, he studied the paltry samples prosecutors had gotten from the accused. B.B. LeBeau had signed a few necessary forms and a brief handwritten statement submitted by his defense team before sentencing.

Still, that was enough for Diamond to get a horrifying peek under the Eel's mental covers. Angular, aggressive patterns exposed an obsessive need to dominate and control. Dark, heavy strokes and emphatic underlining revealed a dangerously explosive temper. The extreme forward slant bared his rabid fanaticism. Dagger-shaped "T"s and filled rounds showcased his unrelenting cruelty. Though the samples were not enough to be absolutely conclusive, it was clear that the man behind this writing was totally devoid of compassion and human concern. He could kill an innocent stranger with no more thought or remorse than the average person gave to swatting a fly. Diamond was glad to turn the sample over and move on to the witnesses.

Slowly, he examined the scrawls and signatures, searching for odd or missing notes. Content could be significant, but his job was to see through and beyond it. Still, sometimes, his emotions dug in and demanded to be heard. He was especially moved by a letter to the court from Joe Garmin's mother, delivered before LeBeau's sentencing, which attempted to express the enormity of her loss.

Diamond did not need words to read the woman's grief. Her screaming pain rang in the long, dour descenders and fragile, anguished strokes. Her letters had a morbid slope and desperate, disorganized rhythm that belied a crumpled will and shattered hopes. Patterns like these were only seen in the terminally ill and morbidly depressed.

On his notepad, Diamond jotted a reminder to mention Mrs. Garmin's mental state to the group. If any remnants of this profound melancholy remained, she would need to be managed with extra-soft kid gloves.

Putting that letter aside, he rubbed his eyes and forged ahead. He was determined to finish the task tonight, even if it meant no sleep at all. Given the enormous stakes, the Arcanum had to move quickly.

Methodically, he went through the stacks of papers. Many of the handwriting samples were unremarkable. In the few that caught his eye, all he could detect were understandable traces of anxiety. The majority of people were intimidated by even the most innocent dealings with the legal system. A murder case multiplied that skittishness in all but the professionally experienced—or psychopathically inclined.

He spotted no serious red flags in the statements from the Garmins' neighbors or friends. Nothing suspicious struck him in the handwriting of detectives or courthouse personnel involved with the case. One judge, who had presided in an earlier unsuccessful action against B.B. LeBeau, showed all the signs of a seriously authoritarian personality, but that was not relevant here. Going through the informants' notes, he picked up several with the standard false confessors' exhibitionistic tendencies. No surprise.

The clock read half-past six. The first hints of daylight leavened the glum, pewter sky. Diamond's back ached and his red-rimmed eyes kept drifting out of focus. He had been working steadily, sipping cold, acrid coffee to stay awake. The only break he'd taken was to put in a quick call to Bellevue to check on Harry.

An ER nurse assured him that Harry was fine. "Your friend's sitting up, Mr. Diamond. He's been carrying on most of the night, singing something awful."

"Quintessential Harry. Good to hear. When do you think he'll be released?"

"Soon as we can swing it. That's for sure. My ears can't take it much longer."

"Really? I kind of like Harry's singing."

"You're more than welcome to it. Believe me."

"Did they figure out why he collapsed?"

"Not exactly. He had a goose egg on the back of his head. Could be he took a fall and passed out. These things tend to happen to fellows like Harry."

"'Long as he's okay now."

"Aside from the singing, I'd say he's fine."

Returning to the table, Diamond eyed the shrinking pile of papers that were left to review. Soon, he would need to stop working on the Garmin case, so he'd have time to review his court documents and make it to the kidnapping trial for a final day of cross-examination. He could pick this up again after court recessed, but he was beginning to fear that he'd have nothing more than a sore spine and soggy brain to show for the effort.

Gauging what he had to do for the kidnapping trial, he decided he could afford to devote fifteen more minutes to the Garmin papers. He downed the last of the cold, bitter brew and dug in again.

The next documents in the pile were statements by tradesmen and others who had worked for the Garmin family and had access to the house. Speaking aloud to break the numbing monotony, he examined them in turn.

"Plumber: insecure but nonviolent, something of a loner. Exterminator: sensitive and artistic. Can't take criticism. Oil deliveryman: a major straight arrow." The worst Diamond could imagine that one killing was joy. "Garbage man shows evidence of a compulsive personality. Maybe a gambling problem. Could be into petty theft, no more."

Weaving his thick fingers behind his neck, Diamond could easily conjure a scenario where the family came home and found the guy trying to lift a kid's toy or heist a garden tool, but he couldn't get from there to multiple murders and a grisly ritual aftermath. No way.

The once-a-week housekeeper looked fine. Ditto the young man who made the diaper deliveries and the electric-meter reader and the carpenter who came in to do occasional odd jobs. Diamond detected no problem with the piano teacher who had given Garmin's wife lessons or the old high school friend who showed up once a month to trim her hair, unless you counted a poor self-image and an unhappy childhood.

The next statement came from the regular baby-sitter, a teenager who lived down the block. From the rigid writing, Diamond could tell that she was a highly obedient kid. She was wound a little tightly for absolute comfort, but the worst he could associate her with was a possible tendency toward eating disorders or some other self-destructive response to living in an emotional straitjacket.

As he turned over the next sheet, his heart quickened. The writing belonged to a seventeen-year-old girl named Toby Felder. According to the interviewing detective's annotation, this kid was a good friend of the regular sitter, and was occasionally called in to pinch-hit. She had watched the Garmins' little boys three days before the murders, while the parents attended a friend's surprise birthday party across town.

The Felder girl's writing reeked of lying and monumental stress. The lies were etched as broad loops in her lowercase "o"s. Extreme pressure showed in her heavy, ragged strokes and erratic rhythm. All normal patterns and consistency had collapsed.

This degree of upset had to be acute, a view confirmed by the fact that none of the pathology sank below the midline, which would point toward some cause in the past. Something in this interview or right around it had triggered the disintegration in the girl's writing. Diamond's best guess was that Toby Felder had knowledge of the murders. Given the nature and force of the crime, it was highly unlikely that a seventeen-year-old could have been the perpetrator, especially a girl, but he would place way better than even odds that she could somehow help lead them to the monster that was.

Suddenly fizzing with energy, Diamond dialed the phone in the Calibre Club's solarium. Griffey answered on the third ring, his flimsy voice worn even thinner by fatigue.

"Morning, Solomon Griffey. Aldo Diamond calling. I turned up someone who was hiding something about the Garmin murders."

"Music to my ears, Aldo. Give me the details."

Diamond explained his suspicions about the baby-sitter and recited the particulars he was able to get from the file: full name, parents' names, the family address and phone number at the time of the murders, school and work information on the kid and her parents.

"That's wonderful. We'll track her down."

"Wish I could help, but I'm finishing up my cross-examination in that kidnapping case today."

"You have helped, my friend, and you will. It's your catch, and you get to run with it, wherever it goes. Call when you get a chance. We'll keep you up to speed."

"Thanks, Solomon Griffey. I appreciate that."

"You're the one who deserves thanks, Aldo. I have a feeling this might be the start of a turnaround in this blasted mess. I'm sure LeBeau is as guilty as they come. We've simply got to get to him before he gets to anyone else."

2 8

One Police Plaza crouches like an ugly troll behind New York's majestic City Hall. The building is home to much of the sprawling NYPD administration and many of its more arcane specialty units. In the era of heightened post-9/11 security, the boxy brown building and the plaza whose name it bears, are protected from attack by giant planters, garish blue walls, makeshift fences, police tape, uniformed guards, and strict prohibitions against photographs, suspicious loitering, and intrusive curiosity.

Fortunately, Duffy had arrived before me and cleared our presence with the duty officers in the booth fronting the building's entrance. He stood in the shadows of a giant sculpture composed of large, interlocking, red-metal disks, reminiscent of clotting blood cells. Spotting me, he clicked his teeth like castanets. "Th-there you are, C-c-claire. Zachary should be along any time."

As soon as I stopped walking, the wicked cold burrowed up through the soles of my loafers, and settled deep in my bones. "Couldn't we have had this meeting indoors?"

"Zach's got an appointment inside with the Computer Investigation and Technology Unit in a bit, so he wanted to catch us on the way. You want to deal with this character, you learn to go along. Here he comes now. You'll see what I mean."

A freckled kid in scarlet spandex approached through the City Hall arch. He was perched on purple metallic Rollerblades, barreling toward us at reckless speed.

He tucked in a crouch, poised his elbow like a lance, and kept coming. I recoiled reflexively. Duff held his shaky ground.

"Watch out!" I shrieked.

He stood unmoving as the crazy kid bore down. Faster, grim-faced, head dipped like a battering ram.

The second warning stuck in my throat as the boy zoomed toward a certain collision. I braced for the brutal hit, tensing in sympathetic defense. But then, a breath from disaster, he veered off like a capricious breeze. At the entrance to the arch, he executed an astonishing back flip and landed smoothly on his blades. Then, he circled around and came to a squealing stop directly in front of us.

The kid clapped Duffy's upraised hand. "Hey, Detective. How's it hanging?"

"Isn't hanging at all, Zachary. What hasn't shriveled from the cold has dashed near up to my throat to protect itself from the reckless likes of you. I see you've been practicing. Coming along nicely, I must say."

His smile framed a fence of crooked teeth. "Keeps me out of trouble, Detective McClure."

"Sure, and I believe in the Easter Bunny, too, Zach. Meet my friend Claire."

"Hey."

"Likewise," I told him.

"Zachary's quite the remarkable young man," Duffy said. "Excels at whatever he sets his mind to: music, art, sports, and every conceivable subject in school. Boy graduated from Columbia last year at the tender age of eighteen. He was top of his class with a quadruple major in theoretical physics, computer science, French literature, and international relations. Unfortunately, sometimes he puts that remarkable mind of his to things the law does not allow. That's how we met. Young Zach ran afoul of Lady Justice some years back, and he came to us as part of his community service. Still works with the department from time to time. CITU wouldn't know what to do without him." Duffy tipped his head toward the building, as if that explained it all.

"You made me see the error of my ways, Detective. I was caught up in the glory, riding the high of Zach Hack Attacks. Guess you have to chalk it up to immaturity."

"Don't bother handing out the empty excuses. You could, therefore you did. You can, therefore you will. I don't believe for a second that there's a cure for the likes of you."

The kid made a scout's honor sign. "No fair. You can see for yourself: I'm playing outdoors like you suggested. Having some nice, wholesome, innocent fun."

Duffy sniffed. "Save your breath, son. I'm not in the market for any horse manure today."

The kid circled backwards in a tidy figure eight. "What can I do you for?"

"We're trying to get a line on a hacker named Phelan, with a P-H. You know him?"

"First name or last?"

"Yes. Or none of the above."

"Does Phelan stand for something else? The 'Ph' handles are usually a play on some word that starts with 'F.' 'Failing'? 'Feeling'? Think it could be something like that?"

"Sure, or 'felon,' for that matter. Who knows?"

"Thought you might have some idea," Zach said.

"Your guess is better than ours. 'Phelan' is all we've got. He's about seventeen or so. Bit of a slimy smartass."

"Name's not familiar, but that doesn't mean much. Most of these guys change identities like other people do shirts. Typically, you'll have several spares so you can toss them out when they get dirty. You have anything else on the kid?"

"We tracked him to a rat hole in Alphabet City. Could be a one-time thing or a regular hangout. I honestly don't know."

"Where in the ABCs exactly?"

Duff recited the address.

Zach's face tensed with concentration, clumping his freckles in khaki blots. "Distinguishing features?"

"Not on the lad, but there was something odd on his screensaver," Duffy said. "Thing was shaped like a stick with two points coming off each end and a circle in the middle. Looked like a do-it-yourself job." He pulled out a paper scrap and sketched a crude likeness.

"Interesting." Zachary pocketed the drawing. "What's his deal?"

"That's what we're trying to find out. Identity theft is a good possibility."

The boy sniffed his contempt. "Lowest of the low. Guys who do that are no better than muggers who toss old ladies, if you ask me."

"Oh? I thought he might be one of your playmates."

"Doing crap like that? No way. Anyhow, most of the guys I hung with have long since moved on. Consulting for the white hats like I do, if they've kept it up at all. Once you've climbed all the mountains, it gets a little old. Plus, it's gotten ugly. Not like back when we were into it."

Duffy bit back the smile. "Way back in 2000, 2001 you mean?"

"More or less. The point is we were in it for the sport. Creeps today don't care who they hurt or how badly."

"Look at you, Zach. Standing high up on that soapbox with your halo shining so bright it could blind a person. Never thought I'd live to see the day."

"Just gets me mad, Detective McClure. Gives us all a lousy name we don't deserve." A wry grin cracked through his dismay. "Anyway, if I've developed a thing about right and justice, you're to blame. You and Detective Travis ruined any chance I had to become a legendary rebel outlaw. So now, when I break my neck turning quads on the half-pipe, it'll be your fault."

My heart skipped at the mention of the name. "You knew Noah?"

Zachary nodded eagerly. "Detective Travis and this guy saved my sorry butt. Turned me around and showed me I could put what I had to better use." His pale eyes narrowed and then sparked with recognition. "Wait a minute. You're Claire. *The* Claire. Am I right?"

"She is," Duffy said gently. "Noah's wife."

The boy clutched my hand. "Great to meet you. Detective Travis talked about you a lot. He used to say that maybe someday I'd get really lucky and find someone half as good as you. I'm so sorry about what happened. Really threw me."

I swallowed down a bitter lump. "Me, too."

The boy's face went grim. "Never made any sense to me, the suicide thing."

"No, me neither."

Duffy cleared his throat noisily and shot a loaded glance at Zach. "Before one of us freezes off something he's especially fond of, let's cut to the chase. Can you help us or not?"

"Sure. I'll get on it right away. Put out what you've got to the players and see what floats. Stop by the Pit later today. Around four. I should have some kind of answer for you, one way or the other, by then."

"Standard terms?"

"No way."

"Trying to hold up an officer of the law in broad daylight at police headquarters? Maybe you're not such a genius after all."

The boy's hands shot up, and I noticed a trace of the same keyboard twitch that kept Phelan's fingers dancing in perpetual motion. "I meant no way I'm going to charge you for this, Detective. When it's official NYPD business, that's one thing. I don't take money to do favors for friends."

Duffy coughed in his hand to cover his embarrassment. "That's good of you. But if it turns out to cost a pile of time or you run up expenses, you'll let me know. We square on that?"

"It won't."

"You never know."

"Make you a deal. If I get you what you want, you can come cheer me on at the blading regionals next month. I'm signed on for three events."

"That I'll be glad to do, son, whether you get me what I'm looking for or not."

29

A fresh pile of aggravation awaited me on the foyer table at home. A statement from my teacher's retirement account showed a substantial recent withdrawal that I had not made, along with a staggering penalty for withdrawing the money earlier than the rules allowed. There was a bill in excess of two thousand dollars for a MasterCard account I hadn't opened, an eye-popping invoice for a limousine service contracted in my name, and a fat statement for cell phone charges on a number I knew nothing about. The calls amounted to thousands of long-distance minutes, including several breathtakingly expensive chats with such far-flung locales as Nairobi, Kenya, and Quito, Ecuador.

I called the cell phone company first and heard the drill that by now had become familiar. They needed a letter protesting the charges, plus an official copy of the case information. If I wanted them to investigate, I would have to report the crime to the police.

I felt like the old lady who swallowed a fly. Anything I might do to try and solve the problem threatened to make the problem worse. Before I took any irrevocable action, I had to know whether Rainey was involved. If she was, I had to understand how and why before I could decide what to do about it.

Fixed on that, I drifted down the hall toward her room. Richter followed me warily, catching my reluctance like a yawn. I stopped at the threshold, hating the thing I felt I had to do. Contrary to Rainey's assertions, I had never been inclined to snoop. Growing up, I had experienced far too much of that on the receiving end.

My mother could never bear to be kept on the outside of a secret. When Lottie and I talked behind closed doors, trading sisterly confidences or advice, she would barge in on some pretense and find an excuse to hang around and probe. She went through my notebooks and rummaged through my drawers, never shy about leaving her mark on my things.

Letters that came addressed to me were opened "by mistake" and declared fair game for critical discussion. At her most insufferable, Mom would sniff at me with bloodhound suspicion or peer into my eyes, searching for some unimaginable enlightenment. Sometimes, I even caught muffled evidence of her lurking on the extension phone when I was talking to a friend. When we were sure she was out of earshot, Lottie and I would tease that we were growing up in an Orwellian nightmare, under the harsh, unblinking eye of Big Mother.

I was never going to behave like that, not for anything, not in a thousand years. But here I was, prepared to violate Rainey's privacy and set aside my firmest convictions in the name of parental desperation and concern.

Rainey's room was a study in adolescent dissonance. Pastel-colored little-girl frills still framed the window, and pale print ruffles skirted the bed, but the matching quilted spread had been banished long since to the rear of the linen closet, replaced by rumpled bold leopard-print sheets. Worn dolls and faded stuffed animals perched dejectedly on the painted rocker. Once the object of love and ardent affection, they were now draped by dirty socks and discarded clothes. The walls, save for the Pooh Bear framed needlepoint, were festooned with heavy-metal posters and baby-beefcake shots torn from movie magazines.

From Noah, I had detailed knowledge of many aspects of detective work, including how to question a suspect, how to read unspoken lies in nuances of posture and expression, and how to conduct a thorough evidence search. All those procedures required steady, methodical digging, a keen eye for detail, unwavering patience, and a dogged sense of purpose. Echoes of his voice played in my mind. *Don't overlook the obvious. Be sure to pick up the missing beats.*

Remembering the search process he had described in fascinating, horrifying detail, I went through Rainey's things. I examined her dresser and night table and checked for contraband that might be taped to the undersides of lamps, appliances, furniture, or drawers. I took apart her bed and studied her mattress, seeking unexpected tears or lumps. I went through her closet, piece by piece, digging into pockets and patting inside shoes. I examined the books and other mementos on her shelves, quickly flipping past the predictable and innocent: pages turned down to mark a steamy passage in a novel she'd read, nasty caricatures of a teacher she detested, catty notes she and Danielle had passed in class, a picture of her Hollywood flavor of the week emblazoned with her waxy red lip print.

Next, I took apart the heating ducts, casting my hand deep into dark recesses that were lined with sticky spider silk and brittle insect carcasses. I unscrewed the lighting fixtures and removed the backs from her radio and boom box. I rummaged inside the bathroom fixtures and felt behind the lotions and makeup in the medicine cabinet.

Nothing.

I rolled up the rug and the pad beneath it, leaving a trail of crumbly foam. Pacing in tiny steps, I listened for telltale squeaks in the floorboards and searched for gaps between the planks that might indicate a hiding spot.

Finally, I stood on Rainey's desk chair to reach the top closet shelf. Here, in taped, battered boxes, she stored her assorted "stuff." Noah had described this as a prime hiding place for nuggets of important information. As he told it, people had a near-universal need to preserve important bits of their past, no matter how gruesome or incriminating the mementoes might be. You could learn a great deal from what a suspect deemed worth saving.

I ferried the boxes to her bed and slit the tape so it could be mended in a way that would not be obvious.

The first box was full of tiny play outfits and bathing suits, sized for the beanpole body Rainey no longer had. Several others also contained outgrown clothes. Another held old birthday cards and letters from friends, school papers, artwork, and a rubber-banded clump of perfect report cards.

Finally, I came to a box filled with her most ancient mementoes. Quickly, I scanned the poignant souvenirs on top: baby pictures of Rainey with her mom and Noah, later shots of Rainey and Noah alone. I was struck, as always, by Rainey's uncanny resemblance to her mother: same opal eyes and melting smiles, same oval face capped by a widow's peak, the same slender form. If ever I fantasized for a crazy instant that Rainey was my child, I had only to look at Jenny to stand sharply corrected. Jenny's likeness was etched on her daughter's face and body, ingrained in her most primal memories, inscribed on her genes like a thousand stone-carved prophesies.

I had come into the child's life late, and by default. I'd had no part in her origin or in all those precious moments that these keepsakes brought to mind: the baby book, the lock of fine flaxen hair, the hospital bracelet with the legend "baby girl Travis" wedged in the tiny plastic canal, the imprint of Rainey's minuscule foot beside her mother's fingerprint at birth. Maybe there was no way to get past that and earn a solid place in Rainey's heart. Maybe I'd been delusional to imagine that was even remotely possible. My heart sank, weighted by the crushing probability that it was not.

At the bottom of the box was a thick, legal-sized envelope bound with strapping tape. I memorized the placement of the tape and slit the top. My pulse quickened as I saw what was hidden inside.

This was not what I was looking for, and certainly not what I had hoped or expected to find. It was Noah's last memo book, the one I had thought he'd destroyed. Every cop was required to keep a record of all on-the-job activity in these department-issued pads. Unless higher-ups needed to see them for some official purpose, they remained individual property. Most cops kept these books routinely, giving little thought to the possibility that other eyes might someday read what was there. Most often, no one ever did. The collection of memo books tracked a police career from rookie year to retirement and typically came to their final rest on an attic shelf or at the bottom of a musty, forgotten trunk.

But Noah had been ordered to turn in his final book when he was under investigation by Internal Affairs. As far as I knew, he had been prepared to do so on the day he died. But he had never shown up for that hearing. And later, when I searched for it, the book was nowhere to be found.

Though I remained convinced of his innocence, the book's disappearance had always troubled me. If there was nothing incriminating in his record of events, why would he have made it vanish?

Now the puzzle took a disturbing new turn. Had Rainey found this and hidden it to protect her father? Or had Noah hidden it for me or Rainey to find someday? If he had wanted it permanently gone, wouldn't he have simply destroyed it?

My questions multiplied. Whichever of the above was true, why? Was there a dark secret revealed in these pages that he wanted to keep in the family? Was there something here he hoped we would expose for him someday? Was it the thing that had pushed him to his death? My head reeled, trying to imagine what could have been so dangerous or awful, and terrified that such a damning thing could exist.

There was only one way to find out.

I replaced the box and scrutinized the room. Staring critically, I repositioned the tangle of jungle sheets on Rainey's bed, pulled her sock drawer out several inches, tugged the rug back in proper position, and pulled the closet door further ajar.

Impatient as I was to read the book, I forced myself to take another careful look at the room. As I did, Noah's words came back to me: *Don't overlook the obvious. Be sure to pick up the missing beats.*

As I mutely repeated those cautions, a missing beat announced itself firmly. Two years ago, when Rainey decided to redo the room, she had stripped down everything hanging on the walls, including countless images of her beloved Pooh. Sometime later, the Pooh needlepoint my mother had made found its way back among the garish posters and leering movie idols.

As I took it down, I felt a sharp edge lurking under the taut cotton surface. Shaking the frame, I heard the rattle of a loose object inside. A tidy slit ran across the paper that sealed the back. I was able to slip my finger inside and work the object clear: a manila envelope.

Inside, I found newspaper clippings about Noah's death. Rainey had marked the offending words and scrawled strident protests in the margins. Every mention of suicide had been circled. She had underlined every reference to the charges of his alleged misconduct. *No!* she wrote. *Don't believe this! Lies!*

Grimly I understood that I was looking at some of the poison that poor kid held inside. Rainey had hidden her pain at first behind a phony wall of strength. And now, she kept it locked behind the rage. I returned the clips to the envelope, slipped it back in its hiding place, and hung Pooh, with his pudgy paw in the honey jar, in his place.

Then I went to my office, locked the door, and opened Noah's book. I followed his bold, round writing through every hour of every duty tour he worked during those final months.

April 16, 9:15 P.M. Call to 325 W 23rd. Neighbor reports hearing gunshot. Examination of the premises reveals no suspicious activity.

I read through countless other false alarms. Much of the book reported such routine activity: interviews, follow-ups, and endless meetings and hours of observation that didn't pay off. Real police work is nothing like what is depicted on the big or little screen. Events don't fit into a thirty-minute or two-hour format with the case neatly wrapped at the end.

Other entries made me shudder: *May 22, 11:33 P.M. Call to 14th and Eighth. Suspect strapped with explosives, threatening to detonate, holding woman and child.*

I remembered how that had ended, with a sniper's shot to the lunatic's head. A single second's missed timing or the tiniest other mistake, and Noah could have been blown to bloody bits along with the perp and his hostages.

In harrowing detail, he described the drive-by shootings, violent holdups, hostage standoffs, and the most gut-wrenching for any cop: *Call for emergency backup at 42 and Seventh. Car 145, Ninth Precinct, caught in crossfire resulting from a drug dispute. Two officers down.*

My head rang with imagined siren screams and cries of grief. As a cop's spouse, you were always prepared for the worst, but preparation did nothing to cushion the loss when it came.

I read about the time Noah and Duffy tracked down the lair of Richmond Gray, a photographer who had murdered six young women in his cavernous Tribeca loft: *June 16: 4 P.M. Audio surveillance at Franklin Street loft. Suspect arranges appointment for "photo shoot" with decoy.*

June 16: 8:03 P.M. Decoy inside. Audio contact fixed.

8:10 P.M. Conversation from inside inaudible.

8:12 P.M. Audio down. Force entry to premises. Warning shots fired. Suspect surrenders and is placed under arrest. Suspect read his Miranda rights, which are acknowledged as being understood, and transported for processing at Midtown South.

I followed Noah's account of the harrowing all-night stakeout as he and Duffy waited out a heavily armed, drug-addled suspect in the Bryant Park spree killing. They took out the shooter in a hail of screaming lead, death buzzing everywhere like a blinding swarm of blackflies.

Noah had come home reeking of gunpowder and despair. His eyes were dull with the horror of what he had seen. The bitter, charred stench lingered in the clothes he wore for weeks. Washing couldn't get it out, nor air. An experience like that could only be cured by the salve of forgetting and a thick, broad bandage of time.

June 18, 10 A.M. Henley case closed. Fatal suspect shooting determined to be justifiable.

As I read, I shared Noah's brutal frustration as promising leads fell apart, and I reveled in his exultation when long, vexing cases showed the first glint of promise.

June 23: James Daly's former girlfriend agrees to testify that he placed an ad seeking a mercenary to murder his business partner.

Never did I have a better picture of how the work felt, how terrible it could be or how rewarding, or how these two disparate states could weirdly coexist.

That was the way things had evolved in the monstrous case of B.B. LeBeau. For homicide detectives, there had rarely been a more attractive prize. In the years since he aged out of juvenile custody for the murder of his family, LeBeau had been a prime suspect in at least a dozen horrific slayings, all memorable for their brutality and the cool deliberation with which they had been staged. But each time, no matter how strong the case against him appeared to be, the Eel had slipped the hook and slunk away.

Then, six months before Noah took his life, he and Duffy caught the Lynnwood case.

June 30, 9:12 P.M. Call to 40th and Second. Mother reports multiple child slayings at residence. Perpetrator unknown.

The five Lynnwood kids, ranging in age from six to eighteen, had been slaughtered in their apartment while their widowed mother taught a night class in business law at NYU. Mrs. Lynnwood came home to find her lifeless children posed around the dining table like a grotesque group of gray-skinned mannequins. Scrawled on the wall behind them was the bloody legend: "There's no place like home."

The macabre scene was classic LeBeau, and NYPD Homicide was hell-bent on bringing him down. During the investigation, Noah and Duffy worked around the clock, stopping only to blunt the sharpest edge off their exhaustion. They tracked every lead, ferreted out every possible witness, and milked the city's dregs for informants to make their case.

Slowly, the critical elements clicked into place. Duff and Noah were able to demonstrate that LeBeau had access, history, and an alibi that proved to be full of holes. Most important, he had been spotted leaving the scene by the building superintendent, a skittish soul named Stanley Peake.

From the first time they interviewed Peake, Noah sensed that the man was hiding something. *July 2, 8 A.M. Witness Peake evasive. Did something? Knows something?*

Patiently, he and Duff had worked to erode Peake's defenses and earn the man's trust. It took weeks, but finally, one night when Duff was down with a nasty case of flu, Noah managed to get the superintendent talking.

July 15, 7:38 P.M. Witness Stanley Peake, facility manager at the Chadwick, on East 40th Street, states that he observed a young male Caucasian, approximately 5 feet 11 inches tall, 165 pounds, fleeing the building through the rear service entrance at 7:30 P.M. June 30. Subject's clothing was stained with considerable quantities of a substance which the witness presumes to be blood.

The next day, Noah escorted Peake to headquarters downtown, where the super pored through a computerized file of mug shots and positively identified the blood-spattered man he'd seen racing out the building's back door as B.B. LeBeau. That was enough to secure an arrest warrant from Supreme Court Judge Vincent Maldonado. Noah was tapped to make the collar, a triumphant high point in his career.

July 16, 3:45 P.M. Suspect B.B. LeBeau located at the Sutphen Hotel, Room 1213. Suspect handcuffed, read his Miranda rights, which were acknowledged as understood, and placed in custody. Suspect then transported for processing at the North Infirmary Command, Tier 2C, at Rikers Island. Arraignment scheduled for 10 A.M. July 17th.

Vividly, I remembered Noah's boundless delight at taking LeBeau down and checking him into Tier 2C, which was reserved for New York City's most dangerous and infamous suspects. We celebrated with a special dinner and a night of ardent lovemaking, which, along with virtually everything else, had been put on hold during the exhausting weeks he had spent in pursuit of the case.

Noah remained unflinchingly upbeat as the pretrial motions proceeded without a hitch and the trial date approached. Despite LeBeau's media appeal and high-powered defense team, the case against him looked solid and unassailable. This time, the Eel had no conceivable means to slip away.

But nevertheless, it all came crashing down. The day before the scheduled start of jury selection, Stanley Peake, accompanied by a dour-faced lawyer, recanted. The superintendent claimed that Noah had coerced him into making the damning statement against LeBeau. As Peake told it, Noah had promised favored treatment by the force if he did so and serious personal reprisals if he refused. Peake further claimed that Noah had prepped him for the photo identification and promised to coach him on exactly what to say when he was called to testify. The list of possible charges against Noah grew uglier and uglier: obstruction of justice, witness tampering, harassment, conspiracy. I remember watching the super's appearance on the evening news. Every damning word struck Noah like a blow.

Duffy, who had been home in a fevered delirium with the flu when Peake finally decided to talk, was powerless to help. Given that he was likely to be called to testify against his partner, he was ordered to have no contact with Noah until the Internal Affairs investigation was completed.

Those dark days echoed in my mind. Rainey and I did everything we could think of to get Noah through, to make the endless hours pass less painfully, but the effort was as futile as trying to hasten the end of a storm or speed the cruel, plodding course of grief.

I turned to the final entries.

December 17. Ordered to report to I.A. Offer of reduced charge in return for full admission.

December 22. Formal hearing set for Thursday Dec. 29th, 10 A.M. at I.A. One week and counting. Who got to Peake?

December 26, 11:30 A.M. Visit East 40th. Peake AWOL.

December 29, 2:30 A.M. Now I get it. Last thing I'd suspect. Need to confirm, then open I.A.'s eyes.

December 29, 9:40 A.M. Time running out. Maybe too late already.

The book ended there, about an hour before Noah slipped the noose around his neck and secured the other end around the ceiling fan and stepped off the ladder into the empty air, where I found him dangling an hour later, gray and cold.

Or maybe what I'd just read confirmed what I had long suspected. Maybe it had not happened that way at all.

Just as I was thinking that, the doorbell sounded. It was the Arcanum graphologist.

"Trial's on recess, Claire Barrow, so I thought I'd stop by and see what you found. Hope it's not a bad time."

"No, Aldo. It's perfect. Turns out I found the mother lode." I handed him the book. "If you want to know Noah. This is about as good as it gets."

3 0

Herding Arnie Broder toward the door, Callendar felt like a tugboat try-ing to maneuver an unwieldy barge. He towered over most people, but this patient brought new meaning to the idea of "big." Broder had pier-piling legs, and arms like linked cannonballs. His bulging neck tapered to a coconut-shaped head that allowed precious little space for decent-sized features or brains. "See you Thursday at five, Arnie. You take care."

Broder smacked his own simian brow. "Wait up, Doc. I just thought of something. This business with my old man. It's how it always goes, see?"

"Interesting. Hold the thought, Arnie. We'll talk about it Thursday."

"Come on, Doc. Gimme a break. Coupla minutes ain't gonna kill you. This could be the answer we been looking for. Same thing happened with my boss at the lumberyard. See what I'm saying? Both those butt-holes screwed me the same freaking way."

"It'll have to wait, Arnie. Time's up."

Desperation glinted in the dark, squinty eyes, and the paltry lips curled in a pout. "Five lousy minutes, for chrissakes. You'd think I was asking for blood or something."

"You know the rules."

Callendar held the smile until he had ushered the behemoth across the threshold and locked the door behind him. Arnie's thunderous footfalls started away, but then stopped halfway across the reception area. Hoping to avoid an unpleasant encore, Callendar kept still. Thankfully, the steps soon continued and the outer door thwacked shut.

Fencing with Broder had cost five precious minutes. Callendar grabbed his briefcase and stuffed in the patient files he needed to review. With any luck, he could still make it to the Javits Federal Building in time to meet Trupin's contact from the Phoenix field office.

Trupin had phoned from the Mount Sinai Hospital ER moments before Arnie arrived. His eightysomething mother had taken a fall and suffered a probable broken hip. Callendar had agreed to fill in and meet Special Agent Straley, who was scheduled to leave for London following a pit stop in New York for a meeting at the FBI field office downtown.

Timing would not have been a problem with any patient other than Broder. Arnie had serious attachment issues, and most every session ended with a whiny tug-of-war. Countless times in the year since the guy started coming in for his biweekly gripe fests, Callendar had fantasized about losing him to another therapist. Sadly, he could never think of a colleague he detested nearly enough to saddle with such a roaring pain. Broder was not just a giant barnacle; he was a selfish, self-pitying, irritating bore.

The phone blared as he was headed out the rear. Callendar let it bounce to the machine. A beat later, Broder's grainy whimpering echoed through the office. "Pick up, Doc. Don't play games. I know you're there."

Callendar rolled his eyes and spoke his thoughts aloud. "That's way more than I can say for you, Arnie."

"You've got one hell of a nerve, Doc. You're sure there waiting with your hand out when it's time to pony up your fee. For that, you got plenty of time. You think you can brush me off like some lump of crap, you got another big think coming."

Callendar closed the door behind him, muffling Broder's continuing rant. He charged down three flights and ducked out through the service entrance. His office was in a Gothic-looking prewar building on lower Fifth. To avoid a run-in with the incredibly annoying hulk, he held to the shadows on Waverly Place and cut a ragged swath through Washington Square Park. Emerging on the south side, he caught a cab. The driver spoke English and knew his way to Broadway and Duane. Things were looking up.

Suddenly, his cell phone chirped. He answered quickly, thinking it must be his daughters with news about the tests they'd had in school today.

Bad guess.

Arnie's gravelly voice was shot with splintered glass. "You're pissing me off, Doc. Big time."

"I need you to cut this out, Arnie. Right now."

"How about I cut you out, you sorry piece of shit? So happens you work for me, Doc. I pay the bills. Four bucks a minute in case it's slipped your money-grubbing mind."

"I'm hanging up, Arnie. I don't know how you got this number, but you're not welcome to use it."

"My ass. Nobody tells me what to do, especially not some useless know-nothing like you. Talking to you is a goddamned waste of my valuable time."

"Maybe you're right, Arnie. Maybe the best solution is for you to find another therapist. Why don't I talk to your parole officer and work something out?"

"Do that; I'll cut out your freaking tongue. I'll cut your lousy stones off and feed them to my dog."

Callendar pressed the End button. Almost immediately, the phone trilled again. "Private call" flashed on the digital display. Broder again.

He set the phone to vibrate, so he could monitor things in case the girls did call. As the cab sped south, the missed-call counter soared like a telethon tote board: 7—10—15. King Kong was persistent. You had to give him that.

But not much more.

Broder was a referral from the court. Creep had the longest yellow sheet Callendar had ever seen, maybe the longest and most varied in NYPD history. He could have wrapped himself up in it some Halloween and gone as a giant lemon.

Talk about typecasting.

Unfortunately, none of his offenses rose above nuisance-level infractions and minor misdemeanors, never anything big enough to get him out of society's hair for more than sixty or ninety days of heel-cooling at the Rikers Island jail. Arnie's specialties were harassment and menacing, though he dabbled in drunk and disorderly, petty theft, assault, reckless endangerment, minor fraud, creating a public nuisance, and a bit of basic-to-intermediate stalking here and there. That, and the occasional indecent exposure, which, in Callendar's opinion, should have extended to any time Broder showed his unsightly mug.

Judge McElroy, in his dubious wisdom, had decided that psychiatric treatment should be a condition of Broder's latest parole. Callendar was considered one of the city's foremost experts in dealing with the seriously antisocial mind, and so, by some sadistic quirk of fate, Arnie's intended punishment had become his.

A section of lower Broadway with lousy cell service offered a brief respite from Broder's barrage, but as soon as the signal hit again, the phone quivered like a spooked mouse. Ten more calls from Arnie—fifteen.

Suddenly, traffic came to a halt, backing up like water on a grease-clogged drain. Callendar's anxiety rose as the time on the taxi's dashboard clock edged toward six-twenty. Special Agent Straley had to leave to catch the London flight from JFK by six forty-five, latest. He had secure transport to the airport that might be tough for Callendar to horn in on. Even if he could, the agent's plane was scheduled to push back from the gate at seven fifty-eight. That would leave precious little time for Callendar to collect whatever intelligence Trupin's friend had been able to gather on the courthouse murders and LeBeau's abrupt release. At Trupin's request, Straley had done the digging and talked with critical insiders. The guy was bound to know something beyond whatever documents he had in hand. Callendar hated like hell to miss a minute of precious brain-picking time.

The traffic picked up to a rollicking five miles an hour. In the distance, Callendar spied the flaming pulse of emergency lights. "There's an accident up ahead, driver. Better take a different street."

As they angled out of the jam, his Nokia started trembling again. This time, the display flashed his former home number. Both of his daughters were on the line, chatting in manic unison.

"Hey, Dad. guess what?" Cody said.

"What?"

"I nailed the French test, Daddy. I know I did," Madison blurted. *"Je suis absolutement contente."*

"Tres bien," Callendar offered. *"Muy molto mucho tres mightily bien."*

"Jeesh, Daddy. Mrs. Wyland would flunk you so hard."

"She already did years ago, though her name then was Mr. Letalon. How about you and math, Cody?"

"I can't say I nailed it, but it didn't nail me, either. I'm figuring that I got something around a B-minus, maybe a C-plus. Worst case, a C."

"I'm sure you gave it your best, kiddo."

"Damn it, Ted. That's the last thing she needs to hear."

His ex-wife's voice was the last thing Callendar needed to hear, but he made a strict point of keeping such sentiments to himself. "Hello, Janice. I didn't know you were on the line."

"No wonder she gets mediocre grades when you merrily condone her underachievement. If she applied herself, Cody would be at the very top of her class, where she belongs."

"Why don't we talk about this another time, Janice?" Callendar squeezed the words through clenched teeth.

"The least you can do is encourage her to reach her God-given potential, Ted. Lord knows, everything else falls on me."

Not the right things, Callendar thought bitterly. All it would take was one well-aimed brick. "Sorry, I've got to run. I'm late for a meeting. See you tomorrow night, kids: regular time, same station."

"I don't know, Ted," Janice said. "They have tests right through the end of the week, and your place is far from the ideal study environment."

"Not to worry. There will be total peace and quiet. No distractions. The girls will study nonstop until bedtime, except for absolutely essential bathroom breaks, during which I will require them to look at flashcards. There will be no fun at Dad's place this week. No way, no how."

He heard the muffled trill of Cody's giggle. Madison did a slightly better job of covering hers.

"I'll hold you to that, Ted, believe me. If their grades don't reflect a proper study experience, you'll be the one responsible."

"Good night, kids. See you tomorrow. Can't wait."

"'Night, Daddy."

The sound of their voices melted Callendar's heart. The thought of missing his meager allotted time with them was unbearable. Until he had those incredible kids, he never imagined that such ferocious love—or the terror of loss that went with it—was possible.

The cab finally dropped him in front of Jacob Javits Federal Building, a modernistic high-rise that shot like a triumphant fist into the chill, inky sky. He turned off his cell phone, happily shed of Broder's obsessive presence for a while.

Callendar passed the somber guards and metal detectors at security and scanned the stream of exiting employees, seeking someone tall and dark-haired, as Trupin had described. There were far too many contestants. Anxious to get Straley talking, he pulled a file from his briefcase and scrawled the agent's name on the face of the manila folder.

A brawny guy in a suit sauntered toward him. Callendar was about to greet him, when a pixieish blond woman raced by and launched like a rocket into the guy's waiting embrace. She looped her slender arms around his neck and kissed him deeply. Loneliness and envy lodged like a boulder in Callendar's chest.

While his glance was still fixed on the embracing couple, he felt a light tap on his arm. Turning, he faced six feet of knee-softening perfection crowned by a spill of black satin hair.

"I'm Sandra Straley. Are you looking for me?"

Have been all my life, he was tempted to say. "Agent Straley?"

"Yes. And you are?"

"Friend of Lyman Trupin's. He had a family emergency and asked me to meet you in his place. He sends regrets."

"Nothing serious, I hope."

"His mother had an accident. Looks like a broken hip."

"Sorry to hear that. Thanks for filling in, Mr.—?"

Her hand was an intoxicating blend of softness and strength. "Callendar. Ted Callendar."

"Lyman has mentioned you. Forensic psychologist, yes?"

"Yes." He couldn't imagine saying anything else to her: *Yes.*

"Lyman thinks very highly of you. He says you have X-ray vision. That you cut directly to the bone."

"I try. I certainly don't always succeed."

"Nobody does."

Callendar stared at her full-lipped mouth, wondering how it would taste.

She glanced at her watch. "I've arranged for us to use a colleague's office upstairs. We'd better get to it. I haven't much time."

"Sure. Let's go."

He took in her black ballistic suitcase and scuffed attaché. From all indications, Agent Straley was a seasoned road warrior. Callendar wondered if those travels brought her to New York often.

He followed her onto the elevator and up to a spare, utilitarian space amid the rabbit warren of cubicles on the twenty-fifth floor.

The agent shrugged off her black coat, and Callendar caught the scent of a bright, meltingly perfect spring day. Tailored black slacks and a teal silk blouse showcased a slim waist, proud curves, and long legs. She opened her attaché and extracted a pair of thick files. "What we have here is a serious political hot potato."

"That's no surprise."

"It may surprise you to find out how high up it goes. LeBeau's accusations have them popping Valium in the statehouses and on Pennsylvania Avenue. Lots of politicians have hung their hats on hardline support of the death penalty. Now they're all furiously backpedaling."

"And they'd like to lay whatever blame there is at the Arcanum's door."

"Exactly. You offer several dozen juicy sacrificial lambs for the price of one."

"We don't intend to go gently."

Straley flashed a dazzling smile of approval. "No reason you should. From all indications, LeBeau may have crawled off death row through some nasty sleight of hand."

"How so?"

"Celasphere's chief scientist cops to falsifying evidence, and then he disappears. At Lyman's request, I got someone from the bureau to interview the acting head of the lab early this morning. The guy couldn't imagine how Ronald Sallis or anyone could have faked those DNA findings. Celasphere has strict procedures for preserving the chain of evidence and ensuring unbiased results. Samples are handled anonymously. The identifying codes reside on a distant server, managed by an independent auditing firm, which is buffered in turn by a complex encryption system that's applied to all incoming specimens by yet another company. No one has access to the person behind a given sample until the reports are certified and distributed."

"I don't get it. How did they let LeBeau go without checking Sallis's admission?"

Straley shrugged. "Celasphere processed the evidence for several extremely high-profile cases. I think the powers that be were so eager to contain the situation, they never stopped to look past their own exposed noses. Taking Sallis at his word as a nutcase trying to scuttle the death penalty was definitely the path of least resistance."

Callendar pulled a pad and pen from his briefcase and started doodling. He sketched a crowd of faces, all seriously perplexed. "I'm afraid
my X-ray vision is on the blink. I still don't get why Sallis would hang
himself out to dry this way. He had a big stake in a highly lucrative and
growing concern. Rumor has it Celasphere is slated to go public in the
next couple of years. The guy had plenty of bucks and a pot of major
gold going forward."

Straley ruffled through the papers and pulled out the plum: Ronald
Sallis's medical report from the Graydon Clinic in Chicago. "Sallis was
diagnosed with pancreatic cancer three weeks ago. Given six months,
maximum, to live."

Callendar frowned. "Why would that inspire him to assassinate himself any sooner?"

"His contract with Celasphere called for ninety percent of his stake to
vest over the next eighteen months. He dies before that, and the company
gets to reclaim the unvested piece of the action. His shares revert to the
option pool and get handed to Sallis's successor. Guy has precious little
life insurance, three young kids, a stay-at-home trophy wife, and a
monthly nut that would choke an entire team of horses. I call that central
casting's idea of a perfect candidate for desperate, crazy behavior."

Callendar's head was spinning from the revelation and his proximity
to Agent Straley. "You think someone made Sallis disappear to keep that
under wraps?"

"It's one possibility. Another is that he agreed to make himself
untouchable as part of the deal. For all we know, he's cashed out early, or
he's been stashed in some private clinic under a spanking new identity.
We've got feelers out, checking recent intakes with pancreatic cancer, but
I'd call our chances of finding him a long shot, at best."

"What if we get the acting head of the lab to testify about those security procedures? Wouldn't that be enough to put LeBeau back in his cage?"

"Doubtful," the agent said. "The argument would be that there is no
absolutely foolproof security system, which happens to be the sorry
truth. Also, the head of the lab isn't exactly a disinterested party. He'd be
seen as willing to say anything in a desperate play to save his business.

Unless Sallis resurfaces and recants, it's going to be a very hard sell. And even if he did, the guy has pretty much lost all credibility. You think, given the circumstances, that anyone's going to be in a hot hurry to retry LeBeau?"

"Did you manage to get a line on Martha Garmin?" Callendar had been trying without success to reach the victim's mother. In a bid to have LeBeau retried, a plea from her might have some impact on the court.

Straley went grim. "More rotten news on that front, I'm afraid. We tracked her from Phoenix to Sedona, where she's been living for the past few years under her maiden name. Turns out, she's been AWOL for more than a week. Took off in the middle of the night and hadn't been heard from since. We ran a check and found a woman who matched her description. Blood type and dental records confirm. Martha Garmin was stabbed to death and dumped in a landfill outside of Sedona. Some joker hung price tags from her toe and earlobe that said 'special clearance' and 'as is.'"

"Hand-lettered?"

"Not this time. Standard-issue Wal-Mart. No latents or other trace evidence. Our boy gets high marks for cleanliness and attention to detail."

Callendar sketched another face, this one with wobbly, crossed eyes. "What a mess."

"From the way the numbers seem to be piling up that could turn out to be a major understatement." Straley handed over the current copy of the investigation reports on the courthouse murders. "Judge Montrose, Deakin Barnes, Martha Garmin, and, quite possibly, Ronald Sallis are fresh casualties, and it's only been a week since LeBeau's release. I'm glad the Arcanum is working to sort it out."

"We're going to do our level best, Agent Straley. You've been a tremendous help."

Her smile softened Callendar's knees. "It's Sandra." She handed him her card. "I'd better run. If you need me for anything else, call my cell. It works internationally."

Callendar offered his card in exchange. "Same here. If you think of anything, any time, give me a call."

"You too. Anything. Any time. Sleep is way overrated, if you ask me."

"Agreed."

She was putting on her coat, closing the attaché, taking up her suitcase.

"If you're passing through New York on your way back, maybe we can get together and review the case further."

Straley offered her hand. Callendar seriously hated to return it.

She looked him hard in the eye and a current passed between them. "Absolutely, Ted. I'll need an update, to be sure."

3 1

Duffy kept a stranglehold on the wheel and stared in rapt fury at the road. I did my best to ignore him as well, forcing my eyes away quickly whenever outraged curiosity moved me to glance his way.

Finally, I could stand it no longer. "I can't believe you. I tell you that Noah was on to something that probably got him killed, and you tell me to forget about it."

"I didn't tell you to forget about it, Claire. I told you to let it go. I don't see it the way you do. Plain as that."

"This is not just a little difference of opinion. I'm talking about the possibility that someone killed Noah and made it look like a suicide."

He rattled the copies I had made of the crucial pages before I entrusted Noah's book to Aldo Diamond. "Where does it say that? Where do you find a single word of fact to back that up? You're reading way too much into this. I know you'd like to believe Noah didn't kill himself. So would I. But wishing doesn't make it so."

"It's all right there. Noah said he had found something that would open eyes at Internal Affairs. Obviously, it had to do with the investigation against him."

"There's nothing obvious about it in the least."

"Then how do you explain what he wrote?"

"You're sure you want to know that, Claire?"

"Yes."

He eyed me gravely, and then fixed his gaze again on the road. "Maybe we should drop this right here and now."

"No, Duff. Whatever it is, I need the truth."

"What if the truth is dirty and ugly and covered with warts?"

"I don't care."

"You're sure?"

"I am."

"Okay, then." His chest puffed around a hard-drawn breath. "Noah knew he was going down, and he couldn't deal with it. Wasn't the shame so much. Or even the chance he could do a bit of time. What he couldn't abide was the thought of life without the shield. The job defined him, Claire. He was Noah Travis, hotshot detective, or he was nothing. You had a hard case, one that no one else could crack, Noah was your man. That was how he needed to be seen. And it turned out to be the very death of him."

"I don't understand."

His grip on the wheel tightened, leaching the blood from his joints. "When he saw the chance to nail LeBeau, he couldn't let it pass. So he convinced himself it was okay to bend the rules. A wee bit at first, then harder. Problem is he kept bending, until everything broke."

"That can't be. Noah was as honest as they come."

"And how honest is that? Fact is, the Devil lurks in all of us, just waiting for his chance. Given the right temptation, out he comes."

"Noah wasn't like that."

"Maybe not under ordinary circumstances. But Noah wanted LeBeau like he never wanted anything in his life. He was blinded by the lust for it. Hell-bent on becoming the legend who took down the Eel. He was bound and determined to make that happen, whatever it took."

"You don't know what happened. You weren't even there when Peake talked."

His mouth warped in a bitter sneer. "No, I wasn't, was I? Taken to my bed with the fever I was. Oh, the wicked, wicked pain."

A chill settled deep in my bones. "You weren't sick?"

"Sure, and I was, in a way. Sick to the core that Noah would do such a mad, foolish thing. Yes, LeBeau deserved to be put away, but not like that. I knew what would happen, how it was bound to play out. I begged Noah not to twist Peake's arm, but he wouldn't hear me. I couldn't be a part of it, so I took the only out I could see."

"It can't be, Duffy. Noah wouldn't do that."

"But he did, Claire. That's the fact. And when it unraveled, so did he. Noah believed his life was over, and so he put an end to it."

An anguished cry escaped me. "No!"

"Sorry, sweetheart. But that's the way it happened. The God's honest truth."

"Why didn't I know? Why didn't you tell me?"

"You weren't in a state to hear anything. And what was the point if you were? Noah was gone. LeBeau was off the hook in that case. It didn't matter anymore."

The air spun with dizzying currents. "But it does matter. The truth matters."

"The truth is he never lost the love of you, Claire. You or Rainey. That you have to believe. It was a sickness he had. Something he couldn't control."

I forced air through the anguished knots in my chest. "I hear you."

"You can't let this throw you, Claire. You have to be strong for that girl of yours."

I met his fretful gaze. "I know, Duff. I'll be all right."

"That's the spirit, sweetheart. Now let's see what young Zach has to say."

Duffy turned onto West Forty-ninth Street. Halfway down the block, he eased into a vacant loading zone. The spot fronted a chunky, dun-colored building girdled by battered scaffolding and rusting fire escapes.

A faded sign beside the entrance read, CRAIN TECHNICAL SCHOOL, FOUNDED 1958. Plastered to the door were several notices from the Board of Health, warning that the building had been condemned. Faded circulars for a job fair and professional qualifying exams drooped from a crumbling bulletin board. Looking closer, I saw that they were dated eight years ago.

"Place has been empty since then," Duffy explained. "Bit of a family disagreement. Seems old man Crain founded the school and spent forty years building it up. He left it to his three sons, hoping they'd carry on. And carry on they did, though not in the way he expected. Before the poor soul was cold in the ground, the brothers set to battling."

The building had the aura of a dead, decaying beast. "Over this?"

"Wars have been waged over less, sweetheart. One of the sons had a gambling problem, and he wanted to turn the place into cash he could lay on red. Another wanted to borrow heavily and expand the school and shift the focus from technical training, which was the old man's passion, to liberal arts. The third boy decided that either action would dishonor their dead father, a thought he couldn't abide, so he simply came in one night and wrecked the place. Pulled down walls, punched holes in the ceilings, set off the sprinklers, and trashed the furniture and machines."

"And that was the end of it?"

"Sadly, no. All these years later, the estate is still tied up in litigation. Everybody's suing everybody, and no one's winning but the attorneys. Until the money runs out, it's likely to stay exactly as is. Meantime, Zachary and some like-minded souls squat here from time to time and use it as a sort of clubhouse."

Following Zach's directions, Duffy felt behind an exposed drainpipe and found the key. It opened a door at the rear of the loading dock. We passed through a cluttered storeroom to the first-floor hall. Everything was twisted, torn, and splattered with filthy debris. Doors lay trampled to kindling or dangled precariously from broken hinges. The furniture in the former classrooms had been reduced to splinters and scrap. Taped cardboard bandaged the broken windowpanes, but cold, heat, and dampness still leaked through, staining and buckling the walls.

Near the end of the corridor, Duffy turned into a low-ceilinged stairwell and led me down a steep, rickety flight. At the base was a long, rectangular crawl space, redolent of rust and musty earth. Duffy ducked in a near crouch and still narrowly missed scraping his head on the decaying ceiling, which exuded dense, powdery mold.

Struggling to clear my mind of Noah's death, I followed him through a graveyard of outmoded equipment. There were ditto machines, Selectric typewriters, adding machines, massive mechanical calculators, Epson dot-matrix printers, black key set phones, blueprint files, surveying gear, oscilloscopes.

At the center of the space loomed a makeshift fortress, walled by antique mainframe computer carcasses. I spotted vintage '60s IBM 700 Series cabinet models and later, sleeker, 360 Series machines that were merely four feet tall. We pressed through a tiny opening to the center of the so-called Pit, where Zach perched on a makeshift seat, comprised of several TRS 80 computers covered by worn cushions. He was working a keyboard linked to a patchy sprawl of alien-looking electronic gear. Stony concentration etched his face. The monitor's glow blanched his freckles and bleached the meager color from his eyes.

"So, Zachary. What's the good word?" Duffy said.

The kid didn't blink. Except for the jerky play of his fingers, he was inert.

Duffy's lips pressed in a rueful seam. "Worse than heroin, it is. More addictive than crack. Even a brilliant soul like Zachary hasn't a chance once it takes hold. Look at him, Claire. Completely lost."

Zach had no awareness of our presence. He leaned closer to the monitor, fingers working like a swarm of nervous gnats.

Duff cleared his throat loudly. He clapped beside Zach's ear, but the kid remained impassive. Catching my eye, he shook his head gravely. "That is his brain on high-speed access. Boy might as well be made of the chips and plastic himself."

To me, the screen appeared to be filled with gibberish, but whatever the jumble of data meant was obviously fascinating to Zach. A poke of Duffy's finger to his ribs failed to draw the boy's attention. Duff tried to pluck his fingers from the keys, but the kid simply swatted the annoyance away.

"Enough!" Duffy placed his hands between Zach and the screen.

The computer whiz swelled from the chair in outraged disbelief. He wheeled around and came at Duff, face contorted, fists flailing. "Stupid son of a bitch!"

Duffy trapped his wrists and deftly sidestepped his flying feet. "Easy, Zachary. This is your old pal Detective McClure and Noah's wife, Claire. You asked us here. Remember?"

Suddenly, the kid stopped struggling and blinked hard. "Detective? Hey, sorry about that. I didn't hear you come in."

"You fell off the planet, Zach me boy. That's what happens when you allow yourself to wander too near the edge."

"I was doing some research. In fact, I've got some things I think you'll find of interest."

Duffy's look stayed harsh. "If you've got a lick of sense, you won't go there anymore, Zachary. I should never have gotten you involved. It's playing with fire. I can smell the burning, son. Could be your eternal soul turning on the spit."

"Fire makes heat, Detective. Heat and light. Without it, cavemen would have had to eat those woolly mammoths raw."

"For a certified genius, you show a startling lack of sense, Zach. Now tell us what you've learned, so we can get out of here and be done with the pitiful sight of you."

"I asked around about that Phelan guy. No one I spoke to knows him firsthand, but a couple of my friends know of him. Kid's got a pretty nasty reputation."

Duffy's frown deepened. "What sort?"

"Cracking and hacking, like you thought. Rumor has it he may have been behind the monster mixup last year at that Chicago medical center."

"The one where the medication orders were switched and two patients died?"

"Exactly."

"You remember that, Claire? One of the fatalities was a newborn. The other was a woman in her thirties with three little kids. If that was Rainey's friend, the good news is he'll soon be well out of the way—for ten years to life, at a minimum."

"Maybe yes, maybe no," Zach said. "The word is that he's got some sort of big-time protection. Apparently this Phelan, if it's the same kid, is pretty much untouchable."

Duffy's face heated. "I didn't come here for fairy stories, Zachary. Don't be trying to sell me some bill of bogus goods."

"Whoa, easy. I'm not trying to sell you anything. I'm just repeating what I heard. Could be bogus like you say, but the story is that some people are in a position to get away with things and that this Phelan kid is one of them."

"What position? What things, Zachary? One of whom? Just spill the lot of it. I'm not of a mind to play 'Twenty Questions.'"

"That's all I've been able to come up with so far. Bits and pieces. I can't even say for sure if the kid I heard about is the one you're after. But if he is he looks like seriously bad news."

"You get anything useful? Whole name? Address?"

"That's what I've been trying to nail down." Nimbly, Zachary swung back onto his perch. A few keystrokes filled the screen with Web site names and virtual addresses. Several more pulled up people named Phelan he had found through those sites' directories or in their underlying subscriber bases. Next, Zachary culled the Phelans linked to the New York metropolitan area and further refined them by sex and age. Still, there remained screen after screen of possibilities. The candidates ran to hundreds of names.

"That's enough. I get the picture," Duffy said.

"That's only part of it. We still don't know if Phelan is the kid's name or his handle, which is more likely. Plus, whatever he's called for real, I'd lay odds he runs his Web activity through an anonymizer, a service that masks the subscriber's underlying information, so even if we managed to pick our Phelan out of this mob, chances are we wouldn't have anything much."

Duffy sighed. "So it goes. Thanks for trying, Zach. We'll be heading out now. Take my advice and do the same. You need to give it a good, long rest."

"Wait, Detective. There's one more thing. I found some information about that screensaver you saw on Phelan's machine." The kid's eyes locked again on the monitor.

Duffy drifted closer as an image wafted into view. "That's it. What's the story?"

"It's called a Heretic's Fork." Zack brought up a gruesome stream of illustrative sketches. "They were used as instruments of torture in medieval times. Someone accused of a crime would have this thing strapped around his neck. One end of the fork would be pressed into his breastbone and the other one dug in under his chin. Suspect could only move his head enough to say he was guilty. If the guy gave in and confessed to his alleged crime, he was usually still executed, only they'd put him in some fancy costume first. I don't know about you, Detective, but if I was about to get offed in some gruesome, bloody way, I don't think I'd care a whole lot about my wardrobe."

Duffy cringed. "Doesn't look like much fun."

"Some people think it is. Check this out." Zachary brought up the home page of a private, guaranteed secure, members-only group and easily slid through the site's protective walls.

Zach sniffed in disdain. "Guaranteed secure, my butt."

The home page featured another replica of the draconian device Phelan had as a screensaver. Beneath that was the single word, *Abiuro.*

"*Abiuro* means 'I recant,' in Latin. That's the word the suspect was expected to say to admit he'd been lying about his innocence. This site is a clearinghouse for information on torture methodology. They offer step-by-step instructions for the manufacture and the use of such handy-dandy gadgets as the ones pictured here. That's the Breast Ripper, the Cat's Claw, the Judas Cradle, the Iron Maiden, and my personal favorite, the Chair of Spikes."

The gruesome drawings of victims locked in those horrid rigs, screaming in mortal agony, made my skin crawl. "Phelan has some connection to this group?"

"He's on their subscriber list. Posts to their chat room as well."

"How did you track him here?" I asked.

A light flush set his freckles in high relief. "Took a little doing. No need to bore you with the technical details."

Duffy's head swung in a rueful arc. "That's Zach-speak for not wishing to let you in on his nasty little secrets. You don't want to know anyway, Claire. It's all in a whole different neighborhood from anything legal."

"Can't get what you're looking for by following the scout manual, Detective McClure."

"You find him anywhere else like this?" Duffy asked.

"Couple of places." Zach gave us the virtual tour. Phelan's online address appeared on the roster of visitors to sites that sold and exchanged torture paraphernalia. He frequented group discussions of physical and psychological torment, where the goal was ever more diabolical and dramatic cruelty. The postings were positively gleeful, as if the subject was some childish prank, like phony phone calls, and not the infliction of unthinkable pain.

"So that could be our Phelan or not," Duffy observed. "If it isn't, he still looks like a bad piece of work. And if it is, he may be way worse than we thought."

My mind was reeling. "Now what?"

Duffy shook his head. "Good question."

"Leave it to me, Detective. I've got an idea," Zack said.

"I know your ideas, Zachary," Duff said gravely. "If it's one of those, forget it right now."

"You want Phelan? I believe I have a way to get him for you. That's all I'm going to do, Detective. Cross my heart and hope to die."

3 2

Rainey dumped her book bag on the foyer floor and strode in a tight-lipped snit toward her room. Richter watched her warily, like a fierce, approaching storm.

Girding for a tempest myself, I called after her. "Aunt Amelia had to cancel for tonight. There's some problem with the renovation on her Connecticut house. She needed to go and straighten things out."

"No-o-o-o!" she wailed. "That sucks."

"I know you were looking forward to it. Sorry it didn't work out."

"Right. Like you give a damn."

"I do, Rainey. Honestly. I'm sorry you're disappointed."

"Sure."

"Any requests for dinner?"

Her eyes skittered frantically. "Since I'm not going out with Aunt Amelia, I'll probably go to Dani's."

"I'd like you to stay home tonight. You've been running around too much lately."

"So now I'm a prisoner?"

"No. I'd just like to spend some time with you."

"How about what I'd like? Doesn't that count for anything?"

"It won't kill you to stay home for a change." I winced at the words and the tone, echoes of my mother at her whiny worst.

"Whatever." She withered me with a look, stormed down the hall, and slammed her door.

I managed to coax her out for dinner, but it was hardly worth the trouble. She stared at her plate and picked halfheartedly at the current favorites I'd concocted: shrimp cocktail, stuffed Cornish hen with wild rice and sautéed asparagus. I had set the dining-room table using the good china and silver and a pressed linen cloth, trying to lift the mood. But the elevator seemed to be out of service.

We ate awhile in strained silence, broken only by the metallic clank of our silverware, rounds of listless chewing, the dry thunk of food struggled down.

Finally, I dared to risk a bit of neutral chat. "How are things at school?"

"What things?"

"Did you get any feedback yet on that project you did with Melinda?"

"The science fair is not until after vacation."

"I didn't realize."

"You would if you bothered to read the damned newsletter."

"I did read it, Rainey. What I can't read is your mind. You didn't tell me the earthquake model was for the fair."

"Right. So you figured we're doing it for what? Our health?"

Her dripping sarcasm killed the meager remains of my appetite. I stood to clear the plates. "Want dessert?"

She brightened. "Good idea. I'll go out and pick up some ice cream."

"I have three kinds in the freezer. You can pick it up there."

"Haven't we had enough dumb discussion?"

I set down the plates and sat again. "Yes. We have. I agree with you."

"Then I can go to Dani's?"

"No. We can change the subject to something more important."

She blew a breath. "What now?"

"How much do you know about Phelan?"

"Don't start on him again, Claire. I mean it."

"I just want to be sure you know who he really is, what he's really into. Sometimes there's a lot more to people than you can see."

She drilled me with a look of pure disgust. "Oh, I see. I see more than you'll ever imagine."

"Meaning what?"

"Meaning I know who you really are and what you're really into, and I hate your guts. I wish you and Daddy never met."

My voice shrank to a pained whisper. "I'm sorry you feel that way. I loved your dad with all my heart; and I love you, too, Rainey. I love you and I care about you. And I'm going to be there for you, no matter how you try to push me away."

"You're so full of it." Her features contorted with rage. "All you love is yourself, Claire. That's all you care about—*you!*" She lurched to her feet and raced from the room.

I sat listening to the nasty slap of her footsteps and then, the hard, dismissive smack of her door. In the bristling aftermath, Richter sidled over, eyed me lovingly, and licked my hand.

I scratched beneath his muzzle. "Thanks, pal. I needed that."

He trotted alongside me to the kitchen, where I spooned the choicest leftovers into his bowl. There was definitely something to be said for unconditional adoration, especially when Cornish hen and rice were all it cost. The dog hovered faithfully at my side while I cleaned up and turned out the lights.

In my room, I sat on the bed, took up Noah's picture from the nightstand, and stared into his clear, unflinching eyes.

"You're supposed to be here to help me with her, with everything. That was the deal—remember?"

Anger seeped in to fill the painful hollow in my chest. "It was only a job, Noah. It was only a case, for God's sake, one of hundreds. How could you throw your life away for that?"

His image blurred behind the stinging tears. "What about Rainey? What about us? Wasn't there anything you considered worth living for beside your goddamned work?"

I lay back, muffling the sobs, clutching his image to my chest. I knew the answers to those terrible questions, and I understood the cruel depths of the joke. He had loved us, and he had done the best he could. As far as our deal went, he had slipped through the escape clause. Our bargain expired when he stepped off that ladder into the empty air, and the rope crushed his windpipe. Death did us part, and the contract was null and void.

Suddenly, Rev. E Train's mournful plaint rang out across the street. *"Woe to the obstinate children, declares the Lord, to those who carry out plans that are not mine, forming an alliance, but not by my Spirit, heaping sin upon sin."*

"Hurling stones and shattering egos," I breathed. "Don't forget those."

"Your children who do not yet know good from bad, they will enter the land. I will give it to them and they will take possession of it. Take these lost souls in hand, brothers and sisters. Upon you it falls to open their blind eyes and lead them in the ways of righteousness."

"Upon me it falls," I said bitterly. "Yea, and I am verily buried beneath it."

The Reverend's voice went liquid-light. *"Where there are prophecies, they will cease; where there are tongues, they will be stilled; where there is knowledge, it will*

*pass away... And now these things remain: faith, hope and love. But the greatest of
these is love. Follow that, lambs and rams; warriors and worriers. Go where love leads
you. No matter how bleak or despairing the path, love will show you the way."*

33

The burst of static through the speaker system startled Diamond awake.
"Ladies and gentlemen, those lights you can see coming up to the left of
the aircraft are the famous Las Vegas Strip. We'll be touching down in
just a few minutes. For your safety and comfort, please keep your seat-
belts firmly fastened until we come to a full stop at the gate."

Diamond yawned and rubbed his grainy eyes. The last he could
remember was the noisy takeoff from JFK. From the dampness on his
shoulder and his parched, raspy throat, he could tell that he had been
mired in drool sleep, snoring harshly, ever since.

His seatmate, a trim, dapper man, wore a puckered scowl of serious
distaste. Diamond caught his eye and flashed a sheepish smile. "Guess I
was really out. Hope I didn't bother you."

The man drew his head back like a finicky bird. "Actually, you
reminded me of my wife, who passed on last month. Celia snored exactly
like that: with gusto."

"Sorry."

"Sorrier than you can imagine. Didn't have one decent night sleep in
thirty-five years. I can't tell you how often I was tempted to suffocate that
woman in her sleep." He went wistful, savoring the fantasy. "Once or
twice, I actually went so far as to place the pillow over her stupid face.
How easy it would have been to simply squeeze and keep squeezing. She
wouldn't have offered any resistance. Celia had no muscle tone to speak of,
except in that jaw of hers that was forever nagging at me or gorging on
junk. Just one long, firm squeeze and that would have been that." He
sighed. "If only the law had the sense to recognize the perfect logic of such

an act. But now, it's all water under the bridge. No more Celia; no more sleepless nights." He brushed his hands free of the expired annoyance.

Diamond smiled stiffly and stared out the window. The call from Griffey, reporting that they had tracked the Garmins' former baby-sitter to Las Vegas, now seemed like part of a dream. So did the last of his cross-examination in the kidnapping case and the hurried trip from the courthouse to Kennedy Airport, where Griffey had arranged to have an electronic ticket waiting in his name. On the ride, Diamond had studied Noah Travis's memo book, especially the last entries in the days before his alleged suicide. He detected several off notes, but he couldn't identify their precise nature or source.

Diamond so wanted to help Claire Barrow get the answers and closure she sought. He knew how impossible it was to live with the *what ifs* and *if onlys*. He couldn't undo that day for Em and Willy at the bus stop, but young Claire might still be able to rid her husband's ending of its terrible question mark.

The plane banked hard, swooped toward the runway, and touched down smoothly at McCarran Airport. As soon as the jet way was locked in place and the doors slid open, Diamond scurried off the plane, eager to avoid further contact with his homicidal seatmate.

This was Diamond's first trip to Sin City, or "Lost Wages," as it was sometimes aptly called. Given that he was booked on the first return flight in the morning, he primed himself to take in as much as he could.

That was no simple feat in this blazing, twirling, dizzying monument to greed and excess, which could boast nine of the world's ten largest hotels and seemed to have cornered the international market on scream-colored neon. Elvis impersonators abounded, as did other living caricatures of every conceivable stripe: blue-haired ladies, oil-baron types in ten-gallon hats, sugar daddies and their overstated armpieces, business tycoons, mob bosses, happy hookers, Hollywood hopefuls, and legions of the dissolute and disturbed. He never could have imagined the magnitude of the hype or the astonishing cornucopia of money-losing opportunities. A visitor could blow the vacation budget, or the family fortune for that matter, without ever leaving the airport.

On the cab ride, Diamond got an even more startling eyeful. The taxi drove past a giant replica Sphinx, another of the Eiffel Tower, a slightly scaled down New York City with a roller coaster zipping through its core. Towering water jets surged as they passed the sparkling Bellagio. Beckoning lights and empty promises flashed everywhere. *Win! Big Jackpot! $$$$$ and More!* Finally, the cabbie dropped him at the door of the aptly named Mirage, a soaring monster surrounded by gigantic palms.

Using his considerable contacts, Lyman Trupin had secured a coveted reservation for the evening's headline show. Diamond uttered his name; and the maître d' escorted him to a prime stageside table. As he settled in his chair, the orchestra sounded a triumphal fanfare. Soon, dozens of stunning young women streamed down the aisles and onto the stage. They swooped in, six at a time, on giant glittery swings and descended from above; dangling on unseen harnesses from clear filament line, perched on jewel-encrusted tubes, and posed astride fuzzy pink clouds and gilt stars.

They wore great, spangled, feathered headdresses, and their amazing legs were bound in shiny fishnet stockings. Some of the dancers wore minuscule skirts in scorching sun tones; others sported flame-colored tap shorts. Every one of them, perhaps two hundred in all, was nude above the waist. Diamond tried not to stare, but every place he settled his eyes, there they were: scoops of ice cream, floating islands, mounds of whipped cream, baked Alaskas, cherries jubilee.

Sternly, he turned his mind to business. Pulling out the likeness of Toby Felder, which Griffey had faxed to the court clerk late this afternoon, he scanned the dancers' faces, trying to make a match. The former baby-sitter, now professionally known as Tawny DeeVine, had been dancing in this review for the past eight months. Mentally, Diamond allowed for the changes she might have undergone since this high school graduation picture was taken. He considered the extra makeup and a possible change of hair color. She could have gained or lost weight or indulged in a bit of surgical tailoring, as many of these gravity-defying specimens appeared to have done.

Several times, he lit on one of the dancers, thinking she might be the one he sought, but, given the strident lights, constant movement, towering headdresses, and those highly distracting front pieces, he could not be sure.

Griffey, whose range of knowledge never ceased to astound, had offered tips on how to make contact with the former baby-sitter. At intermission, Diamond did as the great man had advised. He borrowed the waiter's pen and inked a brief note on a cocktail napkin, indicating his interest in meeting Tawny DeeVine after the show. He wrapped the note around a crisp fifty-dollar bill and handed a second fifty to the waiter for delivery service. At Griffey's suggestion, he had raided the airport ATM for eight hundred dollars, the day's allowable limit, before he left New York. He was unaccustomed to carrying so much cash, yet in these surroundings his fat bankroll seemed positively spare.

Diamond sweated through the rest of the show, and not merely because of the searing lights. The second act commenced with a pair of live tigers that bounded across the stage, muscles rippling, snarling and baring their claws, within easy striking distance of his seat. Next, a man juggled flaming swords so close to Diamond's table that he understood how a T-bone felt on the grill. Still, worst of all was the feature that followed: a bawdy comedian who made several excruciating fat jokes at Diamond's considerable expense.

Drumrolls hammered home the nasty blows. "Hey, would you look at this guy. This man was fat from the day he was born, ladies and gentlemen. Saddest thing you ever saw: a stork with a hernia. *Pow!* Instead of the usual christening, his parents broke a bottle of champagne on his side. *Kaboom!* He's so fat, they've assigned him his own Zip code. *Ratatat Tat!* This guy's got more chins than the Hong Kong phone book. *Boom—clang—boom!*"

Finally came the grand finale, and the topless dancers swarmed the stage again. This time, Diamond watched numbly, barely focusing. The spotlight had shifted from him, but he still stewed, with the stiff smile frozen on his face, in the humiliating afterglow.

That's entertainment.

He kept his seat as the audience drifted out and busboys bearing large, unwieldy trays swarmed in to clear the tables. He remained there as the busboys finished clearing and a cleaning crew descended, armed with vacuum cleaners, buckets, and mops.

Nervously, he kept checking his watch. Nearly twenty-five minutes had dragged by since the show let out. Maybe the waiter had made off with both fifties, or, perhaps, Ms. DeeVine had opted to take the money and run. Griffey was rarely wrong, but even he was incapable of predicting every nuance of human behavior.

Fifteen more minutes ticked away, though it seemed far longer. The cleaning crew closed in like an army of seeking ants. Diamond lifted his feet to allow the growling vacuum to slide underneath. Freshening spray and lemon wax filled the air, scents that tickled his nose and set him wheezing.

Finally, the maître d' approached Diamond's table, tapping the rear of his wrist. "Sorry, sir. I'll have to ask you to leave. We're about to lock up."

Desperately, Diamond scanned the empty room. "Can you give me just a few more minutes? I'm supposed to be meeting someone."

"One of the showgirls?"

"Yes, actually."

"Not here, buddy. That would be out at the bar."

"Oh no," Diamond groaned. "I didn't realize. What if I missed her?"

"Easy, pal. If you sent a little token of your appreciation backstage, she'll be waiting."

"Are you sure? This is really, really important."

"Don't sweat it, buddy. Come with me." He led Diamond out of the massive theater and across the steamy, rainforest-motif lobby to the Baccarat Bar. "Which lovely morsel caught your eye, pal? I'll point her out."

"She goes by Tawny DeeVine."

He took a playful jab at Diamond's side. "Excellent taste. Tawny's grade-A, top-notch, prime. One of my very favorites. And there she is, like I said, waiting for you in that booth. Go west, young man. The wild frontier awaits."

Minus the feathers and jewels, the dancer reminded Diamond of a child recuperating from a tough game of dress-up. Makeup traces shadowed her small, skittish features, and her strawberry-streaked hair hung scraggly and limp. She wore tight mock-snakeskin jeans, a stretch purple tank top, and silver spike-heeled sandals. The outfit may have been intended to look sexy, but it delivered precisely the opposite effect. The girl looked painfully young. If Diamond hadn't known she was twenty, he would have guessed twelve or thirteen.

Diamond offered his hand. "Aldo Diamond."

Her shake felt like toothpicks in gel. "Hi there, I'm Tawny. Nice to meet you."

A waitress came by. "Get you something?"

The girl ordered a sea breeze. Diamond quickly consulted the snack menu. Torn between the giant nachos and the fried mozzarella sticks, he ordered both.

As soon as the waitress was out of earshot, the girl smiled coyly. "Before we go any further, let's discuss the rules."

"Rules?"

"This is a looking store, not a touching store—okay? You can window-shop, but no sampling the merchandise. For this, I only charge viewing prices, not audience participation. One hundred an hour, payable in advance. No refunds. Are we clear, big fella?"

Diamond coughed to clear his throat of embarrassment. "I only want to talk, Miss DeeVine."

"Whatever floats your boat, pops. It's a C-note every sixty, just the same. How many shall I sign you up for?"

Diamond peeled off four fifties and handed them over. The transaction was likely to be much quicker, but he didn't want her watching the clock.

Tawny/Toby rolled the bills in a tight cylinder, which she stuffed down the front of her skintight top. The money settled at mid-torso, like an extra rib, and pulsed with the sharp, shallow beating of her heart. "Bring on the words, papa bear. I'm all ears."

"No. I am." Diamond tugged his bulbous lobes to make the point. "I'd like you to tell me about yourself, Tawny DeeVine."

"It's your nickel. Not that there's much to tell. I'm a dancer, which you already know. Have been, professionally, since I got out of school. This place is okay for now, pays the bills and all, but soon as I can swing it, I'm off to the Big Apple. Broadway, if I'm lucky. Off-off or whatever, if I'm not." She lit a cigarette with her jewel-encrusted Bic and blew a cloud of mentholated smoke. "But definitely New York."

"No thoughts of going back to Phoenix?"

Her eyes narrowed. "Do I know you?"

"No. But I know you, in a way."

She pressed back against the seat. "Look, mister. You're creeping me out. Maybe you'd better go."

"Sorry. I don't mean to do that, Tawny DeeVine." Diamond flashed several impressive, though irrelevant, credentials. "I'm an investigator, looking into the Garmin murders. Maybe you haven't heard, but the man who was convicted of those killings has been released."

Her eyes sparked with alarm. "It's been ages. Years. I barely remember."

"You gave a statement to the police." He pulled out the copy. "Maybe this will refresh your recollection."

She scanned the page, then set it down and pulled deeply on her mint-scented weed. "Yes, I baby-sat for them three days before the murder. I changed diapers, read *Goodnight Moon,* gave the baby a bottle, and put the kids to bed. It's all right here. That's all I know."

Diamond fished in his pocket for a photograph of the slain toddlers. "Doesn't seem right for whoever did such a thing to get away with it."

Her voice went shrill. "Don't you think I know that? Christ."

"Yes, I do know, Toby Felder. I know how decent and sensitive you are and plenty more." He stared at her writing. "I know that you love the outdoors and that you're shy. I know that you're a middle child, that you only have a couple of close friends, and that you like to make things with your hands, knitting and the like. You were born in the winter, and you're a morning person. You're accident-prone and troubled by respiratory problems. Asthma, specifically. Smoking is a bad idea, and you know it, but you do it anyway. Sort of a death wish, and not the only one you've got."

"So you're a mind reader. Big deal. This town has more clairvoyants than drunks and liars, of which we have more than plenty."

"I don't need to read your mind, Toby Felder. It's all there, in your writing."

A hard silence settled between them. The young dancer stubbed out her cigarette, then lit another and spewed an angry plume. "What do you want from me?"

"You can get rid of it, Toby Felder. If you help me find out who destroyed those sweet little boys and their parents, you won't have to carry it around anymore. It's destroying you, too. I can see that."

"You can't see anything. You don't even know me."

"I do, Toby. I know you have nightmares. I know you wake up screaming from the image of those dead babies."

She cupped her ears. "That's enough."

"I know you're afraid to have kids of your own. Afraid they'll be taken away to punish you."

Her lip quivered. "They're gone, pops. There's not a thing in the world I can do about it."

Deep behind her eyes, Diamond saw the crouching fear. "That's not true. You can help keep it from happening to anyone else."

She shook her head sadly. "I'm no use. I'm nothing and nobody. Don't you get it?"

"That's not true. I can see it in your writing. You're a good, decent person who deserves to feel that way."

A nervous little laugh escaped her. "I don't feel anything. Good or bad. Haven't in years."

"I think you can again. I think you'll be able to breathe again, too. Let it go, and it'll let go of you."

She snapped her fingers. "Easy as that."

"Yes. It is."

"No it's not. It's not simple at all. If I say I held something back, they could lock me up. You see me in some jail full of tough broads with big attitude and nothing on their nasty hands but time? I wouldn't last a day, pops. Maybe not even an hour."

"You won't be locked up. You'll be set free."

Her eyes pooled with tears. "It's too late."

"It's not, Toby. The time's exactly right. Take a breath and tell me."

"Please—I can't."

Diamond looked at her kindly. "You can. Just tell the story. Start where it starts."

Her face warped in anguish. "I'm afraid."

"Of course you are. Everyone is."

A shudder shook the girl's small frame and her tears spilled over. Diamond listened, unmoving, as the long-buried truth came out.

3 4

I reached Lottie on her cell phone in Paris, where she was out jogging, trying to work off her outsized lunch in preparation for an even richer and more outrageous dinner. In the background, traffic swooshed and blared. Voices burbled in an alien singsong. My sister's breathing came in strident rasps as she bumped across the punishing cobblestones, determined to leave battalions of defeated calories in her wake.

"I was just about to call and check in, Claire. You must be psychic."

"If that's short for psychotic, you've got it exactly right."

"Why, sweetie? What's wrong?"

"Ask me what's right. Much shorter list."

"Poor baby. Rainey still giving you a hard time?"

"She's not giving me any time. Just a lot of lip."

"Teenagers."

"She's hurting. I get that, Lottie. I just don't know what to do about it."

"I know, honey. It's hard." Her sigh gave way to a horrifying shriek.

"Lottie? What happened? Are you okay?"

"Sorry if I broke your eardrum. They're not big on pooper-scoopers here. I just ran into a steaming mound of *merde de chien*."

"I've been doing that a lot lately myself. Doesn't even take a dog."

"Tell me everything, sweetie. I'm all ears."

"I'll wait to bore you with the gruesome details when you come home. I just wanted to hear your voice."

"You sure?" She was huffing harder, picking up the pace.

"Much as I hate to pass up a whining opportunity, what I really need to do is get to work. I still have miles to go on the new proposal."

"You'll get there."

"Where?"

"I'm serious, honey. Whatever you're going through is temporary. You'll get to be a few days older, and things will change."

"What if it's for the worse?"

"Watch it, Claire. You're starting to sound like Mom."

"No please. Anything but that. I'll be a good little optimist. I promise."

"That's better. Now get to work on that proposal. I'm going to call in a couple of days, and I expect to hear that you've got the damned thing done."

"Somehow, when you say that, it sounds possible."

"It is, and you're going to make it happen. Now get to it. Go."

Heartened by her reassurance, I settled at my desk. I spent the next four hours re-creating the work I'd lost to the weird, file-eating computer worm. The scenes I sketched gradually eroded my protagonist's footings and sent her life spinning in a grim downward spiral.

I decided to call her Laura, the name I would have given myself had I been allowed to choose. She would have a solid marriage, a pair of terrific kids like Lottie's, and a syndicated humor column that has been steadily gaining in popularity. When I started writing, I sold a few humor pieces, and going back to that someday has remained on my to-do list. Even the most dismal situations can be leavened by a dose of laughter. So I decided that humor would be Laura's gift and salvation. She could mine precious nuggets of irony and absurdity from almost any situation.

And then—

The downhill progression was clear. Someone assumes her identity and invades her finances. As Laura is grappling with that, the thief starts committing crimes in her name. The accusations that follow threaten her career, her relationships, her reputation, and, finally, her freedom and her sanity. The evidence against her grows more and more damning, until even her staunchest allies defect. In the end, she is alone in her bleak desperation, seemingly out of resources and options.

What crimes? What evidence? What happens next?

The cursor beat like the tap of an edgy foot. My story had drifted into an inescapable ditch. I was stuck.

The common but alarming malady known as writer's block has inspired a remarkable variety of home remedies. Some of my colleagues claim they can break the logjam by checking into a writers' colony like Yaddo or Ragdale for a month or two. Of course that takes a life you can walk away from by simply canceling the paper and throwing out the milk. Others find it effective to switch from computer to longhand or vice versa. Lottie swears by a long, hot bubble bath. For me, this results in nothing more than frizzy hair and shriveled digits. I have also tried doing laundry and straightening up and paperwork and dental appointments, reasoning that writing would seem irresistible by comparison. But it turns out that a really bad case of mental constipation can be worse than having your gums scaled or even a root canal. Plus, there are anesthetics for those.

Today, I decided to try and walk my way out of the slump. The weather was brisk and clear, perfect for a long stroll. With no particular destination in mind, I allowed the Walk and Don't Walk signs to guide me. They propelled me north, through the Flatiron district, east, along bustling Twenty-third Street, and then north again, up Second Avenue.

I traversed the neighborhood known as Kips Bay, crossing to First Avenue, where I passed a straight flush of medical facilities: the VA hospital, Bellevue, Brookdale, the Medical Examiner, and, finally, NYU. This is the bounty of New York. Everything is so plentiful and convenient; you can be mildly sick, chronically ill, critically stricken, deceased, and autopsied—all without ever having to cross the street.

At the corner of Fortieth Street, the Walk sign sent me ricocheting west again, toward Second Avenue. There, I stalled in front of a modest twelve-story dwelling sheathed in chunks of chocolate cement. The place looked nothing like the horror house it had been for the five Lynnwood children and the mother who had found them, posed around the dining-room table, dead.

I tracked the narrow walkway that meandered toward the door. Chipped stone pavers buckled beneath their burden of winter-brown weeds. Beside the entrance, I scanned the resident directory. Quickly, I came upon the line marked: s. PEAKE—1c.

A jab at the button brought a grating squawk. When I stopped, the silence settled thickly.

I waited awhile, mired in doubt. I knew that this was ill-advised, verging on reckless. But reason had nothing to do with my aching need to verify the facts. Noah was not here to tell his side of the story, and Duffy's view, no matter how stubbornly firm, might not be complete or even accurate. I was prepared to swallow the truth, no matter how harsh or unpalatable it turned out to be, but first I had to be certain I knew what it was.

I pressed the button again.

No response.

The super could be anywhere in the building. Committed now, I decided to find some way inside. Peake was the only resident on the first floor, so I began buzzing the names that were listed on two.

Nothing.

Working my way up systematically, I pressed and listened. Finally, after I rang C. Dribben in apartment 6B, a disembodied voice crackled through the intercom. "Who's there?"

"Sorry to bother you. I'm looking for Mr. Peake."

"That's 1C."

"I know, but he doesn't answer. Any idea where else he might be?"

"Basement, probably."

"Thanks. I'll try that. Can you buzz me in?"

"Sure." I waited out a lull. "Wait. You selling something?"

"No. I just need to talk to him."

"Good luck."

Finally, a grating razz spat through the intercom. I wrenched the door open as the signal fell away, and entered the dingy lobby.

The furnishings were grim. Bald spots and dark, oily stains pocked the surface of a green plush sofa. The couch was flanked by rickety wooden tables that were chained, like risky prisoners, to the floor. The mock-Oriental lamps were bound in place as well, as was a large terra-cotta planter and the cheesy, yellow-streaked plastic fern it contained. A cloud of lemon freshener hung over the stench of old cat litter, cooked onions, and spoiled milk. Holding my breath, I hurried to the staircase at the rear.

My footsteps resounded in the cool concrete well. As I descended, the light grew dimmer still. The basement was a dark rectangular crypt. Oversized machinery clanked and trembled in its midst, and I caught the acrid smell of gas fumes.

"Mr. Peake?"

I had to duck beneath damp, corroding pipes that snaked and angled everywhere. My hand dislodged a thick drape of cobwebs.

"Mr. Peake?"

"Yeah, what?" The gruff voice that answered loomed directly behind, startling me so I whipped straight up and whacked my forehead.

My hand flew up to cradle the throbbing pain. The super was younger than I'd expected; a brutish character with buzz-cut hair and stained crooked teeth. He wore a soiled sleeveless T-shirt and low-slung jeans and gave off the rank scent of sweat and tobacco. His huge belly slopped over his belt, wriggling like a scared piglet as he moved.

I tore my gaze away from that astonishing gut. "You're Mr. Peake?"

"Who wants to know?"

"My name is Claire Barrow. Is there someplace we can talk?"

His look went coy. "What about?"

"You knew my husband. He passed away."

"Name of?"

Thick webs of shadow gave the space an eerie, sinister feel. "Can you please turn on some more light?"

"Name of what, I said. Could be you're wasting my time."

"His name was Noah Travis."

He stepped closer, swallowing my air. "That cop?"

"Yes."

"What makes you think I want to talk about him?"

"I need to know what happened. I need to hear it from you."

"Who gives a damn what you need?"

"Please, Mr. Peake. I'll pay you." The fifty dollars I peeled from my wallet was all that remained of the emergency cash I'd had in the house. The rest had gone for the computer repair at J&R and to settle my debt for the dress and shoes I'd bought at Nicole's.

Peake crumpled the bills and shoved them back in my purse. "You want to trade favors? I got a better idea."

I caught the wicked glint in his eye, dark wheels turning. He stepped closer, swallowing my space.

"Get away from me."

"You want something, I want something. Simple as that."

Turning, I ran, ducking below the weave of pipes. Frantically, I raced up the stairs. The air throbbed with his low porcine grunts.

As I neared the top landing, he caught my ankle and wrenched me off balance. I slipped, cracking my shin against the riser's edge. Spiking pain seared through me. Desperately, I scrambled to my feet, hobbled up the remaining steps, and threw open the heavy fire door to the lobby. I felt Peake closing in behind me, bearing down. As I stepped into the foyer, he caught my arms and held me in a vise grip.

"Let me go!"

He stood behind me now, chest heaving. I felt the press of his grotesque flab, and the hardness rising beneath it.

"Relax, lady," he whispered in my ear. "I'm ready to talk now. Nice and friendly. All you like."

I stomped his instep with my heel. Hissing a curse, he hopped back.

Wrenching free of his grasp, I started for the door. I tried to run, but my injured leg went soft.

Peake caught me again. He lifted me off my feet, and forced me, writhing and kicking, toward the cellar door.

"No!"

I fought with everything I had. Butting backward with my head, I caught his nose with a sickening crunch. But still, he lumbered toward that staircase; intent on getting me down in the dark, noisy basement again, where no one could hear my shouts for help.

He was at the door now, turning the knob.

I filled my lungs as best I could and screamed.

"Shut up," he rasped.

I kept screaming, howls of raw terror.

"I said, shut the hell up!" His filthy fingers clamped my mouth. I forced my jaw open, grasped the fleshy heel of his hand, and bit down hard.

As his hand jerked away, I howled so hard my throat seared and my head rang with the ungodly noise.

Suddenly, he released me and stepped away, eyes stretched with fear.

"What the hell's going on here, Sid?"

His hands flew up. "Nothing. Just fooling around."

Turning, I saw a grim-faced hag in a housecoat. Her hair was a stringy gray mass, and her drab skin hung in spongy folds.

"Woke me up, you stupid fool. Barely slept the whole damned night."

"Sorry, Mama."

"Sorriest thing I ever saw." She turned to me. "What'd you come here for? Can't be a friend of his, that's for sure."

"I was looking for Stanley Peake."

She snorted. "Good luck finding him. Son of a bitch took off on me going on three years ago. Said he was going out to buy a pack of cigarettes and never came back. Left me with this rat hole to run and nothing but that useless lump to run it with."

Sid pointed at me accusingly. "She's that cop's wife, Mama. The one who started all the trouble."

She wagged a gnarled finger at him. "Don't get harping on that foolishness again, Sidney. Load of crap."

"Isn't either. Pop's only gone on account of him. 'Cause of that cop coming around here, hounding all the time. Scared Pop off is what happened. I know it."

"What'd I tell you?" She trundled closer and slapped his face. "Now shut the hell up."

His lip curled, on the verge of tears.

I aimed for the door. "Good-bye, Mrs. Peake. I'll be going now."

"Go on. And don't come around here again, if you know what's good for you. This one can't be trusted. Never could."

"I won't be back. Don't worry."

"You get a line on Stan, let me know. If that creep's not dead already, I'd give the world to wring his stupid neck."

3 5

Griffey drove with shocking ferocity. He swerved deftly from lane to lane, squeezing every possible second from the trip.

Diamond kept bracing against the glove compartment and stomping an imaginary brake, wishing he had insisted on taking the wheel. He had noticed the odd gleam that invaded Griffey's eye when they rented the car at the Avis on East Forty-third Street, but who could have imagined that the diffident, gossamer-tongued old man harbored a perilous streak of urban cowboy?

Rockaway, Queens, was normally a good hour's drive from midtown, but with Griffey at the helm, they made it in forty-five minutes flat. He screeched the maroon Buick Century to a jarring stop in front of the Behringer house on Beach Channel Drive, a small white jewel overlooking the broad, choppy expanse of Jamaica Bay. As they stepped from the car, a jumbo jet swooped low overhead with an earsplitting roar on its descent into nearby Kennedy Airport.

Diamond, still soft-kneed from the ride, followed Griffey up the driveway. He studied the house, trying to get some measure of the man Toby Felder had told him to see.

Waning sunshine glinted sharply off the windows, which were

rendered in old leaded glass. A small skiff on a trailer; a scatter of bright, plastic toys; several dirt-crusted lawn tools clustered behind the family SUV. From inside came the voluptuous strains of a Chopin nocturne broken by the cacophonous chatter of a power saw.

A pallid young woman answered the door. She wore a ruffled apron over a prim white blouse and dark skirt and carried a wan-looking toddler on her hip. The little boy was runny-nosed and pink with fever behind the brave little grin and Spiderman pajamas.

Diamond cleared his throat. "Hello, ma'am. Name's Aldo Diamond and this is Solomon Griffey. Mr. Behringer's expecting us."

"Howard's out back, in the studio. You can go right around."

The sawing noise grew louder as they circled the house. Down a short flight at the rear was Behringer's workshop. Peering through the amber-tinted fanlight, Diamond saw a bearded man hunched over a piece in progress, a complex carving depicting the Last Supper. Behind him, a young apprentice, dark eyes swimming behind dense safety goggles, cut fine shapes from mahogany panels with a scroll saw. Diamond's sharp knock was swallowed by the din.

The door was unlocked. Griffey turned the knob, and Diamond followed him inside. They dawdled uneasily near the door until the bearded man took notice and set his chisel down on the worktable.

"Mr. Diamond? Didn't hear you. Come on in."

"Thanks for agreeing to see us, Mr. Behringer. This is my colleague Solomon Griffey."

Behringer brushed his palms on his khaki cargo pants and proffered a calloused hand. "Good to meet you. You said you have a message from an old friend?"

"Yes. From Toby Felder."

Behringer's eyes flashed. He turned to his assistant and tipped his head toward the door. "Go out and get some Diet Coke, Tomás, *por favor*. A six-pack and the *Post*. *¿Comprende?*"

"*Sí.*"

"And take your time."

The kid pulled off the goggles, snatched the bill from Behringer's hand, made a pit stop in the bathroom at the front of the workshop, and loped out the door.

Diamond scanned the cluttered space. Perched against the walls were more religious scenes destined for altar pieces. He recognized Jonah and the great fish, Daniel and the lion, Moses staring awestruck at the burning bush. Other projects in various stages of completion poised everywhere. Parts for a chancel rail, a broken rood screen, the front piece of a pulpit, a row of pews, and a pair of ark doors. At the center of the shop, dividers held wood panels and scrap. Hand tools nestled in a hive of cubicles and hung from hooks embedded in perforated board. Table saws and finishing tools occupied the rear half of the space.

"Toby Felder thinks about you a great deal," Diamond said.

"Can't honestly say I think about her. That was a different place, different life, different me."

Diamond's eyes narrowed. "What about the Garmins, Howard? You think about them?"

"Sometimes, sure. Of course, I didn't know them personally, but it was such a terrible thing."

"You say that as if you had nothing to do with it."

"You suggesting I did?"

"I'm suggesting that you stopped in to see Toby Felder while she was baby-sitting at the Garmin house. While she was busy with the kids, you took the house key. You made some excuse and left long enough to make a copy. Toby saw you when you slipped it back on the pegboard in the kitchen, but she was too afraid to say anything. She knew she shouldn't have let you in, that she could be in big trouble, but she never imagined how big. Later, after the murders, she was paralyzed by guilt and fear; sure they'd lock her up if they found out her part in it. It's been eating her up ever since."

Behringer laughed dryly. "Toby always had some imagination."

"Maybe so, but in this case, she was telling the truth. You gave that duplicate key to someone or used it yourself. Which was it?" Diamond demanded.

Blots of hot color scaled Howard Behringer's neck. "You can't think I killed those people."

"No? You took the key, and I can prove it. There's Toby's statement, plus it wouldn't take much to track down whoever made that dupe for you."

"Taking a key doesn't make me a murderer. It was nothing close to that."

"I wonder what a jury might think," Griffey said. "You steal a key from the Garmin house and three days later, the family is slaughtered. There's no evidence of forced entry, which there wouldn't be, since the killer had the key that you stole. I'd say that adds up to a nice, tidy case against you, Mr. Behringer, the kind of 'nothing' that can lead to a life sentence, or even the death penalty."

"I'm a God-fearing man. I would never take an innocent life."

Diamond shrugged. "Maybe so, but like you said: that was a different place, different life, different you. Maybe the old Howard Behringer was a whole different breed. Maybe he was capable of baby-killing."

His face went taut with alarm. "No. I've done things I'm not proud of, but never anything close to that."

Griffey nodded gravely. "That's for a jury to decide. In case they happen to find the case against you credible, Mr. LeBeau's release has left a convenient vacancy on death row at the Florence Penitentiary."

"Please," he wailed. "I've got a wife. Two little kids."

"Just like Joe Garmin did," Diamond said.

Tears streamed down Behringer's cheeks and settled in his wiry brown beard. "I didn't kill those people. You've got to believe me."

"If you want to convince us, I'd recommend the truth, Mr. Behringer," Griffey said.

Behringer slumped against a worktable. "I guess there's really no way to escape the past, no matter what you do."

"You have to know where you've been to understand where you are or where you're going," Griffey said.

Behringer wiped his eyes and faced the old man's unflinching gaze. "I met Toby at a bar about a year before the Garmin thing, and we got to be friends. It wasn't romantic, at least not for me. She claimed she was twenty-two, but I could tell she was younger. Way too young. Plus, she was such a sad, serious kid. I kept thinking if I made a wrong move, she would break."

"She may still," Diamond said.

Behringer went on, "I was boozing heavily back then, working for a cabinetmaker downtown when I was able to see straight enough. He paid me piecemeal, a lousy hourly, which was probably way more than I deserved. So I was always desperate for cash, always looking for ways to make an extra buck.

"Anyway, this guy starts coming into my favorite watering hole. He's a strange one, creepy, but he always has plenty of green to throw around, and that's all I cared about back then. He has me do these little jobs for him, and he pays like you wouldn't believe. I get him a pack of cigarettes, he tosses me ten bucks. Twenty bucks to give some guy a message. Fifty to call some old lady and tell her he's going to be late or something. Fifty to send someone an e-mail. Like that."

"What did he have to do with Toby Felder?" Diamond said.

"I was getting to that. This guy was spooky, the way he knew things. Somehow he found out Toby was a friend of mine. He knew she was going to sit for the Garmin kids, so he asked me to get him a copy of the house key. A hundred dollars for a few minutes work. That's how I saw it. No big deal."

Griffey shook his head. "I don't buy that, Behringer. You had to know he wanted that key for some nasty reason."

"I didn't, honestly. He said he was a friend of Joe Garmin and his wife, that he was planning a surprise for their anniversary. I thought he was talking about a party. Really I did." His face collapsed in anguish. "What do you want from me?"

"As we said, Mr. Behringer, nothing but the truth," Griffey said.

"That is the truth. I know it sounds dumb and crazy now, but I believed him."

"Was it LeBeau?"

Behringer ran a sleeve across his sodden beard. "Didn't look like him. But I honestly can't be sure."

"Why is that?" Diamond asked.

"The guy who paid me to get the key had a ropy scar on his chin, a mustache, short, dark hair, and glasses. And his face seemed fuller than LeBeau's. At least, fuller than the way LeBeau looked in the papers during the trial."

"Still you're uncertain?" Griffey said.

"Wish I wasn't, but my guy could have been LeBeau in disguise. If you know how, it's easy to make something look like something else. Fatter, flatter, darker, different in so many ways. It's the same for wood and faces. There are all kinds of tricks you can use to fool the eye."

"So the man who paid you to get the key and LeBeau were the same size? Same age?" Diamond asked.

"More than that. My guy had the same something missing, if you know what I mean."

Diamond frowned. "'Fraid I don't."

"He was dead behind the eyes like LeBeau. Like he didn't have a soul."

Griffey nodded and handed him a card. "Thanks for your help, Mr. Behringer. We'll be going now. If you think of anything else, give us a call."

They were in the car, ready to pull away, when Behringer came running down the drive.

"Wait!"

Diamond had reluctantly acceded to Griffey's eagerness to drive back to Manhattan. He opened the passenger window. "Yes?"

Behringer passed him a folded slip of paper. "I kept this note from the guy. Can't say why, but something told me to hold on to it. It was a message he asked me to relay. Maybe it'll help."

"Maybe it will, Mr. Behringer. Thanks."

"No. Thank you." Tears pooled again in his eyes. "I was wrong. I should have come forward years ago."

"You did now. That's the main thing."

As Griffey pulled onto the road, Diamond took the page and opened it. His eyes gobbled every scrap of information: slant and rhythm, shape and pressure, unique letter forms and clusters, loops and connectors, dots and slashes. Hungry for more, he inverted the page and then turned it upside down. This would take considerable study and comparison. Even the paper bond and ink might yield critical information. If it proved useful, he could even make studied judgments about the age and manufacture of the pen.

The more he looked, the more questions reeled through his mind. The deeper he probed, the more he needed to dig even further. As with food, he had little hope of achieving satiety any time soon. He would gorge on this frayed four-by-six-inch scrap until it offered some merciful release. And hopefully, at the end of it, they would be closer to putting LeBeau away.

3 6

Callendar stared again at the autopsy photos. He had spent every spare minute of the last twenty-four hours reviewing the file, and, by now, he knew Judge Gretchen Montrose and Bailiff Deakin Barnes intimately. Montrose had been a well-nourished, five-foot-ten-inch-tall, one-hundred-fifty-pound, fifty-three-year-old female, and Barnes was a forty-eight-year-old male, six feet tall, who weighed in at two hundred and eight. Montrose had been healthy except for a tiny calcium deposit in her left descending aorta and some mild arthritic degeneration in her knees.

Barnes had minimal congestion in his lungs and minor scarring to the left leg from an early motorcycle accident. If not for the multiple incised and transected stab wounds, seven to Montrose and nine to Barnes, both might have lived to ripe old age. Each of them had suffered gross defense wounds to the hands, indicating that neither had succumbed without a fight. From the absence of blood spatter and the pooling pattern of fluids in the corpses, it was clear that the murders had been committed elsewhere and the bodies moved to the courtroom posthumously.

As Callendar reviewed the facts, the same questions continued to plague him. He viewed the list he'd made, tracing over the persistent, maddening question marks. Where were they killed? Why were they moved? When would he see Sandra Straley again? How could he make it sooner? How were they moved undetected? When would he see Sandra Straley again? How could he wait until then?

Callendar peered up from the file and gazed at the muted TV. What he saw there launched him like a rocket from his favorite chair. He stood railing in rabid pantomime, swearing mutely as his beloved Knicks blew the last of what had been a cozy sixteen-point lead. Lonnie Jonze, the team's newly acquired star center, was tossing the game away with both gigantic hands.

The guy looked only half there. Maybe it was the shock of all those dollar signs. In an idle moment Callendar had calculated that Jonze pulled in somewhere around 2,054 dollars a minute during the average game, plus revenue from ads, product endorsements, and autograph fairs, where he could bag a crisp fifty for nothing more strenuous than scrawling his name.

Callendar's own John Hancock was worth exactly as much as the face value of any given check he wrote, except the ones he scribed monthly for alimony and child support. For those, his ex-wife saw that he got way more than his money's worth in aggravation.

He gazed lovingly at his kids. Madison and Cody perched like bookends on the living-room floor. They were surrounded by textbooks, notebooks, markers, pens, and Callendar's idea of brain food: cheddar cheese Goldfish. Both wore looks of intense concentration, though, knowing Cody, hers was probably staged. Still, he was keeping his word to hold their pert little noses to the grindstone. Janice would have to find some other way to try and screw up his visitations.

Not that he doubted she would do everything in her nasty power to do so. Anything to make him miserable. Ending the marriage had not changed her unstinting dedication to that.

Jonze bobbled an easy layup. A scrappy rookie half his size stole the rebound, ran it down the court with long, fluid strides, and sent it breezing in a graceful arc through the hoop. The stands erupted, one side jubilant, the other lusting after Jonze's zillion-dollar hide. Callendar burst to his feet again.

"He sucks. Don't you think, Daddy?" Cody opined. "I mean give me a break. The guy makes what? Ten million?"

"So I've read."

She frowned, thinking. "At eighty-two regular season games, that's almost $122,000 a game."

Callendar was not surprised that she had managed to catch Jonze's lousy performance while appearing to stare intently at her books. Nothing got past that kid. "You'd better watch that if you want to keep up your reputation as a crummy math student."

"That's not math, Daddy. It's basketball."

Madison, whose social conscience was sprouting along with the rest of her, sniffed in disapproval. "I think it's disgusting that he makes all that money for throwing a ball around while people are starving."

"If you can say that in French, you get my vote, kiddo," Callendar said.

Still enjoying her recent parole from the imprisonment of orthodontics, Madison flashed a brilliant grin. *"Je pense qu'il est dégoûtant qu'il fait tout cet argent pour lancer une balle pendant que les gens meurent de faim."*

"Show-off," Cody railed. "Big shot, genius, know-it-all, teacher's pet, goody-two-shoes, geek."

Madison, posturing to the full limits of her one-year seniority, patted her sister's head. "Thank you, Cody dear. That's very secure of you to acknowledge my superior intellect."

"Like hell I did, you flea-brained little dope."

Madison kept up the maddeningly patronizing calm. "Poor thing. She tries so hard. But she simply can't keep up."

"Keep up with this, creepo." Cody lunged for Madison's notebook, flipped open the back cover, and then laughed in spiteful delight. The pressed-paper surface held a riot of stylized hearts pierced by arrows. *Madison loves Scott* they read. "Check it out, Daddy. Madison's in love with a kind of toilet paper."

Madison ripped the book from her sister's hands. "That's better than *being* toilet paper, you immature twerp."

Callendar sat back and fixed on the game. He believed in letting them work through their sibling quibbles alone. These early wrangles and subsequent negotiations struck him as excellent preparation for coping with outsiders later on. Having grown up with three sisters and two brothers, Callendar had plenty of practice in dealing with opposing agendas and differing points of view. Often, the best solution lay in some middle ground, where everyone was disappointed to a more or less identical degree.

Janice, it went without saying, was an only child.

Jonze redeemed himself on the next play, snagging a tough pass and then swishing a three-point long shot through the net. After that, a neat steal put the ball back in their court. The Knicks appeared to be on a comeback trail. Callendar was pumped.

During his few seconds of inattention, the girls had reached a truce. They were in the giggle phase that marked the conclusion of most every argument. Naturally, that's when Janice called to check up on them.

Callendar signaled frantically for them to be quiet, but they were in that hyper-silly mode that kept popping out in bursts. He kept his hand cupped around the receiver, but when it came to even the smallest screwup on his part, Janice's radar was infallible.

"That hardly sounds like a serious study environment, Ted."

"They've been at it for hours, Janice. They're just letting off a little steam."

She sniffed. "I don't remember that as part of our deal. But then, commitments are not exactly your strong suit. Are they?"

"The girls are doing their work. Everything is fine. Would you like me to put them on?"

"Let me guess, Ted. You're watching the game."

"Nice of you to ask, Janice."

"Watching some idiotic game and looking at disgusting sadistic photographs. Isn't that right?"

"No. Not at all. It's not in their way."

"I beg to differ. There is no way the girls can concentrate properly with all that foolish nonsense going on. Not to mention how inappropriate it is to expose young children to grotesque criminal behavior."

"I know that," he said with preternatural calm. "I don't."

"Look, Ted, you have your priorities, and I happen to believe the children's education is more important that some stupid game or those bloody, revolting crime pictures you get off on. You care about those things, I care about the girls. Call it an honest difference. No hard feelings, okay?"

The kids' ebullient spirits had dissolved. Both of them were staring at Callendar, trying to gauge what was transpiring on the phone.

He tuned his voice to a cautious neutral. "Nope. None of those."

"Great. I'll be by to pick them up in a half-hour."

"No. They have everything they need for school tomorrow. Don't you, girls?"

Cody hitched her shoulders. "I do."

"Mommy knows we have everything. What's going on?" Madison demanded.

"Cut the crap, Ted. You broke our agreement, and that's that. Have them ready."

"They'll see you after school tomorrow, Janice. Good night."

"They'll see me in thirty minutes!" she shrieked. "You'd better have them packed and ready, or we can discuss it in family court. I'm sure Judge Frankel will be delighted to hear that you're encouraging them to watch ball games and look at bloody murder victims instead of doing their schoolwork."

"They're studying, Janice."

"I'm sure the judge will be amused by your definition of studying. Now, I will be by for them in thirty minutes, and that's that."

Callendar could read the kids' distress. If he didn't agree to let them go, Janice would barge in and stage an ugly scene. "Okay. I'll have them ready."

"And for Christ sake, don't let them go downstairs before I get there. Last time you did that—"

"Okay." Callendar hung up. He didn't need to hear the rest. More than eighteen months had elapsed since that terrible night when some lunatic lured his daughters off to deliver a scare and a threat. Janice was determined not to let him forget it. Not that he needed reminding.

Until that creep was caught and locked away, Callendar had spent every waking hour watching over his girls. When he slept, which was rare and fitful, lurking monsters infested his dreams.

After the crisis passed, Janice had hauled him before Judge Frankel and accused him of deliberately placing his daughters in jeopardy through his participation in the Arcanum. The fact that he had taken a leave from the group held no sway with her. Fortunately, the judge, a smart and reasonable soul, had dismissed the argument and Janice at her most incensed, with unflinching firmness.

Frankel did not buy the idea that Callendar had been responsible for the abduction either. The judge ruled that hazardous work did not negate a parent's custodial rights, though he had admonished Callendar to keep the girls at a safe distance from that work and its potential consequences. An investigator from the Department of Social Services had confirmed that he was more than capable of providing adequate parental care and a suitable environment for the girls. But none of that made the slightest dent in Janice's resolve.

"Why do we have to go?" Madison demanded as he hung up.

"Mom wants you home tonight."

"How come?" Cody asked.

"She just does. No biggie."

"You always give in to her," Cody accused.

"She's bigger," Callendar quipped. "Seriously, it's just a matter of where you sleep. After your tests are done, we'll be able to hang out as usual."

"It's not fair," Cody said.

"It's okay, honey. Honestly," Callendar said.

Madison caught the pleading in his look. "Come on, dork head. Let's not make a federal case out of it."

"Don't call me dork head, dork head."

They headed for the spare bedroom to pack their things. Thoroughly disgusted, Callendar flipped off the set, dissolving Jonze in the middle of a foul shot.

He took up the courthouse file and slumped in his chair. Frog-marching the tantalizing Agent Straley out of his mind, he pondered the vexing questions again. Where were they killed? Why were they moved? How were they moved undetected?

First question: Where were they killed?

Suddenly, it seemed obvious. They had to have been murdered on the premises. Callendar had a complete rundown on the Maricopa County Courthouse and its safety precautions. Security at the facility was ultra-tight, state-of-the-art. There was no way in or out that avoided the seeking eye of security guards and the ubiquitous pan-tilt-zoom cameras that were equipped to catch everything and everyone.

The murders had been committed on a weekend, when only authorized vehicles were allowed in the lot and all personnel had to pass through a gated security check with the latest in failsafe ID. A thorough review of tapes from that day revealed nothing out of the ordinary. Vehicular and personnel traffic had been light.

Which meant it had to be *in* the ordinary.

His heart raced along with his thoughts. From the record, he knew that only passenger cars had entered or left the garage that day. Given the size of the victims, there was no way their two stiffening bodies could have been smuggled inside in a trunk. Furthermore, all entering vehicles were subject to a thorough search, so it was unlikely that any self-respecting murderer would have taken the chance.

The front desk kept a log of all incoming and exiting personnel and their authorized visitors, and Agent Straley had secured a copy for the day of the killings. The list was routine. There had been a handful of judges and court employees and members of the regular, bonded maintenance crews who worked under the supervision of security. Of course, there were the guards themselves, all of whom had passed complex, rigorous screening procedures before they were hired.

After that, they had free run of the place. Everyone was watched by the guards, including the guards. If one of their ranks was intent on getting away with anything, even murder, he would be in a perfect position to work the system to his advantage. He could find out easily when and where his colleagues would be conducting routine checks and when they would be off on breaks and out of the loop. He would know the range and position of each camera, so he could figure out how to work the weak and blind spots. If necessary, he could engineer diversions.

Which brought Callendar to the next question: Why had the victims been moved?

Callendar had to believe that was not the killer's plan. Setting them up in the courtroom with the bloody legend behind their backs was an obvious attempt to imitate LeBeau, but killing them elsewhere struck him as an unnecessary and probably unintended complication. Murderers were every bit as lazy by nature as anyone else. They didn't purposely create extra trouble for themselves. Somehow, Judge Montrose and Barnes must have changed their normal pattern and messed up the plan. Either that, or some unexpected outside force had changed the course of things. The assailant could have been delayed by a traffic jam or a flat tire or an unexpected visit by the boss. Even the best-laid assassination plans sometimes went astray.

Which led to question number three: How had they been moved?

Barnes and the judge were not small people. Together, they added up to almost twelve feet of height and more than three hundred and fifty pounds. Dead weight was harder to manage, especially when the moribund flesh was compromised by multiple stab wounds and slick with blood.

The tumblers kept on clicking into place. Aside from Judge Montrose's courtroom, no blood had been found in the building or on the courthouse grounds. No traces could be detected on the stairs, in the elevators, or on the corridors leading to the courtroom. That meant the killer had cleaned up at the scene and then found some clean, hidden way to transport the bodies. Either that, or any stray spatter had been expunged.

"Clean" was the operative word here. A cleaning crew would have the means to eradicate all evidence of blood, which was a difficult substance to eliminate completely. Commercial crews had industrial-strength vacuums, floor washers and polishers, disinfectants and bleaches, heavy carts, plastic sheets, drop cloths. All it would have taken was a cleaning crew working with a guard. In other words: an inside conspiracy. Which meant—

Madison reappeared with Cody at her heels. Stopping in her tracks, she pointed mutely.

Cody grabbed her sister's hand and started tugging her toward the door. "Hurry, Daddy. Look. There's a fire!"

Wispy smoke traces filled the room, gathering thickly near the ceiling. Callendar caught the acrid stench of burning rubber and the crackle of hungry flames.

"Wait right there," he ordered. "Don't move."

The door to the hall felt cool, but he wasn't taking any chances. He wet a stack of paper towels and pressed them against the crack above the sill. "Come with me." He held each of his daughters by the hand and herded them to his bedroom window.

"Out you go, fair damsels."

Gently, he helped them onto the fire escape. Then he ducked out himself and led them down the open metal stairs.

"I'm scared," Madison said.

Cody squeezed his hand tightly. "What's burning, Daddy? How did it start?"

"First, let's get to the street. Then we'll figure it out."

He saw no sign of trouble in any of the neighboring apartments. Smoke billowed from his open window alone. He flipped on his cell phone and dialed 911. As soon as the girls were safely away from the building, he ventured into the lobby and sounded the alarm.

Soon, they were joined on the sidewalk by neighbors in various states of bewilderment and undress. Janice appeared in tandem with the cacophonous arrival of an engine company, two ladder trucks, and a Fire Department ambulance.

Shrieking, she grabbed the children to her chest. "My babies! My God, are you all right?"

Callendar heard Cody's muffled protests. "We're fine, Mom. It's nothing. There was just a little smoke."

"Where are your coats? What is wrong with you, Ted? How can you let them out like this in the dead of winter?"

Callendar was talking to the company chief, explaining what he'd seen. He rolled his eyes, summing up his domestic situation.

The chief raised his voice so Janice wouldn't fail to hear. "You did exactly right to call and evacuate immediately, Mr. Callendar. No one was hurt. That's the important thing. You people wait here. Just take us a couple of minutes to check things out."

The fire crews fanned out and swarmed the building. The driver of the ladder company remained at the truck on standby. Callendar caught the sector reports as they came in over his intercom. *All clear in the basement. No sign of fire in the stairwells. Lobby's clear. Nothing on the first or second floor.*

They were in Callendar's apartment now. *Found it, Chief. Fire in what looks to be a garbage can in the hall closet. Totally contained. It's out now.*

"A garbage can? There's nothing like that in my hall closet."

"Someone planted it, you think?" the chief said.

Janice went on high alert, awaiting his response. Whatever he said, she would be sure to use it against him.

He kept his look deadpan and shrugged. "Could be something of mine. Like you said, all that matters is that everyone's okay. No harm done."

The chief offered a knowing nod. "That's the ball game, sir. You'll probably get a call from the inspector. Just routine."

"Sure."

Janice herded Cody and Madison toward the street. "Come with me, girls. Let's get you home where it's warm and safe and there's none of this craziness. I hope you're not too upset by all this to concentrate on your exams."

"We're not upset, Mom. You heard the man. It was nothing."

Janice clamped Cody's mouth before she could make any more reasonable statements and hustled her into a cab.

The neighbors drifted back inside and Callendar followed. In his apartment, he surveyed the destruction. His blue down jacket was seared and his camel topcoat was singed around the hem. There were two incinerated mufflers, a charred catcher's mitt, and the stinking, blistered remains of his favorite briefcase. Fortunately, he had removed the files he'd gotten from the very special Agent Straley. On almost any other day, that briefcase would have contained confidential tapes and papers that would have been difficult or impossible to replace.

His closet hung with musty dampness and the stench of charred wool. The gray rubber garbage can, scorched and filled with murky water, was not familiar.

Eyeing the mess, he shuddered from the depth of the violation. Someone had stolen into the apartment while his kids were here. That fire could have raged out of control in the stifling confines of the closet, and then burst free, ravenous for oxygen, in a lethal show of force. Madison and Cody could have been trapped in the searing flames, horribly injured or worse.

He thought at once of Arnie Broder, who had been haunting him relentlessly on the phone. But several other ruthless candidates came to mind. In this line of work, there was no shortage of nasty enemies.

 3 7

A long, hot shower failed to wash away the specter of Sid Peake. My head swam with his rank, feral stench. Again and again, I saw him coming at me in the shadow-webbed cellar. I felt his coarse fingers grab my ankle and pull me off balance as I tried to flee. His raspy panting thundered in my ears.

My right calf throbbed where I had crashed against the step. Hot swelling radiated from the raw, dusky center of the wound, and each gingerly stride I took was a nasty reminder of my foolish recklessness.

The phone rang as I was toweling off. Moving at an awkward hobble, I caught it on the third ring. My hair was still soaked, dripping down my back.

"Hi, Claire. How are things?"

"Things are fine, Jed. People are another story."

"I have the perfect antidote: a nice relaxing dinner out tonight with me."

"Thanks, but I can't tonight. I need to be here with Rainey."

"Tomorrow?"

"We have an appointment with Dr. Bruno tomorrow."

"When then?"

"I don't know, Jed. I'll call you, okay?"

Awkward silence bristled on the line.

"Okay?" I asked again.

His tone went tight. "So I'm the people problem?"

"No. It's not you at all. Honestly."

"Then what is it?"

"It's complicated."

"Try me, Claire. I bet I can understand. Maybe I can even help."

"I can't right now, Jed. There's too much going on. I just need some time, okay?"

"Time?" He snickered darkly. "A kiss-off by any other name."

"I'm not kissing you off."

"Did I use the K word? Shame on me. You like brushing off better? Is that cold and distant enough for you?"

"Please. It's not like that."

"Yes it is. It's exactly like that and has been since I got to New York. I suppose I should have gotten the hint way earlier, but I guess I'm more than a little dense when it comes to you. Sorry for bothering you. I won't do it again."

He hung up with a jarring smack before I could answer the charge. I stared at the dead receiver, trying to figure out how that short, casual chat had escalated into a train wreck. Jed had been one of the precious few upbeats in my recent existence.

I started to call him back, but thought better of it. What I'd said was true. Things were too complicated right now. I didn't have the time, energy, or spirit for a budding romance. My dance card was way over-booked with work problems and Rainey problems and financial problems and the crushing revelations surrounding Noah's death. If Jed couldn't deal with such chronic messiness, maybe the derailment was inevitable.

I pulled on my sweats and slippers and limped to the office with Richter hovering at my heels. I reread the proposal in progress until I came to the dangling end.

Conventional wisdom dictates that you should write what you know, and I decided to do just that. If I was to be blessed with such a bounty of misery, why not use it to my professional advantage?

I trashed my heroine's long, stable marriage and traded her two model kids for one hostile, rebellious, maddening teenage daughter. I changed Laura from a humor columnist to a novelist and had her foundering on the overdue proposal for a new book. I even replaced the editor she adored with a testy, unreasonable, undermining bitch. I judiciously named her Eleanor, after considering more hazardous possibilities like Pat or Peggy. To cover my butt further, I endowed her with bee sting–sized breasts and a massive rear end that jiggled when she walked like two boisterous kids scrapping under a blanket. Paige Larwin, with her perfect, trim figure, would never claim that this was supposed to be her.

Peering up, I was surprised to find that more than an hour had passed. My leg still ached hotly, as did the breach with Jed; but for a while, the work had given me welcome distance.

Plunging back into the story, I decided that the first crime committed in Laura's name had to be plagiarism. The person intent on destroying her submits a purloined story in her name and then publicly exposes the work as someone else's. Some highly established writers have been able to recover from such revelations, no matter how damning and humiliating, but Laura's career would not be nearly solid enough to get her past the crisis. Worried about legal consequences, her agent and publisher would drop her from their lists. She would be reviled by other writers and crucified by the media.

The cursor pulsed on a fresh blank screen, inviting me to up the ante even further. One more horror would deliver my hapless heroine to the brink. At that place of total desolation and desperation, she would be left to outsmart her faceless nemesis or be destroyed.

Clearly, I envisioned the climactic episode. Laura's daughter has run away and she has reason to believe the child has gone to stay with a favorite aunt in upstate Connecticut. No one answers when she calls the house, and Laura presumes that they must have gone out to dinner.

Determined to bring the girl home and heal the rift between them, she rents a car and drives to the country. When she arrives, the aunt is home, but she has not seen or heard from Laura's daughter. They call the police to report the girl missing.

Imagining the worst, Laura heads home. A light snow intensifies as she tracks the maze of dimly lit back roads. Several times, she skids out of control. The third such episode sends her careening into a tree, where she smashes her front grille and fender and injures her leg. My own aching limb and shaky situation provided compelling details: skin drawn painfully tight across the hot thump of the wound, mind skidding over its own wild, risky patches.

On this narrow, winding ribbon of pavement, there is no place to turn for help. She sees no houses or other cars, and her cell phone registers no service. Laura angles the car back onto the rutted, ice-pocked pavement and continues on her way. Shakily, after several more harrowing skids and wrong turns, she makes it back to the highway and drives home. There, she finds her daughter sprawled on the couch, chatting on the phone and watching television, as if nothing had happened.

They have a terrible fight; Laura's maddening helplessness and fear are pitted against her daughter's rebellious contempt. It ends as usual, in a technical knockout. Exhausted, Laura falls into a dark, dreamless sleep.

Early the next morning, she awakens to thunderous pounding at her door. She finds a pair of detectives, armed with a warrant for her arrest in the fatal hit-and-run of a seven-year-old Connecticut girl. The child's mother, who witnessed the appalling accident, has identified Laura's rental car and reported the plate number.

The cops arrest her and escort her out to their waiting squad car. On the way they pass the rented Taurus she had parked at the curb. In the harsh morning light, the bashed grill reads like a leering accusation. The metal is twined with fine blonde hairs and spattered with dried blood.

Richter had been snoozing beside my desk chair. As I typed the word "blood," he shot to his feet and howled.

"Hush, damn it!"

The dog hunched low, mewling.

I scratched the slackened fluff beneath his muzzle. "Sorry, boy. I didn't mean to yell. You just spooked me."

As I said that, I realized it was not entirely true. What had spooked me was slipping so fully into my character that I had experienced the horrifying events and brutal helplessness firsthand.

When the work was going that frighteningly well, it was possible to lose sight of where the story ended and reality began. A writer could get trapped in that murky twilight between her invention and herself. The line could grow too indistinct to see.

3 8

Zachary strapped on the harness and faced the toughest section of the wall. The ascent ran a sheer vertical, punctuated by yawning crevices and gravity-defying outcrops. The fabricated surface was deliberately slick and large gaps loomed between the shallow hand- and footholds. He cast a longing glance at the beginner's face on the far wall, where whimsical protrusions in bright primary colors and pastels offered the equivalent of a paint-by-numbers amble to the peak. Unfortunately, that would not provide the necessary effect.

The spotter was a squat, muscled sneer. He dispensed the required cautions and directions with mechanical dispassion and signaled his itchy boredom with a sharp tug on the belay. "You ready or what?"

Zachary answered with a rush of speed. He mounted the wall and scrabbled up crablike, moving so quickly the spotter had to hustle to reel in the slack.

Despite the breathless rapidity of his climb, Zach's brain zipped several steps ahead of his darting form. Approaching the base, he had memorized the complex landscape. In a flash, he had calculated and catalogued the optimal route to the top. Eyes closed, he tracked that mental map without a bobble or misstep. Watching him, no one would believe that this was his first attempt at a climb.

Reaching the top, he swung out, caught the belay, and drifted to the base like a spider riding its own extruded silk. A dozen gap-jawed observers had gathered to watch. They cheered him on, hooting and applauding, eager to treat him to a feast of adulation.

But that was not on the carefully crafted agenda.

Zach stared past his rabid admirers at the shadowy figure slouching near the door. Crossing toward him, he worked a fresh set of calculations. By the time he reached the stranger, he felt calm and utterly prepared. "You're late."

"I see you managed to pass the time."

"That's beside the point."

"What is the point?"

Zach faked a trace of paranoia. "Not here."

"Anxious?"

"Just ready."

"Good." The kid bumped the door open and strode out. He loped down the three long flights to the main floor and continued to the last door on the left. In seconds, he breached the lock on the door to the office marked MARCUS OLEN, PRESIDENT, EXTREME ASCENT, INTERNATIONAL, INC. Inside, he looked around briefly and then slumped in the oversized leather chair at the head of the glass-capped conference table.

Zachary stayed on his feet, claiming a different power position.

The kid's mouth curled with amused contempt. "So you like pain?"

"I find it interesting."

"Interesting how?"

Zach affected a pensive frown. "Mostly how little people understand about it. Everyone thinks pain is a response to some aversive physical or emotional stimulus. In fact, it's much more than that, and far simpler."

"Meaning what?"

"Pain in pure form—I mean the essence of it, the distillate, if you will—reduces the recipient to the most primal basics: fear, dependence, acquiescence, resignation, trust. In a perfect exchange, the receiver is completely regressed. At that point, the giver can effect a nearly godlike transformation."

Phelan was nodding now, running with the hook. "I like that. The distillate, that's what you go for."

"It's not about the *what*. All that matters is *where* you go," Zachary corrected sternly. "The essence of fear is the destination, the arrival point. Go too far or not far enough, and the process is utterly destroyed."

Phelan's fingers tapped a nervous cadence on the tabletop. "So you're saying that the main thing is control."

"Not the main thing. Control is everything," Zach chided. "It's the opposite of extremes, which is what almost everyone shoots for. That's why almost everyone fails."

The kid leaned in, still tapping. "I get why they say you're a genius. You're good with words."

"Words are nothing. All that counts is what's behind them."

Phelan blinked slowly. "Care to show me what's behind yours?"

Zach still detected a little play in the line. "How do I know I can trust you?"

The kid's laugh was dry and mirthless. "You think I'm a cop or something? Think I'm a ringer for CITU?"

"You could be."

"Sure and you could be Jesus Christ, but given the odds, I'm willing to take my chances."

Zach studied the kid's unflinching eyes. They were steel-hard and cold as a slap. "Not good enough."

Phelan snickered. "Okay. I'll show you mine, and then you'll show me yours."

"Deal. Where to?" Zach tensed, hoping for a nugget of good information.

"Your place is closer."

"You know this how?"

"Just a guess. Mine's in a whole different country."

"Okay. *Mi casa*, then. It's not much, but we won't be interrupted."

"Good enough. Lead the way."

Zach started out, keeping his pace slow and easy, taking pains to mask his mounting eagerness. This had gone way better and faster than he'd hoped. Phelan had responded quickly to his carefully targeted posting on the torture site. After a brief exchange, they had escalated to instant messaging, and then agreed to meet. The climbing club had been Phelan's choice for some reason Zach had yet to define.

For the time being, Zach was content to let the kid lead. Each choice he made revealed something about him. Sooner or later, all the bits and pieces would add up to a tidy picture he could hand like a gift to Detective McClure.

The Pit was two blocks west and ten blocks south. Phelan trailed silently behind, leaving Zach to his thoughts. Mostly, he mused about where he would be if not for McClure and Noah Travis.

Where and what.

Despite his swagger, Zachary was terrified by the fragility and regular failure of his will. Hacking had sucked him in like quicksand. It had taken getting busted to pull him out, clean him off, and get him straight again. Strong, steady hands and lots of patient determination had kept him that way. Still, he lived with the constant need for vigilance. He understood that he had to view himself as someone who could not be trusted.

He caught the hard, screw-you swagger in Phelan's footsteps. The pathetic little creep was trying to cover his weakness with the pose. But for the grace of McClure and Travis, that would be him. As with any addiction, you came to crave bigger and harder jolts, more frequent doses. Filling that insatiable and growing need was all that mattered, and over time, that got harder and harder to do. Eventually, you turned into a jangling lump of ugly desperation.

Phelan's fascination with torture would follow a predictable course. Sooner or later, the creep would step over the line, move from theory to practice, if he hadn't made the leap already.

Hopefully, before it could go much further, Zach would be able to arm Detective McClure with enough ammunition to bring the kid down.

Who knew? Maybe someday soon, the little creep would be working the right side of the street.

Zachary tracked the final block to the long-defunct Crain Technical School. He retrieved the key from behind the drainpipe and opened the loading-dock door. Phelan followed like a phantom along the wreckage-strewn corridor and down the stairs. Zach led him through the fortress of antiquated equipment to his makeshift workstation.

"Make yourself at home," he said.

Phelan surveyed the complex electronic array. "You were right. She's not much to look at."

"True, but she more than makes up for it in performance. Go ahead and fire her up. See how she runs."

The kid perched on the ancient TRS carcasses and booted up Zach's machine. He jumped online and worked through a ritual warm-up. Zach watched unblinking as Phelan keyed in the magic codes that let him slip into a stunning range of unauthorized places: top-secret FBI files, Cedars-Sinai Hospital patient records, the nuclear power plant at Indian Point, private account information at the First National Bank, a couple of far-flung American embassies.

"Not bad," Zach said grudgingly.

Phelan tossed his long stringy hair in dismissal. "Old news."

"So what's new and exciting?"

"Real-life torture sessions. The *American Idol* of pain. Interested?"

"Definitely."

Phelan keyed onto the *Abiuro* site. The picture of the Heretic's Fork floated into view on the home page. Working deep into the site's hidden recesses, he opened a page titled "The Bitter End."

The video that followed was murky, but Zach could see more than well enough. The scene featured a gray-haired woman on a dark road-way, pleading hoarsely for her life. Blood spouted from a trail of stab wounds on her neck and torso as a disembodied hand delivered more.

Slowly, the camera pulled back. The killer's arm came into view, and then his shoulder.

A nervous laugh escaped Zach. "Snuff films? Wouldn't exactly call that new."

The camera trailed slowly upward, revealing a slim neck under a drape of long stringy hair.

Phelan's hair. Zach was looking right at it. He erupted in a chill, clammy sweat.

The killer's chin came into view; the hard, stingy lips.

Phelan's laugh was a hissing taunt. "Funny how everyone claims those are faked."

Zach could barely muster the breath to speak. "Funny, yeah."

"Look closer." The kid rose from his perch and pressed Zach toward the screen.

Too stunned to resist, he sat and stared in mute horror as the killer's nose came into view, and finally, the eyes.

Then, the hair came off—just a wig. Two fingers pinched off rubbery prostheses that lengthened the chin and widened the cheekbones. Another pinch dislodged the obfuscating contact lenses.

"Wait. That's not you," Zach said. But then, the naked face was oddly familiar, too. His mind reeled with dizzy confusion.

Phelan chuckled. "Is it or isn't it? That is the question."

On the screen, the hand came down again, wielding a long, ugly blade. The fierce tip pierced the old woman's windpipe, silencing her scream.

"What is real, and what's illusion?" Phelan taunted. "Is he or isn't he? Come on, Hacky Zach—guess."

Zach wanted to strangle the little asswipe, but, keeping his gift to Detective McClure in mind, he restrained himself. "I'd guess—isn't. Good joke, bud. You really had me going there for a minute."

"Good joke is right." Phelan slapped him hard between the shoulder blades. "And guess what, genius? The joke's on you."

Zach felt a deep, searing pain where he had been slapped. Warm liquid dribbled down his back. "What the hell?" Looking up, he saw the blade in Phelan's upraised hand, and then he felt it plunge again, deep between his ribs.

Phelan was laughing in earnest now, thoroughly enjoying himself.

Zach registered that fact as a workable advantage. The kid was so busy with his premature celebration; he had taken his eye off the ball. Through his fading senses, Zach saw a possible escape. All he had to do was broadcast a distress signal. One of his buddies lived a block away. With any luck at all, help would come in seconds.

He shut his eyes and drew an excruciating breath, trying to fill his punctured lung with air. His heart stammered wildly, and his chest rattled like a fistful of loose change.

The kid was shaking with laughter, tears streaming down his face.

Mustering the last of his strength, Zach lunged toward the keyboard. His fingers found the necessary characters, and he pressed.

Staring, he waited for the letters to appear on the screen. His pinky rested on the Enter key, ready to send the alarm.

Why was it taking so long?

He was running out of time, growing hazy. In desperation, he pressed Enter. As soon as he did, his muscles gave way, and he sank onto the cold concrete floor. That was when he saw the plug for the keyboard, dangling from Phelan's hand.

Zachary managed a rueful smile. He, of all people, understood the rules of engagement. Strategy was everything. He had missed a crucial move at a critical juncture.

Game over.

3 9

Diamond drifted into the late-night brainstorming session with a major tempest raging between his ears. Erin McCloat and Perry Vacchio hunched over a table at the far end of the Calibre Club solarium, studying the copies of the courthouse-murder files that Callendar had circulated. Lyman Trupin and Griffey manned the table at the center of the room, which was strewn with records and speculation about the Garmin case.

Griffey peered up over his glasses as Diamond cleared a meager space among the sprawl of documents for his laptop. "Glad to see you, Aldo. Everything all right?"

"Sorry I'm late. I've been working on the detective's memo book and analyzing that note we got from Howard Behringer. Afraid I lost track of the time."

Trupin's brow peaked. "What you found was that interesting?"

"That *perplexing* is more like it," Diamond said. "I'm still trying to see if there's a hidden subtext in the Noah Travis suicide note, but I'm not there yet. Behringer's note has some really weird inconsistencies." He shrugged off his navy topcoat and draped it on the coatrack. Returning by way of the snack-laden sideboard, he scooped up a handful of jelly beans and tossed them deftly into his mouth.

Griffey's head cocked with curiosity. "Inconsistencies in the writing or the author's personality, Aldo?"

"Both," Diamond mumbled, chewing. "Let me show you. It'll be easier to explain with the visual aid."

He opened his laptop and coaxed the slim Toshiba out of Standby mode. A scanned image of the note wafted into view. The paper scrap had moth-eaten edges and traces of several sharp folds. The message Howard Behringer had been hired to relay was scrawled in black ink on blue-lined yellow paper. Detailed delivery instructions were printed at the top. Behringer was to rewrite the message on a plain sheet of white paper, fold it in quarters, write the intended recipient's code name— "Stryker"—on the front and then slip it behind the men's-room sink at ten P.M. Tuesday at the Bluebell Diner in Scottsdale.

The body of the message was three-lines long, rendered in choppy script. *The plan is proceeding as scheduled. Request unexpected additions. Will contact through standard channels in one week.*

Heidi Cohen, who had just arrived, peered over Diamond's shoulder. "What's that, Aldo? Sounds very *Mission Impossible.*"

"A new piece of evidence in the Garmin case."

At that, Erin McCloat and Perry Vacchio dropped what they were doing and joined the others who had gathered around Diamond.

"Where did it come from?" Erin asked.

"Through one of the witnesses: a girl who baby-sat for the Garmin kids days before the murders," Griffey explained. "It could be the missing link between Garmin and LeBeau."

Diamond raised a tempering hand. "I'd like that as much as anyone, Solomon Griffey. But I'm afraid we don't have it here."

"You couldn't match the writing to LeBeau's?"

"Yes and no. Certain elements matched quite well, but others didn't at all. Might help to have more samples from LeBeau. Aside from signatures, all I found in the file was a short handwritten statement."

"What about the threatening letter sent to Joe Garmin?" Griffey asked. "The dueling experts disagreed, but at least two on the prosecution side attested that it was from LeBeau."

"I didn't find it in the file," Diamond said.

"You sure?" Trupin asked.

"Positive. I went through everything, piece by piece. It wasn't there."

Griffey nodded grimly. "Let me look into this. I have a good idea where it might be."

"Can we back up a minute please, Aldo?" Erin McCloat tucked her hair behind an ear. "You're saying it is LeBeau's writing but it isn't?"

Diamond felt his cheeks redden. "Sounds crazy, I know."

Griffey set a comforting hand on his back. "Some things simply don't make sense, my friend. You mustn't blame yourself."

Diamond enlarged the image on the screen, magnifying each letter to a towering angry slash. "I don't know, Solomon Griffey. Feels as if I'm missing something. In my experience, even a seemingly total lack of graphological logic follows certain rules."

Griffey settled back in his chair and meshed his fingers behind his neck. "Such as?"

"Emotional and physical factors can cause the writing to break down so that it becomes virtually unrecognizable. A serious stroke, for example, can alter the handwriting profoundly. Same thing with a psychotic break. It can cause a complete collapse in the graphological identifiers. After my uncle Leonard's nervous breakdown, his writing changed so drastically, he had to file new signature cards at the bank. Lenny had to have his wife attest that he was really him so he could get his driver's license renewed. Got really messy."

Griffey's brow ruffled with bewilderment. "There's no such thing as a partial collapse in those identifiers?"

"There can be, of course. But it would be a partial collapse in all of them. The writing would deteriorate across the board. You wouldn't have perfectly stable descenders and ascenders while the connectors underwent drastic change. And you certainly wouldn't have what I see here. Some patterns match LeBeau's writing well and others simply don't fit at all."

Trupin squinted at the screen. "What if LeBeau used one hand for part of the note and the other hand for the rest of it?"

"I'd be able to tell."

Heidi Cohen leaned closer, squinting through her pale eyes at the screen. "Couldn't he have messed up part of the note on purpose, knowing it might turn up in evidence someday?"

"That would show in unexpected breaks and pattern shifts as well. I see none of those." Diamond cast a longing glance at the jelly beans. With a knowing nod, Vacchio retrieved the bowl from the sideboard and set it beside the laptop.

Diamond dug in, aching to fill the restless void. Sugary flavor bursts added to the sensory chaos he had been suffering all day. A rush of raspberry, a splurge of vanilla, a tangy lemon leap.

Griffey removed his glasses and pressed his eyes with the heels of his palms. "Did you try running the note through your EDGE analyzer, Aldo?"

A deeper flush stained the candy-puffed cheeks. "I didn't. Of course I should have, Solomon Griffey. How could I be so dumb?"

Griffey pressed his lips in mock rebuke. "You're nothing of the kind. You were simply absorbed in pursuing other avenues."

"You're way too kind, Solomon Griffey. Give me a couple of minutes, and I'll run the program right now."

As everyone peeled away, Ted Callendar came through the door. He wore a thick cardigan over a turtleneck sweater, but no coat. An acrid smell, like charbroiled tires, trailed him across the room.

Heidi Cohen wrinkled her nose. "Hi, Ted. New cologne?"

"Yes. I believe they call it 'Eau de Arsonist.'"

Trupin got to his feet. "You had a fire, Ted? Anyone hurt?"

"Fortunately not. Someone started a blaze in a garbage can in my closet. I got the kids out and called for help. They were able to put it out before it spread, though sadly not before it spread to my ex-wife's attention."

Erin McCloat set down the page she was reading and frowned. "Any idea who it might have been?"

"Several."

"LeBeau you think?" said Heidi Cohen.

"I considered him, naturally, but this was nowhere close to his style. It was too subtle and far too contained. If LeBeau got into fire, it would be major conflagrations. He would start kerosene floods and spark them with industrial-sized flamethrowers, not toss a match in a trash can to take out a lousy briefcase and couple of mufflers and coats."

"Whose style do you think that would be?" Griffey asked.

"The more I think about it, the harder I lean toward a particular patient. In fact, I'd like to ask Russell to put the squeeze on this character if that's okay with everyone here."

"Fine with me," Trupin said.

The rest agreed quickly, and Callendar called in the request to Russell Quilfo. Hanging up, he slumped in a chair. "Quilfo is sending a team of detectives to interview the jerk and sniff around. Hopefully, they'll find enough to send him on a nice, long, state-funded vacation."

"I imagine that must have taken it out of you, Ted," Griffey said. "Are you sure you wouldn't be better off at home tonight?"

"Positive, Griffey. I'm much better off keeping my mind on other things, like figuring out which of the Maricopa County Courthouse guards and which member of the cleaning crew might have been in on the murders of Judge Montrose and her bailiff, Deakin Barnes."

"Security guards and the cleaning crew? Do tell," Griffey said.

Callendar laid out the links in his logic chain. There was clear evidence that the victims had been murdered elsewhere and moved to the courtroom. The most sensitive detection techniques had failed to turn up any traces of blood or violent struggle anywhere else in the courthouse complex. Moving the bodies within the heavily monitored space without leaving a trail had to require privileged access, specialized equipment, and more than one pair of powerful hands. Everything pointed to a carefully choreographed inside conspiracy.

Perry Vacchio took the ball and ran with it. "Excellent work, Ted. It shouldn't be too difficult to check out the security and cleaning personnel. They must all have their fingerprints on file. Lyman? You can help us with this?"

"I can get us a priority run-through on AFIS that will turn up any priors or outstanding warrants, but given the security checks these people are put through before they're hired, I wouldn't think we'd be likely to find any of those."

"You're right, Lyman," Griffey observed. "Still, I like Ted's theory. Having one or more confederates would explain a lot, including how LeBeau could be making very public appearances in New York while murders mimicking his precise MO were being committed in Arizona."

Diamond's computer beeped to signal the completion of the report. Everyone clustered to see the results.

Staring intently, Diamond scrolled through the complex analysis. "The EDGE software examines internal and external influences that can have an impact on handwriting," he explained. "The objective is to bring new layers of information to the document analyst. For example, the program can deduce meteorological conditions at the point of authorship. It offers information about wind velocity and direction, ambient temperature, humidity, and the level and vector of atmospheric pressure."

"Which allows the examiner to assess whether the sample was generated indoors or out, not to mention providing information about season and location," Griffey said.

"True," Diamond said. "We can link the EDGE results to meteorological data banks for outdoor samples and match them to readings taken at suspect sites for the indoor ones. We've been able to kill more than one alibi and track down several kidnap victims from the ransom notes alone."

"But that's far from all. Describe some of the other factors the EDGE is able to detect, Aldo," Griffey prompted.

"Physical attributes, for one. See there, for example." He pointed to the center of the current screen display. "The EDGE finds that our subject is a right-handed male, twenty-one to thirty years old, of Eastern European extraction, approximately five feet ten inches tall, weighing between 160 and 165 pounds, with well-developed musculature."

"You can tell all that from a few lines of writing? Incredible," said Erin McCloat.

This time Diamond flushed with humble pride. "The EDGE algorithms were drawn from analysis of tens of thousands of carefully calibrated samples. We can make pretty decent assessments about age, ethnic and cultural background, education, and, of course, many emotional and personality factors."

"Beyond what you've told us, what do we know about this particular subject, Aldo?" Griffey asked.

Diamond scrolled through more screens full of dense, complex data and analysis. Finally, he came to the summary and conclusion section of the scan. "What I should have been able to see at once, that the writing is a composite. Two, perhaps three, people contributed to the sample. That's why it makes no sense."

Perry Vacchio read over Diamond's shoulder. "I don't understand. How could they do that without those unexpected breaks and pattern shifts you mentioned?"

"They used a machine, a computer-generated scriptwriter and compositor." Diamond leaned closer and squinted hard. "I know of nothing on the market or in development that could produce these results. Had to be an incredibly sophisticated prototype they developed themselves, which would take very particular engineering capabilities and some fairly expensive fabrication."

"Which translates into considerable resources," Perry Vacchio observed.

"Definitely. It's a possibility I never considered. Fortunately, the EDGE software doesn't get confused by what it expects to find. In this case, I'm afraid, the invention is a lot smarter than the inventor." He trolled for consolation in the jelly-bean bowl. His mood was decidedly lime.

"Now all we need to do is identify the subjects behind those other samples," Griffey observed. "I believe the brilliant invention and its equally brilliant inventor are more than equal to the task."

"We'll need to get the employment applications for courthouse security and the cleaning service," Callendar observed.

All eyes turned to Trupin. "I should be able to swing that. Let me make a few calls."

Griffey dipped his chin in satisfaction. "This is excellent, my friends. We're getting closer."

Diamond sat out the round of celebratory backslapping. True, they were getting closer. The question was, closer to what?

4 0

From our front-row-center seats, it was a short hop over the orchestra to late-nineteenth-century Japan. I was drawn to the set: a modest house whose gracious simplicity held the cruel, empty promise of comfort and peace. Massive shoji screens parted to welcome the dreamy summer sky and the face of a radiant moon.

From this intimate distance, I could see the delicate plum-and-silver embroidery in the scarlet silk of Madame Butterfly's marriage sash, or obi. Slivers of a bloodred robe peeked from beneath her virginal kimono. Her hair was a complex, mysterious landscape, and her traditional wooden *geta* sandals tapped with each delicate step. I watched the breathy flutter of her chest and the quavering tissues deep behind her gaping red lips as she reached for the high notes. As the opera progressed, her stubborn hopes washed over me, and I felt the stab of her husband's unthinkable betrayal. The tears that trailed her rice-colored cheeks somehow spilled over onto mine.

When I last saw Puccini's masterpiece, I was Rainey's age. The tickets had come then, as they did today, courtesy of Aunt Amelia. If I remember correctly, her chauffeur had dropped them off as a last-minute surprise all those years ago, as her current city driver had late this afternoon.

My most powerful memory of the opera back then was my horror and mortification at my mother's weeping at odd intervals during the performance. I couldn't bear to be associated with that moist, blubbering spectacle in a shapeless dress and sensible shoes, who would suddenly erupt in syncopated breaths and keening sobs.

I remember scrunching in my seat, trying to retract my molecules, wishing I could somehow disappear. My face burned with the powerful certainty that everyone in the enormous hall was staring at us, peering through their tiny bejeweled glasses at the spectacle of my mother's humiliating angst. I imagined that all of them were thanking their lucky stars that their mothers were far saner or more restrained or blessedly absent or, failing all of those, mute.

Now, I struggled to contain my own boiling sorrow as I watched lovely Cio-Cio-San, the fifteen-year-old geisha known as Butterfly, whose deadly downfall is utter faith in the honesty and fidelity of her two-timing, rat-bastard husband, Lt. Benjamin Franklin Pinkerton. Pinkerton professes eternal love for her, but his actual interest is purely hormonal. As an American naval officer stationed in Japan, he views his Nagasaki house and Cio-Cio-San as temporary comforts to be used for the length of his stay and then discarded.

Soon after their marriage, Pinkerton leaves for America, promising ardently with his forked tongue and both of his faces to return. In his absence, Cio-Cio-San secretly gives birth to Pinkerton's child, whom she gives the apt name: Trouble.

I glanced at Rainey, my own little bundle of sadistic joy, who seemed to find Butterfly's plight both pathetic and amusing. She smirked and sniffed and rolled her eyes, even during the showstopper aria *"Un Bel di*

Vedremo," in which Madame Butterfly expresses her unshaken, unshakeable conviction that her beloved Pinkerton will return someday.

The opera was fast approaching its tragic end. After several years, Pinkerton does show up—with his American wife in tow. The slimy worm lacks the nerve to face Cio-Cio-San and admit his duplicity. Claiming unbearable remorse, he flees and leaves the American consul, Butterfly's maidservant, and his wife to do his dirty work. They confront Madame Butterfly, tell all, and advise her to hand little Trouble over to Pinkerton, whose wife promises to raise the child as her own. Cio-Cio-San sees no cure for her despair and disgrace but to commit hara-kiri. In the final scene, she blindfolds her little boy and slashes her throat.

My tears spilled over as Butterfly succumbed to her mortal despair. Rainey had a very different take. When the houselights went up, she looked positively gleeful.

Amelia's spit-shined Bentley waited in a long line of cabs and limos in front of Lincoln Center. As we approached, my aunt's boy-toy chauffeur popped out and installed us in the buttery backseat. As he angled into the stream of southbound Broadway traffic, the privacy screen slid shut.

Rainey turned her face away and pressed as far from me as the sumptuous space allowed.

The waters appeared to be shark-infested, but I jumped in nonetheless. "Did you enjoy that?"

She tossed her head vaguely in response.

"Didn't you love Butterfly's voice?"

"I guess."

"Want to call Aunt Amelia and say thanks?"

Gingerly, she extracted the cell phone from my grasp and flipped it on. I was fishing in my purse for my small portable address book when I saw that Rainey had Amelia's Connecticut number memorized.

"Aunt Amelia? Hi. Yes. We just got out! It was terrific! Thank you soooooo much!"

She listened intently; hanging on Amelia's every word. "It would have been perfect if you were there," she said pointedly. "When are you coming back? I miss you. Great. Absolutely. Okay. Good night."

Hanging up, she fell into a brooding silence. As soon as we rolled to a stop at the brownstone, Rainey dashed from the car. By the time I got inside, she was blockaded in her room. Richter perched outside, howling with the pain of her rejection.

I shed my coat and kicked off the pumps, which had made it even harder to limp around on my battered leg. Three messages registered on the answering machine. They were all from a worried-sounding Duffy, urging me to contact him as soon as possible.

I was dialing his cell phone number when a hard thumping sounded at the door.

Richter bounded ahead of me, growling. He calmed immediately at the sight of Duffy's broad, ruddy face.

"Thank the Lord you're here, Claire. You're all right?"

"I'm fine, Duff. Why?"

"I've spent the whole evening trying to get hold of you, trying to think where in the Lord's name you could be. Your cell phone was turned off, and nobody home for hours. Near to out of my mind I was with worry."

"Amelia arranged for us to have dinner out on her and go to the opera. I don't get you, Duff. What's wrong?"

"It's Zachary."

"What happened?"

He inhaled sharply. "Boy was stabbed five times. Could have been worse, but one of his friends happened to show up at the Pit and his assailant took off before he could do any more damage. Ambulance took him to Emergency at New York–Presbyterian. I made sure he was registered under my old man's name, in case whoever did this shows up looking to finish the job."

"My God. I'm so sorry. Is he going to be all right?"

"Who knows? Boy's lost a lot of blood. Has a collapsed lung and Lord knows what else. They're still running tests to figure out the extent of it."

"Oh, Duff. I don't know what to say."

"There's nothing to say. It's my fault, plain and clear. I brought him into this; put him in harm's way. Every drop of the blood that boy spilled is on my hands."

"You think he was attacked because he was looking for Phelan?"

"No, Claire. I think it was because of what he happened to find along the way. Could have been Phelan, but it looks like something even worse. Wounds look to have been made by a ten-inch K-Bar."

"What would LeBeau have to do with any of this? I don't understand."

"You don't have to understand. All you need to do is stay the hell out of trouble. Do you think you can do that, Claire? Do you?" He gripped me by the shoulders and spat the angry challenge in my face.

"Cut it out. You're hurting me."

He backed off, muttering in a fury. "Don't need to do that, now do I? You're more than up to the task of hurting yourself."

"I understand that you're upset, but there's no reason to take it out on me."

"When I couldn't reach you, I thought sure you'd gone and gotten yourself attacked as well. Sure you'd pulled another damned fool stunt like dropping in on the Peakes."

"How did you know?"

"Mrs. Peake called in a complaint. The cop who caught it recognized the name, and he was kind enough to pass it on to me."

"That gorilla son of hers attacked me, Duffy. What right has *she* to complain?"

"Every right. You showed up in the woman's home uninvited, which means you were trespassing. You used devious methods to gain entry to the building, which happens to be illegal as well. If her son felt threatened and decided to defend himself and his dear old mother, I do believe most judges would call his behavior reasonable and justified."

"He was trying to get me alone in the basement so he could rape me. You think that's reasonable and justified?"

"You saying he announced what he was planning to do?"

"No, but—"

"Ah. So you read the boy's mind, did you? My mistake. Didn't know you had the second sight."

"I didn't need to read his mind. It was obvious."

"Sorry to rain on your omniscience, Claire. But obvious doesn't cut it in a court of law. Especially when you're trespassing after entering someone's private premises under false pretenses. Especially when you've been told by someone who knows the facts that going there, trying to turn black into white and up into down, was a fool's errand, at best."

I searched for the Duffy I knew and loved, but he was locked behind a cold stone wall. "Don't you care that the creep attacked me?" I lifted the leg of my best black slacks to show him the ugly swelling on my calf. "I tripped when I was trying to run away from him. I didn't ask for that."

"Yes I care, damn it. I care too bloody much."

"What can I say? I'm sorry."

"You take care of that leg? You clean it right and put some antibiotic on it?"

"I did."

"Think it needs looking after? I can take you to Emergency."

"No, Duff. Thanks. It'll be fine."

His look darkened. "Mrs. Peake doesn't want you coming around her place again. Said her boy holds Noah to blame for his father running off and that she couldn't blame him if you turned up and he took his anger out on you. She'll go for the restraining order if you refuse to comply on your own, which is the next step on the road to some very serious charges."

"Don't worry. I won't go there again."

He threw up his hands in disgust. "You will or you won't. I've had it with trying to talk some sense into you. I can't stop you if you're hell-bent on putting yourself in harm's way like that fool husband of yours, maybe get yourself killed."

He stormed out and drove off in the shelter van. I stood on the front stoop, watching the shrinking trail of his taillights. The chill slipped through my pale silk blouse and burrowed beneath my skin, but I stayed rooted in place, staring until he turned off the street and the wind stole the last of his wispy exhaust.

When I turned back inside, Richter pressed close. I led him to my room, grateful for the company. He jumped on the bed and set his muzzle gently on my lap.

I rubbed his flanks, trying to calm my pounding pulse and clear Duffy's rage from my mind. Still, I kept hearing his parting shot. *Putting yourself in harm's way like that fool husband of yours. Maybe get yourself killed.*

In venom *veritas,* I thought bitterly. From his anger, came the truth. Duffy wasn't convinced that Noah had taken his own life. The facts were still unknown.

4 1

Griffey paused in front of Frame's ornate fence and pressed the buzzer. Moments later, a disembodied challenge spat through the sneering mouth of a wrought-iron gargoyle.

"Who's there?"

"It's Griffey, Melton. I need to speak with you."

Frame's nasty snicker poured through the gargoyle's lips. "*Quel* surprise, Griffey. I've been expecting you."

The buzzer sounded, unlatching the electronic gate. Griffey trod lightly up the rough-edged cut-stone walk. Atop a shallow flight, scowling replica library lions flanked the gleaming mahogany double doors. As Griffey reached the landing, the doors swung open and Frame appeared. He wore a fawn-colored paisley robe over matching pajamas, and black velvet slippers embossed with an elaborate golden crest.

"Come in, Solomon. Can I get you something? A nice piece of humble pie, perhaps?"

"Thanks anyway, Melton. I'm actually quite fed up."

Griffey trailed the windbag through a mirrored foyer to the study. Frame's portrait hung over the massive desk amid a cluster of framed fawning letters and certificates of award. Glass-fronted bookshelves held the three-dimensional prizes: statuettes, engraved crystal slabs, and trophies, along with copies of the many books in which Frame claimed complete, partial, or indirect but indispensable authorship.

Griffey's eye fixed on the advance reading copies of Frame's latest work, which lay on the couch in an open carton. "I see you've finished *From a Murderer's Mind.*"

"Indeed." Frame preened like a proud new father. "My publisher is quite over the moon about it. Won't be out for months, but it's already generated a remarkable buzz."

"I'm sure you're pleased."

"Too bad the benefits won't flow to the Arcanum this time. Naturally, I'm having all references to the organization expunged from my bio, my Web site, and my press releases."

Griffey dipped his chin. "Naturally."

Frame struck a Napoleonic pose. "If the subject arises, as I sadly suspect it will during my extensive international tour, I'll simply have to admit that I regrettably no longer find the society worthy of my association."

"As you wish."

"Precisely, Solomon."

Griffey sighed. "Unfortunate unpleasantness."

"Unfortunate and unnecessary. A few simple actions on the society's part could rectify the situation."

"Is that so?"

"It is. Actually, I've given this quite a bit of thought. Probably best if you take notes." Crossing to the desk, he handed Griffey a pen and a memo pad. Both were stamped with his stylized likeness and the legend: SUITABLE FOR FRAME-ING.

Frame circled the desk and stood behind his throne-like black-leather chair. "What I require is an informal apology from you now, followed by a formal written admission of its error and a proper expression of remorse from the society ASAP. You had best take this down, Solomon. The devil is in the details, as they say."

"I'm taking it in, Melton. Every word."

"Onward then." Frame coughed into his hand. "The bylaws must be altered immediately to reflect the value of my extraordinary stature and contribution. I want veto rights in critical society business. From this point forward, I shall have the final say in which cases we take on."

"The final say," Griffey repeated. "Is that all?"

"Not quite. You'll need to rescind Mr. Diamond's membership and provide me with a guarantee in writing that no future additions to the Arcanum roster will be made without my express consent."

A hulking figure in a black turtleneck and leather jeans appeared at the study door. He was armed with a .44, a stun gun, and a Blackberry pager. "Everything okay, Mr. Frame? Need anything?"

"If I do, I shall let you know, Rodney. How many times must I tell you not to interrupt?"

Frame's lip curled. "Which reminds me: Because my work on behalf of the Arcanum placed me in serious jeopardy, I have had to engage a cadre of rather costly round-the-clock personal bodyguards. Naturally, I'll expect reimbursement."

Griffey smiled pleasantly. "Anything else?"

"For the time being, no. That would be the general shape of my demands."

"I understand, Melton. And here's the general shape of mine. You helped yourself to the threatening note sent to Joe Garmin, and I need it back at once."

"Threatening note? I haven't the foggiest idea what you're talking about, old chap."

"You pocketed the original when you were afforded privileged access to the police file on the society's behalf."

"My, my, Griffey. I never fancied you as having such a whimsical imagination."

"You were entrusted to review the Garmin documents and make relevant copies, Melton. That in no way entitled you to co-opt those critical documents for your personal gain. Did you intend to broker the letter privately, or is eBay the better market these days?"

"How dare you make such accusations? This is the final straw, Griffey." Frame pounded the desk. "The very last!"

"Have it your way. I thought I'd give you the opportunity to avoid serious criminal charges, but it's your absolute right to be as mule-headed and self-destructive as you like. I'll simply turn my evidence over to the Phoenix prosecutor's office and let them deal with those pesky obstruction-of-justice and evidence-tampering charges. Good night, Melton. Pleasant dreams."

Frame padded hurriedly beside him. "What evidence? That's absurd. You're bluffing."

At the door, Griffey looked him sternly in the eye. "You've known me for over thirty years. Have I ever been one to make insupportable assertions?"

Griffey stepped out and started down the walk. He could hear Frame's caustic wheeze behind him.

"Wait, Griffey. No need to go off in a huff. Perhaps you're right. Perhaps I inadvertently misplaced that note among some papers of my own. I'll certainly be willing to take a quick look around. No guarantees, of course."

Griffey checked his watch. "You have five minutes, Melton. I'll wait here."

"Now let's be reasonable. I'll have to go through my files. It could take days, maybe weeks."

"Four minutes, forty seconds."

Frame scurried back into the house. He returned in three minutes, carrying the anonymous death threat Joe Garmin received two days before he and his family were brutally slain. "Marvelous stroke of luck, Griffey. I found this in my travel folder, stuck to the hotel bill from my visit to Phoenix to get the Garmin file."

Griffey took the note and left without a word. Frame's pleas trailed him through the gate and out to the street. "Those proposals I made were just a framework, old boy. Naturally, I'll be open to discussion."

Griffey hailed an approaching taxi and slipped inside.

"I'm flexible, Solomon. Glad to talk. All a silly misunderstanding I'd say. Wouldn't you?"

The driver took down Griffey's address.

Frame's voice ratcheted up to a desperate shrill. "When should I expect to hear from you, Griffey? Couple of days?"

Returning to the house, Frame mustered a nice fresh head of righteous indignation. He made for his study, where he poured a stiff brandy to steady his nerves. Cradling the snifter, he ambled slowly around the paneled room, seeking comfort in the many testaments to his stellar career.

Slowly, the degrading interlude with Griffey receded. His ferocious ego brushed off, straightened up, and cast its chin proudly aloft. Flush with imagined applause and alcohol, Frame stepped up to an imaginary microphone. "Thank you, thank you all. You are too kind. May I say how honored I am to stand before you today and accept this recognition of my many outstanding and revolutionary contributions to the field of forensic science." Rising from a grandiose bow, he waited for the roar of the fantasy accolades to subside. "Thank you. Thank you so much." Still, they clapped and cheered. Such adulation.

As Frame ducked in another deep bow, the foyer lights sputtered and went out. A moment later, the study went dark as well. Squinting hard, he detected a lurking silhouette in the hall. "Rodney? What the hell happened? Get those lights back on immediately."

"What's the matter? Scared of the dark?"

He whirled around, trying to trace the source of the voice. It seemed to come from behind him, but he saw no one there. "That will do, Rodney. Lights! Now!"

Suddenly, a blinding beam shone directly at his eyes.

Frame recoiled. "Turn that off this instant, you flea-brained imbecile!"

"What's the problem, wig man? You want light or don't you? Can't make up your little mind?"

Now he recognized the voice. "LeBeau?"

"Guilty."

Warm terror rushed down Frame's legs and pooled in his velvet slippers.

"Sorry to interrupt you in the middle of your curtain call, baldy, but I've already waited way too long to pay you back."

Frame backed away stiffly until his spine struck the bookshelves. His trembling hand groped for a weapon, but all the spheres and trophies were safely ensconced behind locked glass. "Rodney?" he croaked.

"Looking for your bodyguard, big mouth? I'd get him for you, only he's way too busy being dead."

A nervous giggle escaped Frame as the knife's point nibbled teasingly at his chest. The button shot from his robe with a playful pop, and then the blade sliced smoothly through his pajamas.

"No need for anyone to be hurt, LeBeau. Take what you want. Anything at all. I've got gold. Money. Valuable jewelry."

The knife was scraping off his chest hair now, rasping harshly at his skin. "Please. Everything, anything. All yours. I swear I won't even tell anyone you were here."

"That's true, pig face," crooned the voice as the blade plunged deep. "In fact, you won't tell anyone anything ever again."

4 2

I awoke at my desk with my cheek stuck to the Mickey Mouse mouse pad and a paper clip entangled in my hair. My neck ached, my injured leg pulsed fiercely, and the clock on my computer accused me of sleeping past nine.

The events of last night clung like a noxious fog. The argument with Duffy had left me wide-eyed and churning. At about one in the morning, I abandoned my futile flirtation with sleep and decided to work on the proposal instead.

Now, I trained my bleary eyes on the late-night additions I had made to Laura's world-class collection of woes. Her burgeoning romance, the first she'd dared to chance since her divorce, ends with a bitter phone conversation. An ugly argument with her dearest friend threatens to fracture that solid, crucial, longstanding relationship for good. The sister she adores goes off on an extended business trip, where she is largely out of reach. Meanwhile, Laura's problem child grows ever more problematical. All the constants in her world are crumbling, leaving nothing but vexing variables and fearsome unknowns.

I had found it both seductively simple and impossibly hard to draw like this, from undigested reality. I had only to look at my growing pile of bogus bills and dunning letters to deepen my heroine's financial plight. Yesterday alone, two statements for unauthorized charge accounts had come in the mail. One, which weighed in at over 11,000 dollars, included first-class airline tickets to San Francisco, where my impersonator had enjoyed an opulent weekend stay in a suite at the Fairmont Hotel, a luxury car rental, and stunningly expensive dinners at such gourmet pleasure palaces as Masa's, Boulevard, and Chez Panisse. The other bill, for a mere 9,356 dollars, chronicled a marathon shopping excursion with an emphasis on high-end boutiques. The purchases included heavy helpings of cashmere, leather, and exotic skins. Both men's and women's items were represented in a staggering variety of styles.

Still, Laura's decimated credit rating and mounting debts prove to be the least of her worries. She stands accused of several unthinkable offenses, including plagiarism and a fatal hit-and-run. The evidence against her grows more and more damning, until even her staunchest allies defect. Inevitably, Laura begins to doubt herself. She fears that she has fallen off an emotional cliff, as she had some years before, and lost the ability to distinguish truth from lies.

There, I came to another dead end. My protagonist was out of allies. Friends and family saw her horrifying descent as self-inflicted. The police found her story incredible; and she lacked the funds to retain a good lawyer. How could she prove her innocence and reclaim her stolen life? The solution continued to tease beyond my reach.

Craving a hit of caffeine, I hobbled toward the kitchen. Rainey had long since left for school. Richter stood sentry at the window, barking his challenge at every passing motorist and pedestrian. Mrs. DiMarco's cane tapped in furious protest overhead, setting a strident backbeat for the dog's throaty bass.

"I'm calling the police, Claire. You shut that mutt up, or I'm calling. I mean it."

Halfway through the living room, I spied the frantic pulse of the answering machine. Richter abandoned his post to trot over and snarl at the blinking light, containing the situation. I couldn't imagine who had called this early, but the odds of rotten news were overwhelming

The message counter registered six. My heart did a drumroll as I waited for the playback to begin. The first call was from Paige at a little after seven. From the background din and the sharp, shallow cadence of her breathing, I placed her at the gym. I imagined her honing her compact form before heading to the locker room to shower and sharpen her fangs.

I had to get to you right away, Claire. It was simply great. Hilarious. I didn't know you had it in you. Why didn't you tell me, you naughty girl?

Beep!

My mother's voice was leavened, like Paige's, by a terrifying hint of playful cheer.

Oh, honey. Sorry to call so early, but I just couldn't wait to tell you how proud I am. What a smart, talented girl you are. Let's go out for a special lunch to celebrate. How about I take you to that little French place you love downtown? The one that specializes in mussels.

Out? Downtown? Mom? The whole world had obviously gone mad.

Beep!

Hey, Claire. It's Paige again. I keep thinking you need to put some of that humor in your book. Make that lots of humor. Let yourself go, girlfriend. Have fun!

Girlfriend?

A lump of panic lodged in my throat.

Beep!

Hi, Claire. It's Jordana. Remember me from that writing workshop four years ago at the Y? You probably don't. That thing I was working on was simply awful. Anyway, I meant to contact you after your last book came out, which I loved by the way. But you know how things go. I've been swamped at the day job and still trying to find the time to write [giggle, sigh]. And then there's the new baby. Oh, my God. I can't believe how early it is. Molly had me up for a feeding at four, so it feels like lunchtime here. Anyway, I simply had to call before this one got away from me. I've never read anything funnier, Claire. Honestly. You're like a blender drink made of one part Erma Bombeck, two parts Dave Barry, and just the perfect dash of Candace Bushnell. And to have your piece in the New York Times, no less. Wow!

Frantic now, I limped outside in the oversized T-shirt I had worn to bed. The chill poked sharply through my bare feet. It had rained during the night, and my paper rested in an ice-skinned puddle on the walk.

I carried the roll of cold, sodden newsprint inside and stripped off the brittle rubber band. The pages threatened to disintegrate when I tried to peel them apart. I popped the paper in the microwave and cooked it for the requisite three minutes and thirty-three seconds on High.

I flipped through the sections in an anxious frenzy, scanning the bylines for my name: National, Metro, World Business, Business, Circuits, Arts, House and Home. I searched Sports and even Classified, then Arts again.

Nothing.

My mother's phone rang busy. No doubt she was calling everyone she had ever known to brag about this terrific article I had not written.

It had to be a mistake. That kept running through my head: a simple mistake. This was just a strange, if highly disturbing, coincidence. Despite my imagined scenario for the new book, fictional events did not leap off the page and come to be.

Jordana's number had not registered on my call log. I could not muster an image of the woman, much less her last name or any useful identifying information. No help there.

I tried my mother again and again, stabbing the Redial button, but the busy signal persisted. I kept flipping through the newspaper as I dialed, but I could barely see past the rising dread.

Finally, I limped to the office and accessed the paper online. Using the search feature, I input my name.

The query yielded seven hits. Quickly, I scrolled through a few short articles I'd written early on for the education supplement, the review of my last book, and a mention of my participation in a *Times*-sponsored book-and-author breakfast last fall. The listings appeared in chronological order. The final reference was from today's Op-Ed page. There, halfway down the first column, was an essay titled "Teen Tyrants Beware: Your Parents May Be Planning to Rebel" by C.J. Barrow.

My gaze swerved to the biographical data at the end of the piece, hoping to find that this C.J. Barrow was an anthropologist from Wisconsin or the headmistress at a girls' boarding school in Vermont. Instead, it described the author of the piece as a writer who lived with a teenage daughter in New York.

I dialed the main number at the *Times* and waited through a maddening string of voice-mail options. If I knew my party's extension, I could press it at any time. I could do the same if I knew the name of the person I was trying to reach. Pressing three would give me access to home delivery, mail subscriptions, and back copies. For addresses of their main and Washington, D.C., offices, I should press four. If I pressed five, I would be connected to human resources or someone in charge of the neediest cases.

Finally, I reached an operator, who transferred me to the Op-Ed information line. A pleasant recording informed me that they would accept submissions on any topic in a suggested maximum length of six hundred fifty words. They preferred e-mail, with the text included, not attached. They offered a fax number for those averse to e-mail, promised to read all submissions, and expressed regret that they could not call to deliver rejections personally; though they would call if a piece was slated to run. The editor's name and two contact numbers were listed at the end of the tape. In a ragged hand, I wrote them down.

I dialed the same wrong number twice, infuriating a hapless stranger whose voice was slathered thickly with sleep. Finally, I got through to yet another tape. If I left my name, number, and a brief message, Ms. Han, the Op-Ed editor, would get back to me between ten A.M. and six P.M. Eastern Standard Time.

I resolved to wait calmly, and I managed to do so for nearly thirty seconds. Then, I shambled to my room, dressed up as best I could to resemble a sane person, and headed out.

The *Times* editorial and business offices occupy a sprawling building on the north side of Forty-third Street between Seventh and Eighth Avenues. Back in my tour-guide days, harboring secret aspirations to write professionally someday, I had taken special note of the building's history. The structure had gone up in three stages between 1912 and 1932. The original tower consisted of a limestone base, and a brick shaft capped by an elaborate terra-cotta cornice and parapet. As the newspaper's operations outgrew the existing space, two major additions were tacked on. Architects attempted to preserve the original idea: neo-Gothic with a dash of French Renaissance, but to my untutored eye, all aesthetics had been overwhelmed by the ponderous trucks that clattered in and out of the broad string of delivery bays, and the worker bees who streamed through the entrance doors.

I joined them and waited my turn to pass through security. A pimply, gum-cracking guard rummaged through my purse with unabashed curiosity and frisked me rudely with his eyes.

Employees and authorized personnel flowed smoothly through to the elevator banks. Lacking credentials, I was stopped again by a guard. "Help you, ma'am?"

"I need to see someone in Op-Ed."

"You have an appointment?"

"No, but they printed something with my byline that I didn't write. I need to clear it up right away."

He scowled. "Can't let you up without an appointment, ma'am."

"I understand. My name is Claire Barrow. Please call up and tell Ms. Han that I'm here and that I need to see her immediately about a piece in today's paper."

He ran a finger over the directory and found the editor's name. Holding me in his wary sights, he dialed the extension. "Claire Barrow to see Ms. Han. Says it's about something in today's edition. Right. I see. I'll tell her."

Hanging up, he dipped his chin. "Ms. Han is in a meeting. Her assistant says to leave your name and number and she'll get back to you soon as she can."

"This can't wait. I need to see someone now."

He showed me his palms as if to demonstrate that he wasn't hiding any executives, and then he turned his attention to the next visitor.

I pressed closer, refusing to be dismissed. "If she's not available, I want you to call the president's office. Or call the publisher or the editor in chief or whoever is in charge—please."

"Calm down, lady."

"I'll calm down as soon as I get to see someone in authority and straighten this out."

"Nothing I can do right now."

"That's not true." I reached over, picked up the receiver on his phone, and brandished it, like a gun. "You can call the head office. You can call right now and tell them you have a writer here named Claire Barrow who is very, very upset."

He wrenched the receiver from my hand and shoved it back in the cradle. "I'm asking you, lady, nice and polite, to leave."

"And I'm asking you to call the executive office. I will not stand by and allow this newspaper to ruin my reputation and possibly my career. I don't care if you're the goddamned *New York Times*! You hear me?"

Of course he had. Everyone had. The screeching tirade rang in my ears and left my throat raw.

People had gathered to stare, as they always did at the sight of twisted wreckage. Hot with embarrassment, I struggled to rein in my runaway temper. "Just call upstairs. Please."

"That's exactly what I'm going to do." Smiling smugly, he picked up the phone. "This is the desk. That's right. We need someone down here from writer relations right away. Writer relations, yeah. Lady named Claire Barrow. Sure, I'll have her wait right here."

Seconds later, two uniformed men rushed at me.

"That's it, lady. Out you go."

"Please listen to me. There was a serious mistake in today's paper. I was named as the author of something I didn't write. All I want to do is speak to someone in charge and make sure it's cleared up."

"If you won't go voluntarily, we'll have to help you, miss." The guards pressed closer, leading with their bellicose chins.

"That won't be necessary," I said with lethal calm. "All I wanted was to give the paper the opportunity to clear up an unfortunate error before it leads to serious liability. If you won't let me do that, so be it. When the lawsuit goes to court, the judge will know I tried."

The guards traded mute questions, and then ruled against me. "Come along now, miss. Time to go."

They gripped my elbows and ushered me toward the door. Halfway there, a silver-haired man in a camel cashmere topcoat over a dark suit and mirror-polished brogues approached us.

"What is this?" His accent was purebred, his bearing made regal look plain.

"This woman was making a disturbance, sir, demanding to see someone upstairs."

With a stern look, he dispersed the curious onlookers. "What seems to be the problem?"

"There was a piece in today's Op-Ed section with my byline, but I didn't write it. I came here to try and clear it up."

The broad brow furrowed. "I see. Ms.—?"

"Claire Barrow."

"Boyd Howell, president of the news division," he said, shaking my hand. "Ah yes. Barrow. "Teenage Rebels Beware" . . . Center page, Section A, page twenty-six. This was mistakenly attributed to you?"

"Yes. It was."

"Kind of you to bring this to our attention, Ms. Barrow. Please come with me, and we'll get to the bottom of it." Now his fearsome gaze fixed on the guards. They backed off, muttering excuses.

Howell called ahead, and then led me to his top-floor corner office, which had a panoramic eye on the flashing mania of Times Square. "Please have a seat, Ms. Barrow. Ms. Han will join us in a moment. Can I offer you anything in the meantime? Some coffee or a soft drink, perhaps."

"Plain water would be wonderful."

In less than the promised moment, a fine-featured young woman entered, carrying a lawn-green folder. Her dark eyes swam behind dense, silver-framed glasses, and her ebony hair huddled in a stern round bun.

"I'm Lucy Han, the Op-Ed editor, Ms. Barrow. I'm afraid there's been a misunderstanding."

"So it seems."

She sat on the plush chair beside mine and extracted a page from the file. "This is the piece in question?"

I scanned her copy of the column. "Yes. I didn't write it."

"I know that." She read from another page in the folder. "The piece was submitted by a man named Carl Joseph Barrow, a single father who lives on the Upper West Side. He's a retired naval officer who just began writing recently. We loved his humorous take on his daughter's terrible teens."

"Another writer in New York named C.J. Barrow with a teenaged daughter?"

"Exactly."

"I don't know what to say."

Both of them smiled kindly. "It's an honest mistake," said Ms. Han.

Howell nodded in gracious consent. "Indeed it is. I'm forever astonished by the never-ending coincidences we encounter in the news: people with the same names, identical birthdays, and even strikingly similar careers."

"It never occurred to me. I feel like such an idiot. Please forgive me for taking your time. I can see myself out."

I limped to the subway stop at Forty-second Street and caught the southbound local. As we pulled out of the station, Rev. E Train ambled in from the adjacent car. I had only seen him in the past on uptown trains, but it stood to reason that he had to make the southbound return ride as well. He wore an NYPD T-shirt and baggy beige corduroys and had a ratty green muffler bound like a parody noose around his throat. He wove between the passengers, passing the word and his Ronald McDonald collection plate.

"Good morning, brothers and sisters, mothers and misters, saplings and saps. I come bearing the question of the day, asking you to answer my offering with a generous one of your own."

A chunky kid, one of a grungy, loose-limbed trio, tossed an empty Coke can at the reverend's head. E Train deflected it neatly and smiled. *"The Lord said, let there be blight, and so it came to be."*

A blowsy woman across the car laughed heartily and tossed him fifty cents. "Tell it like it is, brother."

The reverend tipped an imaginary hat. *"The question that we ponder today is this: How is she become as a widow! She weepeth sore in the night, and her tears are on her cheeks."*

I looked away. *"All her friends have dealt treacherously with her, they have become her enemies."*

He stopped in front of me, and I felt his heated gaze. *"Her enemies prosper; for the Lord hath afflicted her for the multitude of her transgressions."*

Anxious to be rid of him, I fished through my meager remaining funds and pressed a worn dollar bill into his plate.

A harsh grin played on his lips. *"He hath turned aside my ways, and pulled me in pieces: He hath made me desolate."*

"Stop," I rasped.

"I was a derision to all my people; and their song all the day."

"Enough," I said again. "Leave me alone."

He leaned closer, and my head filled with his rank, sour smell. *"No such thing as enough of the Lord's truth, sister. Makes the blind girl see."*

I stood, slipped around him, and pressed through the crowd to the other end of the car.

Laughing softly, he called after me. "Only cost one measly dollar and I'm giving you the gift, girl." His hands rose in benediction and his mirth fell away like a stone. *"Heed the words and hold them and be saved."*

43

Diamond reached the Calibre Club before the rising sun. Dense, low-hanging fog smudged the contours of the brownstone and gobbled its fine slate roof. Lights from an approaching car split the haze and stabbed him harshly in the eye.

He entered the lobby, his vision still swarming with luminescent spots. As they cleared, he saw Griffey, Callendar, and Erin McCloat huddled near the solarium door.

"Morning, Aldo," Callendar said. "You wouldn't happen to have a key?"

"It's locked? Strange."

"Colin must have ducked out for some reason," Griffey said.

Trupin glanced at his watch. "Let's give it five more minutes. I'm sure he'll turn up."

Diamond shifted on his feet like a roostless bird, trying to contain his eagerness. He had spent the past seven hours analyzing employment applications from the Maricopa County Courthouse security squad and cleaning crews. Trupin had secured the records through the Phoenix field office, and a courier had delivered them to Diamond's apartment shortly after ten o'clock last night. He couldn't wait to share his findings with the group, but first he needed to get inside and set up his planned demonstration. "It isn't like Colin to take off like this and leave the place unattended."

Perry Vacchio came in, followed closely by Heidi Cohen. She caught the outer entry door as Vacchio opened the inner one, admitting a chill swoop of air.

"What's going on?" Vacchio asked.

"We're locked out," Griffey said.

"Pity. I left my burglar's tools in my other purse," said Heidi Cohen.

Pale light leaked from under the solarium door. "Obviously, someone was here not long ago. The heat is on, and I can smell the coffee perking." Griffey's nostrils tensed, absorbing more detailed information. "I'm quite sure that's Colin's blend of one part hazelnut and two parts finely ground Italian roast. The percolator holds thirty cups and takes about forty-five minutes to complete its cycle. From the sound of things, it's still brewing, so he can't have been gone for very long."

"I must say I would kill for a cup of coffee right about now," said Erin McCloat.

"And I would kill to get started. I have to leave in about an hour," Callendar said.

"That makes two of us," said Vacchio.

Trupin checked his watch again. "Perhaps we should call the club manager. You have his number, Griffey, don't you?"

"I do. But it's so unlike Colin to be less than one hundred percent reliable. Let's give it just a few minutes more."

"Why don't I check the men's room?" Perry Vacchio said.

"Good idea. I'll take a look around upstairs," said Heidi Cohen, shedding her pea coat.

Erin McCloat followed as Heidi started toward the stairs. "I'll help you, Heidi. It'll go faster if we split things up."

Trupin shrugged. "I suppose it can't hurt to take a walk around the block and see if perhaps he's ducked out for a paper or a bite to eat. Ted, why don't you go east? I'll start west and we can meet halfway?"

"Works for me." Callendar loped toward the door, trailing the charred ends of his muffler.

Griffey and Diamond remained. "That would leave this floor and the basement to us, Aldo. Any preferences?"

"Your call," Diamond said.

"If you're sure, I'll pass on the stairs. My knee has been acting up a bit."

As he strode around the glum subterranean space, Diamond could hear the others overhead. There was the soft tick of Griffey's stride, the clack of Erin's slender heels, and the slurping clunk of Heidi's thick-soled boots.

The basement corridor formed an elongated capital L, with small storage spaces jutting like serifs at the elbow and the ends. Off the long arm, two doors opened into the large, rectangular kitchen, which contained a wall of steel-fronted refrigeration units, an eight-burner stove, four ovens, and a huge utility island, capped by charcoal granite. Copper pots in every conceivable size and shape dangled from a large oval rack. Glass-fronted cabinets held small appliances and implements.

Diamond strode through the pristine space and then moved on to the wine cellar. Several thousand bottles lay on racks and bins behind the locked wooden door. He peered in through the small eye-level window. Everything appeared to be in order.

The same was true of the trio of cramped storage rooms, which held all manner of equipment and supplies. Diamond scanned each room until he was thoroughly satisfied that the desk man had not wandered in and gotten injured or fallen ill or asleep.

He found nothing amiss, but still, Diamond could not shake a mounting sense of unease. Something nagged at him like a deep, indefinable ache. He climbed the stairs quickly and shut the door behind him.

As he did, Griffey emerged from the library. "No luck?"

Diamond caught the subtle signs of worry on Griffey's face. "Very peculiar, don't you think?"

"Yes, but it could be perfectly innocent, nonetheless. Perhaps we should take a look around outside."

"Can't hurt."

The sky had lightened from pewter to ash. The fog was lifting, trailing cottony wisps and long spectral tails. The two men strode in tandem over the slushy lawn, threading between the frigid puddles. Diamond shivered with the chill and a rising, faceless fear.

"What do you think, Solomon Griffey?"

"Can't say for sure, Aldo. First prize would be for nothing to be wrong," Griffey said.

"And second prize?"

"That would be for nothing to be nearly as wrong as I'm beginning to suspect."

In addition to the solarium, Griffey had found the music room, a small conference room, and two of the administrative offices locked. They paused first outside the music room, pressed close, and exhaled sharply to open view holes in the frosted glass. Griffey cupped his brow and surveyed the space. Squinting, Diamond looked past the pair of grand pianos at the cases filled with reeds, brass, and woodwinds that lined the wall. Behind the instruments ran files filled with printed sheet music and hand-drawn notations of compositions by Calibre Club members.

They moved on to the conference-room window. Diamond ran his sleeve across the glass to clear a swath. Together, they scanned the meeting space, which was sparsely furnished with an oval mahogany table and a dozen Hepplewhite chairs. They strained to see into the murky corners and searched for crouching forms behind the drapes.

The two locked offices were empty as well, but still Diamond's apprehension grew. Pressure mounted in his skull, building to a painful spear as they approached the solarium windows. Instinctively, he slowed, and then, suddenly his legs balked, locking at the knees.

"What's wrong, Aldo?" Griffey asked.

"Nothing. I mean something. I don't know." He clutched his head, trying to still the screeching pain.

"I feel it too," Griffey said.

The old man continued, and Diamond ordered his feet to follow suit. One step. Another.

Griffey reached the solarium first. The windows perched above his eye level, and he lurched awkwardly on tiptoe, trying to see inside.

Diamond's pulse thundered as he came up beside the old man. He stood several inches taller than Griffey, comfortably clearing the sill. He couldn't see the entire room, but he was able to make out the tops of several heads.

"What do you see, Aldo?"

"Looks like some sort of meeting."

"In the dark?"

"Sounds crazy, I know. But there are people in the room. At least three. Could be more."

"Try to get their attention."

Diamond rapped his knuckles hard against the glass. No response.

"Very strange. Let's get to the bottom of this," Griffey said.

The women and Perry Vacchio awaited them in the lobby. Trupin and Callendar followed close behind.

"Apparently, the solarium is occupied," Griffey said.

Trupin did a double take. "You're joking."

Griffey's lips pressed in a grim line. "Wish I were."

Erin McCloat backed away instinctively. "Who could it be?"

"Only one way to find out." Callendar hammered on the door. "Who's there? Open up!"

"Careful, Ted," Diamond warned. "What if it's—"

Before he could complete the thought, Callendar kicked at the flimsy lock. The door burst open. Trupin followed Callendar in and flipped on the lights. The others filed in, squinting in the sudden glare.

Vacchio's hand flew to his mouth. Callendar gasped.

"Dear God," Griffey said.

"Poor Colin," said Heidi Cohen.

"And poor Frame," said Perry Vacchio.

Erin McCloat grimaced. "That's Frame? I honestly didn't recognize him without his hair."

Diamond found the rusted, shrill remains of his voice. "Who's the other one?"

"That's the private guard Frame hired for protection. I saw him when I stopped by the house last night to pick up the Garmin death threat."

Heidi Cohen edged closer. "Frame had it?"

"He did. I was hoping Aldo would be able to use it to connect LeBeau to the courthouse murders."

Diamond had slipped on his professional armor; the thick wooly swaddling that enabled him to function in the face of such horror. Pulling a sharp breath, he absorbed the scene. Frame had been posed at the head of the table with a microphone pressed to his lips. Dried blood from an arterial spurt dotted his silk pajamas and matching robe. Gore speckled his skin as well, except for the smooth pink patch of scalp that had always huddled out of view beneath the oil-spill toupee. Diamond averted his gaze from that naked obscenity, the shiny badge of Frame's final humiliation.

The desk man and Frame's bodyguard sat opposite Frame with their heads bowed. The guard's corpse had the pale sheen of a trout's belly. Crimson rivulets still seeped from Colin's wounds. His fingers coiled like vines around a cocked .45.

Diamond searched for a bloody legend, and he finally spotted one on the wall behind the coatrack. "Caution: Wild Bore."

"This has to stop," said Diamond numbly.

Callendar was on the phone summoning the police. The others drifted toward the door, taking pains not to compromise the scene. Griffey alone moved further into the room, tracking a subtle scent he had discerned. He circled the stacked evidence boxes and dipped stiffly from the waist. "I do believe it has stopped, Aldo. At last."

The others approached. They drifted past the crates and huddled around the crumpled form on the floor. A single gunshot had pierced the skull, tracking an oblique path from the entry wound at the corpse's nape to the spiky scarlet bloom on the forehead.

Perry Vacchio sniffed his contempt. "So much for the unsinkable B.B. LeBeau."

Griffey knelt to make certain that all signs of life had expired. "Amen to that. I suspect that even the Eel won't be able to find a way out of this particular predicament."

4 4

I phoned my mother to explain the mixup about the *Times* piece, and did the same, by e-mail, to Paige. They would both be disappointed and annoyed with me again, back to blessed normalcy.

After trading my grown-up clothes for a pair of sweats, I headed to the office. The solution to Laura's plight continued to elude me. I went back to the beginning and read through the proposal again.

Writing requires a delicate balance between self-delusion and self-doubt. Too much or too little of either, and the process is doomed. Somehow, you need to convince yourself that you can pull an interesting story idea out of the ether, populate it with compelling characters, and then tell the tale coherently from start to end. You need to cling to this belief despite your strident inner critic, the one determined never to let you forget for one instant how mightily you suck.

That nay-saying voice was in rare form today. No surprise after the spectacular fool I had made of myself at the *New York Times*. The entire story line now struck me as unbelievable. How could the things Laura was writing about mysteriously invade her life? Why would anyone set out to ruin her? None of it made any sense.

I mustered a blank screen and tried to sort out the mess. The identity theft rang true enough. I had the raided accounts and bogus bills to back that up. I could use the particulars of Laura's job and family constellation as well, though I considered that it might be much easier and more tolerable to deal with someone a lot less like me.

For hours, I sorted and discarded, argued with myself, and then reconsidered, resurrecting certain scenes and eliminating others. The exercise absorbed me completely. Even when I stopped for a quick bite or to let Richter out in the yard, my mind stayed fixed on the proposal.

Suddenly, it struck me that the room had gone dim. Wavering shadows stretched across the floor. I was startled to note that it was nearly six. No sign of Rainey, and we were due to leave in an hour for our appointment with Dr. Bruno. She had agreed to be home on time, or so she'd said.

I checked the usual places for a message or a note. Nothing.

Another half-hour passed without a word. I paced in a fitful circuit, watching for her from my bedroom, then through the living-room window, and finally stepping out the front door, where I could scan the block to its limits in both directions. On one of my many treks through the foyer, I ran into Dr. Midori.

"Miss Claire have look of bad balloon. Stress like rock crush chi energy bug." He hefted an invisible boulder overhead and brought it down, grunting, to make the point.

"I'm okay. Just waiting for Rainey to come home."

"Worry like spleen fire. Must abdominal breathing—in, out. Ten times slow."

Richter sidled into the foyer and gazed at the doctor luridly, tongue drooping, eyes sparked with lust.

"No!" I told him sharply.

"Daughter age where stuck like moth cocoon. Time pass, soon fly free."

"I'm sure you're right. Twenty or thirty years from now, I bet she'll be a breeze."

"Shiatsu massage make no worry. Miss Claire come soon. Have table free one hour. Seven sharp."

"Thanks. I can't tonight. I'll see you soon though, Dr. Midori. I still owe you those flyers."

"Time no matter, Miss Claire. Peace only thing."

I was certainly having none of that at the moment. I stared down the street until my eyes ached, but I couldn't make Rainey appear.

If we didn't leave soon, we'd be late for our appointment with the psychiatrist. Finally, I gave in and called the usual friends. There was no answer at Dani's house or Melinda's. Grace picked up on the second ring.

"Oh hi, Claire. You calling for the math? Is Rainey feeling better?"

"Was she sick?"

"She wasn't in school today, so I thought—" She stopped dead; trapped in mid-betrayal. I heard her nervous giggle, followed by the breathy rush of frantic backpedaling. "I probably just missed her. I've been such a major space cadet lately. Totally fogged."

"Please, Grace. I won't say a word. I just need to find her. Do you have any idea where she might be?"

"I don't. Honestly."

"What about Dani or Melinda? Could she be with them?"

"Don't think so. Dani's out for dinner for her dad's birthday and Melinda was going with her mom to pick out a dress for her brother's wedding. Vera Wang. Isn't that totally totally?"

"Totally. Look, this is really important. If you have any idea at all of where she might be or who with, you have to tell me." My mind ran a gruesome slideshow: Rainey with Phelan, Phelan with Zachary, Zachary bleeding from five stab wounds at the Pit.

The kid held silent for so long, I thought she'd hung up.

"Grace?"

"She said something about going to visit Aunt Amelia in Connecticut. But it was just talk."

"Thanks. I'll try that."

"Please, please don't tell Rainey I told you. She'll kill me."

"Don't worry. She reserves all her homicidal feelings for me."

The machine picked up at Amelia's country house. Her cell phone rang through to voice mail as did the one I had given Rainey in a futile attempt to keep her in touch.

Uncle Walter, Amelia's sixth or seventh husband, depending on how you counted Uncle Manny, whom she divorced and then remarried, made his mammoth fortune in commercial real estate. I found him at his headquarters on Madison and Fifty-fourth, where I was connected immediately after invoking a family emergency.

I explained the situation. I was pretty sure Rainey was with Amelia in Connecticut. I had to reach them, but I couldn't get through.

Walter laughed heartily, as he did in response to most everything. "That's Amelia all right. She gives kids her full, undivided attention. No interruptions."

"What about calling a neighbor?"

More raucous laughter. "Like I said. Won't do you any good. If she's with your girl, Amelia won't answer the phone or the door. She believes in concentrating on a youngster completely. You want to speak to Rainey, I'd say you'd do best to take a ride up there."

"I don't have a car." I didn't have the means right now to rent one either, but I saw no point in sharing that with him. "Anyway, I barely slept last night. I'm honestly not up to a two-and-a-half-hour drive."

"No problem. My driver can take you. You can curl up in the backseat and rest up on the way. That's what I do. Takes quite a bit of doing to keep up with that firebrand aunt of yours."

"Thanks, but that's way too much to ask."

"Don't give it another thought, sweetheart. Arch will come by for you in a few minutes." He chuckled in punctuation, and hung up.

I left an apologetic message on Dr. Bruno's machine and got dressed. As I raised the shade on my bedroom window, the driver pulled up in a navy Lincoln Town Car and double-parked.

Following Walter's advice, I leaned back on the plush leather seat and sank into dreamy oblivion. I awoke to a chill rush of air when Arch rolled down his window to gain access through Amelia's electric gate. We tracked an endless brick chevron drive flanked by towering evergreens that tossed a menacing gauntlet of spiky shadows in our path.

The "cottage," as my aunt called it, turned out to be a sprawling gray Victorian mansion, replete with gingerbread trim, peaks and turrets, numerous chimneys, and a seven-car garage.

In stark contrast to my aunt, the place had an air of studied tranquillity. Only a scatter of lights broke the darkness of the elegant façade. Amelia answered the door in a long scarlet robe and matching mules.

"Claire dear, come in, come in. I checked home and Walter said you were on the way. Pity you missed the party. I had some local people in to meet your charming child. But they have this utterly dreary work ethic around here. Early to bed on school nights, if you can believe. It's all so positively *Little House on the Prairie*."

"Where's Rainey?"

"Soaking in a nice, hot bubble bath. She traveled hours and hours to get here. Poor child took the subway, bus, train, cab, and Lord knows what else. I can't imagine why she didn't simply call and ask me to send a car. Even you had the sense to do that."

"Why didn't you tell me she was here?"

"You didn't know?"

"No, I didn't. I was worried sick."

She tossed off that notion as she breezed inside. "Come have a little bubbly to calm those silly nerves."

A very little bit of bubbly did just that. A bit more had me close to sharing Amelia's highly amused and utterly dismissive view of the situation.

Her laugh rang with disbelief. "This is honestly the first time she's taken off? My word. I used to run away at least twice a week. More often when the weather permitted. After a while, I simply kept a bag packed so I'd be ready to go whenever the impulse struck."

"Didn't your parents get frantic?" I had no direct memories of my maternal grandparents, who had died before I was born. Still, my image of them was far closer to my mother's grim cautious manner than

Amelia's tendency to stomp in and seize what she wanted like a marauding Visigoth.

"Frantic? Hardly. They were positively thrilled to have me gone. Given what a little hellion I was, my absence must have felt like a vacation."

"Rainey has to come home. She has school tomorrow."

"And tomorrow and tomorrow." She filled my crystal flute again, raising a crackling head of foam. "That young lady is more than bright enough, Claire. Missing a day here and there won't hamper her education in the least."

"Maybe so, but I can't just let her think she can run off at will. That's not okay."

"Rainey is overwrought, dear. And obviously, so are you. You need a break from one another, time for the dust to settle and the air to clear. Let her stay with me through the weekend. She'll have a chance to relax and let off a bit of steam, and you can concentrate on that book thingy you need to turn in." She snapped her fingers, trying to summon the missing word.

"Proposal."

"That's it. Won't it be easier to finish whatever that is without any distractions?"

"Of course, but—"

"It's settled then. This is precisely what you both need."

The champagne had my brain fizzing. So did the heady prospect of a weekend free of Rainey's animosity and in-my-face contempt. "She has to be back for school Monday morning."

"Don't give it another thought, dear. You just run along and enjoy. I shall have her delivered in plenty of time for school."

I gazed warily at the ceiling. "I should talk to her."

"Don't, Claire. Trust me: given the current state of things, she's better off not even knowing that you've been here. I'll tell her that we spoke and you're aware that she is visiting with me for the weekend."

"I need you to promise you'll keep an eye on her."

"Of course I will."

"She stays strictly with you. And I don't want her anywhere near that kid Phelan, not even on the phone."

"Not to worry, darling." Amelia sipped daintily at her champagne. "Up here, the biggest risk she'll face is lethal boredom. Walter insists we have a country place, but I strongly suspect all this space and air and down-home pleasant folks may pose a serious hazard to one's health."

45

Diamond gave notice to the Tudor City management office that he would not be renewing his sublet. He canceled his local phone and electric service, effective in a week. He tipped the doorman and the handyman and left forwarding instructions with the postman for his mail.

Venturing into the crisp Saturday morning, he squinted and sighed. There was so much here that he hated to leave: his brilliant colleagues at the Arcanum who had accepted him as an equal and a friend; the thumping urban energy; the deli, where he could satisfy his hunger for food or company at any hour. He would miss the small, cozy apartment. He would even miss crazy Harry, and his wonderfully awful singing. As he prepared to leave it, Diamond realized that this felt closer to a real home than any he had happened on in years. His shoulders slumped, and a wedge of loneliness lodged in his chest.

At the deli, he ordered bacon-and-egg sandwiches, a couple of cheese Danish, and a pair of large coffees, light and sweet. He crossed to the park where Harry sat on a bench, perusing last week's news.

Diamond set the picnic out between them on the bench. "This is a farewell brunch, buddy. My work here is finished. I'll be taking off soon as I get things sorted out."

Harry peeled back the sandwich paper and gazed fondly at the poppy seed–flecked roll. He snapped off a crisp bit of protruding bacon and popped it in his mouth. His eyelids drooped with wistful pleasure, and he crooned, "If ever you would leave me. It wouldn't be in sunshine—"

"Believe me, buddy. I'd rather stay. But I've got to go where the job takes me. You know how it is. "

"You've got to be a part of it. New York, New York."

Diamond took a boisterous bite, savoring the heady meld of flavors. "It's a good town, Harry. I agree. Can't say I'd mind settling down here, if I could figure a way."

"Get back. Get back. Get back to where you once belonged," Harry sang.

"Who knows? Maybe something will turn up and I'll get to come back here and stay someday. Would be nice, I have to tell you. This nomad business gets a little old."

They ate and sipped awhile in silence. A pigeon strutted close to catch their fallen crumbs. When they were finished, Diamond crumpled the wrappers, crushed the empty Styrofoam cups, and stuffed all the garbage in the bag. He stood heavily and shook Harry's rough, reddened hand. "I want you to take care of yourself, pal. I'll be counting on that."

Harry got to his feet. "Take good care of yourself, you belong to me."

"See you around, Harry. *À bientôt.*"

Returning to his apartment house, Diamond found the expected package awaiting him at the desk. The American Society of Forensic Document Analysis fielded and forwarded requests for his services. Diamond had checked in with them yesterday, after the last body bag was carried out of the Calibre Club, the crime-scene unit had finished collecting evidence, and he'd been debriefed fully by the homicide detectives who caught the case.

With a weary sigh, Diamond slit the top of the envelope. On the elevator ride, he scanned the contents. One case involved a suspected terrorist cell in northern Wyoming. If he took that assignment, he would be working with a Farsi interpreter on documents he could not even read. Winters in the region were elk- and moose-friendly, but highly inhospitable to two-legged, cold-averse creatures like him.

His second option involved an anonymous threatening letter sent from Folsom Prison in Represa, California, to the daughter of a media tycoon named Wendell Manes. Diamond had worked for the man before, and it was not an experience he was in any hurry to repeat. Manes was a tyrant, explosive, unreasonable, and unabashedly flatulent to boot.

The third and sole remaining choice was reviewing documents for a school system in Missouri to ferret out the party, or parties, who had been sending anonymous letters to the local newspaper, accusing several teachers of stealing supplies.

So little time; so many numbing possibilities.

Diamond slumped in the armchair and put up his feet. He closed his eyes and conjured a cherished image of his late wife and son. For a moment, Diamond toyed with the memory, trying to envision Willy grown up, as he would be by now. But his son was frozen in childhood, a gangly boy with outsized feet, improbably large front teeth, and a stubborn cowlick. Em would be forever thirty-two, fine-boned and pensive and wise. Clinging to their memories, he drifted off. The dream took him back to their warm, tidy house and the verdant yard, rimmed by bubble-gum-pink rhododendron, where he'd taught his son to catch pop flies. He pictured the boy weaving backward on his pale, knob-kneed, soda-straw legs, squinting up to track the soaring orb.

Suddenly, a mass eclipsed the sun. Willy screeched in terror as a huge black bird swooped down and carried him off. As Diamond watched in mute horror, the child shrank to a fleck in the distant sky and disappeared. Diamond raced inside to find Em, but instead of a house, he stepped into a bottomless churning funnel. He was trapped in the howling maelstrom, tossed painfully about, sinking by excruciating degrees.

Suddenly, he startled awake. The room was steeped in inky darkness. He must have been out all day and well into the night. Not surprising, given his current state of exhaustion. Still, something felt oddly out of place. Peering around, it came to him. Someone had drawn the blackout shades.

Fear trilled along his spine. "Anybody here?"

"Only you and me, Dumbo."

The voice was a taunting hiss. Diamond wheeled quickly, searching in blind terror for the source. "Who is it? What do you want?"

"I want you to take a little walk with me, get a little exercise. Maybe work off some of that unsightly flab."

Sharp metal teased at the back of Diamond's neck. "Please. Just take what you want and go."

"Trouble with your ears, fat man? Like I already said, what I want is you. Now get up and haul it."

The point pressed harder, nipping the flesh at the base of Diamond's skull. Shakily, he stood and started toward the door. He twisted the knob and stepped into the hall. He tried to turn and see his intruder, but the flat of the blade stopped him cold.

"You know what curiosity did to the cat, chubbo. Just look straight ahead and keep walking."

The tip of the blade prodded Diamond into the stairwell and down two flights to the lobby. Once he emerged, his frail hopes evaporated. The doorman was nowhere to be seen. The lobby was deserted. At this hour, most everyone would be asleep. There was only the slimmest chance that they would encounter a neighbor returning from a late night out.

Crossing the lobby, Diamond caught a glimpse of his assailant in a mirror on the wall. He could barely speak the word. "LeBeau?"

A dry laugh crackled behind him. "Don't be silly, Pillsbury Doughboy. How could I be LeBeau if he's dead?"

"But he *is* dead. I saw—" Diamond's words trailed away as the terrible truth sank in. The dead body on the solarium floor was a decoy. Someone surgically altered to look like B.B. LeBeau. That followed the conclusion he had finally reached while he studied the employment applications from the courthouse. The most logical answer for all the illogical events was a double. A look-alike would have provided the perfect alibi and a handy way to trounce even the most expert investigation. Since the DNA evidence had been discredited, all they'd need to find was someone with the same blood type. One thing they couldn't easily fake was LeBeau's handwriting, so, to get around that, someone had devised an obfuscating machine.

"Where are you taking me?"

"You'll see soon enough, elephant man. Now march!"

Diamond tensed against his terror and the blustery chill. Stiffly, he followed the walk and turned left into the heart of the Tudor City complex. The lights in the deli loomed a block away. If they got close enough, he might be able to signal for help.

LeBeau seemed to read his desperate thoughts. "Actually, that's just where we're going. Unfortunately, the counterman looked tired, so I put him down for a nice, long nap."

Diamond groaned. "Why?"

"Gets my juices flowing, Porky. Some people paint, I take out garbage like you. Sort of a public service."

They were nearing the deli now. Diamond went woozy with fear.

"Good thing you could get here under your own steam, balloon butt. Figured I shouldn't lug your fat carcass any further than necessary. Hate to hurt my back and get laid up when there's so much more good work for me to do."

Diamond walked shakily into the store. The night clerk lay crumpled on the floor beside the snack shelves. His eyes gaped with shock, and a spreading pool of blood stained his apron. As they crossed toward the cash register, the man emitted a low, gurgling moan.

"He's still alive. Let me help him."

"No need, fat man. I'll take care of him right after I take care of you."

"No!" With a sudden surge of fury, Diamond spun around and caught the monster with an elbow to the ribs.

LeBeau staggered back and knocked into a snack-cake display, toppling it with a jarring din. For a beat, he looked startled. Then he sprung back in a superhuman fury, the blade aimed directly at Diamond's heart.

Diamond caught the hand clutching the knife and struggled to hold it away. But LeBeau had all the leverage. He forced the tip of the K-Bar closer and closer. Diamond was losing ground, muscles quavering at the brink of collapse.

The bloodstained metal slashed his shirt. LeBeau's smoky eyes held a cruel glint of triumph. "Any final words?"

Diamond's mouth fell open and his eyes bulged. A split-second later, the shot rang out. The knife fell from his assailant's hands. LeBeau made a sound like a popped balloon and dribbled to the floor.

Diamond filled his chest and took in the miracle standing at the door. The gun was a dainty .22, the lapdog of firearms. The man holding it looked steady, resolute, and perfectly clear.

"Thank God for you, Harry. You saved my life."

"You are the wind beneath my wings," Harry warbled.

"How'd you get a gun, buddy?"

"He's got a ticket to ri-ide."

"You still have the carry permit from your time with the Secret Service? Is that it?"

A broad smile dawned on Harry's face. "You've got to accentuate the positive, e-lim-in-ate the negative, latch on to the affirmative, and don't mess with Mr. In-between."

"Can't argue with you there, pal, but I'd ditch the piece before the cops come, just in case. Speaking of which, I need to call right now and get some help."

Diamond dialed 911 and asked them to send an ambulance and the police. The counterman was holding on, but LeBeau had gone dead-still.

Maybe things were finally looking up.

4 6

Despite Amelia's prediction, Rainey's absence was no magic pill for my book proposal. I was grateful for the interruption when Aldo Diamond stopped by. So was Richter, who had a hopeless crush on the man and preened for him shamelessly.

"Hope it's not a bad time," Diamond said.

"Couldn't be better. I was just hitting my head against a wall. Always feels so nice to stop."

"Hitting your head?"

"Not literally. I've been trying to finish my book proposal. I can't, for the life of me, come up with an ending."

"This is the one you mentioned about identity theft?"

"Exactly. I've painted my protagonist into a corner. Now all I have to do is get her out."

His thick lips pursed. "It'll come, Claire Barrow. Give it time."

"Time is what I don't have. My editor has me on a very short leash."

"I'll get out of your way then. I'll be leaving town in a few days, so I wanted to return your husband's book. Also thought you'd want to know that B.B. LeBeau's finally gone for good."

"What happened?"

"He was trying to add to his body count. Got caught in the act and shot. He was DOA at Bellevue."

"That's wonderful news, Aldo. I was starting to believe he was indestructible."

"Good to have him in the past tense, that's for sure. Been nice knowing you, Claire Barrow."

"You, too. Did you find what you were looking for in Noah's writing?"

"Nothing definite. These things tend to take time."

"Why don't you hold on to the book for a while then? If you get somewhere, fine. If not, you can send it back whenever."

"Be glad to. If that's okay with you."

"It's more than okay. If there's a way to find out what happened for sure, it would mean more than I can say. The hardest thing is not knowing, Aldo."

"That I understand completely, Claire Barrow. I'll see what I can do."

I worked nonstop all weekend and still failed to find the elusive solution to Laura's plight. Several alternatives occurred to me, but none passed the test of further scrutiny. By Sunday evening, my thoughts shifted to alternative careers. After Paige dumped me for failing to meet her deadline, I would need to find some other means of support.

On a break, I called Amelia to find out when Rainey would be home.

"Monday morning, darling, as you said. I've arranged for one of Walter's people to pick her up and drive her directly to school."

"That's crazy. She'll have to get up at four in the morning. It's better if she comes back tonight."

"That's moot at this point, Claire. It's far too late to rearrange everything now."

"I wish you'd checked with me, Amelia. This makes no sense."

"I didn't want to disturb you, dear."

"Since when?"

"Come now, Claire. Don't be so grumpy. The weekend was simply delightful. Rainey is such a bright girl. So sensitive and amusing. And her insights are so well considered and mature. I honestly can't imagine why on earth you have such difficulty getting along with her."

"I get along with her. Just not well."

"You simply need to be more open to the child."

"I've been open. Believe me. I can show you the scars."

Amelia puffed her exasperation. "Claire, Claire. There you go sounding like your mother again. You know, she had precisely the same tiresome complaints about you when you were Rainey's age."

"I've asked you not to go there, Amelia. What's between you and Mom has nothing to do with me."

"Of course it does, dear. It's all intricately connected. Someday you'll understand that."

"Whatever. Right now, I need to get back to work."

"You didn't finish that thingy you were working on?"

"Not quite. I'm having trouble with the end."

"Everyone does, my dear. Endings are the most challenging part, to be sure."

47

Sometimes the answer would come in a dream. If I framed the question correctly and fell into a fortunate sleep, my subconscious might serve up the elusive solution to a problem that had plagued me for days. Out of other ideas and on a collision course with my deadline, I decided to try that now. I kissed Noah's picture, slipped between the cool sheets, and focused hard.

How could Laura find out who was trying to destroy her and put a stop to it?

I fell asleep clutching that thought. I awoke to strident pounding and a gruff, insistent voice shouting my name.

"I know you're in there, Claire. Now, open up!"

Duffy?

I slipped on my robe and headed to the door. Duff stood in the foyer beside a squat, balding stranger.

"This is Detective Brill, Claire. Have to ask you to come with us."

"This isn't funny, Duff. You're scaring me. What's going on?"

He and the squat cop swapped loaded looks. "You're wanted for questioning in connection with a hit-and-run fatality late last night a few blocks from here."

"This is a joke, right?"

"Not hardly, Ms. Barrow. Young woman was killed and her boyfriend's critical. Witness saw the vehicle fleeing the scene and recorded the license plate. Description and plate number match that Taurus outside that you rented yesterday afternoon."

My head was reeling. "I didn't rent a car yesterday. I haven't been out of the house all weekend."

"Save it until you talk to a lawyer, Claire," Duffy warned.

"You don't understand. This has to be more of that craziness I was telling you about. Like the phony bills and unauthorized credit cards. I write things for my book and they happen. Someone has to be tapping into my computer."

Duffy eyed me harshly. "I strongly advise you to say nothing until you have a chance to consult with an attorney."

"Please, just go look at the file named 'New Proposal.' It's all there. My main character is framed in a hit-and-run. Someone's been doing all these crazy things to me for some reason. Maybe it's that kid Phelan, playing mind games. You said he was a hacker, remember?"

"Get dressed, Claire. We have to take you in."

"You know me, Duff. I would never do a thing like that."

Outside, car doors slammed, and I heard the swell of animated voices. Brill tipped his head toward the door. "Must be the evidence techs. Keep an eye on her. I'll go have a word with them."

Duffy clamped my arm and steered me into the apartment. "LeBeau's dead."

"I know. That handwriting expert from the Arcanum told me."

"At least something good's happened in the midst of all this lunacy."

"You have to convince them this is all a crazy mistake, Duff. I know you're mad at me, but come on."

"I'm not mad. But there's nothing I can do. This thing is in motion, and we'll have to see it through. Just don't say anything, will you please? Not another word. Opening your mouth will only deepen the hole."

"But it's insane. I'm telling you, I didn't do anything wrong."

He set his meaty hands on my shoulders. "Listen to me, damn it. You've got to get yourself under control and handle this the smart way. I'm going to help you all I can, but it won't count for anything if you refuse to help yourself."

"What can I do?"

"Keep still, like I said. Concentrate on getting hooked up with the best defense lawyer money can buy."

"What money? I told you, my accounts have been raided."

"Everything I have is tied up in the animal shelter. You'll have to talk to your mother or sister, or that wealthy aunt of yours."

"This can't be happening. It just can't. It's a nightmare."

He nodded gravely. "You're right. It's exactly that. But it's not the kind you cure by waking up."

Through the window, I saw Brill and the evidence techs huddled at the front end of a spinach-green Taurus. As Brill peeled away, I spotted the shattered headlight and the bashed, twisted metal. The grille looked like a grimace, streaked with blood.

Dizzy disbelief washed over me. "What's going on, Duffy? Why is this happening?"

He caught my elbows and kept me from crumpling to the ground. "Ssh, sweetheart. Go on and get dressed now. Have to take this step by step. In time, it'll all come clear."

4 8

Brill and Duffy walked me to the squad car and installed me behind the bulletproof glass. I hadn't been formally arrested, so they didn't put on the cuffs, but otherwise, my humiliation was complete. Neighbors and passersby gathered to watch. As we pulled away, Mrs. DiMarco stuck her head out the second-story window and chortled in spiteful delight.

"Always knew this would happen, you shameless harlot. That's what you get for all that carrying on."

They drove me to the Sixth Precinct, sirens wailing, and led me in through the side door, which was reserved for suspects and cops. Upstairs, they led me to an interview room and barraged me with questions that Duffy kept mutely cautioning me to dodge.

Brill's patience quickly expired. "You're not doing me any good here, McClure. How about taking a hike?"

Duffy continued to stall for time. Amelia had promised to send a top-notch mouthpiece soon. "The woman has a right to wait for her attorney."

"She's not under arrest. This is just fact-finding."

"So you'll wait and find your facts with the help of her counsel."

"Her failure to cooperate will be noted, Detective. It's not going to do her any good."

Duffy planted his hands on the scarred table and looked down his ruddy nose at Brill. "Twisting Ms. Barrow's arm is not going to do *you* any good."

"Screw you, McClure. I don't care if she's a personal friend. Point is she ran down a couple of innocent kids. Probably drunk or drugged to boot from the look of things. What are you? A cop or a goddamned nursemaid?"

Duffy turned his face to the broad-mirrored wall. "Smile for the camera, Brill. That little performance could prove to be quite the classic."

"Oh yeah? We'll see what I.A. thinks of yours," Brill hissed.

I cringed in my hard-backed chair. At any moment, I expected them to go for each other's throats.

Before they could, the door opened and a young woman in uniform appeared. "I need to speak to you outside, detectives."

Brill scowled. "Both of us?"

"Yes." She smiled my way, obviously mistaking me for a person. "Excuse us please."

They were gone for seven minutes by the clock, though it felt far longer. I heard voices, but I couldn't make out what they said. Instead, I tried to read the dueling tones: angry, incredulous, outraged, disgusted, amused.

When the door opened again, I realized I had been holding my breath. I filled my lungs quickly as Duffy and the female cop reentered the room.

"I'll take you home, Claire," Duffy said.

"Now?"

The woman smiled again. "Sorry to have troubled you, Ms. Barrow. I'm Lieutenant Marchetti. Please accept our apologies and regrets."

"The signature on the rental agreement was an obvious forgery, Claire," Duff said, consulting a note. "And the blood on the bumper turned out to be phylum *Chordata* from the order *galliformes*, family *Thesienidae*, genus *gallus*."

It sounded terrible. "What's that?"

They erupted in hysterical laughter. Duffy went cranberry-red, and tears of hilarity rained down Marchetti's sallow cheeks.

Another long minute passed before Duff was able to get out the word. "Chicken, Claire. It was chicken blood. Seems you were framed by the likes of Frank Perdue."

"Chicken blood," I repeated dumbly. I struggled to see it as he did, as a side-splitting gag. But I could not.

Duffy dropped me off at home. As I walked inside, the phone was ringing. I picked up to Aldo Diamond's eager voice. "Sorry to bother you, Claire Barrow, but I had a thought about an ending for your new book. If someone is spying on your character through her computer, why doesn't she simply turn it around?"

"Meaning?"

"Why doesn't she plant something to make them think she's figured out who they are?"

"Set herself up as a decoy to draw them out, you mean?"

"Exactly. It'd be way too dangerous in real life, but this is fiction, so I figured, why not?"

I felt that wonderful electric rush that signaled an idea was right. "That's perfect, Aldo. Brilliant. How do I begin to thank you?"

"No need, Claire Barrow. My pleasure."

As I hung up, another chilling revelation bubbled to the surface. I understood what Laura had to do, and what I did as well. There was only one way to get to the bottom of this, and, dangerous or not, that was where I needed to go.

4 9

The patient known as Seamus McClure was allowed no visitors. The plump, owlish, white-haired woman behind the New York–Presbyterian Hospital information desk remained adamant despite my urgent pleas. She was unmoved by my claim to be a relative who had come from great distance at remarkable expense to cheer him up. She barely blinked at my assertion that "Cousin" Seamus would be devastated if I didn't get to see him and that, since he was neither infectious nor immune-suppressed, the ban on visitors had to be a mistake. Rules were rules, she repeated with mounting impatience. The only one who could change the doctor's orders was the doctor himself.

Patient Seamus McClure's physician of record was Patrick McClure, aka Duffy. When the woman read that information off the computer screen, my spirits slumped in defeat. Duff was the last person I could go to for help with this. If he got the slightest hint of what I was planning to do, he would do everything in his considerable power to stop me. He would view my plan as lunatic-quality, at best. When Duffy drove me home after my release from custody for the bogus hit-and-run, he'd made it clear that my sense and sanity were the prime suspects in my current plight. Worse, he'd more than hinted that he thought I might have doused the car in chicken blood and reported the accident myself, looking for attention or something equally pathetic and absurd. His parting shot still stung: *It's not true what they say, sweetheart. Not all publicity is good publicity. Remember that.*

I tensed at the memory, angry all over again, but I had no time to waste on that now. Running through my meager options, I dialed the page operator from a house phone and asked for Jed.

A moment later, his name reverberated over the loudspeaker. *Dr. Slattery, call 325.*

After a short wait, his breathless voice came on the line. "Slattery here."

My throat went dry. "Hi, Jed. It's Claire."

I waited through a long, bristling silence. "Yes?"

"I'm in the hospital lobby. I hate to bother you, but I need your help."

"Of course. Why else would you be calling?"

"I know you're disgusted with me, and you have every right to be, but this is really important. Please, Jed. I don't know where else to turn."

He sighed. "I'll be right down."

Stepping off the elevator, he eyed me with guarded curiosity. "What's going on?"

I forced myself to face him squarely. "I told you, it's complicated."

"Try me. As I've told you, I'm not nearly as dumb as I sometimes act."

I peered around, not trusting anyone. "Not here."

"All right. We'll go up to my office."

He led me through a maze of corridors and up the elevator to the pediatric cardiology suite. His office was at the rear, a cozy space furnished with colorful plush chairs and a bright profusion of books and toys. I was sorely tempted to sit on the floor and erect a Lego fortress. How I ached for a warm, safe place to hide.

Instead, I perched stiffly on the chair facing Jed's desk. "Someone has been trying to destroy me. They invaded my charge accounts, raided my bank accounts, and now they've started playing with my mind. I know it sounds paranoid."

"It would, but you're not."

"You honestly don't think so?"

"No, Claire. You're lots of things, but not that. Any idea who?"

"No, but whoever it is has found some way to get into my computer and use what they find there against me."

I could see his anger softening. "How can I help?"

"There's a patient here who can help me, but he's not allowed visitors." I gave him a condensed, bowdlerized version of Zachary's background and of the circumstances that had landed him in the hospital under a phony name.

"There's no other way?"

"None that I can think of. Believe me, I wouldn't be here if there was. I understand how you feel about me."

He shook his head. "That I seriously doubt."

"Meaning?"

"Now's not the time, Claire. To quote a famous thinker: It's complicated."

He called on a house phone, got the necessary information, and led me out. We walked in silence back through the maze and up the elevators in another wing of the mammoth medical complex. Jed carried my briefcase, which contained my laptop, a variety of plugs and adaptors, extension cords, an array of software, and phone cords of various lengths. I had no idea what Zach would need, but I wanted to have whatever it might be on hand.

At the nurses' station, I hung back while Jed talked his way through security to get us entry to Zachary's room. The process took several calls and a hasty conference between the head floor nurse, the resident in charge, and two somber men in stern, navy uniforms.

After we finally got the okay, Jed walked me to the room marked "McClure, Seamus." Our fingers brushed as I took the briefcase. He recoiled as if he'd been burned.

"Take care of yourself, Claire."

"You, too. And thanks." I didn't bother to voice a last good-bye. Somehow it went without saying.

Alone in an oversized room, Zachary reclined on a hill of pillows, watching the muted play of a daytime soap. Half a dozen tubes snaked into lines that ran into his arm and under the thin cotton blanket. Dense bandages, stained with wound seepage and bile-colored antiseptics, were visible through the flimsy cotton of his hospital-issue gown. A monitor on the wall tracked his vital signs. Every so often, it screeched like a startled crow.

When Zach spotted me, the glaze of boredom in his pale eyes fell away. "Claire. I can't believe they've let in an actual person who isn't on official medical or police business. How'd you manage to get past the goon squad? My mother couldn't do that, even armed with her legendary semiautomatic mouth."

"People in high places. You know." I searched for a neutral place to fix my eyes. I kept landing on bare skin, effusions, bruises, sparse sprouting hair, things that felt too intimate to view.

"You can't imagine how good it is to see you."

"You too, Zach. I'm so sorry about all this. How are you feeling?"

"More than ready to blow this joint, that's how. Any chance you can sneak me out in that bag of yours?"

Eyeing the drips and dressings, I felt a mounting weight of guilt. I wanted to be anywhere but here, leaning yet again on this poor kid who'd been injured trying to help me and mine. "I wish I could, Zach. I'm ashamed to even say it. But I came to ask you a favor."

He propped his hands behind his head. "Shoot. Be great to feel I had some use beyond propping up the covers and playing human pin-cushion."

Riveted, he listened as I explained what I needed him to do. I'd composed an e-mail that had to look as if it had been sent from my computer to the Computer Investigation and Technology Unit without actually hitting the unit's In basket. The short note claimed that I had hard evidence about the people who'd been hacking into my computer. Further, it said I would be out until nine P.M. tonight, and available to meet with the computer investigators and turn over what I had uncovered first thing in the morning. I also needed him to send a shorter return note, routed from CITU to my e-mail address, acknowledging receipt and agreeing to meet with me at One Police Plaza, tomorrow at eight A.M.

Zach frowned up at me. "But you don't really have any evidence. Right?"

"I don't, but I need whoever is behind this to think I do."

"So you want me to send this to you as if it came from CITU, but it can't really come from there?"

"Yes. It has to carry exactly the right transmission data. These people are too sophisticated to be fooled by anything less."

I could see the gears twirling as he applied his massive talents to the task. He caressed my laptop with reverent affection and walked me through the proper way to hook up to his bedside phone. Pausing for an instant before he set the plan in play, he searched my face. "You sure about this?"

"Positive. It's the only way. And please, Zach, Duffy can't know."

A shadow crossed his face. "Could be dangerous."

"What isn't? Did you know a kid can drown in six inches of water?"

"Makes sense, theoretically."

"Do you have any idea of the hidden dangers in the ordinary lollipop?"

"Aside from sticky hands, you mean? Rotten teeth?"

"That's nothing, kiddo. I'm talking mutilation, possibly death. According to my mother, those things should come with warnings from the surgeon general." I kept my tone light and even, though my heart was lashing hard against my ribs.

"Okay, Claire. I guess you know what you're doing."

His guess was wrong. All I knew was that I had to do something and that this was the only course of action that made any sense. I watched as he sent my message to the CITU and then hacked into their computer to send a return response to me. Finally, he cleaned up all potentially incriminating signs of the tampering. Seconds later, Zach shot me a thumbs-up, confirming that things had been set in motion.

Now, there was no turning back.

5 0

Nothing would happen until after nine tonight. I had made a point of planting the notion that I would be out until then. That left me several hours to get physically and mentally prepared.

I went to a local Starbucks to place the necessary calls. First, I made arrangements for Rainey to go from school to her friend Danielle's and spend the night. I told Dani's mom, Shari Auer, that my mother wasn't feeling well; a statement that pretty much covered the fact of her life.

Shari assumed that I needed the time to take care of Mom, and I simply let her believe that. Always a sweetheart, she asked nothing else except what she could do to help.

"Thanks. There's nothing really. If Rainey wants to, she can reach me on my cell."

Next, I left a similar message at Rainey's school. She was to go home with Dani and sleep over.

On the extremely off chance that Rainey might call my mother to check on her health, I called Mom myself.

"How's it going?" I asked.

Her answer was the typical low groan.

"What's wrong?"

"Nothing important, Claire. You get older, and that's how it goes."

"I have an appointment later uptown. If I get the chance, I'll stop by and visit, okay?"

"Whatever suits you, dear."

"You'll be home?"

She sniffed. "Where else would I be? The weather is dreadful. A person could catch her death."

Hanging up, I tried to shake off the fog of her gloom. My call would serve the necessary purpose. If Rainey contacted her out of some perverse burst of empathy, my mother's response would not be quite so off the wall.

I returned to the apartment, stealing in through the rear door. Richter was in the kitchen, cowering under the table. The dog had caught my anxieties, which added to his own, reducing him to a quivering, piddling pile of nerves. Gently, I prodded him out of the apartment and walked him to a kennel two blocks south. He whimpered and clung to me in terror until a young man in an industrial apron and waterproof clogs strong-armed him toward the cages and runs out back. Poor neurotic thing kept looking back at me as if he were praying for a call from the governor.

"It's okay, boy. I'll be back for you tomorrow," I said, making a mental note to add Richter information to the note I planned to leave in case things went south. Lottie had agreed to take care of Rainey if anything ever happened to me. Despite the current frost between us, I had no doubt that Duff would do the same for Richter.

Again, I snuck into the apartment through the back door. The shades were drawn, and I padded about noiselessly in my stocking feet, ducking beneath the windows so no hint of my presence would be visible from the street.

Noah's Glock rested in a locked case at the rear of our top closet shelf. I cleaned and oiled the gun and loaded it as I had seen him do so many times. The heft of a weapon felt oddly soothing and familiar in my hand.

I was grateful now for the interest I had taken in every aspect of Noah's work. I wanted to understand what he did, to know as much as possible, and to share the experience as best I could, even if it had to be from a safe distance. At my urging, we had made several forays to a practice range in Connecticut, where I had learned to steady my hand, align the sights, and confront a target head-on.

For good measure and what little protection it might offer, I strapped on Noah's Kevlar vest. The ponderous contraption still held some memory of his form. I imagined it contained some molecules of his scent as well. Inhaling deeply, I tried to take it in.

Moments after nine, I slipped out the kitchen door again, ducked through the dark, still garden, and squeezed through a hidden breach in the fence. I rounded the block, clinging to the shadows, and then made a conspicuous entrance into the brownstone through the front door. As I approached the building, I noticed the lights blazing in Mrs. DiMarco's apartment and the bleak stillness of the Eastern Therapy Center on the third floor. On most nights, Dr. Midori's operation continued into the wee hours, but from time to time, he shut the place down early to make out-calls or give lectures.

My stomach roiled. All day, I had been too jumpy and preoccupied to eat, and now bilious fear bubbled up to fill the void. I flipped on the living-room lights, strode about for a few moments, and then switched the lamps off again, steeping the room in soupy darkness. I padded down the hall, put on the reading light beside my bed, and ran water in the tub.

Despite my racing thoughts and stampeding pulse, I forced myself to move slowly and project no sense of urgency, in case I was being observed.

When the tub was full, I closed the bathroom door and made sloshing noises, running one hand through the tepid water while I clutched Noah's Glock, like a child's treasured blanket, in the other.

Wrapped in a terrycloth robe over my Kevlar vest and street clothes, I padded out of the bathroom and slipped beneath the covers. I blew a kiss at Noah's picture, as I did every night, and turned off the lights.

Silently, I slipped out of bed, crouching below the sight lines from the street. I plumped pillows to approximate a human form and stole down the hall to the dark living room.

There, I settled in an armchair. And I waited for the enemy to come.

 5 1

I sat utterly still. My mounting fear multiplied each creaking floorboard into an intruder's approaching stride, each click of the radiator into a twist of the doorknob or a window yielding to the insistent press of a malevolent stranger's hand. My bristling imagination served up hulking forms, lurking evil, prying eyes.

But nothing real.

An hour passed with glacial slowness. Then two.

From upstairs came the drone of Mrs. DiMarco's television: shrill dialogue, a laugh track, the jarring blast of a commercial, characters nattering again. Outside, cars passed with a loud rush and a rude flare of light. A group of kids went by, trailing jibes and laughter. In the dim distance a baby wailed its mournful verdict on the world.

Midnight came and went. Fidgeting in the chair, I worked to maintain the circulation in my limbs. My eyes went slack and grainy and my chin drooped. Suddenly, I snapped awake, overwhelmed by the horrifying realization that I'd fallen asleep.

A sour taste rose in my throat, and I fought a wave of nausea. I should have eaten, forced down something to absorb the churning acid.

Too late now.

Again, my thoughts went hazy and my eyelids fluttered shut. No harm in resting for just a minute, I told myself.

No harm.

Gorgeous day. So warm and sunny. Noah was bound to be pleased by the surprise special lunch.

Funny that he's home. I bet Internal Affairs came to their senses and canceled. Why don't I go see what he's doing, Rainey? Maybe he's taking a nap.

I follow the corridor through a long, looping tunnel of sun-glazed walls. No end in sight. Somehow, I know I am safe here. The light, relieved laughter is mine.

But then I hear a noise from the front vestibule. The doorknob twists with a plaintive squeal and the hinges yield in scratchy complaint. I snap awake to the sharp strike of approaching steps.

I clutch the Glock. Icy stillness overcomes me. Whatever it is, I am ready to take it on.

But then the footfalls stop dead, the light flares on, and I see what I could never have expected.

And I freeze.

 5 2

"Aunt Amelia. My God. You scared me half to death."

She smiled grandly. "Only half? Dear me. I suppose I'll simply have to try harder."

"What are you doing here? Is something wrong?"

"Don't be silly, Claire. You'd be the last person I'd come to if something was amiss."

"What, then? It's the middle of the night."

She breezed into the room, trailing her signature haughtiness and jasmine perfume. "Is that any way to greet a guest? Where are your manners? Invite me in, for heaven's sake. Offer me a chair and something to drink, why don't you? A bit of that cognac I gave you would be lovely."

I had to get rid of her before my unknown nemesis showed up. "I need you to leave, Aunt Amelia. I have to work in the morning, and I have to get some rest."

She eyed the Glock, which was loosely tented by my hand.

"My, my. What have we here?"

"Nothing. I was cleaning Noah's gun and I fell asleep."

She pouted. "Let me put that dreadful thing away, Claire. You're liable to hurt yourself." She grasped the pistol gingerly and placed it on the highest shelf she could reach. I watched carefully, planning to retrieve it as soon as I got her out the door.

I yawned broadly. "Good night, Amelia. I'm going to bed."

She sniffed at the dismissal and draped herself decorously on the couch. "I'll go, Claire, but first I need to show Rainey a very, very special performance."

"In the middle of the night?"

"It's unusual, I know. But it's the event of a lifetime, and I simply won't hear of Rainey missing it because of your dreary rules and conventions."

I stood and strode purposefully toward the door. "Rainey's not home. She's sleeping at Danielle's."

Amelia ticked her tongue. "My, my. You don't even know your own child's whereabouts. Small wonder she's fallen in with such unsavory influences."

"What are you talking about?"

She extracted a small plastic rectangle from her ostrich clutch and pressed the silver button on its face. In seconds, the front door swung open, and two lanky figures in broad-brimmed caps and tinted glasses strode in. The one on the right had Rainey flung over his shoulder. As he settled her on the couch, my heart seized.

She looked slack, boneless. "Rainey, my God. What have you done to her?"

Amelia's laugh was a spite-ridden trill. "No need for such histrionics, Claire. The child is perfectly fine. After we fetched her from Danielle's, I simply gave her a little something to relax her. She's not even fully asleep. Simply *very* relaxed."

"You drugged her? Are you out of your mind?"

"It's only a mild sedative, dear. Must you make a federal case of everything?"

"I need you to leave, Amelia. Right now!"

"Sit, Claire," she said. "Take a nice, deep breath."

"Get out of here. All of you. I mean it!"

"As do I." She tipped her head toward the two men, who shoved me down roughly next to Rainey on the couch. "Now listen and perhaps you'll learn something." With a coquettish smile, she regarded the stranger on the left. "Are you ready, dear?"

"Good to go."

"Splendid. What have you planned for our entertainment pleasure, Phelan?"

Phelan?

When he removed his cap and glasses, I saw to my horror that this was indeed the creepy kid Duffy and I had discovered Rainey hanging out with in Alphabet City.

I could barely get the words out. "You know him?"

"That would be a considerable understatement, dear. I helped to make him the splendid creature you see before you today. Isn't that so, darling?"

A vicious smirk split Phelan's lips. "Amelia took care of me when I got in trouble, arranged to make it go away. Ever since, she's helped me develop my particular skills."

I stroked Rainey's hair and watched the slow, even tides of her breathing. "What is he talking about? What's going on here, Amelia? You must be insane."

"Insane? Hardly. I am perfectly attuned to reality, Claire. The difference between me and pitiful souls like you and your mother is that when reality doesn't suit me, I simply alter it so it does. I find the most gifted young people to assist me in setting things right. Justice is the main thing, don't you agree?"

"Agree with what? This is all too crazy. Please. Just get out and leave us alone."

She crossed to the sideboard and poured herself a drink. "Claire, Claire. You always need to have things spelled out for you, and even then, you fail to see what's right before your eyes." She took a demure sip of amber liquid. "I suppose you inherit that particular form of blindness from your mother as well. She has been so very unsatisfying as a target."

"Target for what?"

She sighed. "It honestly never occurs to her that all her greatest misfortunes have been carefully orchestrated. Hard to believe, but the fool still believes that her precious Charlie's death was a simple accident."

"You're saying it wasn't?"

"Hardly simple, Claire. Rigging brakes and setting up a fatal collision takes considerable work and creativity."

My throat closed. "You killed Charlie?"

"'Killed' is such an inadequate word. Let's say that I took him out of the equation. Actually, his death was your mother's fault, not mine at all. I told her I intended to have that man for myself, but the stupid cow refused to listen. And then she flaunted her grotesque contentment, always taking pains to express how much in love she was, what a happy home she had, and what darling little girls. I had no choice but to relieve her of all that unseemly happiness, which, by right, belonged to me. Justice demanded that I do so."

"To hurt her? You are out of your mind."

"Not in the least, Claire. Revenge happens to be my hobby. Perfectly lovely way to pass the time. I've spent countless satisfying hours making sure your mother got what she deserved. I considered taking you apart a bonus."

"You stole my accounts?"

"With clever Phelan's help, of course. Bless the Internet. It has added immeasurably to my fun. I also arranged for your editor to be fired and replaced, for that piece in the *Times* that would appear to be yours, the mock hit-and-run, all of it. Everything was meant to challenge your fragile equilibrium, as well it did."

"But why? What did I ever do to you?"

"You didn't need to do a thing, my dear. I simply find you loathsome, and did so enjoy seeing you slowly, and most painfully, undone. Designing the details of your demise was particularly satisfying. I had all those charges run up on your accounts, and I arranged it so that collection agency would mix you up with a deadbeat who had a similar name. I knew you'd be upset, intimidated, and unbalanced, Claire, and so you were. Exactly as I wished. Power and means are so very handy, I must say."

"Noah?"

She raised her glass. "Brava, Claire! At long last, you're beginning to catch on. Setting Noah up was a most entertaining exercise. I had only to plant the notion that he'd coerced Stanley Peake to talk and then see to it that Peake disappeared. And one of my other talented young men made Noah's actual death appear so very authentic. I thought the hanging was such a lovely touch. Watching the devastation his presumed *suicide* caused you made it all the more enjoyable."

Fury bubbled up inside me. But I refused to let it erupt. All that mattered now was finding a way out, keeping Rainey safe. I placed a protective hand on her slender back. "Leave now, and that will be the end of it, Amelia. Just get the hell out of our lives!"

Outrage blazed in her eyes. "I shall say when this ends, Claire, when and with whom." Softening, she cast a glance Rainey's way. "Pity about the child though. I was so enjoying her transformation. I had only to insert dear Phelan in her life and have him convince the girl that you drove her father to his grave. I would have loved to see how that played out, but your foolishness in contacting the authorities has forced us to bring this to a conclusion. We saw that unfortunate e-mail from the Computer Investigation and Technology Unit. We couldn't have them involved. Surely, you're not too dense to understand that."

It took every scrap of my will to keep from lunging for her tight, scrawny neck. "No, Amelia. I get it perfectly."

She downed the last of the cognac. "All right then, we shall dispose of you and the child now. Then I have only to make sure your precious mother knows exactly what she has caused before she receives her own, long overdue, final payment."

5 3

My eyes skittered to the Glock. Somehow, I needed to get the weapon and use it to get Rainey out.

Amelia turned to Phelan. "You're prepared, dear?"

"Completely."

"I can't wait to hear about your glorious plan."

Amelia nodded at the second stranger, who until now had stood silent. "Graduation is here at last. I'm so eager to see how our young Phelan has progressed, darling. Aren't you?"

The mute stranger doffed his hat and glasses and fixed his smoky eyes on my aunt. My heart raced frantically, jolted by the fact that my brain could not absorb. B.B. LeBeau wasn't dead. He was standing ten feet away. "He's nothing and nobody, golden girl, like I've told you again and again."

Amelia wagged a playful finger. "Mustn't be jealous, dear B.B. Auntie has plenty of love and attention to go around."

LeBeau's face warped with contempt. "Jealous of him? I think you're losing it, Methuselah. Little jerk's not worth wiping my butt with. You'll see."

Amelia beamed. "We'll all see. Tell us, Phelan dear. How will the story play out?" She held up a restraining hand and turned to me. "So you understand fully, Claire. I challenge my star pupils to develop their own unique approach. A trademark, if you will. B.B.'s masterworks have all involved the K-Bar knife and titled tableaux. Young Phelan has been exploring various means of torture in the interest of developing a signature method of his own. You and Rainey shall have the privilege of starring in his debut performance." Now her gaze swerved to Phelan. "Do tell, darling."

"I found myself particularly drawn to accounts of people being boiled alive, either in a form of ritualized cannibalism or as a particularly wicked means of capital punishment that was practiced in various parts of the world from the first millennium through the early eighteenth century."

Amelia clapped her hands like an elated child. "I love it!"

Now it was Phelan's turn to raise a restraining hand. "Then, it occurred to me that steaming is a much more efficient way to go. In fact, they happen to have a handy-dandy facility right upstairs. All it would take is disabling the safety cutoff valve and pumping up the heat. The death is slow, terrifying, excruciating, and highly original. Perfect in every dimension. So that's what I've arranged."

"Wonderful," Amelia said. "Let the games begin."

LeBeau sniffed. "Bunch of crap. Perfect from a little turd like you, scat man."

"Yeah right. You wish you'd thought of it," Phelan sniped.

Amelia stood and set her hands on their shoulders. "Boys, boys. Let's not ruin the fun with silly arguments."

Using the distraction, I bolted up and grabbed the gun. "Don't move!" My eyes swerved from Amelia to Phelan to LeBeau and then to Rainey, who was beginning to stir.

Slowly, I edged toward the phone. I clutched the Glock as I lifted the receiver and punched 911. Breath held, I waited for the call to connect.

Before it did, LeBeau wheeled around and kicked the pistol out of my hand. Phelan caught my wrist and twisted furiously. I heard a sickly snap and felt a searing pain. Rough hands caught me by the shoulders and wrenched me out the door.

Phelan flashed a gleaming knife, and then settled the blade at the small of my back. The point bit through the Kevlar. "Upstairs, bitch," he spat.

LeBeau followed him, carrying Rainey, who was muttering in confusion. From below, I heard the scolding strike of Amelia's heels.

As we neared the second landing, I thought to call out to Mrs. DiMarco. But Phelan was a step ahead of me. He pressed the blade harder, until I felt a probing pinch. "Make a sound, and I'll gut the kid right here."

We passed Mrs. DiMarco's door and climbed another flight to the Eastern Therapy Center. The knifepoint nudged me through the door and down the hall. I smelled the heavy must of eucalyptus-scented steam. And my legs refused to take another step.

5 4

A searing, suffocating mist engulfed me as Phelan opened the door to the steam room. He shoved me inside, and sent me sprawling on the slick tile floor. Reflexively, my hands shot out, and exquisite pain seared through my injured arm.

I groped blindly through the stifling heat with my good hand, recoiling as I happened too near a roaring jet and scorched my fingers.

"What is this? Where am I? I can't see."

I tracked Rainey's tremulous voice through the thrumming wall of steam. Perched on the tile bench, I hugged her hard. For once she didn't stiffen or pull away.

"Ssh, Rainey. We're in Dr. Midori's steam room."

"It's too hot. I can't breathe."

"I know, honey. Try to stay calm."

"They locked us in?"

I had heard them nail the door to the frame, hard, striking thwacks, driving the steel rods home. "Don't worry. I'm going to find some way out."

"Why would Aunt Amelia do this? What's wrong with her?"

My lungs seared with each blistering breath. "Let's not think about

JUDITH KELMAN

her now, honey. Heat rises, so stay as low as you can, but be careful of the jets."

I felt my way around the tile walls, searching for a switch or something I could use to break the glass. It was bound to be safety-grade and impossible to crack without some strong metal object.

Hissing steam kept pouring into the room. The heat was growing more and more intense.

"Please, Claire. I can't stand it. Get us out now."

"I'm trying, honey. Hold on."

Struggling to focus, I thought back to last week, when I came here with Richter for a massage. During my tour of the place, I had taken special notice of the emergency valve. Bringing up a mental image, I felt my way toward it.

Scalding drips beat from the ceiling. Every drop was a sharp, painful jolt.

"I'm so thirsty," Rainey said. Her voice was shrinking, melding with the roasting mist.

"I know, baby."

At last, I came upon the valve. The metal was too hot to touch. I stripped off my blouse and the stifling vest beneath it and used the fabric to protect my still-functioning hand as I desperately worked the valve.

Nothing.

The steam kept boiling through the jets. The heat took on the fearsome force of a rabid beast. Phelan had disabled the safety cutoff. In a rage, I shook the metal stem one final time, and it came away in my hand.

I groped blindly back to the door and stood facing the murky light of the window. An inhuman cry escaped me as I brought the metal down with every shred of remaining strength. But the glass was tempered, as I'd known it would be, and I couldn't break it.

"Water," Rainey wept. "Please."

"Wet your hand on the tile and lick it, honey. The water will be hot, but it should help."

"Please, Claire. I don't feel well."

"I know, sweetie. Just hold on."

I pounded the valve against the unyielding glass, railing at my unbearable helplessness. I kept bashing, clanging furiously until my strength lapsed and I sank to the floor. That's when I heard the rabid tapping of Mrs. DiMarco's cane.

"What are you doing up there? You nuts or something, you pervert? You woke me up."

Gasping, I managed to raise my hand and hammer the valve against the tile.

"That does it, Dr. Sleazebag. I'm calling the cops right now."

"Yes," I rasped as I pounded again. "Do that. Call the cops."

I was getting weaker, losing touch, but I kept raising my hand to bring the metal down on the floor. Again and again, I struck, even as my muscles screamed with pain.

Call!

All I could hear was the persistent tap of her cane. Terror filled me as I thought of all the times her threats had been empty. Only a couple of times had she actually called in a complaint.

My strength was giving out. My arm was a cement block, too heavy to lift. I was out of ideas, hopes fading.

Please, no. This can't be. I have to get Rainey out.

But then, as my thoughts dimmed, receding from the pain and agonizing heat, I caught the distant shrill of a wailing siren. Coming closer. Screaming in the night.

 5 5

Amelia smiled wistfully as she listened to the fading pleas and useless pounding from inside the steam room. Phelan sat beside her on a slatted teak bench, and she turned to stroke his cheek. "Brilliant, my dear. Simply marvelous. You have exceeded my most optimistic expectations."

LeBeau hung back, slouched against the wall. "Looks like you set your bar mighty low, Granny."

Amelia's grin curled in a taut-lipped rebuke. "I've asked you not to dampen the occasion, B.B. Must you act so childish?"

"Me? I'm not the one playing Suzy Homemaker, he is."

Phelan bristled. "What the hell are you talking about, LeBeau?"

The smoky eyes narrowed with spite. "A cooking demonstration. I mean give me a break. Couldn't you come up with something better than playing cartoon cannibal?"

Phelan rose from the bench, hands balled in white-knuckled fists. "You can't stand it because it's better than anything you ever did."

LeBeau snickered cruelly. "Yeah right. You've really got me on the run with your people-soup recipe. Never could have come up with something quite so *original,* no siree. Tell me, what did you use for spice? Just pepper and salt? Or did you go in an Italian direction, with garlic and oregano?"

"Shut the hell up, LeBeau. I've had about enough."

"Oooh. Now I'm really scared. What are you going to do to me, Julia Child? Whip me into a meringue pie? Puff me in a soufflé?"

Amelia glowered at LeBeau reproachfully. "This is Phelan's performance, B.B. Now behave."

LeBeau leaned in and nuzzled Amelia's ear. "I am behaving, baby. Just like you taught me."

The old lady issued a girlish trill. "Stop, darling. You know how that tickles."

He rubbed Amelia's neck and scribbled languid circles down her back. "Of course I know. I know everything you like. Don't I, Auntie dear?"

"Yes, you do, you big naughty boy."

"Cut it out, you lump of crap. You're making me sick," Phelan said.

The sounds from the steam room had faded. Now nothing but the hiss of the jets played as background to LeBeau's fawning advances and Amelia's increasingly ardent response.

"I spent weeks putting this together. Shut the hell up and watch," Phelan whined.

Again, LeBeau chuckled dryly. "You should really be proud of that little guy, baby. Look how he's into healthy living. Nothing fried or fatty, just plain steamed."

Amelia chortled in delight. "How true."

"You're ruining everything, you rotten scum," Phelan railed.

"Jealous, jealous," chided Amelia.

"Don't be ridiculous. Why would I be jealous of that useless, no-name hack?"

LeBeau stiffened. "What'd you say?"

"Just the truth, LeBeau. You're so useless your parents couldn't even get it up to give you a goddamned name. That's why they call you B.B., because on your birth certificate, all it said was 'baby boy.'"

"That's the last thing you get to say, you little turd." LeBeau lunged at Phelan.

"Stop!" Amelia demanded. "You silly boys are spoiling all my fun."

Suddenly, LeBeau whipped out his K-Bar. "Say good night, Gracie," he said as he reared back to strike Phelan. He faked left, and then whipped his right arm around with lightning speed.

Phelan folded in on himself, clutching his slashed, gushing abdomen. "What the hell?" Surprise registered on his face, then shock, and finally, as he fell to the ground—nothing.

LeBeau held up his K-Bar, now agleam with crimson gore. "You didn't even see it coming, did you, you little lump of crap? That's one thing Suzy Homemaker should have learned: better knife skills."

Amelia railed. "You stupid fool. You've killed him. He was the best I've ever found."

"You said I was the best."

"No longer. I'm finished with you, B.B. Get out of my sight."

"You can't dismiss me like that, you ugly old bitch."

"You heard me. Out!"

"You can't do this."

"I can do precisely as I please. You are to leave, this instant, or I shall be forced to destroy you."

LeBeau shot a single high-pitched blast of incredulity. "Destroy me? You?"

Amelia read the feral glint in his eye. "Now, darling. You know I'm not being serious. You've always been my absolute favorite, after all." She caught the distant wail of sirens. If only they were coming here. She could finger LeBeau for the murders and be done with this needless unpleasantness. *Just a bump in the road,* she told herself. "I was just a bit upset about your silly spat with Phelan. It kept me from fully enjoying the performance, darling. Surely you understand."

LeBeau stopped his menacing approach and smiled. "I'm really your favorite."

"Always, darling," she crooned. "You're my number-one big baby boy."

LeBeau was on her in a blink. And with a stab to the heart, she was done. "And you were my number-one rich bitch. But sooner or later, all good things come to an end."

5 6

Strong restraining hands. Grim-eyed strangers. Cruel, piercing lights.

"No! Let go of me! Stop!"

"Now, and would you listen to her screeching like bad brakes. Calm yourself, Claire. You're in the hospital. Everyone here is a friend."

"Duffy?"

"The very same. You've been out for a few days, darlin'. But you're going to be fine. Burns are healing nicely, and your lungs are on the mend. Still, from the sound of it, there may be a serious problem with your disposition."

Through the dense medicinal fog, the scorching horror in the steam room drifted back. "Rainey?"

"She's going to be fine, too, Claire, thanks to you. She's down the hall.

Itching to get out of here. Driving everyone crazy, so you know she's about back to herself. Now that you're up, I'll bring her around for a visit."

I brought his ruddy face into focus. Struck me as a true work of art. "Water?" I croaked.

He held the plastic cup and I pulled greedily on the bent, plastic straw. The liquid was so smooth and deliciously cool. Nothing had ever tasted better.

My throat was painfully raw. I sounded like the last crackling trace of a fading transmission. "Phelan and LeBeau? Amelia?"

"Thank the Lord all that blight has finally been cleared, Claire. Young Zachary had a bout of conscience in the middle of the night, and he called to warn me about those phony e-mails you had him send you from the CITU. I was on my way to come and give you a good talking-to when I caught your neighbor's noise complaint on the two-way.

"When we showed up, we found your aunt and Phelan slashed and posed in the dry sauna. The bloody writing on the wall said 'Some Like It Hot.'"

"Phelan and LeBeau had a really bad case of sibling rivalry," I rasped.

"If that's what it was, makes Cain and Abel look positively brotherly. Anyhow, we put out a call to all units, and a cruiser spotted LeBeau three blocks north, trying to hail a cab. Seems this wasn't his normal well-planned and executed job. The Eel still had blood on his clothes, and was quite the raving fury, according to the officer who took him out."

"Honestly dead?" I repeated for my own assurance.

"This time, for sure. The B.B. LeBeau look-alikes came courtesy of Amelia's protégé, the plastic surgeon. This one was the genuine item. Been verified through fingerprint and dental records, the works."

"Hallelujah," I exulted as best I could.

"Amen to that." Duffy offered me another soothing sip.

"Richter?"

"He misses you, but he's fine. Sends his love, in fact. Can't wait to get you home, so he can protect you."

My chest ached, everything did. But then, aching confirmed that I was still very much alive. Confusing emotions washed over me and bubbled up in my eyes. "Noah didn't kill himself, Duff. It was Amelia."

Taking care to avoid the needles and tubes, Duff set his broad soothing hand over mine. "I know that, sweetheart. Rainey told me."

"Rainey heard?"

"I did," she said from the doorway. "I heard it all. Dr. Bruno says Amelia was sick, but I think calling her that is unfair to sick people." Lottie pushed Rainey into the room in a hospital-issue wheelchair. She rolled close and kissed me gently on the cheek. "I'm sorry, Claire. I was a total dope, so wrong about everything. Can you ever forgive me?"

"There's nothing to forgive, honey. Are you okay?" I took a quick survey. Her feet were bandaged and bright-pink patches scaled her arms.

"Except for being bored to death."

"Honestly?"

"Yes. The burns don't hurt anymore. My eyes were messed up, but they're much better now. Other than that, everything's fine."

Lottie's lovely face came into view. "Except the food. That is definitely not fine. Starting right now, Claire, your job is to let me know everything and anything that appeals to you in the eating department. Whatever it is, I'll get you the very best of breed. Rainey wanted a burger, so I got her the one stuffed with short ribs and foie gras from DB Bistro Moderne."

"It was totally amazing," Rainey said.

My mother hovered anxiously. "In moderation, Lottie. You don't want her to overdo."

Lottie winked at me. "You're absolutely right, Mom. I believe in moderation in all things, especially moderation."

A rangy redheaded nurse paused at the door. "Everything okay here?"

"Fine," I said hoarsely.

"Easy on the partying, Claire," she said. "You still need to rest."

My mother seized the point. "What did I tell you? You mustn't overdo."

This time Rainey raised the water to my lips. "We have to keep you hydrated," she said gravely, showing off the fresh vocabulary that I wished she had never needed to learn.

Lottie cleared her throat and tipped her head meaningfully. I was still too foggy from the painkillers to read her signal. "Duffy has been amazing, Claire. Hanging around here every spare second," she said pointedly.

"Thanks, Duff."

Duff flashed a crooked grin. "Just enjoying the silence with you off in Dreamland. How often does a person get the chance at that?"

Lottie eyed him harshly. "Enough of your blarney, Duff. It won't kill you to admit that you care."

His ruddiness deepened and he coughed into his hand. "Of course I care. Claire and I go way back. Don't we, Rainey darlin'?"

Rainey rolled her eyes. "Leave me out of this. Okay?"

"What's going on here, Duff?" I asked gently.

"Your sister thinks that just because I've been keeping an eye on you, making sure you don't get yourself in any more fool trouble, that I must have gone soft in the head."

I looked him hard in the eye, and he looked back. And something undeniable passed between us. "So have you?"

"Maybe a little." Duff turned to Rainey. "How would that be for you, child, if an old fool like me happened to develop a bit of a case for Claire?"

Rainey hitched her shoulders, reverting to her cool, unflappable teenage mode. "Knock yourself out."

His gaze drifted back to me. "Any thoughts on the subject?"

I beckoned him close and kissed him lightly on the lips. My head filled with the scent of sweet coffee and lime-menthol shaving cream, and my mind spun with pleasant possibilities.

The lights went dim behind my slumping lids. The sounds in the room settled at a gentle remove.

"Looks like she's drifted off again. Thank the Lord we've got her back," Duffy said.

"Ditto," Lottie sighed. "She's the best."

"I am awfully proud of her. I must admit," my mother said grudgingly.

"You're sure you're all right with my courting Claire, Rainey? Might feel a bit strange for a time," Duffy said.

I treaded water at the edge of consciousness, waiting for Rainey's response. It seemed forever before she broke the bristling silence. "Courting? Give me a break, Uncle Duff. You want my Claire to like you, you're going to have to be way, way cooler than that."